Praise for Chevy Stevens

'An **astonishingly well-crafted** debut novel.
Still Missing will have you spellbound from the first
page until long after you close the book'
KARIN SLAUGHTER

'**Frank, fierce,** and sometimes even funny,
this is a dark tale pinpricked with light and told
by an **unforgettable heroine**'
GILLIAN FLYNN

'**Crackling with suspense** . . .
will have you glued to the page'
PEOPLE

'*Still Missing* runs deeper than the
chills it delivers, the surprises it holds and
the resilience of its main character'
NEW YORK TIMES

'Chevy Stevens writes in a fresh, truly authentic
human voice, gripping you and **tearing your heart**
from the very first page to the last'
PETER JAMES

THOSE GIRLS

CHEVY STEVENS

SPHERE

First published in the United States in 2015 by St Martin's Press
First published in Great Britain in 2015 by Sphere
This paperback edition published in 2015 by Sphere

3 5 7 9 10 8 6 4 2

A CIP catalogue record for this book
is available from the British Library.

ISBN 978-0-7515-5506-6

Printed and bound in Great Britain by
Clays Ltd, St Ives plc

Papers used by Sphere are from well-managed forests
and other responsible sources.

MIX
Paper from
responsible sources
FSC® C104740

Sphere
An imprint of
Little, Brown Book Group
Carmelite House
50 Victoria Embankment
London EC4Y 0DZ

An Hachette UK Company
www.hachette.co.uk

www.littlebrown.co.uk

For Piper,
my favorite girl

Author's Note

Though there is a town called Cache Creek in British Columbia, my 'Cash Creek' is fictional and in a different location. The town of Littlefield is also fictional. All other locations are real.

Part One

JESS

Chapter One

July 1997

We'd only been on the road for an hour but we were almost out of gas. The white line of the highway blurred in front of my eyes, my lids drooping. It was three in the morning and we'd barely slept for days. Dani was driving, her face pale, her long dirty-blonde hair pulled under a baseball cap and out the back in a makeshift ponytail, her eyes staring straight ahead. Her name was Danielle, but we just called her Dani. The oldest at almost eighteen, she was the only one who had her license. She'd barely said a word since we left Littlefield.

On my right, Courtney was also staring out the window. When her favorite country song, 'Wide Open Spaces' by the Dixie Chicks, came on the radio, she turned it off, then stared back out into the dark night.

She brushed at her cheeks and I could tell she was crying. I gave her hand a squeeze, and she gripped it back. Her hair was down, one side pushed forward, trying to hide the burn that had left an angry red mark along her jawline.

None of us had ever traveled this far from home before. We'd found a map at the hardware store – Dani had stolen it while Courtney and I kept watch – and carefully planned our route to Vancouver. We figured we could make the drive in about eight hours if the truck held up. But we had to stop in Cash Creek first and borrow some money from one of Courtney's old boyfriends.

It was the middle of July and so hot you couldn't walk outside without feeling your skin cook. We were golden brown, freckles covering our faces and upper arms – a family trait. Forest fire warnings had been out for a month, and a few towns had already been evacuated. Everything was dried out, the fields pale yellow, the weeds in the ditches covered in gray dust. We were in jeans shorts and T-shirts, our skin sweaty even this late at night, and the air smelled hot.

I touched the camera hanging around my neck. My mom had given it to me when I was ten, just before she died. Dani hated it when I took her photo, but Courtney loved it – *used* to love it. I didn't know now. I glanced over at her again, then down at my chewed nails. Sometimes I imagined that I could still see the blood under them, as if it had soaked into my skin like it had our floors.

'We're going to need gas soon,' Dani said suddenly, making me jump.

Courtney turned back from the window. 'How much money do we have?'

'Not enough.' Before we left town we'd siphoned a little gas from a neighbor's truck and gathered what food we could, picking fruits and vegetables from the farm's fields, taking eggs from underneath the hens and storing them in our cooler. Our cupboards were empty by then – we'd been living on soup, Kraft dinners, rice, and the last few pounds of ground deer meat in the freezer from the buck Dad had shot that spring. We pooled our money – I had a few dollars from babysitting and Dani had a little money left from when she helped during hay season, but she'd used a lot of it already that year trying to keep us afloat.

'We could get some money for your camera,' she'd said.

'No way!'

'Courtney sold her guitar.'

'You know why she really sold it,' I'd said. Dani had gotten quiet then. I'd felt bad but I couldn't do it, couldn't let go of my one good thing.

'What are we going to do?' I said now.

'We're going to steal some gas,' Dani said, angry.

Dani always sounded pissed off, but I didn't pay any attention to it unless she was really mad. Then I got the hell out of her way.

She had a right to be angry. We all did.

We found a gas station in the next town, an old Chevron with two ancient pumps and a lone shadowy figure visible through the window. Was he the only one working? We pulled around back, gravel crunching under our tires. Dani switched off the engine and we sat there while it ticked. I held on to my camera tightly.

'Jess, go in and make sure no one else is there,' Dani said.

I darted a look at her but her profile was rigid. 'Okay.' I tried to sound confident, but we'd never done anything like this before – only shoplifted food and makeup, small items. Of course it would be me. Courtney was too pretty – she had the same dirty-blonde hair we all had, but she used peroxide and gave it highlights and had our father's blue eyes that looked even brighter against her tanned skin. And now, with her burn, people would remember her. But I was small at fourteen, with plain toffee-colored hair and green eyes. People forgot me.

The door jingled when I opened it. The guy behind the counter glanced up. He was young, maybe in his early twenties, with long sideburns and acne. I looked around, didn't see anyone else working. The store was empty, and there were no security cameras or monitors. I cleared my throat.

'Can I have the key to the bathroom?'

He pushed the keys across the counter, then looked back down at his magazine. I browsed the shelves, then made my way outside around the back of the store, where a sign pointed to the restrooms. A laundry room for truckers was beside the washrooms. I pulled out the slots, checked for spare change under the machines – sometimes you get lucky, but nothing today. In the garbage can, I found a few cans and a pizza box with a couple of crusts. My stomach growled, but I left the box and went into the bathroom, used the toilet, and washed my hands. I glanced in the mirror. My eyes looked big, scared. The fluorescent light above my head was humming loudly, the bathroom seeming suddenly cold and empty.

I turned my face so I could see the bruise on my jaw. The makeup was smeared. I rubbed at it with my finger, spread it smooth. I stepped back, staring at my reflection. I tried to narrow my eyes and squared my shoulders, pulling my hat down hard, making myself look tougher, more like Dani. It didn't work.

I returned the key and walked back to the truck.

'What did you find?' Dani said through her window.

7

'Just one guy at the counter – he's reading a girlie magazine.'

She nodded.

'Now what?' I said.

'Courtney, you go talk to him.'

'Shit, why me?' Courtney said.

Dani gave her a look. Courtney heaved a sigh, undid the top button of her shirt, and got out of the truck.

'I'm going too,' I said.

'No. Stay in the truck, Jess.'

'But I'm hungry!'

'Jesus Christ.' Dani bitched all the time about my 'hollow leg', but she still gave me extra helpings.

I followed Courtney into the store. She leaned over the counter and began talking to the guy, who immediately put down his magazine and turned to face her. Through the corner of my eye, I saw Dani pull the truck around to the pump. Quickly, I walked down the aisles and shoved chocolate bars and snacks into my pockets. Courtney glanced out the window once in a while, waiting for the signal. I was also keeping an eye on Dani. Finally she lifted her hat and wiped her brow.

I left the store and jumped in the truck. Courtney took the pen the guy was holding out, wrote something down on a piece of paper. He was smiling big. She made like she was checking the pocket of her jeans shorts, then shook her head and nodded at the truck.

Now she was heading back to us, walking slow, letting her hips sway. I could see the guy inside staring at her, riveted. She got in the truck, made it look like she was reaching for her purse, then slammed the door behind her. Dani pounded the accelerator. The truck fish-tailed onto the road, swerving on the dusty, dry edge. I watched behind as the guy ran out of the gas station, his hand on a phone, already calling the police. Our license plate was covered in dried mud, but my heart was still pounding. If we were caught, we'd be brought back to Littlefield and the cops would have questions – lots of questions.

I turned around and pulled out my chocolate bars. We ate, silent in the dark.

'Remember when Dad used to buy us Caramilk bars every Christmas?' Courtney's voice was small, the memory big.

I chewed slower now, my eyes filling with tears. It had been years since Dad had brought us chocolate bars, not since our mom had died.

It had only been three days since I'd killed him.

Chapter Two

Littlefield

Three Days Earlier

Dad had been gone a month this time, working in Alberta on the oil rigs. Before that job he mostly worked construction around town and on the ranch where we lived. Littlefield was a small town near the Alberta border and it didn't have a lot of jobs – mainly farming or logging since the mill had closed down – so a lot of men worked in Calgary, a couple of hours away. Dad said he'd make better money in Alberta, and maybe he did, but we never saw any of it. He worked three weeks in and one week out. He'd stop at a couple of bars on the way home from the rigs, then usually didn't quit drinking until it was time for his next shift.

I was sure this time things would be different, though. My fifteenth birthday was coming up and he'd told me he'd bring me something special. I'd been thinking about it all week.

'He's not bringing you diddly-squat,' Dani had said that morning.

'He promised,' I said.

'So?'

I didn't look at her, just shoved another spoonful of scrambled eggs into my mouth. Across the table Courtney was practicing some chords on her guitar, scribbling into a little notebook. She gave me a smile.

'I'll write you a song,' she said. 'For your birthday.'

'That'd be cool.' I smiled back at her.

'Jess, I just don't want you to be disappointed,' Dani said from the other end of the table.

'I know, but I've got a good feeling. I think he's going to bring something for my camera — maybe a new lens.'

'You're such a dumbass.' Dani was always telling me I was too hopeful, Dad would never change. But sometimes he went weeks without drinking. Maybe one day he'd quit for good.

I was half expecting to see Dad's truck in the driveway now as I walked toward our house, or have him roar past me, laughing as he left me choking on the dust. I glanced behind me. In the distance I could hear calves mooing and a tractor out in the fields. I aimed my camera at a pretty bird sitting on the fence, then took another shot of our house. Dani was home. I could tell she was in a mood by the way she'd parked the truck – sideways, windows down, the grille almost touching the front steps – and by the music blasting from inside the house. I slowed my pace.

I didn't mind living on the ranch, but I wished it was ours – the bank had foreclosed on our old place. That house had been pretty – I still remembered the front patio swing, the white fence that went down to the road, how Dad would repaint it every year. This was just an old ranch hand's house on a cattle farm, but we had lots of room, a big yard for Dad's stuff, and we needed the work. After Mom died – she was hit head-on by a truck carrying a load of hay – Dad lost his job. He took off to Calgary for months. I'd just turned ten. Courtney was eleven and a half, and Dani almost thirteen. We ended up in foster homes.

They couldn't find one willing to take all of us so I got put with a family that already had six kids, two of them handicapped. There never seemed to be enough food for everyone. I'd wait until my foster mother wasn't looking, then slip some of my mashed potatoes or whatever onto the little kids' plates, shaking my head to warn them to keep quiet about it. If one of them forgot and yelled, 'Thank you!' my foster mom would whip around and we'd end up with nothing. I ran away once, trying to get to my sisters, but got picked up by the cops. I found out later they'd tried to run away a few times too. None of us made it.

Finally, after five months, Dad came back, promising to stay sober.

Courtney told me a little about her foster family, how the father peeked at her in the shower, how the mom used to slap her when he wasn't watching.

Dani didn't talk about her foster home much, just said the people had been old and couldn't take care of their farm and wanted a helper. I don't know if they were mean to her – she never said. Sometimes I wondered if she wished she was still there. 'Did you like it better than taking care of us?' I said. She cuffed me lightly across the head and said, 'Don't be a dumbass.'

When I walked into the house she was sweeping the kitchen and I could smell pine-scented cleaner. All the windows were open.

'Where've you been?' she said. 'I looked for you at the barn.'

'Ingrid needed help in the fields.'

During the school year we worked on the farm at night and on weekends, but in summer we worked whenever they needed us. Our arms and legs were muscled, our hands blistered – Courtney was always putting lotion on them or doing her nails. Dani would spend all day in the fields if she could, riding the tractor with a smile on her face, her hair under a big cowboy hat. Sometimes after school she'd even go over to her boyfriend's place to help – his family had the neighboring farm. I didn't mind working in the fields, but I preferred working with the animals. Spring was my favorite, all the babies being born, but I refused to eat the meat, which made Dad furious. I took a few beatings for that.

'We've got to get this place cleaned up before Dad gets back,' Dani said.

'Okay.' I started washing some dishes that had been on the counter for at least a week, scraping at the dried food, imagining a big dinner when Dad got home. I hoped he'd take me grocery shopping with him.

After Dad got us out of foster care, he'd found this place and kept himself together for months. Then the beer cans started piling up. The cops came by a few times, asking if we were okay, but we kept our mouths shut. When teachers asked about a black eye or a bruise we couldn't hide, we'd say we fell or hurt ourselves on the ranch, tangled with a mean horse. If Dani heard someone teasing us, she delivered what we'd gotten good at taking. I didn't tell her when a kid gave me a hard time about the smell of manure on my shoes or called Courtney names. It just made Dani feel bad.

'Where's Courtney?' I said.

Dani shrugged. 'Where is she usually?'

So she was off with another boy. I wondered who it was this time.

Dani and I had the house clean by the time Courtney got home. We were out in the backyard, setting up beer cans to do some target practicing. Dad left us his rifle when he was out of town – an old Cooley .22 semi-automatic he'd gotten from his father – and made sure we had enough bullets. He said he wanted us to be able to take care of ourselves. We didn't have much time to just kick around, but we liked shooting stuff or going fishing. I squinted, took aim on the can, held my breath, and squeezed the trigger. The can flew into the air.

'Good shot!' Courtney's husky voice said from behind me.

I lowered the gun and turned around. Courtney had a case of beer on one hip and a cigarette in her hand. Her long hair was damp and tangled, and her baseball cap was on backward. She was wearing dark sunglasses too big for her face, which looked cool, and a bikini top under a black tank top.

'She's always a good shot,' Dani said. She didn't give a lot of compliments, so it meant something when she did. I liked shooting, liked that moment when everything came into focus, came down to a split second. Same with my camera, seeing the frame, lining up the shot, taking a breath, then boom!

'Jesus, what's with your shorts?' Dani said. Courtney's

jeans shorts were cut so high you could see the bottom of her front pockets.

Courtney laughed. 'You like them? They make the boys go *craaaazy*.' She sang out the last words. Courtney was always laughing or singing. Mom used to say Courtney sang before she talked. She was a pretty good guitar player too, had bought a second-hand one and taught herself by listening to the radio.

'They just about show everything.' Dani wore cut-offs – we all did – but Courtney's were always the shortest, the frayed bleached-out edges contrasting with her golden skin. I glanced at her legs, then down at mine, wondering if I could get away with taking my shorts up an inch.

'Here, take a beer and shut up already,' Courtney said.

Dani grinned and grabbed the beer, opening the can with a pop, and took a long swallow.

'God, that's good.'

Courtney handed me one. I took a slug, savoring how cold it felt going down my dry throat on a hot day. I liked beer, the fuzzy feeling it gave everything, the malty taste, but the smell always reminded me of Dad.

'Where did you get the beer?' Dani asked.

'A friend.'

Dani just shook her head. There wasn't much you could say to Courtney. She did what she wanted. Dani would get mad at her, but Courtney would grab her in a big hug or sing her a silly song or get her laughing somehow. She worked hard but she played hard too. If Dani got after her about how she needed to sleep, she'd say, 'I'll sleep when I'm dead.'

Dani pointed to the cigarettes and Courtney threw her the pack. Cigarettes were another luxury. Sometimes we'd steal a couple from Dad's pack when he was home or from one of the farmhands. Then we'd sit out on our porch, sharing drags. We sat now on the rock edge of what used to be a nice garden running around the house. It was just weeds these days. Dani kept trying to grow vegetables in the backyard, but Dad kept driving over her patch.

Courtney passed me a cigarette, lighting it with the end of hers. I set the gun against the warm rocks and took a drag, watching to see how Dani did it, her mouth parting slightly to let the smoke out in a long, lazy exhale. I leaned back so she couldn't see, tried blowing it out the same way.

Only the middle of July and the grass was already dead, same with the flowers we'd planted. Most of our front yard was dirt. Dad was always dragging home stuff from the junkyard, and scrap metal and wood littered the property. The house was in bad shape – in the winter we had to board up the windows – but I liked the sprawling deck on the front. I was going to ask Dad if we could paint it.

I didn't bring any friends home, and we kept to ourselves at school. Dani was usually with her boyfriend, Corey, who was kind of cute in a redneck farm-boy way with his tanned skin, white teeth, and dimples. Courtney was always skipping or hanging out with a boy; most of the other girls didn't like her. I tagged along with my sisters or worked on my homework during breaks. Dani put my report card up on the fridge, like Mom used to. I helped with their homework sometimes. Courtney would just get me to do hers if she could, but Dani wouldn't allow that.

Dani moved over to sit on the tailgate of her truck. It was an old Ford, and silver where it wasn't rusted out. She'd bought it from her boyfriend's dad for cheap, then worked it off. It was usually broken down. She kept it cleaned out, hung a coconut air freshener on the rearview mirror, but it didn't hide the stink of manure from our boots. I always kicked my boots on the fender, trying to get the dirt off before I climbed in or she'd yell at me.

Courtney took a long drag. 'I'm going out again later.'

'You nuts?' Dani said.

'If he's back, he won't be home for hours.'

'You don't know that for sure,' I said. Sometimes he stopped at Bob's, his friend in town, and they hit the bars, but other times he came straight home.

She tugged the back of my hair. 'Don't worry.'

18

Courtney acted like she didn't care what Dad did to her, but I knew she was scared of him. Mom was the only person who'd ever been able to keep him under control, but he'd still go on benders with his friends, then come home yelling and throwing stuff around, breaking dishes. She kicked him out a couple of months before she died, but he sweet-talked his way back in, sober and swearing he'd stay that way. Mom was really happy for a while – we all were. Dad stayed sober until the night we found out she'd died. Sometimes I think about how sad she'd be over what happened to us, how pissed off she'd be at Dad.

I looked down the road again, imagined his truck getting closer.

'*Promise* you'll come home early?' I said. The last time Dad caught Courtney sneaking in, she hadn't been able to sit for days.

'Promise,' Courtney said.

'He told you what would happen if you mess up again.' Dani dropped her cigarette onto the dirt, ground her heel into it. 'He *warned* you.'

'God, you guys are paranoid,' Courtney said. 'He's not even in town.'

But I'd seen the way she glanced at the road before she picked up the rifle.

'Come on, let's shoot some more cans.'

Chapter Three

We shot cans until we'd finished the case of beer, moving each one farther away to make it more challenging, trying to distract whoever was taking aim. We were all good shots – Dad had taught us. When we were younger he liked to make us set the cans up for him – he'd shot one when I was reaching for it. I fell back, crying, and he laughed. I didn't flinch the next time.

The rest of the afternoon we did laundry, hanging it outside to dry because the dryer was broken again, then made dinner, adding some rice to the last of the tomato soup to make it more filling.

After dinner, Courtney headed upstairs to get ready for her date.

'Want to keep me company?' she said.

Courtney didn't like being alone much and often asked me to hang out with her. I didn't mind. I liked sitting on the side of the bathtub listening to her talk about her new boyfriend and watching her do her hair

20

and makeup. We'd shoplifted most of the makeup – we figured stealing samples wasn't as bad – but we shared what we had. It led to a few fights, mostly because Courtney left a lid off something, but usually we were okay. Dani didn't use makeup unless she was going out with Corey, but I liked playing around with it.

Courtney was leaning toward the mirror, carefully shaping her eyebrows with an old pair of tweezers. I perched on the side of the tub, the porcelain cool against the backs of my legs. The window was open, blowing the curtains with a faint breeze, but it was still damn hot. The scent of the cedar shingles baking in the sun on the roof drifted in, mixing with Courtney's hairspray and perfume.

'You going to see Shane?' I said.

She paused, looked confused.

'That guy with the blue car,' I said.

She made a face. 'Ugh, no. I got rid of him last week.'

Courtney didn't keep boyfriends around long. The only guy she'd ever gotten sort of serious with, Troy Dougan, had moved away in May. She said she didn't care because she was going to move to Vancouver as soon as she graduated. She figured she could make enough money to move down to the States in a few years, somewhere like Nashville, and become a country singer. When I graduated I was going to come live with her in Vancouver – I couldn't wait to see the ocean. We talked about it a lot, how I'd go on tour with her and take all her photos. I took one of her now, her tawny skin bathed in warm evening light from the open window that turned the side of her face gold.

I didn't actually have any film in the camera, hadn't had any for weeks. Sometimes Dad would bring me home a roll, same with Courtney – she stole it or got boyfriends to buy it. She liked the thrill of grabbing it right under the clerk's nose. Dani kept telling her, 'You're going to end up in jail before you're twenty.'

Courtney stepped back, straightening her sundress. We didn't have many clothes, and what we did have we'd bought at the second-hand store. Courtney spent hours mixing and matching stuff, trying to make it look like pictures from magazines. Dani and I mostly wore jeans and T-shirts, but Courtney was good about lending us her things.

Courtney fluffed her hair over her shoulder. I smiled and took another photo, thinking of our mother, how I'd watch her brush her long hair in the mirror. But Mom never wore makeup, letting her freckles show. We'd still had some of her clothes until we went into foster care. Dad had gotten rid of just about all her things – even her wedding ring. I'd managed to save a couple of photos and the camera, Dani kept her recipe cards, and Courtney clung to an old bottle of perfume that was dried up now.

'Where are you going?' I said.

'Out.' Courtney usually shared more, so she was probably seeing someone she shouldn't, like one of her friends' boyfriends. Mom used to call Courtney her wild child, but she'd say it in a proud way. Dani was her worker bee, and I was her dreamer. I never felt like she had a favorite, more like she loved each of us for different things. She'd said we were all the best part of her, and that if anything ever happened to one of us, her heart would break.

Courtney smiled in the mirror. 'Where's *your* boyfriend?'

I rolled my eyes. Courtney knew perfectly well that Billy wasn't my boyfriend – he was just the guy who lived down the road. We hung out sometimes, but it wasn't like that, though he was always trying. I'd let him kiss me one time, just to see what it was like. He tasted gross, like barbecue chips, and his skin smelled like sweat. I didn't tell Courtney or Dani about it, but I liked listening to their talk. Dani had only slept with Corey – they'd been together since the eighth grade – but Courtney slept around and had told me enough about sex and what boys like that I wasn't sure if I ever wanted to go through with it myself.

It was after midnight when Courtney finally stumbled home, smelling like cologne and cigarettes, giggling as she pulled on her nightgown in our room – we'd shared a bedroom since we were babies. Often we'd end up sleeping in the same bed, curled together like puppies, her long hair wrapping around us. On really cold nights Dani would pile in too. We'd talk about our mom, our dreams, Dani and her farm that would stretch for acres, Courtney and her music, the crowd screaming her name. I just wanted to take photos, of anything and everything. My sisters were my favorite subjects, but I liked it best when they didn't know I was there. Dani fussing over the tomatoes, wandering among the corn-fields, Courtney with no makeup and her hair messy, strumming her guitar.

Courtney pulled her blankets over her head and passed out. I drifted back to sleep.

Hours later, I woke to a crash downstairs.

I jerked up and fumbled for the lamp on my night table.

'The fuck was that?' Courtney said.

'Is it him?'

'I don't know. Did you hear his truck?'

'I was asleep. I heard something downstairs.'

I found the light just as Dani slipped into our room, her face anxious. The three of us stared toward the door, not moving a muscle, listening. Was that the fridge opening? We heard something drop. Someone cursed.

Now heavy footsteps were coming up the stairs. I got

out of bed, stood beside Dani. Courtney was sitting up, blankets pulled off, one foot on the floor, ready to run.

Dad pushed open the door. His white tank top was sweat-stained, blood or ketchup dotting the front, his shoulders covered in dark freckles and sunburn.

He gave us a big smile. 'There's my girls!'

I watched him, waiting to see if his smile would disappear and he'd start shouting insults. Dad started off happy when he was drinking, but it never lasted long.

'Well, come on, where's my fucking hug?' He was still smiling, but anger simmered in his eyes.

Dani and I walked up to him, Courtney lagging behind. Dad crushed us to him in a hug, enveloping us in the smell of beer and sour sweat and cigarettes.

'Come on, let's play cards,' he said when he let us go.

'It's late, Dad,' Dani said. 'Walter wants us up early, and—'

'I don't give a shit what Walter wants,' Dad said. 'I want to play cards.' Sometimes invoking Walter's name would make Dad shut things down a little faster. He didn't want to lose another place. But tonight he was too far gone, his blue eyes glassy, his sandy-colored hair damp on his forehead.

His eyes focused on Courtney. 'Come on, Court. You're always up for some fun – right, girl?' There was an edge to his voice, testing, like he knew something. Courtney looked terrified.

25

'Sure, Dad. Let's play some cards.'

He was pissed at her. I could see that now. What had she done?

She started walking past him, but slowly, her body tense, like she was bracing for him to hit her. He pretended to lunge at her. She screamed and he laughed, his deep voice filling the room.

'You girls are a bunch of chickenshits.'

We followed him down the stairs, his broad back filling the space. He pulled one of the chairs out at the table, slapped his hand down on the wood.

'Sit your asses down.'

We all sat around him, and he gave me a grin. 'How you been, Peanut? Miss me?'

'Yeah, Dad.' I felt like crying, hated the sound of drink in his voice, his phlegmy cough, his red-rimmed eyes.

He pulled a deck of cards out of his back pocket, started to deal them. When we all had a hand, he pulled a pack of smokes out of his other pocket, lit a cigarette, letting it dangle out of his mouth, one eye squinting from the smoke.

'We'll play for cigarettes,' he said, throwing a few in front of each of us.

We all looked at each other.

'You think I don't know you bitches steal my smokes?'

Dani said, 'Dad, we don't—'

'Save your bullshit.' He looked at me. 'Get me a beer out of the fridge.'

I got up quickly, yanked a can free from the plastic ring. There were only two left.

I handed it to him and sat down. He opened the can with a loud pop, took a gulp, beer dribbling out the corner of his mouth. He didn't wipe it off. Courtney and Dani were studying their cards. Dani's forehead was shiny with sweat. Courtney's eyes were still scared, flicking to Dad and back to her cards.

He caught her looking. 'You trying to see my cards?'

'No.'

He slammed his fist down again, leaned over the table. 'You trying to see my *fucking* cards?'

'No, Dad!' she cried out.

He leaned back, gave her an assessing look. 'You think you're pretty smart, don't you?'

She shook her head. 'I'm not smart at all.'

He looked around at us. 'Worthless – the whole lot of you. I work my ass off for you three, and all you do is embarrass the shit out of me.'

'I'm sorry, Dad.' I didn't know what I was apologizing for, but it didn't matter.

His gaze settled back on Courtney. 'Are *you* sorry?'

'Yeah, Dad, I'm really sorry.'

'Then get your sorry ass over to the stove and make

me a fried egg sandwich.' He laughed, then started coughing, choking on cigarette smoke.

Courtney got up and turned the stove on, set a frying pan on the burner, got eggs out of the fridge.

'We don't have any bread,' Dani said, her voice calm, but her hand shaking slightly on the cards.

Dad snatched the cigarette away from his mouth. 'You don't have any *bread*?'

'We didn't have any money.'

'Where's the money I left you?' A hundred dollars. The three of us had stood in the store, studying the prices on the cans and boxes. Apples were on sale – we'd bought a big bag.

'We used it all,' Dani said. 'We needed groceries.'

He was shaking his head now, a slow, dangerous movement. 'You fucking useless bitches. A man comes home from working for weeks and he can't even get a decent fried egg *sandwich*?'

Courtney was frozen next to the fridge, waiting.

'I can make you scrambled eggs, Dad,' she said. 'I make good eggs.'

He turned and looked at her. 'You make good eggs?' He laughed. 'At least you can do something right.'

He was watching her now, staring as she cracked the eggs into the bowl with a shaking hand. She kept giving him nervous looks. He took another hard drink of his beer, sucked on the cigarette, almost biting it with his teeth.

28

'You better make sure that pan is good and hot.'

'It's hot, Dad,' she said.

'Really hot?'

'Yeah.' She gave him another scared look.

My heart was up in my throat, and I was getting that sick feeling of dread. Something was going to happen. I could see it in my dad's face, the way his hand was gripping the beer, his boot tapping under the table.

'What've you been up to, Courtney? You working hard?'

'Yeah, every day.'

'What about every night? What've you been doing then, Courtney?'

I saw the fear on her face.

'Just hanging out,' she said. Some of the eggs slopped out of the pan and hit the burner, filling the air with the smell of scorched eggs. She frantically tried to brush the crumbled egg away from the burner.

I looked at Dad, who was still watching Courtney. I waited for the explosion, but he was silent, just took another drag of his smoke. She turned the burner off, scraped the eggs onto a plate, then got a fork out of the drawer.

She walked over, carefully set the plate in front of him, and sat in her chair again. We all watched as he took a bite, pieces of egg falling off his fork and landing on the table. His cigarette was still burning in his other

29

hand, the smoke drifting into Dani's eyes. She didn't move, didn't cough.

Dad grunted, gave a nod, then took another bite.

I felt Courtney's body relax a little beside me, heard her take a breath.

He stopped chewing, got a disgusted look on his face, then opened his mouth and let the whole mouthful slop back out onto his plate.

'These are fucking rotten!'

'We just collected the eggs yesterday!' Courtney said.

'It's true!' Dani said.

'Maybe *you're* the rotten egg,' Dad said, staring at Courtney, his eyes raging. 'Everything you touch tastes like shit.' He picked up his plate and threw it at her. She jerked her body to the right, making the chair topple over, spilling her onto the floor. The plate shattered behind us. Dani and I leapt out of our chairs.

Dad took a lunging step toward Courtney, his huge body towering over her. Dani pushed me behind her as she reached for Courtney, but Dad was already grabbing her arm and hauling her off the floor.

Courtney screamed and tried to pull away. He dragged her toward the stove. I tried to go after them but Dani held me back.

'Do you know what it's like hearing that shit about my kid?' he roared.

Courtney was begging, 'What did I do?'

'Bob calls me in camp, tells me my good-for-nothing daughter's screwing a married man!'

Dad had Courtney close to the stove. She was screaming. I was sobbing and yelling, 'Dad, let her go!'

Dani released my arm and ran for the rifle, pulled it out from under the couch, grabbed the box of shells.

Dad picked up the frying pan, held it close to Courtney's face. She squirmed, frantically trying to get away. I threw myself at his back, pounded against him, clawed his neck, any flesh I could find. He hit backward with his elbow, catching me in the jaw and sending me to the floor.

He gripped Courtney's face tight in one fist, her eyes bulging.

'Dani!' I screamed. She had the gun up to her shoulder, aimed at Dad, but she was just staring, her face shocked and white.

Dad pressed the pan against Courtney's jaw. She shrieked, the sound stabbing into me. Dani stood there, the gun quivering in the air.

I scrambled to my feet, yanked on Dad's arm, pulling the frying pan away. He lashed out, smacking me hard across the face. I stumbled backward, crashed into the table. The pan slipped out of his grasp and thudded to floor.

'Fucking bitches!'

He wrapped his hand in Courtney's hair and dragged

her down the hall to the bathroom. Her back was sliding on the hardwood, legs kicking out uselessly.

I chased after them, grabbed on to his belt with both hands, pulled back. He swatted at me with his free hand but I didn't let go. He was at the bathroom.

'I called the cops!' Dani yelled. 'They're coming!'

Our phone had been disconnected two weeks ago.

She was running after us, still carrying the gun. 'Stop! Dad, stop!'

Dad flipped up the toilet lid, held Courtney's face over the bowl. Plunged her down, brought her up so she could gasp at the air, then held her down again. Her legs kicked out.

I beat on his back, picked up the garbage can, slammed it down on his head, but he didn't stop. Dani held the gun up again.

'Get out of the way!' she yelled, and I dropped the can, moved back to the doorway.

'Let go!' she screamed. 'Let go!'

Dad laughed. Water streamed from Courtney's face. She was gagging and gasping, clawing at his hands. He plunged her head down. The moment stretched out. I couldn't tear my gaze away. Dani was screaming, but she wasn't pulling the trigger. Courtney's hand was loosening. Her legs stopped kicking out.

I grabbed the rifle out of Dani's hands, aimed for the fleshy part of Dad's shoulder, and pulled.

The shot echoed in the small space. Dani shrieked. A bloody gash opened on the side of Dad's neck.

He let go of Courtney, who crumpled to the floor. He clasped his neck, looked at the blood. He turned and came at me, hands out, his face ugly with rage.

'I'm going to fucking kill you!'

Desperate sobs coming out of my mouth, I pulled the trigger again. A small hole opened in his forehead and he dropped to his knees, fell forward. He made a couple of weird sounds, gasping breaths from his chest, then silence. Blood flowed onto the linoleum floor, pooled around his head.

'Oh, Jesus.' Dani ran over, checked his pulse. 'He's not breathing!'

My hands were shaking. I fell to my knees and stared at my dad's body. Dani had flipped Dad over and was holding his face between her hands, blowing into his mouth, then pounding on his chest, but I knew it was too late. Courtney crawled past Dad, her face and hair wet. She got to me, and I dropped the gun. We gripped each other tight. Finally Dani stopped and sat up on her heels.

'Fuck, fuck, fuck.'

She turned to look at us, tears dripping down her face.

'You *killed* him,' she said, her voice stunned and shaky.

I'd killed Dad. I'd killed Dad. I couldn't believe it. I swallowed hard.

'I had to. Courtney was *drowning*!'

She looked away then, a flash of shame in her face. She wiped at her nose, staring down at Dad's body again. She put her hands to her head.

'What the fuck are we going to do now?'

I looked at the blood around Dad's head, his open eyes staring up at the ceiling. I thought of all the times I'd worried he was going to kill one of us, all the times I wished he'd just disappear and we'd no longer have to live in fear. I'd thought our lives would be better then, that we'd finally be free.

But now, looking at my father's body, I was more scared than I'd ever been in my life.

Chapter Four

We left Dad and the gun in the bathroom and closed the door. In the kitchen, Dani helped Courtney flush the burn with cold water. She was bent over the sink, crying and shivering, her hair and the top of her nightgown wet.

'Maybe she should go to the hospital.' I couldn't stop staring at the burn on her jawline, a puckered angry mark about four inches long. It looked painful.

Courtney shook her head, splashing water everywhere. 'They'll put us in foster care.'

Dani was pacing the kitchen now, her shirt covered with red splotches, her face and hands with streaks of bright red. She stopped and stared at my shirt, her face haunted. I looked down, saw the drops of blood. My lip felt puffy and I tasted blood in the corner. Dad must've split it when he hit me.

She started pacing again. 'Shit, this is bad, really bad.'

'Should we tell Walter and Ingrid? Maybe they could help or—'

'No, we have to think.' She sat down. 'You'll be arrested. Maybe us too, if they think we're accomplices or whatever.'

'Walter might check on us – the gunshots,' I said. The .22 didn't make a loud shot, but it had echoed with the cast-iron bathtub and the window was open. I imagined him getting dressed, pulling on his boots, searching for his truck keys.

She was nodding. 'We have to figure this out fast.'

'I'll tell the police the truth – I did it.'

My legs felt shaky. I braced my hands against them, holding them down or holding myself up. I wasn't sure. My gaze flicked to the bathroom door. Everything was so quiet now. The air felt electric, thick. I could smell blood.

Dani was also staring toward the bathroom. I wondered if she was thinking about how she couldn't pull the trigger.

Her head snapped back toward us, her face grim and determined.

'We should hide his truck until we know what we're doing.'

'Okay,' I said. We looked at Courtney.

'Okay,' she said.

*

While Courtney and Dani changed their clothes, I ran outside. I didn't have my license but Dani let me practice sometimes. I climbed into Dad's truck, moved the seat forward. The truck stank of spilled beer and Dad's cologne – we'd bought it for him last Christmas. I tried not to notice the small plastic cowboy hat dangling from the rearview mirror, one of his work shirts tossed on the floor, the empties rolling around, the old cigarette pack, one corner of the silver paper folded down. I thought of how when I was little he'd make me animals with the thin foil.

Then I noticed the plastic bag on the seat. Inside I could just see a corner of a yellow box. I lifted open the top of the bag with my finger.

One of the boxes had an image of a camera lens on the front, the other one was film. I squeezed my eyes shut.

Don't look at it, don't think about it.

I pulled the truck into a thicket of trees far behind the house, using the moonlight and memory to guide me, scared to use the headlights in case Walter and Ingrid were already coming down the hill. I hesitated, then grabbed the plastic bag and ran back to the house. Courtney was standing by the front door, wearing a fresh T-shirt, a long one.

'Dani's trying to clean up,' she said. 'You should change too, but put on something you'd wear to bed.

Make it fast.' She was talking through gritted teeth, her face strained like every movement hurt.

I washed my face and pulled on an old nightgown.

Downstairs, Dani had grabbed a bunch of old towels and placed them around Dad's head to soak up the blood. Courtney was cleaning the kitchen, putting away the frying pan, picking up the chairs that had been knocked over. I gathered the playing cards and cigarettes strewn across the table while she stuffed Dad's empty beer can to the very bottom of the garbage can.

We found Dani in the bathroom, on her knees, staring at Dad's body.

'What do we . . . what do we do with him?' I said.

'I don't know.'

Courtney stood beside me. 'Should we move him to the back bedroom?'

'He'll leave blood,' I said.

A vehicle pulled up outside. We stared at each other, our eyes panicked.

Dani got to her feet, ran to the front window, peeked through the curtain.

'Is it the police?' I whispered.

A door slammed.

'Walter,' Dani hissed. 'Pretend you're making tea.' She turned to Courtney. 'Don't let him see the side of your face – sit on the couch in the corner where it's darkest and turn away.'

We ran to our positions, our feet soft on the floor, while Dani walked to the door and opened it.

'Hi, Walter.'

I couldn't see him from where I was in the kitchen but heard his voice say, 'You girls okay? Heard some shots.'

'Yeah, rat was in the cupboards again – got him this time.'

'You girls need to be careful with that gun.'

'We are – Dad taught us.'

'Thought I heard his truck earlier.' My hand froze midair as I reached for a mug.

'That was just Courtney getting dropped off.'

I took a breath. *Good thinking, Dani.*

'When's your daddy coming home? He's late on rent.'

'Should be any day. Anything extra we can do around the place?'

'Don't know, Dani. We've found you just about as much work as we can, you know?' Silence for a moment, then he said, 'What's that smell?'

Shit, could he smell the blood?

'What smell?' Dani sounded calm but she was gripping the door so tight her knuckles were white.

'Like something's burned.'

'Oh, that's just Jess. She left a pan on the stove too long, burnt some eggs. We're all up so we figured we'd make a snack, but Jess is useless in the kitchen.' She laughed.

I called out, 'Evening, Walter.'

He called back, 'Evening, Jess.' Then, to Dani, 'You kids should get to bed. Big day tomorrow on the farm.'

'Yes, sir.'

'Okay, then. Let me know when your daddy shows up.'

'Sure will.'

She closed the door, sagging against it, then peeked through the side window until we heard his truck driving away.

She turned back around. 'We have to get rid of the body.'

We found an old plastic tarp in the garage and rolled Dad onto it. It took all three of us to move him. Then we pulled the tarp around him, wrapping duct tape around his ankles and upper body to hold it in place. We shoved the bloody towels and rags into a garbage bag. We worked quickly, not speaking, but Courtney kept sniffling and Dani's face was pale, her eyes angry.

I kept seeing Dad's smile when he called me Peanut, how he took us four-wheeling or shooting, remembered to get me film, bought Dani seeds. He taught us that being girls didn't mean we needed to rely on men, showed us how to change the oil and tires on the truck and fix things at the house. When he was around we weren't scared of anyone or anything. But we were always scared of him. I thought about the cigarette burns on my legs, the time he threw Courtney out of the truck, how his eyes would turn to slits when he'd been drinking. I felt like he was glaring at me through the tarp, could hear his voice in my head.

You fucking useless bitches.

'Should we put him in the quarry?' Dani said. The old gravel quarry, now full of water, was half a mile away, so deep people said there were logging trucks at the bottom.

Courtney shook her head. 'We have to bury him or he could float up.'

'Somewhere no one will look,' Dani said. 'It can't be near our house.'

We were silent, thinking.

'What about the pig field?' I said. 'Under the trough. The ground is always wet because of the mud – and they haven't moved that trough in years.'

Dani was nodding. 'It will help with the smell too.'

I flinched, but Dani's mouth was a tight line.

We lifted him, groaning under his weight, and carried him to the back door. We set him down while Dani ran to the shed and came back with the wheelbarrow.

We walked him down the back stairs, then laid him across the wheelbarrow, resting the sack of rags and a couple of shovels on top. We took turns, two pushing while one forged ahead. We had to take a back trail that connected our house with the farm. Normally a ten-minute walk, it took us twenty minutes of pushing and we were covered in sweat and breathing hard. We moved the trough, slipping and sliding in the mud, then started to dig. The ground was dry once we got through the mud, and we were filthy and exhausted by the time we had a deep enough hole.

We pushed the wheelbarrow closer and rolled our father out. He landed partway in the hole and we had to shove him the rest of the way. He barely fit. Dani threw the garbage bag into the grave. It made a thud and we looked around. The night was silent except for one of the farm dogs barking up on the hill. I hoped Walter didn't come out to investigate.

'Should we say something?' Courtney whispered.

We looked down at the body, the black shroud shiny in the moonlight.

Worthless – the whole lot of you . . .

I dug into the dirt and threw a shovelful down the hole, then another, faster and faster, crying with each toss. My sisters joined in.

When we were done, Dani grabbed me and Courtney for a hug. We held on tight, our skin and breath merging.

'It'll be okay,' Dani said.

*

It was almost morning, the sky already getting light, and we had to work on the farm in a couple of hours, but we scrubbed the floor in the bathroom with bleach, using old blankets for rags. Finally we had to stop, too tired to do another thing. We couldn't get out all the blood – the grooves in the linoleum showed rust-colored stains.

We hadn't patched the wall where my first shot hit, so we hung a small painting from the living room over the hole. We threw the rags into garbage bags, burying them in the hall closet until we figured out how to get rid of them, then shut the downstairs bathroom and locked the house, making sure every window was closed. We collapsed onto our beds, trying to get a few minutes of rest before we started our day, but I could only toss and turn. I heard Courtney moving around too. She'd been taking ibuprofen but I could tell by her breathing and occasional moans that she was still in pain. My jaw hurt where Dad had elbowed me – my teeth even ached – but we didn't have many pills left so I'd given them all to Courtney. When Dani came to get us for work, her eyes were red-rimmed.

We left the windows closed for the day. It would be hot as hell by the time we got home, but we had no choice, couldn't risk someone snooping around until we finished cleaning the bathroom and got rid of the bleach smell.

My lip wasn't puffy anymore but it stung when I

spoke and my jaw was bruised. We figured we could cover it up with makeup.

We weren't sure what would arouse more suspicion: Courtney missing work or showing up with the burn, which looked even worse in the daylight, the skin red and blistered. Dani figured it was a second-degree burn. None of us wanted to risk going into a hospital. They'd want to talk to our father for sure.

'I'll just say it was an accident,' Courtney said. 'We need the money.'

'We need to not get caught,' Dani said.

'We have a lot of accidents,' I said. 'If we say she's sick, Ingrid might come check on her. Even if she doesn't, they'll figure it out if they see her in a few days and she still has the burn on her face. They'll know we were hiding her.'

Dani was nodding. 'Yeah, you're right. Better we just act normal.'

We were working on different parts of the farm that day but agreed that if anyone asked, Courtney would say she was bending down to get something out of a lower cabinet that morning and I'd walked by with a hot pan.

I mucked out the stalls, trying to focus on the work. *Clean that corner, pick up the shovel, load the wheelbarrow . . .* But I couldn't stop thinking about the shovel in my hands, Dad's body slumped in the wheelbarrow, how it had rolled out. *You're a murderer. You're going to jail.* My body ached, my eyes and throat felt dry, my hands were blistered – I'd put on gloves that morning, but every shovelful ripped them open, making them sting and burn. I licked the split in my lip, tasting blood. My gaze kept drifting down to the pig field.

It didn't feel real, what we'd done. What I'd done.

'You in here, Jess?' It was Ingrid.

I turned away, scraped some manure in the corner. We'd put makeup on my bruise, toning down the color, but a faint shadow showed through.

'Yeah, last stall.'

Ingrid leaned over the open door, chatting about one of the horses – a vet was coming out later and she wanted me to move the horse to a different field. As she spoke, I had to turn to dump the manure into the wheelbarrow. I hoped she was too distracted to see my face, but she stopped talking. I looked up.

She was staring at the bruise. It wasn't the first time I'd come to work banged up, but I worried she was thinking about the shots last night.

'What happened to you?' she said. Ingrid was a farmer's wife through and through. She wore men's jeans and shirts, kept her hair up in a bun, could nurse a lamb with a bottle while baking a pie and throw a hay bale as hard as any man.

She also didn't miss anything that happened on the farm.

'This?' I rubbed my jaw. 'Angus got me.' Angus was

one of the Clydesdales – he often knocked his big head into someone, usually on purpose.

'Told you to stay away from his front end.'

I forced a smile. 'His back end's just as dangerous.'

She chuckled. 'True enough.' Her face turned serious, the leathery tanned skin pulling at her eyes. 'Walter said you kids have some rats . . . '

'We're getting them.'

'Maybe it's time to try some poison.'

'We don't want them stinking up the walls.' I felt sick, thinking of the blood still on the floor in the bathroom, the bag of bloody rags, flies circling.

'We'll talk to your daddy about it when he gets home.'

'Yes, ma'am.'

That night we heated up the last can of tomato soup. Courtney told us Ingrid had asked about her burn.

'Did she believe you?' I said.

'I don't know. She asked weird questions, like why you'd been cooking and not Dani, and if we went to the hospital. She said it wasn't good, us being on our own so much, but I said Dad was coming home soon.' Ingrid could be nosy, and she had no problem sharing your personal business with anyone who would listen. She'd more than likely already told a few people that we were still alone. People who might decide to be neighborly and check on us.

Courtney looked at Dani. 'We should just get out of here.'

Dani thought it over, taking so long I wanted to shout at her, but the more I pushed, the longer she'd take. She liked to look at all sides of stuff, weighing the options, but I thought she should listen to her guts more. I agreed with Courtney, but if I told Dani what I thought, she'd just tell me to shut up.

'If we split right after those gunshots, they're going to wonder,' she finally said. 'Maybe even send the cops after us. Let's just hold tight for now.'

When we were finished eating, we ripped up the linoleum in the bathroom, which had already been peeling in places. We didn't know what to do with it, so we shoved it into the shed until we could figure something out. We dug the bullet out of the wall – it had lodged in one of the beams – then patched the hole with some drywall putty we also found in the shed. We repainted the whole bathroom and the plywood floor with some old paint Dad had stolen from one of his buddies.

Around midnight we took Dad's truck to the quarry, sticking to the back road. Dani drove, wearing one of Dad's cowboy hats and a big coat, making her look bulkier in case anyone passed us. Courtney and I stayed low on the passenger side. At the quarry we drove around, checking that no one else was out there for a late swim. It was quiet. We went to one of the highest spots, put the truck in neutral, and pushed it over the edge. It didn't sink right away.

'Shit! It's not going down,' I said. 'We should've opened the windows.'

'Wait,' Dani said. Finally it started to move, sinking below the surface. Bubbles rose.

'What if someone sees it? Like swimming down or something,' I said.

'They won't,' Dani said. But she didn't meet my eyes.

We decided to ditch the bleached rags and ripped-up linoleum at a neighbor's. The man had more junk in his yard than our father, and stacks of building debris behind one of his shops – Courtney had fooled around with his son and remembered him saying the stuff had been there for decades. Best case, if he ever did clean up, it would get hauled to the garbage dump for us.

We drove Dani's truck, our cargo under some other garbage, and parked near the bottom of his fields, where he brought the tractor through, turning our headlights off and coasting in. We couldn't get too close – he might hear us up at the house – so we followed the tractor road on foot, each of us carrying an armload, the moon lighting our way. Courtney tripped and dropped her load with a thump.

We all froze, waiting to hear if anyone had noticed. The night was still.

We spread the garbage among the plywood, drywall, and scrap metal, carefully placing the sheets of linoleum between everything, trying to make sure it was at the back of the piles. It was hard work because we had to move some of the scrap, which was heavy, and we were trying to be quiet so we had to move slowly, our muscles screaming with tension. We didn't know what to do with the bag of rags. Courtney and Dani argued in hushed whispers – Courtney thought we should just bury them, but Dani said an animal might be attracted to the blood and dig them back up. Finally we shoved them into an oil drum, then ran down the tractor road to the truck, my sister's bodies dark shadows in front of me.

Back at home, we lit the last of Dad's cigarettes and talked about what we should do.

'We could get jobs,' Courtney said.

'Doing what?' I said. 'And who would hire us?'

There weren't many opportunities in this town for three teenage girls, just farm work and maybe waitressing or working at the grocery store.

'You guys are missing the point,' Dani said. 'They won't let us stay here without Dad – people, his boss and his friends, are going to start looking for him. If we say he skipped out on us again, they'll put us in foster care.'

'You're almost eighteen, maybe they'll let you keep us,' I said.

'I'd have to show that I could support you.'

'Walter and Ingrid might let us stay if we kept working on the ranch.'

'It's not enough money and Dad's already behind,' Dani said.

'We could go on welfare,' I said. 'Or maybe Corey's parents would let us stay there?' Dani was pretty close to her boyfriend's family and they were nice.

'They don't have room,' she said. 'And we can't stay anyway. We don't know if Dad stopped somewhere before he came home. Someone might've seen him in town.'

'Should we leave tonight?' Courtney said.

'No,' Dani said. 'It'll look like we didn't give him a chance to come home, like we know something.' The way she said it told me she'd been thinking about this for a while. 'In a few days we have to say that he's taken off again, and we're going to stay with family.'

'If no one sees him for years, won't they suspect something?' I said.

Dani took a long drag of her smoke. 'Yeah, so we need to buy ourselves enough time to get out of here and settle somewhere else, then we'll have to get fake ID. If anyone finds the truck or catches on, we'll be long gone.' She looked at Courtney. 'What about that married man

Dad said you were messing around with? Is he going to be a problem?'

'Who was it anyway?' I said.

'Ben Miller,' Courtney said. 'I broke it off last night, just told him I didn't want my dad catching on.'

'Ben *Miller*?' I said. 'He's, like, thirty.' He owned one of the construction companies in town and had a wife and a couple of kids. I didn't know how Courtney had hooked up with him, but no wonder Dad had freaked out.

'Doesn't matter now,' she said, her face flushed. 'It's over.'

'What about Corey?' I said. He'd come by once since Dad had come home, pulled his truck up with some friends and asked Dani if she wanted to come for a swim, but she said she was too tired. He was going to get suspicious soon.

Dani blinked a few times, her lower lip trembling, until she caught it with her top one, pressed hard. I was almost relieved – I'd thought for a minute she might cry. I hadn't seen her cry for years. Not since our mom's funeral. I don't know what I would've done if she had broken down.

'I'm going to have to break up with him.'

'No!' I breathed out in a hushed whisper.

'You sure?' Courtney sounded shocked too. Dani looked stunned herself, like she couldn't believe what she was saying. We all thought they'd get married. They'd been friends even before they dated and I couldn't remember a time when they weren't together. Corey had been like a big brother to Courtney and me, teaching us how to drive his truck, taking us to the lake or movies with them, never acting like it was a pain in the ass to have his girlfriend's sisters around.

'Won't he think it's weird?' Courtney said.

'Probably not.'

'Have you been fighting?'

Dani nodded, taking an angry drag off her smoke, blowing it out hard.

'Why didn't you say anything?' Courtney looked as surprised as I felt, and also a little hurt.

'It wasn't any of your business.' Dani's chin jutted up now.

'But he's always talking about you guys getting your own place ...' Courtney looked confused now, then understanding came over her face. 'He's been bugging you to move out and you wouldn't because of us.'

Dani shrugged. 'Whatever.'

My eyes filled with tears. 'Sorry, Dani.'

'It's not your fault.' Her voice was tight, like she was trying to squeeze out the words. 'We're getting together Saturday night. I'll do it then.'

'Where are we going to go?' Courtney said.

'It should be a big city, so we don't stand out,' Dani said.

'Vancouver,' I said.

Courtney and I looked at Dani.

'Okay.' She knew how much we wanted to go there, but it had been our dream, not hers. I felt bad about how much she was leaving behind.

She was staring at the bathroom again, the cigarette burning down in her hand. None of us had been able to go in there since we'd cleaned up.

'I'm sorry, Dani,' I said again. This time she didn't answer.

Chapter Five

We agreed that we'd give it a few more days. We were walking home from the farm the next afternoon, hot and tired, with Dani leading the way, her long hair swinging with each step, her body stiff, angry. Was she thinking about how she had to break up with Corey? I fiddled with my camera, clicking the shutter over and over again but feeling out of it, spacey from lack of sleep. Courtney's fingers grazed her burn. Dani kept telling her to leave it alone, it would get infected, but Courtney kept poking at it or looking at it in the mirror.

Dani stopped abruptly and I looked up. A police car was waiting in the driveway. My fingers froze on the camera. Dani didn't look at us.

Barely moving her lips, she said, 'Let me do the talking.'

The sergeant got out of his car and we walked toward him. He was tall and lean, his belt hanging low.

'Sergeant Gibbs,' Dani said. 'What can we do for you?'

'Just wanted to make sure you girls are okay.'

'We're fine.'

'Heard you guys have a rat problem.' So he knew about the shots. Ingrid or Walter must've called him.

'We're staying on top of it.'

'Your father home?'

'Soon.'

'Been a long shift this time. He sending you money?'

'We're okay.'

'Heard you're getting behind.'

'We'll get caught up.'

He glanced down at the driveway, his eyes scanning the dirt, like he was looking for tracks. He looked back at the house, then us. 'Mind if I look around?'

'What for?' Dani said. Her voice was calm, but she had her chin lifted.

'You girls here all alone, just want to make sure the house is safe.'

'I don't think our dad would like it.'

'Well, we don't have to tell him.'

I glanced at Dani, my stomach muscles tight.

'Look all you want,' Dani said, shrugging.

She walked up the steps, pushed open the door. We came in behind, standing awkward in the kitchen. Courtney ran the tap, poured herself some water. Her gaze flicked to me, then back to the sergeant. She leaned against the counter, acting casual, but her hand on the glass was shaking slightly. I sat down at the table, thinking about the gun under the sink. Dani was behind me. I could feel her heat, the nervous energy in her body.

The sergeant walked around, checking windows, his boots heavy on the floor. He fingered a broken lock on one of the back windows.

'You got someone to fix that?'

'Dad will do it when he gets home.'

He grunted, walked over to the bathroom, pushed open the door. I held my breath. His head tilted as he studied the fresh paint on the floor.

'Been painting?'

'We thought if we fixed things up a little, Walter might knock some money off.'

He left the bathroom, walked toward us, eyeing Courtney, the burn on her face.

'What happened there?'

'Jess burned me with a pan when I was bending over.' She laughed, but it sounded nervous.

'Looks pretty bad. You go to the doctor?'

She shook her head.

He stared at her face. 'Usually takes a while for a burn to go that deep.'

'It was a really hot pan,' I said.

His gaze flicked to me, lingered for a minute on the

bruise on my jaw. I could feel my face flush and knew I looked guilty. I hoped Ingrid had told him about the horse. If he asked me anything, I was sure I'd be a terrible liar.

He turned away and opened our fridge, his eyebrows lifting when he saw how empty it was. He leaned over, moved a few things around. I thought about the beer Dad had brought home, the leftover can. We'd never taken it out of the fridge. I gripped my hands tight in my lap.

'Why you looking in there?' Dani said.

'If you kids aren't eating properly, might have to get social services to help out.'

'We're eating fine.'

He stood back up, closed the fridge. 'How old are you now, Dani?'

'Almost eighteen.'

'You're all minors. None of you should be here alone like this. There are some good foster—'

'We're not going back to foster care.'

'Your dad don't come home soon, I'm going to have to make some calls.'

'He'll be home.'

He sniffed the air again, the smell of bleach and fresh paint lingering. I waited, holding my breath. Was he going to figure it out?

'You girls aren't supposed to be using that gun

without a parent around. I could take it away from you.'
He was looking at Dani over my head.

'We're careful,' she said.

My heart was beating so hard now I worried he could hear it, or see the panic on my face. Finally he turned and moved toward the door.

'Keep it locked up until your dad gets home. Don't want you shooting your foot off or something.'

'Yes, sir.' Dani exhaled softly behind me.

At the door he turned. 'I'll send the wife over with some food, should tide you over for a little while.'

'We don't need any food,' I said.

Dani gave me a shove. 'That'd be great,' she said. 'Just until our dad comes home. Then we'll pay you back.'

'Just until your dad comes home.' He held her gaze for a second, then walked to his car. He stared down again at the ground near his foot, scuffed his boot in the dirt. What was he seeing? A drop of blood? A tire track?

He looked back up at us one more time, then climbed into his car and drove off.

We were quiet that night as we ate our soup. Dani had used some of her money from doing odd jobs and bought a case of Mr Noodles – you could get four packages for a dollar. I liked to make mine just noodles, using the package of spices as flavor, and mixing it with butter. But we were out of butter and Dani said I should make the broth so it filled me up longer. She fried up some of the remaining deer meat and added a couple of carrots we'd taken from the field to the pot she'd made for her and Courtney – she tried to convince me to eat some of the meat but I'd seen deer in the fields, their big brown eyes, and I couldn't do it. I made a separate pot of soup for myself, just noodles, broth, and carrots.

'We're going to have to leave in a couple of days,' Dani said. 'He won't let us stay – he'll put us in foster homes.'

'You don't have to go – you're almost eighteen. You could move out with Corey. We could just go into a home together, me and Courtney.'

Courtney looked like she was going to cry. 'It would just be for a couple of years,' she said. 'We could make it work.'

'No,' Dani said. 'We have to stay together and it's too risky staying here.'

'We don't have any money to start over anywhere else,' Courtney said.

'I should just turn myself in,' I said.

Dani grabbed my shoulders hard.

'No one is going to the police. You're not going to jail, and you're not going to foster care.'

'This is my fault,' Courtney said.

'No, it's Dad's fault,' Dani said. She let go of my shoulders, but looked in my eyes. 'He was going to *kill* Courtney – you had to do it.'

I pushed my bowl of soup away.

'I'm scared,' I said.

'We're all scared,' Dani said, pushing the bowl back to me.

Courtney and Dani were waiting for me outside the barn after I finished work the next day. We used to walk home alone or Dani would go to her boyfriend's, but now we stuck together. When we got to our house, a box was on our front steps. Inside there was some food, dried pasta, canned meats, soup, and even a few pairs of old jeans and some shirts. I remembered that the sergeant had some daughters a few years older than us. Then we noticed the dusty boot print on the porch. He'd dropped off the box himself. Had he been looking through the window? We checked around the house for footsteps. There was a boot print near the shed.

It was time to leave.

Dani drove to Corey's. When she got home, her eyes were red-rimmed and puffy. She went straight into her room and wouldn't come out for hours.

Courtney shouted through the door that she was taking the truck and Dani didn't say anything. Courtney grabbed her guitar and headed out the front door.

'Where are you going?' I yelled after her. 'Can I come?'

'Stay with Dani.'

I wondered if she was going to see a boy and felt frustrated, helpless. She was going to get us in more trouble. Dani should've stopped her. I paced the house until I calmed down. It would be okay, Courtney was smart.

I walked to the farm and stole some eggs from the henhouse, then picked some chives from the garden and some tomatoes and green peppers from the greenhouse, hoping Ingrid and Walter didn't see me. I shooed one of the border collies who was following me around, his tail wagging.

I made Dani scrambled eggs and knocked softly on her door.

'Made you some dinner, Dani.' No answer. I went back downstairs and fed myself but left her plate under a cover.

She came down five minutes later, her face splotchy, and picked at her eggs, then gave me heck for leaving a mess in the kitchen.

'And what the hell were you thinking, stealing that stuff? You should always have one of us with you for a lookout.'

'Sorry, Dani.' I smiled, happy that she was angry at me. Meant she was feeling better.

Courtney came home when I was doing the dishes. She gave me a wan smile and a 'Hey.'

'Where you been?' Dani called out from the living

61

room, where she was packing some of our framed photographs into a box.

'Selling my guitar.'

Dani came in. 'What the hell? Why?'

'We need the money and I don't plan on singing anymore.' She touched her burn. 'I'll never make it big with this on my face.'

'That's stupid, Courtney,' I said. 'You're still beautiful.'

'No. I'm not. And even if I were, I'm done with singing.'

Dani and I looked at each other.

'We should go to Cash Creek first,' Courtney said. 'Troy, he'd lend us some money. We're going to need a lot for fake ID.' Cash Creek was a small town about two and a half hours southwest of Littlefield. We'd heard it was nothing but farmers and fields. Everyone had felt sorry for Troy when he had to move.

'We can't let anyone know where we're going,' Dani said.

'He wouldn't say anything – especially if he gives us money.' Troy dealt drugs, mostly just weed, but he always had cash on him. 'He told me they were moving to a trailer park – I'm sure we can find his car easy.'

Dani thought it over for a minute. 'Okay.'

That night we packed up. I had some books, clothes, my camera, envelopes full of photos – we didn't have any

62

family albums. Dad had trashed them all when he was drunk one night. But I had my favorite photo of Mom from when she'd won a fishing derby and posed in front of the tackle shop, her hair wild under her hat, a big smile on her face. I tucked the photo inside one of my books, then shoved everything into a packsack. I also still had the camera lens and film Dad had brought home for me, but I pushed them to the bottom of my bag.

Courtney packed almost all her clothes and cosmetics. She was going to leave her songwriting books, but we made her take them. We stored a few things in the shed and dragged out the old tent and camping equipment.

We argued about whether to tell Ingrid and Walter or just leave a note. I wanted to tell them.

'They depend on our showing up,' I said. 'And Ingrid will be upset, she'll be worried.'

'That's exactly why we can't tell her. She'll have too many questions.' Dani mimicked Ingrid's rough voice, her hands on her hips. 'Where are you going? What aunt? How come you never mentioned her before? Maybe we should talk to the sergeant and see if anyone's heard from your father lately.'

'We have to write a note, Jess,' Courtney said.

'They're going to think it's weird,' I said.

'They're going to think whatever we do is weird,' Dani said. 'But if we leave tonight, we have a few hours' head start before anyone starts looking for us.'

I hated it but they were right. We rehearsed a few different ways of saying it, and in the end they got me to write the note – I had the best handwriting.

Dear Walter and Ingrid,

Thanks for letting us stay. We really appreciate everything you've done for us and are really sorry to be leaving you. Our dad hasn't come home and we're out of money, so we're going to stay with our aunt in Edmonton. If he shows up, tell him we're at Helen's.

Love, Jess, Dani, Courtney

We waited until two in the morning, when we figured the streets would be the quietest, taped the note to the front door, and drove off. As soon as we got out of town and the wooden sign for Littlefield disappeared in our rearview mirror, I was filled with apprehension. What was going to happen to us? Would Walter send the cops after us? Would they find some blood in the house? Had we missed something? We'd taken the gun – it was under the bench seat. If we got pulled over we'd be in trouble for having it, but that was the least of our problems.

'You should try to get some rest,' Dani told us.

But we couldn't sleep. We talked a little about what Vancouver would be like, where we'd stay. Dani figured we'd find a youth hostel. Then we'd find jobs, maybe cleaning or waitressing. Dani wanted to see if there were any farms on the outskirts that were looking for workers. We'd have to get new ID right away – none of us had a social insurance number – but we didn't know where to start. Dani said we'd just have to find out where the rough section of town was, like where drug dealers hung out, then we could ask.

After we stole the gas we drove for another hour, through small towns and farmland, lakes and valleys lining the roads. The towns were dark at this time of night, our only company on the road the occasional truck. Dani fell asleep at the wheel once, swerving onto the dry shoulder, only waking when we yelled at her, so we pulled off onto a side road and spread out our sleeping bags in the back of the truck. We'd planned on getting up early, but we were all exhausted and woke with the sun beaming down on us, our bodies stiff and sore. We drank some water, ate some of our food, brushed our teeth – spitting into the ditch – and got back on the road. If we found Troy without too much trouble, we figured we could still make it to Vancouver by the afternoon.

'We'll go to the beach on your birthday,' Dani said.

'That'd be cool.' I tried not to think about my father's presents, how days earlier they'd been all I wanted.

A half hour later when we were getting close to Cash

Creek, steam started coming up through the hood, then billowed out in big gusts.

'What the hell is that?' Courtney said.

'Fuck if I know,' Dani said as we pulled onto the side of the road. We all piled out and looked at the truck. Water was dripping out from below.

'Is it the radiator?' I said.

'Probably. Shit.' Dani kicked the tire.

'We're going to have to hitch to town,' Courtney said.

We grabbed what we could out of the back – water, our packsacks, some of the food – and started walking. We had to leave the rifle under the front seat and I worried about someone breaking into the truck. We hadn't gone far, could still see the truck, when we heard the rumble of an engine – a black Ford pulled alongside us. Two guys, maybe in their early twenties, were smiling through the window. The driver, a dark-haired boy with a baseball cap and a white tank top, leaned over the steering wheel.

'Truck break down?'

Keeping her distance from the truck, Dani said, 'Yeah, steam started coming out.'

'Probably your radiator or the water pump. I can look at it – I'm a mechanic,' the dark-haired boy said. The other one had brown hair and a big toothy smile, no shirt. He had a farmer's tan, lines on his neck and arms.

Dani turned, met our eyes.

Courtney shook her head. 'We should just walk to town.'

Dani whispered back, 'It'll take too long.'

The boys glanced at each other. The dark-haired one shrugged.

'It's cool if you don't want help. We can send the tow truck back, cost you about a hundred.'

The other boy chimed in, 'Or if you want to walk, probably take you an hour.' The heat was already waving off the road, sucking at our skin.

Dani said, 'If you could take a look, that'd be great.'

Chapter Six

'Yep, it's definitely the water pump,' the dark-haired boy said, his head under the hood. His name was Brian and he was tall and thin with dark round eyes, dark eyebrows and lashes, a small nose and mouth, and a necklace with a bullet on it. His faded jeans had rips in the knees and old stains, and his boots were scuffed and coated with dried mud. He smelled of grease and cigarettes.

His brother, Gavin, didn't really look like him, with lighter hair and a wide mouth full of white teeth. He was also bulkier, broad shouldered, and moved slower, but he was tall too. He had a different way of looking at you. Brian's eyes were lively, and he spoke quickly, breaking into laughter a lot. His gaze darted around, his hands fast and confident as he checked things under the hood. Gavin was more watchful, quieter.

Gavin was sitting on the tailgate now, taking long pulls from a beer. They'd handed us each one – ice-cold from a beer cooler, condensation dripping down the sides, and we guzzled them eagerly while I kept a wary eye on the boys. My camera was around my neck, and I rested one of my hands on the strap, the worn leather familiar and reassuring. I could tell my sisters were also uncomfortable. Courtney kept her face turned away, her fingers playing with the label on her beer. Dani's answers were stiff when they asked where we were from – she said Golden, a town a couple of hours north of Littlefield. She'd told them her name was Leanne, and we'd also given fake names. Courtney was Sandy and I was Heather, the name of a girl who sat behind me in class for years.

The boys didn't seem to notice our nerves, or didn't care. They were friendly and smiled lots, Brian telling us about how he worked at his uncle's garage in town, Gavin teasing him for being a grease monkey.

'Our dad's got a big spread,' Gavin said. 'Three hundred head of cattle but we've got some horses, too. Brian, he's always working on the tractors. Can't keep him away from an engine.' He laughed.

With country music playing on their truck radio, empties rolling around in the back, and cigarettes hanging out of their mouths, they could have been any of the kids we grew up with, and I began to relax. Courtney started smiling once in a while at something they said, and Dani asked a few questions about their ranch.

'I might be able to find a water pump in the wrecking yard,' Brian said. 'But it'll take a couple of days. You girls in a hurry?'

'Yeah, we're meeting with our aunt,' I said.

Dani shot me a dirty look, annoyed at me for answering first. 'How much will it cost?'

'Fifty for the part if I can find an old one, but it could be tough. New one will cost you about a hundred fifty, and a couple hours' labor. Then there's the tow truck. So maybe about three hundred altogether.'

Dani winced. 'We don't have any money.'

Brian glanced at Gavin. 'We could probably find some work for you on our ranch,' he said, 'fixing fences or cleaning stalls for cash. And we got a spot where you girls could camp.'

Dani gnawed her lip. 'You know a guy named Troy Dougan?'

'Troy?' Brian laughed. 'Everyone knows Troy. Why you asking?'

'He's a friend of a friend. If you give us a lift to town, we can give him a call.' I was relieved. I liked that idea a lot better than staying with these guys.

'Too bad. Troy just left to go camping for a couple of weeks.' Brian said it like he felt bad for us, but I kind of got the feeling he was maybe a little happy.

Courtney looked upset, and Dani just looked pissed off.

'If we camp on your property, your parents won't mind?' Dani said.

'We won't tell them you're camping,' Gavin said. 'As long as you don't have a fire, should be all right.'

'You can make enough to buy the part,' Brian said. 'My uncle will want you to pay for shop time, but I'll chip in my labor for free.'

'Why would you do that?' Courtney said, frowning.

He smiled big. 'I'm a nice guy.'

'You gonna say we owe you something else?' she said.

He looked confused. I was starting to think he might not be all that smart about people, just trucks.

'What else would you owe us?' He shrugged. 'I just like working on stuff.' I glanced at his hands, the grease under his nails. His pinkie fingers were strange – they curved in toward the fingers next to them.

'We need a minute to talk,' Dani said.

'Sure, gotta take a leak anyway.' The boys walked into the woods. We could hear them breaking branches, then silence. We took a couple of steps to the other side of their truck, the music playing behind us.

'I'm not sure about this,' Courtney said.

'Me either,' Dani said. 'But we need the truck.'

'We could take the bus,' I said.

'We don't even know if one stops in town.'

'We could hitch to Vancouver,' I said.

'The cops might see us on the road and too many

71

people will remember three girls – we stand out. Same with the bus, the cops can track us.'

Dani was sounding annoyed, but I couldn't stop my questions. 'What about the gun under the seat? We'll be stuck here for a couple of days.'

'They don't have any reason to look under the seat. Once the truck is fixed, we can get the hell out of here. No one knows where we're heading.'

I glanced back where the guys had gone into the bushes, saw them walking out.

'You think *they're* okay?' I whispered.

Dani turned and looked at them. 'Yeah, they're just typical boys hoping to get lucky. If they want to be nice, fine, but we don't have to do anything else.'

We climbed into the back of their truck, throwing our gear and the cooler in with us. The boys had helped us load the remaining boxes into the cab of our truck so we could lock it up. Brian said he'd come back with a tow truck later in the day. It would be added to our bill but he said he'd get his uncle to cut the rate.

They brought us through town. It looked even smaller than Littlefield, and it was obvious the guys knew everyone – people waved at the truck as we drove past, giving us curious looks. I focused my camera and took a few pretend shots of downtown, which had only a couple of stoplights. I noticed a few stores, a diner, a brick motel. Between a pizza shop with some plastic chairs outside and a florist, a bulletin board was crammed with notices like no one had ever taken anything down. The hardware store had a sign for the post office. There only seemed to be one garage: 'That's where I work!' Brian yelled through the rear window. He pulled in front of one of the shop bays and got out.

'Just have to talk to my uncle and make sure he's cool with everything.' Gavin got out and went inside with Brian.

We stayed in the back of the truck. The sun was beating down, reflecting off the black metal, hot to the touch. Courtney had her head resting against the plastic box under the rear window. It ran the length of the cab and had a padlock. Some of the men in Littlefield had the same boxes in their trucks for tools. Courtney's hand was covering her burn. Dani was watching her and chewing her nails.

I noticed a pub beside the garage, or at least I thought it was a pub, with music thumping and the smell of greasy food. The back door opened into an alley between the two businesses. Above the pub an open window looked down on the garage. Some curtains blew in the breeze and I wondered if people lived up there.

The back door opened and a boy came out. He looked about my age, with blond hair that fell into his eyes. He brushed it away. His face was flushed like he was hot, his white apron stained. He glanced around and lit a cigarette, leaning back against the wall, his eyes closed as he took a long drag and slowly exhaled.

Brian and Gavin came out of the shop, voices loud, door banging shut behind them. The boy in the alley stood straight, looked right at me.

Our eyes met, held. Then he glanced at the boys. Something in his face, the way his eyes narrowed, told me he didn't like them.

Gavin gave him the finger. The boy didn't react, just took another long, slow drag. An older man with a full beard and silver-streaked hair came out, looked like he was about to say something, then noticed us. Brian and Gavin climbed back into the truck. The man watched us pull away.

The boys stopped outside a general store. Brian hopped out of the truck.

'Gotta get some beer.'

'Is there a bathroom?' Courtney said.

''Round back.'

We piled out and went around the back of the store. Through the window I could see the boys picking up a couple of cases of beer. Gavin was elbowing Brian and they were laughing at something. I glanced at Dani – Courtney was in the bathroom. Dani was also watching the boys. I gave her a look.

'They're just being guys,' she said, but she sounded worried.

Courtney came out and also noticed the boys. They glanced up, feeling our gaze, and gave us big smiles, lifting up a case of beer like a trophy.

'See?' Dani said as she moved toward the bathroom. 'Typical boys.'

We left the town and drove through some farms, then down a winding country road, the pavement cracked and rough. We passed a tractor, the old man giving us a nod. The air was filled with the scent of hay from recently cut fields. Dani's eyes were sad, and I knew she was thinking of Corey.

The road changed to dirt and we hunkered low but still got coated with a fine layer of dust, coughing and rubbing our eyes. Finally the boys turned off onto a smaller road and stopped at a metal gate. Gavin jumped out and opened it.

'Almost there,' he said with a smile.

We pulled into a grassy field and bumped over the rough ground until we stopped at a grove of trees by a creek that had dried to a slow crawl.

Brian got out of the truck. 'This is all part of our land. You girls can set up here. We'll get your truck. In the morning, we'll bring you up to the ranch.'

He grabbed one of the cases of beer, handing us each

a bottle and opening one for himself. He also handed us a bag of jerky. 'Liquor store didn't have much else, but you guys look hungry. We can bring you some more food tomorrow.'

'What are you going to tell your parents?' Dani asked.

He shrugged. 'Ain't no big secret. You're some girls we met passing through who need to make some money so we can fix your truck.' He noticed us exchange looks. 'I don't have to say nothing if you want.'

Gavin added, 'We can just tell them you live in town.'

'We'd appreciate that,' Dani said.

'You girls running away or something?' Gavin laughed.

'We just don't like people knowing our business,' Dani said, her tone angry.

Brian held up his hands. 'Easy, sister. Whatever floats your boat.'

After the boys left, I said, 'I don't like them – they're being too friendly. And they know we're hiding something now. They could steal the truck.'

'If they wanted to steal it, they didn't have to pick us up. Better that they know we want it quiet than them yakking to everyone about us.'

'They still might,' Courtney said.

'I don't think so,' Dani said. 'I get the feeling maybe they shouldn't be helping us out so much. Serves them to stay quiet too.'

I watched the boys' truck driving over the field, then turning onto the road, a dust cloud following them. I looked around the campsite.

'It's sure quiet here. You can't see any houses or anything.'

'That's good,' Dani said, unrolling the tent. 'We don't want anyone knowing we're here.'

I looked back at where the truck had gone, nothing but dust now.

'I guess.'

We spent the afternoon setting up our tent and exploring the creek. We found a couple of pools where it was a little deeper and took baths, rinsing our hair, trying to get the dust out of our skin and from under our nails, but as soon as we'd dried off it felt like we were coated again. That night we were restless, rolling into each other for warmth, the ground uncomfortable. Courtney and I whispered to each other, worried about the truck and the boys. Dani finally told us to shut up.

The boys came to get us early the next morning. We piled into the back of their truck, and they took us up to the ranch. It was pretty, with a brightly painted sign that read LUXTON CATTLE RANCH at the entrance, white fences and flowers lining the driveway, a white Victorian farmhouse that looked like something out of a movie, with a wraparound veranda, a porch swing, and a couple of maple trees. I almost expected a woman to walk out in a pretty country dress and offer iced tea.

I aimed my camera, took a few pretend shots. I caught Brian watching me in his side mirror and put the camera down.

The cattle were out on summer pasture but the ranch had a lot of horses and a couple of barns, a big chicken run. We didn't meet their parents, just a ranch hand named Theo who had a perpetual squint like he was always looking into the sun. He showed us around and explained that we had to walk the fence line to check for any breaks, and for posts that were leaning from the winter snow or from cows pressing their bodies into the fence, trying to escape. We drove two ATVs, pulling a trailer with the rolled-up barbed wire and fence poles behind us. It was hard work, digging in the dry rocky ground, pounding the posts down, our clothes and sometimes our skin snagging on the barbed wire, the sun burning the backs of our necks. We wore gloves, but our hands ached from handling the shovel and the thick wire, the cutting tools. The strap of my camera dug in, the camera heavier with every mile, but I wasn't going to leave it in my packsack.

We turned our baseball caps around, slathered ourselves with suntan lotion, and used up all our water, but it felt good to be making some money. The guys came by once, driving another ATV.

'I couldn't find a pump at the wrecking yard,' Brian said. 'Had to order one in, might take a couple of days. It'll take me a while to get it on your truck, need half a day and my uncle has a bunch of other shit lined up first.'

'So when do you think it will be ready?' Dani said.

'Maybe Friday. I'll try my best,' he said. He seemed sincere and looked like he felt really bad, but as soon as he left, I turned to Dani.

'That's *four* days. There's something about these guys – I don't trust them. We should keep going, I don't like it here.'

'Me either, but we need the truck,' she said.

'We should just get on the bus.'

'How are we going to get back into town? It's miles. We don't even have enough money for three tickets. We've got to work for at least a couple of days.'

'You just don't want to leave the truck – you're being stubborn.' I felt trapped, panicked.

'Screw you, Jess. You're just a kid, you don't know—'

'But, Dani, this doesn't feel right.'

'Like you have ESP.'

'No,' I said, frustrated. 'It just doesn't.'

'I feel the same way,' Courtney said.

Dani looked furious. She hated it when we banded against her. She dug up a few more shovelfuls of dirt for a posthole, her biceps bunching and flexing as she pushed the shovel into the hard ground, using her foot to force it deeper. We also went back to work, but we were waiting for her to say something.

'We'll stay until we have a little more money,' she finally said. 'We also need it for ID. It might be even harder to get jobs in Vancouver. We have to earn what we can now. If the truck isn't fixed by Friday, we'll try to sell it to the guys.'

I didn't like it but there was nothing else I could say. Dani had made up her mind.

After we were done in the fields, we walked the country road back to our campsite, tried to clean our tired aching bodies in the creek. Most of the food in the cooler had already spoiled, so we ate the last of the jerky, some apples, and a sandwich Courtney had found in a lunch box in the barn. We'd filled up our water bottles at the farm but only had enough for the night. An hour later the boys came back to our campsite with some peanut butter sandwiches, granola bars, and fruit.

'Raided our parents' cupboards,' Gavin said with a laugh.

'We'll pay you back,' I said. I didn't want to owe them anything, but we were starving.

'Nah, they'll never notice anything's gone.' He patted his stomach. 'We eat like horses.'

While we ate, the boys talked. Gavin was nineteen,

his brother two years older. They were both still living at home, to help their parents out.

'Not for too much longer, though,' Brian said. 'How old are you girls anyway?'

Dani said, 'I'm eighteen,' adding a few months. She pointed to us. 'They're seventeen and fifteen.' Courtney wouldn't be seventeen until February. My birthday was the next day, I remembered with a jolt.

'Brave hitting the road all by yourself,' Gavin said.

'People know where we're at,' I said. 'We've got family.'

His eyes flicked to me and he seemed amused, like he knew I was lying, but he just said, 'Want to go for a swim?'

They took us to a river a couple of miles down the road where they said all the local kids swam. There was a small sandy beach where teens sunbathed on towels, clustered in little bunches. A few were taking turns on a rope swing, leaping into the water with a splash and a yell. Down the way, on the other side of the river, you could see another beach where some families had towels and umbrellas spread out, toddlers splashing in the shallows, dogs chasing sticks.

We sat a little apart from the other kids, up on a hill. A few of the boys shouted out greetings to the guys as we walked past, but the girls ignored them, whispering to each other, and a couple of them giggled. I glanced at

Brian's face. He looked angry, then smug when some of the girls gave us curious looks.

Brian had brought extra towels and some beer and pot. I took a beer but refused the pot, not liking how it made my head spin.

Courtney took a long toke, her eyes closing as she held the smoke in her lungs, her shoulders finally dropping, relaxed. Dani took the next drag, sucking at it in a quick angry inhale before she passed it to Gavin. He grinned at her.

We spent the afternoon swimming, sloughing the sweat from our skin, rinsing our hair in the water. Across the river some men sat on the hoods of their trucks, staring at Courtney stretched out in her black bikini. I didn't like the nod Brian gave them – confident, like we were theirs.

The boys kept handing us beers. It felt good, not being so hungry, the water cool and cleansing, the beer making everything fuzzy. Even Dani was relaxing, her voice excited as she talked to Gavin about ranching. She smiled and pushed her long hair off her shoulders, then giggled at something he said. I wanted her to put a T-shirt over her bikini like I had – but then I thought about Corey, how she'd never been with anyone else. Maybe it was good she was showing interest in a new boy.

Even if I didn't like him or his toothy smile.

It was getting dark and most people had left. A few voices carried across the river, someone taking a swim on the other side, then a truck started up and drove away. Everyone had gone home now. We sat around a small campfire, the smell of river still fresh on our skin, our feet sandy, beer bottles piled behind us. Gavin was trying to get Dani to walk farther down the river.

'Come on, I'll show you the bridge,' he said. But he was smiling at her in a way that said he wanted something else, and Dani knew it.

'I can't leave my sisters.'

'They'll be okay. Right, girls?' I glared at him. He laughed and stumbled off to pee in the woods but not far enough that we couldn't see him. His white tank top had sweat stains under his armpits, his jeans shorts sagged.

'I want to go back to our camp,' I said.

Dani nodded and started to gather our things. Courtney and I got to our feet, shook out our towels.

'Hold up,' Brian said. 'Let's have another beer.'

Gavin spun back around, doing his shorts up. 'What's going on?'

'We're going back to the campsite,' Dani said.

'What's your problem?' He started walking toward her. 'I thought we were having a good time.'

'We have to work tomorrow.' Dani sounded friendly, still trying to keep the peace.

'That's what you're worried about?' he said. 'Shit, we go to work hungover all the time. Nothing to it, just drink lots of water.'

He sat down on the towel, gripped her arm, and pulled her down beside him. This time she got mad, shoved him.

'Hey, asshole, that hurt.'

He shoved her back. 'Fuck you.'

'Let go of my sister!' I picked up a bottle, ready to throw it.

'Hey, hey. You girls calm down, now,' Brian said.

Dani had wrenched herself free from Gavin and stood up.

'We're going back to our camp.' She started walking up the trail, motioning to us to follow.

Courtney and I jogged to catch up, the camera bouncing against my chest, my hand trying to hold it in place.

The boys were trailing a few paces behind, carrying their towels and the cooler.

'Come on, don't be like this,' Brian said.

'We'll talk in the morning,' Dani said over her shoulder.

'You better if you want your truck back,' Gavin said, his voice mean.

Courtney looked scared. We both glanced at Dani. I could tell she was scared too, but she also looked pissed off. She wasn't going to back down now. I figured she was angry that we'd let the guys have this power over us, that she hadn't listened to me when I wanted to leave hours ago. We walked all the way back to the campsite, the boys following us in their truck, its lights blinding us whenever we looked over our shoulders.

'What are we going to do back at our camp?' I said. 'Should we hide?'

Dani said, 'Shut up, let me think.'

I could hear the truck behind us, a dark beast nipping at our heels.

'Maybe we should just let them think we aren't mad, you know? Like everything's okay?' Dani sounded desperate, like she didn't know what to do either. Which scared me more than anything.

'They're idiots,' Courtney said. 'They might believe it.'

When we got near our site, Dani spun around and walked to the truck.

'Hey, sorry things got out of control back there,' she said through the window. I couldn't see into the cab, couldn't see the boys' faces.

'We're just tired,' she said. 'Tomorrow after work we'll go swimming again, okay?'

'Sure thing, babe.' Brian's voice. 'It's all good, right?' He sounded calm. 'We just wanted to make sure you got home okay.'

'Thanks,' Dani said.

The boys backed into the field, turned the truck around, then drove off.

We zipped up our tent, changed into our sweatpants and sweatshirts. I had a flashlight, but I didn't like the idea of our bodies being silhouetted. I wrapped a shirt around my camera, shoved it into the bottom of my packsack.

'They're still mad,' I said.

'I know,' Dani said.

Courtney was fumbling around. I could hear the zipper on her packsack opening.

'What are you doing?' I said.

'Getting my knife.'

'You think they're coming back?' I hated how scared I sounded.

'No, they'll calm down. Just get some sleep.'

I climbed into my sleeping bag, heard my sisters settle into theirs. I tried to stay awake, listened to every noise outside, but my eyes kept closing.

Chapter Seven

I woke, my pulse racing as my eyes searched the dark. Footsteps outside, the rustle of clothes, something brushing against the side of the tent.

Dani whispered, 'Shhh,' almost too low to hear.

Beside me Courtney was feeling for her knife.

My hands also groped around under my sleeping bag for my flashlight. I touched the cool metal, wrapped my fingers around it. I strained my ears. It sounded like two sets of footsteps circling the tent. Brian and Gavin. Were they trying to scare us?

I remembered the look on Gavin's face earlier. The rage. Now there was silence. Where had they gone?

I rolled over slowly, trying not to make any noise, reaching out for Courtney, touching her arm. She grabbed my fingers, gave them a squeeze. Dani slowly moved to a kneeling position. I could see the faint outline of her body.

Someone moved outside again.

'Come out, come out, wherever you are.' Gavin's voice, low and slurred.

Like this was a game? I gripped my flashlight. If they touched the zipper on the tent, if they moved an inch closer, I was going to smash their hands with it.

'We're trying to sleep,' Dani said loudly. 'We'll party tomorrow, okay?'

'We want to party *now*.' Brian's voice.

Courtney whispered, 'Maybe we should have one beer with them, then they'll leave us alone.'

'I don't think that will do it,' Dani said.

'Just go away,' I yelled. 'You're assholes!'

Dani jabbed me in the ribs. 'Shut up, Jess.'

Outside we could hear the boys moving around like they were setting something up, a couple of thuds, dragging sounds, the hiss of a beer can opening.

'Come on, girls. We just want to say we're sorry about earlier. We were being jerks. We brought some weed to make it up to you.'

A brief flare of light, then flickering flames. They'd built a fire.

'We have to work in the morning,' Dani said.

'We're the bosses. You can sleep in.'

'We need the money.'

'If you come out, I'll put in some extra hours tomorrow night after work – might be able to fix the water pump faster.'

88

'I don't trust them,' I whispered.

'None of us do,' Dani whispered back. 'But they're not going away.' She turned toward the front of the tent. 'Just one beer, okay?' she called out.

'One beer. That's all we want.'

'Come on.' Dani unzipped the tent, bent low, and climbed out, her feet bare. Courtney followed. I lingered for a minute, zipping my hoodie up to my throat, hoping to hide that I wasn't wearing a bra. I debated staying in the tent, but I wanted to be near my sisters. The fire glowed through the side of the tent. I saw a glint of metal next to me. Courtney's knife. I put the knife in my pocket and climbed out.

'There she is,' Brian said. 'Hey, little sister.' He was sitting on an old log. They'd moved a couple around the fire for seats.

I forced a smile. He patted the log near him, but I moved to the other side of the fire and sat on the log close to Dani.

He grabbed a bottle out of the case, offered it to me. I shook my head.

Courtney took one, leaning across to get it. Brian stared at her waist where her shirt rode up. I wanted to reach out and tug it back down.

He smiled brightly. 'See, this is fun, right?'

Courtney and Dani nodded but they were quiet,

89

staring at the fire the boys had built, a rock circle surrounding it, some tree limbs dragged close.

'What's wrong with you all?' Gavin said. He was sitting on an old stump, poking the fire with a stick.

'We're just tired,' Courtney said.

Her voice sounded just like it had apologizing to Dad whenever he would drag us out late at night to play card games, our eyes blurring with fatigue, fetching him beers until he finally passed out on the table.

Gavin drained his beer, opened another one.

'Thought we weren't supposed to have a fire,' I said.

'S'okay. Parents are away for the night. No one will see it out here.'

I caught my breath. *No one will see it out here.*

No one would see us.

'So you girls have a boyfriend waiting back home?' Gavin said, his mouth moving slowly like he was trying not to slur.

'Yeah,' Dani said. 'We all do.'

He looked annoyed. 'Where are your parents?'

'Back home,' she answered.

I didn't like the questions, wondered why they wanted to know.

'Our aunt, she's waiting for us,' I said.

The boys exchanged a look. 'She must be worried, you already being late and all,' Brian said, his voice cold.

'We called her when you guys were buying beer,' I said.

'Oh, yeah. Where'd you call her from?' Brian said, not sounding drunk at all anymore. Had he been faking? I tried to remember if I'd seen a payphone near that store, but I couldn't think.

'Don't worry about it, little sister.' Brian's smile told me he knew I'd lied. 'You'll be home in no time.'

'No time,' Gavin echoed.

'That's it for us, boys,' Dani said, draining the last of her beer.

'Yeah, party's over,' Courtney said.

'Fire's almost out anyway,' Gavin said. 'Getting cold.' He rubbed at his arms. 'Might have to climb into bed with you. Been drinking too much to drive.'

'No way,' Dani said. 'You guys are going to have to sleep in your truck.'

She started toward the tent. Gavin grabbed her arm, his hands digging in.

I got up off the log. 'Let her go!'

Dani tried to yank her arm free. 'Cut it out!'

He pulled her down onto his lap, his arms wrapped tight around her body, one hand reaching up and gripping her throat.

'I'm sick and tired of your games,' he said.

Courtney and I were running toward Dani when Brian grabbed me around the waist, lifting me off my feet. All I could do was squirm as he tripped Courtney, who hit the ground hard. He kicked her in the side of the head. She lay in the dirt near the fire, eyes closed, a low moan coming from her throat. I grabbed the knife out of my pocket, jabbed it into the arm around me.

Brian yelled, then let go of me. I ran, the knife still in my hand, trying to get to Dani. Gavin had pushed her to the ground and was holding her arms behind her back with one hand, taking off his belt and wrapping it around her wrists with the other. She squirmed and kicked. He punched her across the head.

Brian tackled me. I hit the dirt hard, scrambled forward, but he grabbed my ankles, dragging me back as I screamed. I twisted and turned, tried to stab him with the knife, but my wrist was bent backward and the knife dropped to the ground. Brian's large body was lying on top of me, his breath hot in my ear.

He sat up, pressure leaving my upper body, knees crushing the muscles in the backs of my thighs, a fist digging in between my shoulder blades. Sounded like a belt buckle was being undone, then my arms were tied behind my back, my wrists grinding together. Something else now, material tearing. I screamed as loud as I could. Something was jammed down my throat, fabric tasting of grease.

'Tie that other bitch up,' Brian said.

He threw me over his shoulder. His back was naked,

my cheek bumping against his bare skin. He carried me to the truck, then tossed me in. I hit the metal with my back. I tried to shimmy away, kicking out with my legs. Brian climbed in, flipped me over. A knee pressed down on my legs, a hand gripped the back of my neck, fingers digging into the tendons. His body shifted, the weight pressing harder on one leg, like he was reaching for something. I screamed into the rag. He ran something through the belt around my wrists, wrapped it around, and pulled it taut. Felt like a rough rope.

Metal clanging against metal, like he was tying the rope to either side of the truck bed. Tie-down brackets? The weight shifted and pressed on the backs of my legs. Then the pressure was suddenly gone. A thud as he jumped back onto the ground. I wrenched my arms, but the rope was too tight. I tried to squirm around to see what was happening to Courtney and Dani but could only look over my shoulder, neck straining. The tailgate was open and I could see partly out the back, the dim glow of the fire outlining the boys, their upper bodies pale.

Courtney was still on the ground, a dark lump. I could just make out her blonde hair, looked like her eyes were closed. Gavin knelt over her.

'Get her in the truck,' Brian said

He was carrying Dani over his shoulder. He dumped her in and she fell hard, her head smacking onto the truck bed, her screams muffled like he'd put something in her mouth too. He leapt in beside her as she kicked out, dragged her body up beside me. He flipped her over. Sounds again, like he was unhooking the rope from one side. The tension around my wrists eased but then tightened, like he'd threaded the rope through the belt around Dani's wrists too.

Boots scraped on the truck bed as he climbed out. I tried to look over my shoulder again, caught a glimpse of his naked back.

'Get their stuff,' Brian said.

Courtney was tossed in, then dragged up on the other side of me. Her mouth was also gagged, looked like with half of a ripped shirt. Her arms were behind her back, but I couldn't see what they'd been tied with. Our eyes met, hers terrified, the whites bright in the dark. The rope loosened again, then tightened as we were bound together. They'd pulled it even tighter this time. I could feel it pressing across either side of my butt cheeks, the belt and rope pinching the skin on my wrists. I could hear the guys taking down our tent. They weren't talking but they were moving fast, their breathing heavy in the quiet night.

They threw the tent in the back with us, the poles clattering, then thumps as other things landed: our sleeping bags, packsacks, the cooler.

The hiss of water being poured over the fire, boots

94

scuffing as they kicked dirt over the coals, logs being dragged back into the woods.

Making sure there was no sign we'd ever been there.

We bumped over dusty roads for what felt like a half an hour but might have only been fifteen minutes – I couldn't tell, disoriented and panicked in the dark. Our shoulders bumped as our bodies slid each time the truck took a corner, the rope pulling painfully, making me moan and gasp into my gag. I tried to get to my knees, but the rope was too tight, could only lift an inch. On my right Dani tried the same thing. I sobbed helplessly, choking on the gag.

I tried to focus, searching for a scent, noises, big hills or corners, anything, but the road all felt the same. My wrists ached, pins and needles tingling up my arms. My jaw and cheekbone throbbed from where I'd hit the ground, my head pounded. I could hear country music coming from the cab, Gavin's laugh, and moans and guttural noises beside me. I turned my head in either direction, tried to see my sisters' faces. In the moonlight I could make out their lips stretched wide over their gags, their eyes shining.

Tears rolled down my face. I struggled to hold on to the sobs that were making me choke and retch and gag, but my body heaved with terror.

We hit a pothole and bounced up, which made the

rope bite into the flesh at my wrists again. We drove on. Finally the truck slowed and came to a halt. I turned my head, tried to look up. All I could make out were trees.

The front of the truck opened, driver's side. Footsteps coming around.

'We're here, girls,' Brian said.

We heard one of them undo the tailgate, which dropped with a clatter.

The truck rocked as one brother climbed into the back, then rocked again as the other jumped in. I felt a hand touch my calf. I kicked up and out with my bare foot, something hard under my heel, the smack of flesh.

'Fucking bitch!' Gavin's voice. He grabbed my ankles and yanked them down, pulling my legs straight and sitting across them.

Beside me I could feel Dani's body heaving and jerking as she also kicked out. Courtney was doing the same. We were fighting for our lives.

'Stop moving or we'll fucking kill you.' Brian.

We stopped moving.

A noise on the right, the rope being untied, tension easing around my wrist. Dani was suddenly jerked down, dragged by her ankles. The back of the truck bounced, then grunting noises, footsteps stumbling, like Brian was trying to carry her. A loud thump, something hitting the ground.

'Goddamn bitch.' Brian's voice. Smacking sounds.

Gavin grabbed the belt around my wrists. His body shifted as he reached across and untied the rope on the other side of Courtney. His weight left my body. I tried to get to my knees, but my body was yanked backward by my wrists. Beside me Courtney was also being dragged out. He was using the rope around our wrists like a leash. We slid all the way out of the back of the truck, falling with a bone-jarring thud, my teeth biting my lower lip.

Now we were being dragged, still on our fronts, our shirts riding up, rocks and gravel scraping our stomachs. I looked over my shoulder and saw Gavin grinning in the moonlight as he pulled the rope. I tried to get to my feet, saw Courtney struggling to stand. Gavin gave the rope a hard tug.

I landed on my shoulder, pain shooting down my arm. I got back up onto my knees. We tried to shuffle forward. A blow to the back of my head. I fell forward, my vision blurring, everything dark at the corners. I tried to get up onto my arms, but the ground rushed toward me.

Someone was whispering my name over and over.

'Jess, wake up.'

I opened my eyes, couldn't see anything.

I was on a hard surface, rough and cold, felt like cement, my hands still tied behind my back. The gag had been removed but my lips felt tender, bruised, my throat sore and dry. I slowly rolled over, looking for Courtney and Dani. The room was pretty dark, only a bit of moonlight shining down from above me.

'I'm over here.' Dani's voice on my right. I turned in her direction, could make out the shape of her body. 'Courtney's on your other side, I think.'

I heard a groan.

'How long have we been here?' I whispered.

'Couple of minutes,' Dani said. 'Not long.'

I looked around, my eyes adjusting to the dark now, but I couldn't tell how big the room was. It smelled of old fruit, like a storage room. I shuffled forward on my knees and turned around, looking above where I could see the moonlight. It looked like there might be a gap about a foot high at the top of the wall near the rafters, running the length of the room.

'I already stood up – it's at least ten feet high,' Dani whispered.

'Where are they?'

'I think they're outside the door.'

I heard voices to my left, raised with a slight echo, like they might be speaking in a hallway or a big room outside. Sounded like an argument.

Courtney was moaning again. I crawled on my knees closer to her, whispered in her ear, 'Courtney, it's okay.'

Her body jerked away and she let out a scream.

'Shhh,' Dani said.

It was too late. The voices had stopped. A scraping noise, like something was being dragged away. The door opened. The boys walked in, carrying our propane lantern, jeans hanging low on their hips. Gavin had a small belly, the skin floppy, and a dark patch of chest hair. Brian's left arm had streaks of blood, from where I'd stabbed him. Their eyes looked excited and their nervous energy filled the room. I could smell sweat and beer and pot smoke.

Beside me Dani was sitting up, watching. Blood leaked from her nose and her cheek was scraped. On my left, Courtney was slumped against the wall. The room was only about ten-by-ten feet. The bottom part of the wall was concrete, about a foot high, then wood paneling all the way up to the rafters. There wasn't any insulation in the ceiling and I could see that the roof was aluminum. The room was dirty, cobwebs hanging everywhere, like it hadn't been used for years.

'Well, look who's awake,' Brian walked over and crouched down in front of Courtney. He grabbed her face, turned it to the side so he could see the burn mark. Gavin watched from the doorway.

'Someone sure did a number on you,' Brian said. He turned her back to face him and smiled. 'But you're still a sexy girl.'

A tear rolled out the side of Courtney's eyes but she

was glaring at him. He gripped her jaw tighter and tighter until she moaned, then he let go.

He turned to me, still smiling. 'Little sister, you're awake too.' The smile disappeared. 'You've been giving us a hard time. I'd stop that if I were you.'

Gavin came over, gave Dani a kick. She grimaced but didn't cry out.

'You girls should've been a lot nicer to us,' he said. 'A lot nicer.'

'What are you going to do to us?' Dani said, her voice hoarse.

'We're having ourselves some fun,' Brian said.

'People will notice we're gone,' she said.

'Yeah, right. All we've got to do is wait a little bit, then sell off your truck parts, and *poof*, just like magic you bitches were never here.' He looked at his watch. 'But we've gotta get home now. Don't worry, we'll see you later.'

They headed toward the door.

'Can you at least untie us?' Dani said.

Brian turned and laughed. 'No way, princess.'

'What about water?' I said. 'We'll die without water.'

They exchanged a look and Brian nodded. Gavin disappeared while Brian watched us, one of his hands idly rubbing his chest. He could've been sitting at home staring at the TV.

Outside I heard the truck door open and shut. Gavin

came back with a four-liter plastic jug of water like I'd seen at the ranch. He grabbed a dirty pail overturned in the corner, flipped it right side up, and dumped the water into it.

'Let's go.' Brian gave us another lingering look. 'You girls be good, now. Don't get into any trouble.' Gavin laughed.

The door closed with a loud click, sending us back into darkness. Sounds of something being dragged. Brian said, 'Hold it there.' Hammering. A board was being nailed over the door, each blow echoing through the room.

We spent the rest of the night huddled together. We'd tried to undo each other's bindings, putting our backs together, but they were too tight – the guys had retied our wrists when we were unconscious, wrapped pieces of rope around and around, like we were cattle being hauled to a slaughter.

'In the morning we'll try again,' Dani said. 'We'll climb up the wall.'

'You know they'll come back,' I said. My head throbbed where Gavin had hit me. My thoughts were foggy, my vision blurry if I moved fast.

'We'll get out before then.'

'I think we're in an old fruit-packing place or something,' I said.

'Probably,' Dani said.

'I really have to pee,' I said.

'Me too,' Courtney said.

We put our backs together again and shuffled our way to the corner of the room, hooked our hands into the waistband of each other's pants and pulled them down, and took a pee. Then tried to sleep but we stayed awake all night, sometimes resting our heads on each other's shoulders.

'What do you think they're going to do to us?' I said.

'I don't know,' Dani said, but I could tell she was lying.

'Yes, you do.'

'We'll be gone before then,' she said again.

I closed my eyes, pressed my forehead into her shoulder, breathing her familiar scent, feeling the strength in her muscles, in her words.

When it got lighter in the room, sun shining through the gap near the rafters, which we now saw was covered with a clear sheet of plastic, we tried again to untie our hands. While one sister worked on the other's bindings, the third called out instructions: 'Try to get your finger under the knot, pull it to the left.'

But the knots were too tight and complicated, the bindings wrapped around and around in a figure eight.

We also tried to get our legs through our arms, but none of us was flexible enough. Dani walked over to the door, backed up, and tried the knob with her hand, but we already knew it was pointless.

We decided Dani would crouch against the wall, then I'd climb up her back and try to see out the gap. I managed to get up, wobbling and trying not to lose my balance while Courtney and Dani called out encouragement, but I wasn't tall enough – the gap was still over a foot away.

Next we tried my sitting on Dani's shoulders as she slowly stood up, but we didn't gain any height. I could see a bit of the plastic ripped in the corner, a faint breeze moving it back and forth, and treetops outside. She lowered me down.

'We have to try again, maybe with Courtney,' I said, my voice cracking.

'She's only a couple of inches taller,' Dani said.

I screamed up at the gap, 'Help! Someone help!'

Courtney stood behind me, joining in. 'Help!'

We took turns screaming for help over and over until we were hoarse. Then sat, tried to catch our breath.

'What day is it?' Courtney said, her voice raw.

'Tuesday, I think,' Dani said.

'Jess's birthday.'

Tears came to my eyes, then I was sobbing in big desperate heaves. My sisters shuffled over, pressed their shoulders against my sides. I leaned into Dani, crying harder. After a while I sat back up, rubbed my eyes dry on my knees, took a few breaths.

The heat was rising in the building and we were covered in sweat, our hair damp. We couldn't take our sweatshirts off with our hands tied, and the hot air pressed in around us. We had almost drunk the pail dry already.

'We should save the rest. We don't know when they'll be back,' Dani said.

'We have to get out before they come back,' Courtney said, her voice frantic. 'They're going to rape us – they're going to *kill* us.'

We looked at each other, the words hanging in the air. I felt a sob build in my throat, choked it back, and turned to Dani.

'What are we going to do?'

'Get out of here.' She pushed at the door with her body, banged her shoulder into it, then kicked it over and over until I worried she was going to break her foot.

'Stop!' I yelled. 'Stop, Dani!' But she kept kicking, screaming in rage. Finally she stopped, sinking to her knees in front of the door, her head hanging.

'They might let us go ... after,' I said quietly, but I knew none of us believed it.

'We're just going to have to find a way to get away

from them,' she said, lifting her head back up, trying to sound confident, but I heard the fear.

'If we tell them we're on the run, they'll know we won't talk about it,' Courtney said.

'They need to think people are looking for us,' Dani said, getting back to her feet and coming to sit beside us.

'Then they'll have even more reason to shut us up for good,' Courtney said.

Dani looked away, squeezing her eyes shut like she was trying not to cry.

'I'll do it,' Courtney said. 'I'll go first.'

'What are you talking about?' I said.

'Maybe they'll leave you alone.'

'Stop it!' I said, desperate to stop the horrible thoughts and images flooding my mind. 'We'll fight them.'

'We already tried that,' Courtney said.

'We can't just give in!'

'Sometimes giving in *is* fighting, Jess. We can control it.'

'Dani, stop her,' I said.

'Courtney's right. We'll do what they want, but they have to leave you alone.'

'You can't do that!' I was crying. 'This is my fault.'

'It's my fault for messing around,' Courtney said. 'You're young, it'll hurt you more.'

'They'll still hurt *you*.'

'I can shut my mind down. It's like I'm not even there.

I can fake it.' But she sounded like she was faking it right now, trying to sound brave so I didn't get scared.

'Then what?' I said. 'Even if you do that, they're not going to let us go.'

We were silent.

Chapter Eight

The room was almost dark by the time we heard the truck pulling up outside, country music blaring. It went silent, then doors slammed shut. I looked at Dani, fear shooting through my body, squeezing the breath out of my lungs.

'Do you think they'll kill us?'

'They'd have done it already,' she said, but her eyes were wide, her face frozen as she stared at the door.

Scraping sounds: they were prying the board off. We shuffled closer together, standing in the corner, prepared for an attack. The boys came into the room, Gavin carrying our lantern and a brown paper bag. Brian walked over and dumped some water in the pail. We were all thirsty, but none of us made a move. The boys seemed agitated, their movements jerky and fast, rubbing at their faces, their hair, the smell of beer rolling off them. My legs began to shake.

Dani spoke first. 'We know you didn't mean to hurt

us last night – you were just drunk and angry. If you let us go, we won't tell anyone.'

'Sorry, girls, we can't do that,' Brian said. He walked back over to Gavin and took the brown bag from him.

'People are looking for us—'

'Bullshit,' he said. 'No one gives a crap about you girls.'

Brian knelt in front of me, opened the bag, and took out a sandwich. I smelled peanut butter. He pushed it at my mouth, offering a bite. I looked at Dani. She nodded. I took a bite. I didn't want to give him any satisfaction, but I was so hungry I couldn't help chewing it fast, swallowing it down in a big gulp, the peanut butter sticking. He waited, a smile on his face, almost tender, offered another bite. While I chewed, he glanced up at Gavin.

'Feed the other bitches.'

Gavin took another sandwich from the bag and fed Courtney. Her face was angry and I knew she wanted to refuse the food, but we were so hungry. Gavin toyed with her, though, offering a bite, then taking it away at the last second, then giving it again.

'Stop fucking around,' Brian said.

Gavin looked pissed but he didn't tease Courtney again. He grabbed another sandwich out of the bag with his free hand and fed Dani at the same time.

When they were done, Gavin left and came back with our packsacks. He rummaged through Dani's, found her purse. He turned it upside down, the contents falling on the floor. He toed through everything, bent over and picked up her wallet, flipped through, stopped, and stared at her driver's license. I caught my breath.

'Danielle Campbell, huh?'

She didn't answer. Brian grabbed the wallet from him, stared at the license, then pulled it out and tucked it into his wallet. He rummaged through my packsack next, pulled out my photos, flipped through them.

'Boring as shit, nothing but birds and fucking cows.' He paused, gave a whistle. 'Now we're talking.' He held out the photos so we could see them. 'You girls sure are sexy.' They were my shots of Dani and Courtney. He tucked them into his pocket, then ripped the other ones up, dropping the pieces onto the floor and stepping on them. He crouched down and lit the corner of one of them with his lighter, looking at me the whole time, waiting for me to react. I was trying hard not to cry as I watched the photos crumple and burn.

They're just paper. It's okay. It doesn't matter.

He stood back up and reached into my bag again, pulled out my camera. Started fiddling with the buttons, flipped open the back, checking for film.

'Stop it.' The words came out before I could stop them. *Stupid, stupid.*

Brian paused, stared at me.

'You sure love this camera, don't you, little sister?'

109

'Leave it alone. You'll break it.'

Brian started laughing. Gavin laughed too, though you could tell he didn't really understand the joke.

I struggled to hold back the tears.

He pointed the camera at us, pretended to take a few shots, making a loud *snap, snap* noise with his mouth, still laughing.

'Little sister's worried we'll break her camera.' He turned to look at Gavin. 'We better be real careful with it.'

'Real careful.' Gavin laughed.

Brian held the camera out in front of him, like he was going to hand it to me. My body arched forward, hope zinging through me.

He let go. The camera hit the cement with a *crack*.

'No!' I yelled. I could already tell the lens was broken.

Brian reached down and picked it up. 'We make the rules now, girls.'

'What do you want?' Dani said.

He stared at her, then at Courtney, his gaze lingering as he shoved my camera back in my bag. Gavin put Dani's stuff back in hers.

'We want what you owe us,' Brian said. 'We were nice to you, we helped you, but you haven't done squat for us.'

'Whatever it is you want, I'll do it,' Courtney said. 'Just leave my sisters alone.'

He broke into a smile. He was gloating, relishing the power he now had over her. 'Guess we'll have to see how good you are.'

'Courtney, no!' I cried out. 'Don't!'

She got to her feet.

'Let's go,' she said, tears in her voice.

Gavin looked at Brian. 'I want her first. You owe me for those tires.'

Brian glared at him but jerked his head in an angry nod.

Gavin grabbed Courtney's arm tight and led her off.

I called out, 'Courtney!' just before she left the room, but she didn't look back. Dani sucked in her breath. I turned to Brian.

'I hate you! You're assholes!'

He leaned close. I could smell his breath, beer and cigarettes.

'Yes, we are.'

He turned and looked at Dani. She straightened up and squared her jaw, trying to look tough, but her body was shaking.

Brian walked over and gripped her shirt, pulling her up. He dragged her out the door, closed it behind them.

I shuffled forward, screamed, 'Let her go! Please let her go!'

They stopped outside. Dani was talking, her voice fast and frantic. 'You don't have to do this. We won't tell anybody.'

'You're not going anywhere,' Brian said. The rattle of keys and metal clicking shut – they'd brought a padlock. Sounds of a struggle, a muffled scream, then footsteps walking away.

I sank to my knees, staring hard at the door as if I could see through it, sobbing in big painful gasps that shook my body, my head filled with frantic thoughts. Where were my sisters? Were they going to kill them?

Finally I heard footsteps. I scrambled back to my spot on the wall, straining to hear something, anything, that would tell me if my sisters were okay.

Gavin opened the door and walked in with Courtney, his hand on her upper arm partly holding her up – her wrists were still tied behind her back. In the other he held the lantern. A trickle of blood dripped from her nose and she walked in a painful lurch. One cheek was slapped red, the outline of a handprint still visible.

He pushed her to the floor and she crumpled to one side, shivers going through her body. Her lips were bruised and swollen. I tried to meet her gaze, but her eyes filled with tears and she looked away. Gavin was sweaty, out of breath.

He knelt in front of her.

'You keep me satisfied like that and maybe I'll stay away from little sister.' He reached out and tucked a hair behind her ear.

Brian came through the door, dragging Dani behind.

She was walking stiffly, angry red marks around her neck like he'd been gripping hard.

Her face was pale, but her eyes were furious.

'Get them some more water,' Brian said.

I looked up at him. His face was cold, his body language aggressive as he towered over us, but he'd told Gavin to get water. Did he feel bad? I searched his face but I couldn't see anything other than hatred. I glanced back at my sisters. Dani was also glaring up at him, but Courtney had her head resting against her knees, her body a tight ball.

'Why don't you get it?' Gavin said.

Brian spun around. 'I told you to *fucking get them some water.*'

Gavin's face flushed. 'Fuck you, Brian.' But he left, coming back with a water jug. He topped up the pail.

'Get them a bucket to shit in,' Brian said.

'Why can't they just go on the floor?' Gavin said, angry again.

Brian grabbed the front of his shirt. 'Just fucking do it!'

Gavin brushed off his hand, his face enraged, but he left and came back this time with a big white plastic pail, dropped it in the corner of the room.

'See you tomorrow, girls,' Brian said.

They gathered up our packsacks and left.

*

We sat in the dark – they'd taken the lantern.

'Dani? Courtney?' I whispered.

'I'm okay,' Dani said, but her voice sounded tight and strained.

I could only hear sobs from where Courtney was sitting. I crawled closer to the sound, blind in the dark, leaned my body against hers.

'I'm sorry. I'm so sorry,' I said, my voice cracking, tears building in the back of my throat. 'We're going to get out of here.' Courtney only cried harder.

Chapter Nine

We spent hours over the next couple of days trying to undo our ties. We kicked the wall and door, scrabbled at them with our fingers. We paced the room or slumped on the floor, our bodies slick with sweat, staring up at the gap trying to breathe in fresh air that the heat would just steal right back out of our lungs.

At night they'd return, force-feed us peanut butter sandwiches, and sometimes strawberries or pieces of apple. They never untied us. Gavin looked impatient, but Brian seemed to like feeding us, his expression fascinated as if we were a science project. When we were done, they'd take Courtney and Dani away. They traded girls the second night, then back again the next. They each had a lantern now but they never left one in the room, leaving me in the dark. They both also carried rifles, which they used to prod my sisters to their feet, then out of the room. Making them walk to their fate. We were starving, but we never spoke of food. We barely spoke at all. Courtney, her hair matted and tangled, one cheek mottled shades of blue and purple, was silent most of the day, then, as the night came on, she'd start crying so hard she couldn't get her breath. I tried to sing to her once, tried to remember the words to her favorite song, but she shouted at me.

'Shut up, Jess. Just shut up.'

I cried too, but silently, my face turned away, until she crawled close to me and rested her head on my shoulder.

Dani just stared at the wall, her face a hard angry mask.

Before Brian and Gavin led them out of the room, they liked to taunt them, taunt me. 'Remember, girls, you keep working hard and we'll leave little sister alone.'

I hated what they were doing, hated that they were torturing them because of me. The third night I'd snapped.

'Just take me!'

Brian laughed. 'You'll get your turn.'

The next night they came a little earlier with a plastic kid's pool and dumped a bunch of water jugs into it. I panicked, thinking they were going to drown us. Courtney and Dani looked terrified too, but then the boys undid our ties. We stretched our arms. My shoulders ached, the muscles tight. I looked at my wrist, the scraped skin and bruises, wondered if I'd get an infection.

'Clean yourselves up, you're starting to stink,' Brian said.

They watched, rifles perched on their knees, as Courtney and Dani took their clothes off. We'd undressed many times in front of each other, but I looked away. I heard them climb into the pool, the sound of plastic creaking and shifting as they stepped in, quick inhales as they immersed their bodies in the cold water.

Brian pointed the gun at me. 'You too, little sister.'

'Screw you,' I said, but I couldn't help but look longingly at the water.

'Just do what he says!' Dani shouted.

I looked at her and gasped at the bruises on her body. The bite marks across her chest. Courtney was also covered in bruises and bites.

Gavin stepped closer to Dani, pulling her hair back until her neck was exposed, and pressed the barrel of his rifle against a spot behind her ear.

'Better listen to your sister.'

I stood up and took my clothes off, hands shaking, staring at the floor. I couldn't look at them, couldn't look at my sisters.

Brian whistled. 'Look what you've been hiding.'

I was crying, big gasps of fear. I went over to the bath and eased down into the cold water, my arms wrapped around my knees, trying to hide my chest.

They gave us soap and shampoo, dumped cold water

over our heads to rinse us off. The soap stung my wrists, but I soaked them in the cold water, hoped it was flushing out the wounds. One of them kept a gun pointed at us at all times.

'Get out,' Brian said.

We stood, shivering. Courtney and Dani didn't even bother trying to hide their bodies, but I tucked myself behind them. Gavin tossed us some towels.

We dried off, then they handed us some fresh clothes, summer dresses in floral patterns. They looked used, the fabric worn and faded. New underwear – no bras. They bundled our old stuff up.

They had a bag of makeup, said they wanted us to dress up for them. We did each other's makeup, our hands shaky. They surveyed our work.

'More lipstick,' Brian said. We reapplied.

Gavin pointed to Dani. 'Fluff your hair up, like around your shoulders.' She ran her hands through it. 'Yeah, like that.'

He handed us beers. 'Don't know why you had to be such stuck-up bitches. We could've had a lot of fun.'

We sipped at our beers. I was scared they'd drugged it or poisoned it, but the cold liquid felt good. They also gave us sandwiches, which we wolfed down, keeping our eyes on the boys, waiting for the next step.

They brought in a portable stereo, put on some country music.

118

Gavin clapped his hands, kicked the ground a couple of times with his boots. 'Let's dance.' We stared at them.

'Why aren't you dancing?' Brian said.

We danced, and they joined in, twirling us around like we were at a barnyard dance. I could feel my sisters' anger simmering off of them, though none of us said a word. Our hands were finally untied, but while one brother danced, the other sat with the gun pointed at us.

It was hard to keep dancing. Dani and Courtney faltered and I stumbled, which earned me a slap on the butt from Brian. 'Wake up!'

The boys tired of the game and started taunting us, picking on Courtney and me. 'What's your real names?'

'I'm Sara – she's Melissa.' Courtney pointed at me.

'You're lying,' Gavin said. 'You were lying as soon as we saw you in that busted-down truck.'

Brian started laughing. 'Almost got it fixed up.' Dani looked at him. 'Think I might just keep it. Take the plates off, throw a slap of paint on it. Make for a real nice souvenir.'

Souvenir.

I wondered how much longer they planned on keeping us alive.

Brian circled closer to me. 'Your sister said you just turned fifteen.'

I tried to think which one had told him.

Brian was still talking. 'But I think they're lying about that too. That's no fifteen-year-old's body.'

He stood behind me, his breath on my neck. He lifted my hair, nuzzled my neck, grabbed me, and pulled me back. I cried out.

My sisters came toward me. Gavin stepped in with a gun. 'Stay back.'

'Leave her alone,' Dani said.

'She's just a kid,' Courtney said. 'You can do whatever you want to me again – whatever you want. Just let her go.'

He reached around, cupped one of my breasts, gripping it hard. I elbowed him in the stomach, kicked back with my foot.

'You little brat!' He grabbed me around the waist and started to drag me out of the room.

Dani and Courtney were screaming, 'No! Leave her alone!'

Then I heard the sickening smack of metal hitting flesh.

'I'll shoot your sister, bitch!' Gavin's voice.

I looked back over my shoulder, frantic. Gavin had the gun pointed at Courtney. Dani was on the floor, holding the side of her face.

Brian had me out the door. I fought hard, pushing back with all my strength, but his arm was wrapped tight around my body. Was he going to kill me? Crazed with fear, I didn't care. I didn't want to find out what he was going to do. I remembered the sounds from Dani and Courtney as they tried to clean themselves, their moans at night when they tried to sleep, their crying in the dark.

Brian hauled me down a short hallway, then through an open door. He had the rifle tucked under his other armpit, his hand gripping the lantern, which was swinging and casting strange shadows. I looked around, searching for an escape, something to save me. We were in a warehouse, looked like the roof was a few feet higher than our room, with exposed rafters and aluminum sheeting. Clear plastic poly covered the triangle at the top of the walls at both ends of the building. Wooden crates were stacked all over in haphazard towers, a conveyor belt came out of the side of the building. The air smelled of rotting fruit. A rat scurried away from us. Brian startled, then muttered, 'Fucking thing.'

He took me to a room that broke off from the main one. An old cash register sat on a wooden counter, empty shelves lining the wall. A mattress lay in the center, a faded blue blanket tossed over it. I could see spots of reddish brown.

My sisters' blood.

'Please, please don't,' I begged.

'Shut up and get on the mattress.'

I sat down.

He set the lantern in the corner, stroked the gun barrel as he stared at me. Would it be better to fight or just go along? Talking, that's what Dani would do, she'd try to talk to him.

'Please, I'm just a kid – you heard my sisters. We just want to go home. We won't tell anyone. I thought you were a nice guy.'

Brian rocked back on his feet, giving me a calculating look. 'You think I'm not smart enough to figure out that you're playing me?'

It wasn't working. I thought desperately, remembered the way the girls had looked at him down by the river, how angry he'd been.

'If you let me go, I could be your girlfriend.'

'You don't think I can get a girlfriend?' He stiffened, his face flushed.

'I think you'd be a good boyfriend.'

'Yeah?' He smiled. He rested the rifle against the wall, still within his reach but just outside of mine, then sat on the mattress. He put his arm around my shoulders, pulling me toward him. 'Then act like my girl-friend.'

'That's not how it works. You treat me like a *real* girl-friend, then we do that – like how it's supposed to be.' I brushed his arm away.

His face was angry now. 'You want to be my

122

girlfriend, then fucking act like one.' He stood, stared down at me. 'Take off your clothes.'

'Please ... I'm a virgin.'

He smiled. 'That's why I wanted you.' The smile disappeared. He lowered his head, looked directly into my eyes. 'Take your fucking clothes off.'

My fingers shaking, I took off the dress, sat there in my underwear.

'Take it *all* off,' he said.

I pulled the rest off, trying to make myself small on the mattress. I wondered how much it was going to hurt. He was taking off his own clothes now. I squeezed my eyes shut, heard his belt buckle hit the floor.

'Get on your back,' he said.

I lay down, my arm still across my chest and my other hand over my crotch. My body had started shaking violently.

He climbed on top of me, his hands rough as they mauled my breasts, pinching. Tears dripped down the sides of my face. I cried out.

'I thought you wanted to be my girlfriend,' he said.

I shook my head back and forth. 'No, *please.*'

He pushed my legs apart with his knees.

'You're going to like this,' he said.

He had to help me walk back to the main room. I was dizzy, the pain between my legs agonizing. I tried to close my eyes to the memory of what had just happened, but I couldn't stop seeing him grunting, the glazed look in his eyes.

He brought me back to Dani – Courtney and Gavin were gone.

Dani's eyes roamed my face, her expression anxious. I wanted to cry, but I held my face still, didn't want her to see how scared I was, how much it hurt. Brian pushed me down beside her.

'Little sister was telling me how she wants to be my girlfriend.' Dani's face didn't change but her gaze flicked to me again, just for a second.

He knelt close to me, grabbed my face, and shoved his tongue in my mouth, grinding my lip against my teeth.

'Don't worry, baby. I'll let you be my girlfriend.'

He rolled a joint, finished off a beer. Down the hall we heard Courtney shriek. The sound echoed through the building. Dani stood up and I let out a sob.

'Sit the fuck back down,' Brian said. Dani hesitated, staring at the door and then at him, like she was wondering if she could get through it in time.

He casually picked up the gun beside him, pointed it at her with one arm, then swung his arm around until it pointed to me.

Dani sat back down.

He took a long inhale of the joint, let it out with a

coughing laugh. The room filled with the skunky smell of marijuana.

'Gavin's a freak – he likes it rough.' He gave Dani a look. 'Guess you're getting off easy tonight, sweetheart. We'll make it up to you tomorrow.'

'When are you going to let us go?' she said.

He shrugged. 'This weekend? Tomorrow? Never? Maybe we'll just keep you around for a while.'

'We'll starve to death,' I said. 'We can't live on one sandwich a day.'

He nodded, thinking. 'You did good tonight. Maybe we'll bring you some more food tomorrow.'

Another scream down the hall, the sound digging into my bones.

'Please stop him. *Please*,' I said. 'He's hurting her.' She'd never screamed that loud before. The thought of what he might be doing terrified me.

'Sorry, can't do that. Gavin, once he sets his mind on something, he's like a bulldog. And he does like that girl a whole lot.'

'If he kills her, you'll go to prison,' Dani said. 'You'll be murderers.'

'Maybe we'll kill all of you,' he said with a cold smile. 'That'll make things real simple. Hitchhikers are always coming through. We didn't see the possibilities before, but now?' He laughed. 'Our eyes are wide open.'

'It would be easier to keep us than start over with anyone else,' Dani said.

'You don't think we can do this again?' The look he gave her made it clear she was treading on thin ground.

'Why go through the effort when you already have us?' Dani said. 'That's all I'm saying. But you need to keep us healthy.'

Brian's face was thoughtful. He took another drag, walked over and offered the joint to Dani. She took a long inhale. When he offered me a hit I glanced at her. She nodded, telling me to play along. I took a drag.

He sat back down. 'So you think we should keep you?'

It seemed like Gavin had been gone with Courtney for a really long time. There'd been no more screams, which was almost worse. I tried not to think about what was happening to her, just about buying us time.

'Why not?' I said. 'You've got nothing to lose.'

'It ain't easy coming here every day,' he said.

'You don't have to come every day,' I said. It would be a relief if they didn't. 'You could just leave us food and water and come when you want.'

'Like you're our pets,' he said, his voice high-pitched from the weed. Then he laughed. I hated his laugh. Hated Gavin's even more.

'Yeah, like we're your pets,' Dani said. I could hear the undercurrent of anger in her voice, knew she was close to snapping.

Keep it together, Dani.

He leaned closer. 'We've already got everything we want out of you.' He sat back with a lazy smile. 'I'll think about it.'

A few minutes later, Gavin finally brought Courtney back. She could barely walk, and I saw bite marks on her collarbone. There was no expression on her face, just tears and snot leaking down, mixed with dust and blood. Gavin pushed her to the floor. She moaned, brought her knees up to her body.

He grabbed a beer, opened it, and took a long slug. He wiped his sweaty face on his arms as he looked over at us. He lingered on me for a while.

'I'll try you out tomorrow.' He gave Courtney a look. 'Bitch is starting to bore me.' He spit on her. She didn't even flinch as it ran down her face.

Brian laughed. 'You messed her up good.' He walked over and offered her a hit from the joint.

She wouldn't look at him. He gave her a kick with his boot. 'Take it.' She turned to face him and he held the joint to her lips, looking at her almost tenderly as he said, 'There you go.' He gave her a few more tokes, then stood up, turned to Gavin. 'Let's go.'

We crawled over to Courtney, leaned against her thin frame. I could hear her breath, the sound comforting. *She's alive. We're all still alive.* I tried not to think about the pain between my legs, Gavin saying he wanted me next. I wished we had turned ourselves in. Jail would have been better than this.

'Are you okay?' Courtney whispered after a few minutes.

'I'm all right. Are you?'

'I can't do it again. I can't.' She started crying hard.

'You won't have to,' I said fiercely. 'If they untie us again, we rush them and try to grab the guns and . . . and—'

'They're too strong,' Dani said.

'So what are we going to do?' I said.

'They only . . . they only untie us when they're raping us,' Courtney said, the words hiccupping out of her. 'Gavin, he likes . . . he likes to make you do stuff, but he still holds a knife. Brian, sometimes he sets the gun down.'

'Gavin's taking me next time.' I couldn't breathe, struggled to push the words past the lump in my throat.

'I can try to get the gun from Brian,' Dani said. 'Shoot him, then go after Gavin. If Brian takes you, Courtney, you have to try for the gun.'

'Okay.' Her tears had calmed. Her body shuddered as she took a few ragged breaths.

'What if Brian takes me?' I said. 'I don't know where Gavin's room is.'

'It's another storage room, like this one, but it's at the front of the warehouse. Shoot him right away.'

'What if Gavin hears the shot?'

'Even if we only kill one of them, I'll be happy,' Dani said.

We didn't talk about what might happen if our plan failed.

Chapter Ten

They'd brought Kentucky Fried Chicken and fries and coleslaw, untied our wrists so we could eat. We tore into the chicken, gnawing off greasy bite after bite, almost gagging, our mouths were so full, but none of us were able to slow down or stop our moans of relief. I hadn't eaten meat in years but I didn't even think about that now, didn't care. We sucked back the coleslaw, eating it straight from the container, shoved french fries in our mouths.

Brian was leaning against the wall, tapping his gun barrel against his cowboy boots, smiling at me. 'Think I'll take my girlfriend again tonight.' I was shocked – I thought for sure I was going with Gavin.

'Screw you – it's my turn,' Gavin said.

Brian's face was cold. 'You can have her when I say you can have her.' He pointed the gun at Dani and Courtney. 'Take one of them.'

'Fine.' Gavin jerked Courtney up from the floor and dragged her away.

Brian took a step toward me.

'Please,' Dani said. 'She's really sore. I'll do whatever you want.'

He smiled. 'So will she.'

He grabbed me and pulled me up. I didn't look at Dani, scared I'd reveal something and Brian would sense we had a plan, but I could feel her panic.

In the other room, he started to turn me around. If I was facedown I wouldn't be able to reach the gun, and my hands were still tied. I thought quickly.

'What if . . . what if I give you a blow job instead?'

I was terrified, my throat tight. I tried not to think about it, tried to just focus on the plan.

He was quiet for a second. I braced for his rage.

'Yeah, all right.' He spun me around and pushed me down on my knees in front of him, started to unbuckle his pants with one hand.

'Can you sit on the bed?' I said. 'I can reach easier. And I need my hands.' I was sick at the thought of touching him, touching *it*.

'Whatever makes it better for you, sweetheart.' He untied my hands, stood to unzip his pants, then sat on the edge of the bed, propping himself up on his elbows and closing his eyes.

I knelt in front of him, took a breath, and put my

mouth around him, just the top part. I almost gagged, squeezed my eyes shut, trying not to think about anything, his fleshy taste, his man smell. He gripped the back of my head, pushed my head closer to him, forcing me to swallow more. I gagged again, dry-heaved.

His eyes shot open and he held the rifle to my temple, the cold metal pressing hard. Then he slid the safety off.

'You bite me and I'll blow your brains out.'

I nodded. He kept his eyes open, watching me. Finally he closed them, his hand hard on the back of my head. I tried to focus on breathing through my nose. He was moaning, his hand tight in my hair. His other hand was getting relaxed on the gun. I reached out slowly, touched the barrel, and pulled it from him, moving my mouth away and stumbling to my feet in one quick rush.

His hand whipped out, knocking the rifle away before I could pull the trigger. I scrambled after it. He kicked my legs out from under me and I hit the floor hard. His hands were on my legs, yanking me back.

I grabbed at a broken bit of crate on the floor, turned, and thrust it at his eye. At the last second he batted my hand away and instead of the stake going through his eyeball, it gouged his cheek. He let out a yell.

I pulled my legs free, crawled forward a foot, and grabbed the stock of the gun. He was gripping my ankles, trying to drag me backward. I couldn't get enough space to shoot him, couldn't spin the rifle around. I flipped on my side and with both hands on the gun hit him hard in the temple with the butt. He faltered. I hit him again. A thud.

He collapsed on the back of my legs and was still. I didn't know how far away the other room was but hoped Gavin hadn't heard Brian yell.

I squirmed out from underneath Brian and stood over him, pointing the gun at the back of his head. It was a .22 semi-automatic. I hoped there were a few bullets in the clip. My finger hovered on the trigger, my breath tight. I pulled hard – nothing happened. I turned the gun over and spotted the crushed brass bullet casing jammed in the chamber. Shit, shit, shit. I tried to work it free with my fingers, fumbling and slippery with sweat. How much time did I have before Gavin busted through the door? My heart was beating fast, the moment stretching out. It wasn't coming free. I squeezed my eyes shut in despair, then opened them and glared down at Brian.

'You fucker,' I whispered at his back. 'I hate you.'

I used Brian's belt and tied his wrists together, my fingers struggling with the leather as I tried to pull it tight and buckle it, terrified he might wake.

The rifle gripped in one hand, I inched my way out of the room, through the warehouse, skirting around stacks of crates. The lantern hung down by my knees, creating a small circle of light a few feet in front of me. Dani had told me to shoot Gavin, but I still couldn't get the bullet out of the chamber.

I went back to the other room, trying not to knock into anything as I moved around in the dark, and slid Brian's keys out of his back pocket, holding my breath when they jingled, but he was still out cold. I'd felt something else hard in his pocket and slowly slid my hand back in, pulled out a pocketknife.

I wondered if I should get Dani first, but when I left the room I noticed another door off the hallway. It was bigger, more like an outside entrance. I pushed it open. I seemed to be on the side of the building. I pushed my way through bushes around to the front. Brian's truck was parked facing the building.

I started up the truck, turned the radio on – loud blast of music. Then I got out and ran to the front of the building where there was a door. I tucked myself around the corner, switched the lantern off. In the last of the evening's light I could see that the warehouse was in a clearing surrounded by trees. It looked like the driveway went around the side of the building. I couldn't see any houses or lights through the trees. The only noise was Garth Brooks wailing out from Brian's truck.

Gavin came out, holding his rifle. He snuck up on the truck.

134

'Brian? That you? The fuck you doing?'

He was standing still, looking around, about twelve feet away. I tried again to pry the bullet out of the chamber but my fingers were too slippery.

He opened the truck door and reached in.

I moved slowly, my feet light on the ground, trying not to clang the lantern, creeping back to the door. I had to get to Dani, then we could get Courtney. One foot was over the entrance, the second coming in behind. A noise, the edge of the lantern brushing the doorjamb. I looked over my shoulder.

Gavin spun around, aimed at me through the open truck window, took a shot. The wood broke in front of my face. I dropped the lantern, dove back into the building, yelling Dani's name. I heard her call out from behind a door on my right. Another shot went off behind me. I pushed open the door.

'We've got to get out of here,' I said into the dark.

She was beside me, her hands touching me. I grabbed her arm. We ran down the hall, pushed open the door into the warehouse. We kept to the side of the room, following the wall, keeping crates between us and the door.

'Come out, come out, wherever you are,' Gavin's voice echoed down the hall.

We stopped with our backs against the wall, crouched into a corner. I used the knife and cut Dani's hands free. She rubbed at her wrists. I rested my mouth against her ear. 'The gun is jammed, assholes never cleaned it.'

She took it from me, fiddled with the bullet stuck in the chamber. I held my breath, and finally I heard the soft ping as the casing fell onto the concrete.

'We have to find Courtney,' she whispered, passing the gun back.

I gave her the knife. 'I took his keys too. They're in the truck.'

We crab-walked against the wall as cobwebs tangled in our hair and across our faces, trying not to catch our clothes on the crates. Every sound was magnified, every scrape of our feet loud. I heard Gavin's steps at the doorway, the creak of it being pushed open. I could hear his ragged breaths, knew he was also listening for us. We moved slower. I couldn't see any other exit, the room almost dark now. We had to get back through the same door somehow.

Dani grabbed my hand, pointed to the left in a frantic movement.

I pointed the gun in that direction, could just make out Gavin's shadow as he crept closer. I aimed, but he let off a shot first.

I ducked, pulling Dani down with me, then realized he'd shot toward the other end of the warehouse. How many bullets did he have left?

He cursed, then yelled out, 'Brian, where the fuck are you?'

He was crossing the room now, going to the other side, opposite the door.

'I'll throw something,' Dani whispered into my ear. 'When he shoots at it, shoot at *him*.' She felt around quietly on the floor. 'Got something,' she breathed again into my ear. 'Get ready.'

She threw something to the left. Gavin's shadow spun around, a loud crack as he took another shot. I aimed for his shadow, pulled the trigger, heard a yell, then the sounds of him falling, the clatter of crates being pulled down. I didn't know how badly we'd hurt him, but we got to our feet and ran to the end of the warehouse, feeling our way for the door to the other storage room.

'Here,' Dani said.

We pushed open the door. Courtney's small figure was curled on the floor, a lantern beside her. She was naked.

Dani picked her up, gripping her under her arms, and dragged her to her feet. Courtney leaned against Dani, her arm over Dani's shoulder, whimpering in pain.

I grabbed Courtney's dress off the floor and we ran toward the doorway out of the warehouse. Dani was still supporting Courtney's weight, her arm wrapped tight around her waist, me leading the way, the gun against my shoulder.

Where was Gavin? Had I killed him?

We were in the hallway, moving fast for the door. Dani was breathing hard behind me. We got to the truck. I prayed the keys were still in it.

Dani lifted Courtney into the passenger's side. I kept the gun pointed at the exit, glancing around. Was he in the bushes? Could he circle behind us?

Dani climbed in the driver's side. 'Get in, Jess!'

I raced to the passenger side, jumped inside.

The keys were still dangling from the ignition. Dani started the truck, turned on the headlights. Gavin came running out of the building, his shoulder soaked with blood. Brian was behind him.

Dani threw the truck in reverse, backed up a few feet, then jammed it into gear and pounded on the gas as she spun it around, doing a one-eighty and almost hitting one of them. Brian clung to the side window. We were all screaming.

I hit at his hands until he finally let go and fell to the ground.

We raced down the dirt road, gravel shooting out from behind us, the truck fishtailing on corners.

'I don't know which way to go!' Dani yelled. 'I don't know where we are.'

'Just keep going until we get to a house,' I said.

'We can't go to a house. We can't get help,' she said.

'I don't want to see anyone!' Courtney was finally talking – and crying hysterically. 'I don't want anyone to know,' she said between sobs. '*No one can know.*' She yanked the dress out of my hands and pulled it down over her head.

'The police will want our names,' Dani said. 'They'll figure out who we are.' We all knew what might happen after that. I thought of Dad's body under the pigs, his truck in the quarry.

'But they're going to get away with it,' I said.

'I don't want *anyone* to know,' Courtney insisted again.

'What are we going to do?' I was frantic with fear, desperate to get far away from Brian and Gavin. 'We can't take their truck into town. People will recognize it. Can we just drive it to Vancouver?'

Dani glanced down at the gauge. 'The assholes are almost out of gas.'

'Should we try to steal another truck?' I said.

'That'll just send the cops after us. We need to get our truck back.'

'From the garage?' I said.

'Yeah, we'll ditch this truck in town – it's late, not many people will be out on the streets. We can leave it at the bar, then we'll steal ours back. We have the shop keys. They said our truck was fixed – and we know it's got gas. Our rifle is probably still under the seat or they would've bragged about finding it.'

'They might've been lying – they could've gotten rid of the truck,' I said.

'No, I'm betting they kept it.'

A souvenir.

Chapter Eleven

We followed the road for a while, unsure if we were heading away from town or closer.

'What if we're going the wrong way and they're already in town?' I said.

'They're hurt. They have to come up with a plan too.'

'They might say we attacked them – that we stole their stuff.'

'They don't want the cops asking questions either,' Dani said.

I glanced over at Courtney, who hadn't said anything since we'd escaped. She was staring out the window. Once in a while she would look over her shoulder at the road behind us. I grabbed her hand and held it, but hers felt limp.

Finally we started seeing houses, then we crossed a bridge. The tires hummed on the surface.

'That sounds familiar. I think we crossed over this bridge that night!'

'Yeah, you're right,' Dani said.

'We're almost there, Courtney,' I said. 'We made it.'

She met my eyes, but hers looked hollow, defeated.

In town, we slowed almost to a crawl. The clock on the radio in the truck said it was eleven. We hadn't passed any other vehicles on the road, and there were just a few in front of the bar. I had no idea what day of the week it was. Dani circled the block and parked the truck behind the bar. Music and the scent of fried food carried out into the parking lot.

We got out, careful not to slam our doors. I had to help Courtney down. I saw now that her ear was bloodied, like Gavin had bit it. I found a water bottle on the floor, and an old T-shirt. I wet the corner, wiped at the blood.

Dani was in the back of the truck, trying to open the tool case behind the rear window. She was testing different keys on Brian's key chain.

'What are you doing?' I whispered. 'We've got to go.'

She finally opened the case, pulled out our packsacks, held them up.

We crept through the dark alley to the shop. Dani rifled through the keys, opened it up. I held my breath, waiting for the loud peal of an alarm, but there was only silence. There was also only one truck pulled in the garage.

'Shit. It's not here,' Dani said.

'It *has* to be.' I looked around, tugging at a tarp in the corner, excited for a moment. But it was covering an old car. 'Maybe they have some gas. We could fill up their truck and at least get out of here.'

We were checking a jerry can when the front door opened.

I was still carrying Brian's rifle and spun around, pointing it at the door. The man with the beard we'd seen the day we came through town was standing in the doorway. He was big, now that I saw him close up, his shoulders wide and his beard so long it touched his chest. He was wearing a baseball cap with a Harley insignia, and a Harley belt buckle pulled through faded jeans, a white T-shirt under a black leather vest. One of his forearms was scarred badly, the skin pink and raised in big welts like he'd been burned at some point.

When he saw me with the rifle, he put his hands up. He looked at us one by one, took it all in.

'You girls okay?' His voice was gruff, like a smoker's.

Dani stepped forward, pushed the gun down so it pointed at the floor. I hung on for a moment, but she shot me a look. I relaxed my arms.

'We don't want any trouble,' she said, 'just want what's ours.'

'You're looking for your truck.'

She didn't say anything.

'They have a yard out back,' he said. 'Noticed the boys

hiding a truck under a tarp a week ago. But it's a locked yard – with a big dog.'

I wanted to be brave and was angry when tears threatened. My voice thick, I said, 'You going to turn us in?'

He shook his head. He was looking at us slowly, the ill-fitting dresses, our bare feet and messy hair. His gaze lingered on Courtney's face.

'You sure you don't want me to call some help? Looks like you've run into some trouble.'

'No cops,' Dani said. 'We just want to get out of here.'

'Where you trying to go?'

Dani looked like she was debating whether she should lie, but then she said, 'Vancouver. We need food, clothes. Can you help us?'

The man looked hesitant now, like he was thinking.

Courtney raised her head, her voice breaking as she said, 'Please help us.'

We followed him through a back door into the pub and up some stairs. I saw now that his hair was long and braided down the back, and tied at the end with leather. The music was loud, vibrating through air that smelled of grease, cigarette smoke, and stale beer. I pushed away images of Brian and Gavin. I didn't want to be here, didn't want to go into this man's place, but we didn't have any other options.

His apartment was small but tidy. We sat in the living

room, huddled together on the couch. I gripped the rifle across my knees, looked around at the black velvet landscape paintings, the wooden burl coffee table, the glass shelf full of model Harley-Davidsons. On the mantel over a rock fireplace a photo of a woman was carefully placed on a white doily. The woman had long hair, parted in the middle, and a big smile. She was sitting on the back of a Harley.

'My name's Allen,' he said, then paused, waiting for us to introduce ourselves. We were mute. 'Okay, well, let me see about some clothes.'

He disappeared into a back room and came out with a couple pairs of jeans and blouses he handed to Courtney and Dani.

'My wife – she died a few years ago.' He passed me a pair of jeans, a T-shirt, a gray zip-up hoodie. 'These are my son's.'

'Thanks,' I said.

'I'll see if I can find some shoes.' He came back with a couple pairs of old sneakers, scuffed, laces ratty, and some flip-flops that had also seen better days. 'He wears them until they fall off.'

He pointed out the bathroom, which was down the hall a little but still in view of the living room. Dani told me to go in first. I gave her the rifle, grabbed my packsack, then quickly changed and washed my face and hair. Next Dani went in with Courtney, handing me back the rifle. I waited outside the door, my packsack by my feet, the rifle gripped in my hands. I wondered if Gavin and Brian had another truck. If they were already back in town and looking for us.

Allen was in the kitchen, opening a can of soup, watching me. His gaze drifted down, focused on my wrists, his forehead pulling together in a frown. For a brief moment his eyes flicked to the phone at the end of the counter.

'You better not call anyone!' I said. I took a step toward him, glanced over my shoulder, but Courtney and Dani were still in the bathroom. I didn't know what to do. My head felt light, my body shaky from fear and lack of food.

He held out a hand. 'Easy. I was just thinking the cops would want to know if the boys hurt you.'

'You call them, and I'm going to have to hurt *you*.' I brandished the gun.

'Nobody has to hurt anybody, okay?'

Dani and Courtney came out of the bathroom. Their hair was damp. The clothes were baggy on them, but I was glad to see them out of the dresses.

'What's going on?' Dani rushed toward me.

'He was going to call the cops.'

'Why?' Dani said. 'We told you. Nothing happened.'

He looked at us. 'Something happened.'

'We won't talk to them,' Dani said. 'But those boys,

they might hear that you made a call about *them*.' She gave him a look.

The man stared at her, his hands still on the can of soup, weighing her words, then nodded.

He motioned to the kitchen table. 'Let's talk about how we can get you girls out of town.'

Courtney and Dani sat on one side, dumping their packsacks down by their feet. I stayed leaning against the wall where I could see their faces, the rifle still in my hands but pointed at the floor. The man got a pot out of a cupboard, dumped a couple cans of chicken noodle soup into it. My mouth watered. I wanted to eat it cold, wanted to run over and slurp it from the pot. I glanced at Dani's face, noticed her staring at the stove. She looked away, slowly, her neck stiff.

'It's better if you girls leave your truck behind,' the man said.

'We need it. We just have to drug the dog or something,' Dani said.

'The garage, it's got cameras out back.'

'You didn't tell us that before,' I said. The soup was boiling on the stove. The man stirred it, the aroma filling the air. My stomach grumbled.

'Didn't want to scare you. Brian's uncle, he checks that camera all the time.'

'Shit,' Dani said, gnawing on her nails.

'When you don't claim your truck, they'll chop it up

for parts. I don't know where you came from or who you're running from, but you took a chance driving it out here. Trucks need gas, trucks break down. If you leave it, it's like you disappeared here.'

Like we died here. I glanced at Courtney. She was holding her arms tight around her body, her eyes still vacant in that way that scared me.

'How else are we going to get to Vancouver?' I said.

'There's a bus. First thing in the morning—'

'We can't stay here that long.' My voice was frantic.

He looked thoughtful. 'My son can drive you to Armstrong tonight. You can get on the bus there.'

'We don't have any money,' Dani said, her chin high.

'I'll help you. Do you have any family where you're going?'

Dani shook her head. 'No one.'

'So what are you going to do?' He pulled some bowls down out of the cupboard.

'We'll live on the streets or a shelter or something,' she said.

He looked over his shoulder at us. 'Three girls alone on the streets of Vancouver ... That's just asking for trouble.'

'We're already in trouble,' she said.

He nodded, looked like he was thinking something over.

'I have an old friend ... He has a gym, works with

teenagers from the streets. He might be able to find you a place to stay.'

Dani looked at Courtney, who was staring down at the table, then over to me. I shook my head, frowning. She looked back at Courtney, then turned to the man.

'Can you call him? We'd appreciate it.'

'We don't need anyone,' I said. 'We can figure it out on our own.'

Dani glared at me. 'Shut up and let me handle this.'

'We should get a say in this too!'

'Why don't you girls talk it over?' the man said.

Dani and I glanced at Courtney.

'I'll watch her,' he said. 'You can use my son's room.' He pointed toward the back of the apartment.

I grabbed the cordless, giving the guy a look, making it clear I didn't trust him. Dani and I went into a back bedroom with hockey flags on the wall, posters from bands, a couple of carvings on his desk. His bed was tidy, his clothes folded neatly, books stacked everywhere.

'We can get our truck back,' I whispered to Dani. 'By the time Brian's uncle checks the cameras, we could be in Vancouver.'

'We still have to get past the dog – and he's right. For all we know, the cops are already looking for our truck. We should've left town a week ago.'

'What about our rifle?'

149

'We just have to hope if the guys find it, they get rid of it.'

'We don't know anything about this guy's friend.'

'We don't know anything about *him* either. We don't have any other options. Hitchhiking is too dangerous – they might find us.'

I tried to think of some other way we could get out of town on our own, but before I could say anything, Dani had grabbed the phone out of my hand and opened the door.

'He's our only hope, Jess.'

Courtney was slumped in her chair, staring at the floor. The man reached across the table to set down a bag of crackers, and she flinched. He moved to the other side of the room.

'Like we said,' Dani said, giving me a look, 'we'd appreciate if you called your friend.' She handed him the phone and sat down.

'I'd have to dig up his number,' he said. 'Been a long time, but I can give it a try.' He carried two bowls of soup over to the table, handed the girls some spoons. Then he looked at me. 'You want to sit down?'

Dani shot me another look.

I sat at the other side of the table, worried he'd sit beside me, but he just pushed a bowl in front of me, then stood at the counter. I dug in, slurping at the soup, digging my spoon in so fast some of it splashed out.

'Go easy,' he said. 'Might upset your stomach.'

He'd said it kindly, and I tried to slow down. Courtney was spooning hers in pretty fast but methodically, spoonful after spoonful, like a robot. Dani was eating calmly, her hand steady as she dipped the spoon in and brought another mouthful to her lips. But I saw the look in her eyes, the relief.

Allen opened a drawer and rummaged around. He brought out an address book and flipped through it, muttering. Then stopped and turned around.

'Got the number. I'll give him a call now.'

Dani nodded. 'Thanks.'

He picked up the cordless phone at the end of the counter, turning toward us as though he sensed we needed to see his face. I kept my hand near the rifle I'd rested by my legs. If I got the feeling he was calling the cops, I didn't know what I'd do, but I wanted to be ready.

The phone seemed to ring awhile. Then finally the man said, 'Patrick, sorry for waking you. It's Allen ...' He paused, listening. 'Just fine. How you been ...?' Another pause. 'Listen, I got some girls here, they've run into some trouble.' He glanced at us. 'Big trouble. We're going to put them on the bus in the morning. Can you meet them? They need a place to stay ... Thanks, buddy. We'll talk soon, go for a ride, hey?' He said good night and hung up.

151

'He's going to help?' Dani said, her face hopeful.

'Yeah, he'll pick you up, get you somewhere safe.'

Dani's body relaxed in the chair. I felt mad at her, pissed that she was putting us at risk again. She gave me a look across the table.

'It's better for Courtney,' she said.

I looked down, still mad. We could take care of Courtney ourselves. Allen seemed okay but we didn't know anything about this Patrick guy. What if he was like Brian and Gavin? It didn't matter, though. Dani had made up her mind.

'I'm going to call my son,' Allen said. Dani nodded. He dialed some numbers. 'Owen, can you come upstairs?' He set the phone back down. 'Owen works in the kitchen. Why don't you girls go rest in the living room?' He cleared away our bowls.

We grabbed our packsacks and sat on the couch. It was warm in the apartment but Courtney couldn't stop shivering, her arms wrapped tight around her chest. When Allen came back in, Dani was tucking a blanket around her.

'Your sister's in a bad way,' he said.

'We never said we're sisters,' Dani said.

'You're sisters, all right.'

Steps coming up the stairs, then a boy walked into the living room, tall, with shaggy blond hair and ice-blue eyes. It was the boy I'd seen in the alley.

152

'You're those girls,' he said, surprised. He stared at our clothes, his shoes on our feet. His eyes settled on the rifle in my lap, widened in alarm.

I remembered how he'd stared at us in the back of the truck. Did he think we liked Brian and Gavin? Did he think we wanted to be with them? My face was warm, my throat tight. I blinked back tears.

I held my breath when he passed by me to stand by his dad. I leaned back into the couch, tucked my legs up so he couldn't touch them.

'These girls are going to need a ride tonight to Armstrong,' Allen said.

'Tonight?' He looked surprised again but didn't ask any other questions.

'You're going to see them to the bus station.' Allen walked over to a china cabinet at the other end of the room, reached under, and grabbed something.

He pulled out a rifle and a box of ammo.

'What's that for?' Dani said, her voice loud and scared.

'In case someone doesn't want you to leave town.' He walked back over and handed the gun to Owen. 'Load it and put it under the seat.' Owen nodded.

I didn't like the idea of Owen having a gun, but I didn't much like the idea of him not having a gun either. How long would it take for Brian and Gavin to get back to town? The first place they'd look was at the garage. I wondered if they'd gotten rid of all our other stuff or if it was still in the truck. We couldn't get to it regardless. I was glad Dani had found our packsacks. I reached in, felt my camera, and wanted to cry when my fingers touched the broken lens.

I glanced at my sisters. Courtney was still curled into a ball, Dani watching her as she rubbed her leg soothingly like our mom used to do for us.

'You girls should crouch down when he's driving out of here,' Allen said. 'Even in the next town, the Luxton boys know people.'

My body filled with fear. What if the cops from Littlefield were still looking for us? Would they show photos of us to people at the station?

'We should change our looks,' I said.

'Yeah, we need disguises.' Dani looked at the man.

'We should be able to rustle some stuff up,' he said. 'Owen, why don't you go make the girls some sandwiches first?'

'Not peanut butter,' I said, my voice frantic. They both stared at me. My face flushed.

'She's allergic,' Dani said.

The boy left the room. I heard cupboard doors opening and shutting.

Allen sat in the chair across from me.

'You should leave that here,' he said as he pointed to the gun.

'We need it,' Dani said.

'It's probably registered. You get found with it, all kinds of trouble could come up. I'll get rid of it for you.'

Everything was being stripped away, our truck, the gun. Dani was looking at me and I knew what she wanted me to do. I didn't meet her eyes.

'Give it to him,' Dani said.

The man stood, held his hand out for the gun. I thought about what he'd said. He was right, the gun was probably registered and it wasn't like I could get on a bus with a rifle.

I handed it over.

He opened the clip, dumped the bullets into his hand, and put them in his pocket. Then he slid the gun under the couch.

'I better get downstairs before people start wondering. Owen will take care of you now.'

'Thanks,' Dani said, 'for helping us.'

He stopped at the top of the stairs, gave us one last look. 'Take care, girls.'

We were left with Owen. He packed our sandwiches in brown paper bags and handed them to Dani. She shoved them into her packsack. He gave Courtney a curious look, but his face was sympathetic.

'Don't look at her,' I said.

He glanced over at me. 'There's medicine in the back

155

closet, from when my mom was sick. Pain stuff. Do you want them?'

I glanced at Dani. She looked unsure for a moment, then said, 'Yeah.'

He came back with some bottles and handed them to Dani. 'Directions are on the label.' He pointed to a bottle. 'That's for anxiety. It's really strong, though, so don't give her too many.'

Dani turned to Courtney. 'Sweetie, take this.' She held out a small blue pill. Courtney didn't lift her arm or her head.

'Just open your mouth,' Dani said. Courtney opened it up, then closed it as soon as Dani placed the small pill under her tongue. Dani turned to the boy. 'Did your mom have any makeup?'

'I'll look.' Owen went into the back of the apartment. I could hear doors opening and closing, then he came out. 'I left some makeup on the bathroom counter.' He handed me a black bandanna and two strips of black fabric. 'I figured this could kind of go with your outfit, like to cover your hair, and your wrists.' I was surprised, hadn't even seen him look at my wrists. 'If you put on a bunch of dark makeup, maybe you could look like a heavy metal chick or a skater girl, you know?'

I nodded, wrapping the bandanna around my head and the strips of fabric around my wrists, hating how it made me feel bound again, but glad for the protection from prying eyes.

He turned back to Dani and Courtney. 'We don't really have much for you except baseball caps, but they'd look weird with what you're wearing. Those blouses, they're kind of old-fashioned, so I brought some tank tops.' He looked embarrassed, like he wasn't used to talking to girls like this. 'You can wear them under, and the blouses open, like girls do, you know?' He also handed Dani a purple scarf. 'If one of you wears this around your neck, people might remember that and not your face. As long as you don't pull the shirtsleeves up, you should be okay with your wrists. But your hair . . .' He was looking at Dani's long hair.

'I'll cut it,' she said.

'Dani, no!' I said.

'It's just hair,' she said, her voice irritated, already tying the scarf around Courtney's neck.

The boy went into the kitchen and came back with some scissors. Dani stood up, pulling Courtney up with her.

'Come on, sweetie.'

We crowded into the small bathroom. Dani flipped the toilet seat down, eased Courtney onto it. Dani took a breath, picked up the scissors, grabbed the back of her hair in one big chunk, and started hacking at it. I held my hand over my mouth, trying not to cry. When she'd cut off the bulk of it, which she dropped into the

157

garbage, she cut the rest in a choppy style. She wet her hands and ruffled her hair until it was standing up in tousled spikes. It made her eyes look bigger.

She undid her shirt, pulled the tank top down over her head, while I helped Courtney with hers. Then Dani smoothed some foundation onto Courtney's face, wetting the old, cakey makeup so it would spread over the bruises. She pulled Courtney's hair back in a braid. While they were busy, I ringed my eyes with black and coated my face with pale powder. I stared at myself in the mirror.

I looked dead. Haunted.

'Come on,' Dani said.

We walked back out into the living room. Owen stood up from where he'd been waiting on the couch. He looked nervous.

'I was thinking . . . three of you kind of stand out, you know? Maybe you shouldn't sit together.'

I looked at Dani. 'He's right.' Whether it was the cops or the boys looking for us, more people would remember three girls.

'We can't all sit by ourselves.' I knew she was worried about Courtney.

'Maybe you two can pretend to be like girlfriends or something,' I said.

'That's a good idea,' Owen said. 'Like she could rest on you and you could hold her hand, you know?'

158

'We probably shouldn't get picked up together in Vancouver either,' Dani said. She looked at me. 'But I don't want to leave you behind.'

'I can do it. I'll be okay.' I didn't really want to be separated from my sisters, but Dani was right. Then I realized it might look weird if the same vehicle came and got me. 'Or maybe I should wait somewhere else?'

'There's a park I think you could walk to,' Owen said.

'We better hurry,' I said.

We followed Owen down the back stairs and into a side garage. They had a big truck, a black crew cab with seats in the back. Owen opened the back door, waiting for me. I hesitated, remembering.

Want to go for a swim?

Owen was watching my face. Did he know what they'd done to us? Could he tell? I looked away.

'My dad, you can trust him,' Owen said. 'We won't tell anyone.'

'Why?' I said, meeting his eyes.

'He was in prison, for years. He looks out for people now.' I thought about the gun under the china cabinet.

Dani, on the other side of the truck, said, 'What was he in jail for?'

'He killed a man in a bar fight. Self-defense, but he still got time.'

'What about his friend?' I said.

'He was in prison too. He's cool – he taught me how to box. He'll take care of you.'

We pulled up beside the bus station. Owen gave Dani some cash. The light on the dash told us it was three in the morning.

'I'll stay with you until the bus comes,' he said. 'If you want to get some sleep, I'll keep a lookout.'

I was exhausted, my body hurting all over, but I didn't want to sleep.

'I'm fine,' I said.

'Me too,' Dani said from the passenger seat. In the back with me, Courtney was leaning up against the side, sleeping.

'Remember to act like strangers on the bus,' Owen said.

'We're not idiots,' I said.

He glanced back at me. 'Sorry. I'm just trying to help.'

'It's okay,' I said, feeling bad.

'There are a couple of stops,' Owen said, 'but you should be in Vancouver by lunchtime.' He looked at me again. 'When you get to the station, just start walking to the park.'

'How do I get there?' I was nervous about getting off in a strange city without my sisters.

'Stick to the main road and head straight. There are

cameras at the station so you don't want to stay there long.'

'Should I get out now?' I said.

'Yeah, maybe sit on the bench outside the station until it opens. We'll keep an eye on you from here. Anyone bothers you, I'll come get you.'

'Okay.' I took a breath, climbed out with my packsack on my shoulder, gave Dani a look through the window. 'See you on the bus.'

'Don't worry,' she said. 'This is the safest way.'

Owen got out and grabbed something from the back of the truck, handed me a skateboard covered in stickers.

'This'll make you look like a skater chick.'

I stared at the board, then back at him. He flushed.

'I don't need it anymore,' he said.

I felt him watch me walk to the bus station. I sat outside on the bench, huddled in his hoodie. It smelled of boy, but clean – not like Brian and Gavin. A shudder went through my body when I thought of them. Had they made it back to town yet? Were they looking for us? They'd want us dead for sure now.

I looked down at my wrists, the skin sore and aching under the fabric strips. I clenched my hands, made fists, gritting my teeth against the pain.

I was never going to let anyone hurt me again.

Chapter Twelve

A dark-colored truck slowed as it neared the station. I gripped my packsack, ready to run. I glanced at Owen's truck in the dark, then back at the one coming closer. Was it *them*? The truck passed under a streetlight. A glimmer of silver hair, a grizzled face peering over the steering wheel. An old man.

Finally light was coming up on the horizon. An hour later, the bus pulled into sight with a groan of brakes. There was a noise behind the station door as it was unlocked, then an open sign was shoved in the window. A small cluster of people had been gathering for the last hour. They filed in.

The woman behind the counter slurped her coffee and took my money without even looking at me. Her hair was messy like she'd just woken up. I climbed aboard the bus, which smelled faintly of lemon cleaner and vomit, then settled into a window seat. I watched my sisters walk across the road. Courtney seemed off balance, wobbly, like a passing vehicle could blow her over. Dani was gripping her arm. They went inside, then came back out and got on the bus.

My eyes met Dani's when they passed but we didn't smile or speak.

A heavy woman sat beside me, shoving her bag under the seat in front of her, pushing at it with feet that looked like they were going to burst through her shoes, the laces straining to hold all the flesh in. She gave me a look and a disgusted sniff, then pulled out a book. I was happy she didn't want to talk.

It would take six hours for the bus to get to Vancouver. Six hours before we were away from Brian and Gavin. I watched out the window, studying trucks going past, people climbing aboard the bus, catching my breath every time I saw a baseball cap or someone tall. Finally we were loaded and the bus was pulling away. It stopped in the next town, and a couple of others, but we never got off to stretch our legs. I walked to the back once to use the washroom, not even glancing at my sisters, but from the corner of my eye I saw that Dani was leaning against the window, Courtney asleep against her shoulder.

I had to squeeze past the woman in my seat, almost landing in her lap, then settled myself against the window, counting telephone poles zipping by until the sway of the bus finally lulled me to sleep. I woke with a lurch as the woman beside me grabbed my arm. She gave me a strange look.

'You were having a nightmare.'

'Sorry.' My face flushed, my skin felt hot.

I stayed awake after that.

When the bus got closer to Vancouver I stared out the window, my forehead pressed into the cool glass. I was amazed by all the people, cars, buses, the huge buildings.

The bus depot was a large building on the harbor. I'd expected something industrial, concrete and metal, but it was stone. The bus driver intoned over the speaker that it was a heritage building. Behind the depot I could see the wide blue expanse of ocean sparkling in the sun. As I stepped off the bus, gusts of wind blew salt water toward me. When I stopped to inhale the scent, the large woman bumped into me, nearly knocking me over. I hoisted my packsack over my shoulder, gripped the skateboard Owen had given me, and moved on.

Outside the station, I watched people mill about and waited for my sisters to get off the bus. Courtney still seemed dazed and was walking stiffly, but at least she was looking around. Dani had dark circles under her eyes, her shorn hair sticking up on one side. They were holding hands.

Dani glanced at me, her face revealing nothing. Across the parking lot a maroon van started up and slowly came around. PHOENIX BOXING AND TRAINING was written on the side doors. I couldn't see the man behind the wheel, just a shock of white hair and a beefy forearm covered in tattoos hanging out the window. I remembered Owen saying his dad's friend had been in prison.

The van pulled in front of my sisters. I couldn't hear what they were saying, but the side door opened automatically and they climbed in.

Dani's eyes met mine for just a second, then the door was sliding shut.

They were driving off.

I wanted to run after them, screaming, *Stop, don't leave me!*

The van turned onto the road and was swallowed up by the traffic. I looked around. Most of the passengers were gone. The fat woman was climbing into a Jeep, two big dogs in the backseat licking her neck.

Another bus was pulling up, people walking all around me. Car horns honked, tires screeched, announcements came over the loudspeaker. I spun around. Which way was I supposed to walk? Where was the park?

A man across the way was standing near the pay phones, checking me out. I walked away, fast.

Then I remembered Owen had told me to go straight down the main street. I held my packsack tight on my shoulder. Every time a vehicle pulled up behind me, I jerked around. People pushed past me, their shoulders rubbing against mine, giving me curious looks or not seeing me at all. I felt adrift, like a stick being tossed around in water. I saw a park off to the left, the bright bit of green in a sea of gray. I found a bench near the parking lot, pulled my packsack into my lap, and rested my chin on it.

I watched every vehicle come and go, wondering how long I'd have to wait. It was hot, the sun high in the sky and beating down. I was thirsty, my lips chapped, and I'd eaten my sandwich on the bus hours ago. I also needed to pee but was scared to go anywhere in case I missed my ride. Finally, the van pulled up.

The white-haired man rolled down the window. 'You okay, kid?'

Despite the hair, he wasn't that old, older than our dad but maybe just in his fifties, I wasn't sure. His skin was tanned, his eyes pale green.

'Yeah.' I got up and came closer. I could see Dani and Courtney in the back. Courtney still had her head resting on Dani's shoulder.

He stuck his hand through the open window. 'Patrick. Pleased to meet you.'

I shook his hand but didn't say my name. He just gave me a friendly smile and said, 'Climb in.' The door slid open.

I went around the passenger side and took a seat, glancing in the back at my sisters. Dani looked tired, her head resting on the seat behind her, eyes half closed. I turned back around. Patrick's van smelled like vanilla. I eyed an empty Tim Hortons coffee cup, the rim rolled down. There was a pile of scratch-and-wins stuffed in the ashtray, already scratched.

My eyes stung when I remembered the time Dani, Courtney, and I stole some change from Dad's pocket and bought scratch-and-wins, sure we'd win and he'd be happy. We were stunned when all of them were 'not a winner'. I made Dani scratch them all again. But we were still losers.

Patrick pointed to my feet. 'Sandwich in the bag for you. Your sisters already ate theirs.' He put the van into gear and turned back onto the road.

'Where are we going?' I said, pulling the sandwich out of the bag. Turkey and bacon. I ripped into it.

Patrick reached behind him, tossed me a bottle of water.

'My house. My wife will help you clean up and we can talk about your situation.'

'Why are you doing this?' I spoke with my mouth full, too hungry to care.

'Why shouldn't I?'

'People don't do stuff for nothing.' I glanced back, noticed that both my sisters looked like they were asleep.

'This isn't for nothing. I'm paying it forward.'

I looked at him curiously. 'What does that mean?'

'It's when someone did something good for you one day, so then you do good things for other people.' He glanced at me again. 'Someone helped me out once. So now I help kids before they go down the same path.'

I looked at his tattoos. 'You mean prison.'

'Among other things.' We drove in silence for a bit. 'Your sister seems pretty messed up,' he said in a low voice.

'She'll be okay.' She *had* to be okay.

He gave me another look. 'Some people, they deal with stuff differently.'

I didn't know what to say to that. 'We'll look after her.'

He told me we were on the east side and chatted about other areas of Vancouver like Kitsilano, Shaughnessy, Point Grey. The names blended together. He said the east side had some rough spots – where the homeless and addicts lived – but also lots of families who couldn't afford the downtown prices. He stopped at McDonald's so we could use the bathroom. Courtney was only limping slightly, but when I told her she was walking better she said she was still sore between her legs.

When we came out, Patrick had bought us milkshakes.

'You still looked hungry. Didn't want you biting my arm or something.' He flexed his biceps and laughed, a surprisingly light sound for a big man.

I felt the corner of my mouth lift, almost smiled back, then stopped myself. I couldn't let myself like him yet, couldn't let down my guard.

Patrick's house wasn't very big, just a plain box covered in faded cream stucco that someone had tried to paint. We parked on the street in front. Patrick got out. He was muscled all over, with tree-trunk legs, broad shoulders, and a barrel chest. He reminded me of Angus, the Clydesdale. His T-shirt had a logo of a dark bird rising up.

He pushed open a wrought-iron gate, guarded on the other side by a garden gnome with a perky red hat. Someone had tied a doll's scarf around its neck and added a pair of sunglasses. Dani and Courtney walked through. I stopped to look at the gnome.

Patrick smiled. 'I collect them.'

More gnomes lined the pathway around the side of the house, all with different-colored hats. The backyard was an explosion of color, flowers all over the place, statues of mythological creatures cavorting in random locations, some with broken noses or missing arms. Nothing matched, and there didn't seem to be any rhyme or reason to anything. Vegetable beds blended into flower beds, trees wrapped around fences. Metal wind chimes dangled from some branches, wooden ones from others. Flower wheels spun in lazy circles.

Despite the disorder, it was a strange kind of beautiful.

'When I was in prison, I told myself I'd have a garden one day,' Patrick said beside me. I glanced at him. He was smiling with pride. He bent down, righted a gnome that had been kicked over. 'Cats,' he said.

Inside, the house was warm and cheery. Crocheted blankets in bright colors were tossed over mismatched couches. Plants were crowded into every window, their leaves reaching toward the sun. The walls were covered in photos with different-colored frames. Cats were sleeping on the back of the couch and on the chairs, or on a large scratching post in the corner of the room, the carpet frayed. I counted ten cats, then lost track. A bird chirped loudly from a cage in the kitchen – two more cats watching from the floor, their tails flicking.

Patrick's wife also turned out to be in great shape, her skin tanned, her smile big. She looked about the same age as Patrick, but her hair was blonde, pulled back into a ponytail. She was wearing tight black shorts, running shoes, and a hot pink tank top.

'Come in, come in. I'm Karen. Would you like a cup of tea? Something to eat? A hot shower?'

'Do you have somewhere my sister can lie down?' Dani said. Courtney was almost swaying on her feet, her eyelids at half-mast.

170

'Of course.' Karen took us down a small hallway to a back bedroom with two beds. Courtney curled up in one, her hands covering her face.

'I'll make you something to eat.' Karen's voice was hushed, her face solemn. She closed the door behind her.

'I gave her another pill,' Dani said, staring intently at Courtney, as though she were counting her breaths, willing her to keep going.

'You're supposed to be careful with those,' I said.

'She started crying on the bus and kept asking for it. She said it helped her forget.' She looked at me. 'Were you okay, walking to the park?'

'Yeah.' I nodded toward the door. 'What do you think of them?'

'They seem nice.'

'Don't you think it's weird? Them helping us like this?'

'Some people are just like that, Jess. It makes them feel good inside.'

'Where are their kids?'

'I don't think they have any. But I saw some photos of kids at a gym.'

Sounds and scents of food being cooked wafted down the hall.

'She's making lunch,' I said. 'Do you want to come out?'

'I'm going to stay with Courtney.' She sat down on

171

the bed and stroked her hair. Courtney moaned, made a panicked sound.

'Shhh,' Dani whispered. Courtney quieted, her breath deepening again.

'Do you think they'll find us?' I said.

'The police . . . or them?'

'Both.'

A pause. 'No, I bet we're okay.' But I heard the uncertainty in her voice. She curled up next to Courtney, pressed her face into her shoulder.

Chapter Thirteen

Karen heaped my plate full of spaghetti I wolfed down, barely noticing the fat black-and-white cat batting at my bare toes until I was finished. Then I rubbed his warm belly with my foot as I watched Karen move around the kitchen. I liked how she talked to herself while she worked. 'Now, where did I put those tongs this time?' 'Going to have to get Patrick to fix that sink again.' It reminded me of my mom talking to the food when she was cooking, wrestling the chicken into the crock pot and ordering it to stay, dammit!

Mom wasn't a fancy cook, sticking to mostly fried food or meats and potatoes, but the kitchen always smelled good – and the fridge was full. She told me once that she didn't have much money when she was a kid and always dreamed of having a full fridge. She would've liked Karen.

I offered to help clean up.

'That's okay, sweetie,' Karen said. 'You have a shower

or bath or whatever you like and get some rest. You can stay here tonight and we'll talk tomorrow.'

I soaked in the bath. There were still bruises on my inner thighs. I stared at the bite mark on my left breast, covered it with a soap bubble. I shut my eyes, squeezed them tight, but I could see Brian's face, flashes of his body moving above me, could hear the sounds he'd made. I picked up the washcloth and the soap, scrubbed at my body as if it were filthy, trying to hold back the sobs.

When I got back to our bedroom, Courtney and Dani were sleeping, a lamp casting a glow over their faces. Dani looked angry even in her sleep. Courtney's face was hidden by her hair, one hand tucked near her face like a little girl. I crawled into the other bed, looking around the strange room. I startled at the loud sound of a bus going by, people arguing out on the street. I grabbed the pillow and blanket and curled up on the floor close to my sisters.

In the morning Patrick knocked on the door.

'When you girls are ready, we'll talk.'

We came into the kitchen, sat at the table. Food was already out on plates, steaming cups of coffee by each seat. A cat leapt up, grabbed a piece of bacon. Karen scooped him up and dropped him onto the floor.

'Get out of here, Rocky.'

174

Courtney was looking a little more alert, but all her responses were a half step behind and there was a vague look in her eyes I didn't like. She'd asked Dani for another pill, but Dani said it was better if she waited. Dani looked like she could fall asleep sitting, like she just wanted to close her eyes or curl up on the floor.

I'd woken up at two in the morning, my pulse racing when I heard steps creep past our door. I was ready to wake Dani when I heard a toilet flush. Afterward the house was quiet but I couldn't get back to sleep. Dani's hand was hanging over the side of the bed, all her nails chewed to the quick. I studied my own, broken and rough. Then I remembered Brian's, the grease under his nails. I curled into a ball, squeezed my eyes shut, pressed my hands to my ears.

Now I was groggy, shoveling bacon in my mouth, methodically chewing, but my eyes felt like they had sand in them, the lids heavy. Dani picked at her breakfast, tried to get Courtney to eat hers. Courtney just sipped her coffee.

'So what are your names?' Patrick said.

Dani stared at Patrick, her eyes big. Courtney looked scared.

'We can't tell you,' Dani said.

'You need fake ID.' It wasn't a question.

'Can you help?' Dani said.

He nodded like he'd been expecting that, grabbed a piece of bacon, bit into it with a crunch. 'I can get you some, but you need to come up with new names. Use your current initials for your first and last names.'

Fear shot through me. If we gave him our initials, could he figure out our real names somehow? If he discovered where we grew up . . .

'Why do you want our initials?' I said. Dani gave me an impatient look.

'Easier for you to remember, less slip-ups,' Patrick said. 'I'll get birth certificates for you. Should have them in a couple of days. How old are you all?'

I frowned at Dani, scared she was revealing too much. She hesitated, glanced at me, then back at Patrick.

'Look.' He put a few more pieces of bacon on my plate. 'I don't give a shit what you did or where you're from. All I care about is helping you start new lives.' He smiled at Karen, who was pouring him another cup of coffee. 'Thanks, sweetie.' He dumped cream into his cup, turned back to us. 'So. You going to meet me halfway?'

Dani sucked in a breath, released it. 'I'm turning eighteen in a few months.' She pointed to Courtney. 'She's sixteen and a half.' She pointed to me. 'She just turned fifteen.'

'You're young enough people will believe you don't have social insurance numbers yet. But you should get them soon – not all at once.' He motioned to Dani. 'You

176

first.' He looked at Courtney. 'Did you have a driver's license?'

'She only had her learner's,' Dani said.

'She should apply for another. You're both a year older now.'

Courtney glanced at him, her face blank, took another sip of her coffee.

Patrick watched her for a second. Karen followed his gaze. I didn't like the look on their faces, their concern. What if they called the police or took her to a hospital?

Patrick turned back to me. 'We'll keep your age at fifteen. You look young.'

That's no fifteen-year-old's body. I blinked back tears, stared down at the table, the smell of bacon grease turning my stomach now.

Karen got up and started making a fresh pot of coffee.

'Do you have any work for us?' Dani said. 'You've got this big yard.' Her voice was hopeful, pleading. 'We're really strong.'

'What kind of experience do you have?'

'Farming, mostly, but Jess, she's really smart – and we're hard workers.'

'I might be able to find you something at the gym to get you started.'

'We don't have anywhere to stay,' Dani said, her face

flushed. 'Is there a shelter around here? We don't have money ...'

Karen turned around from the sink, gave Patrick a look. I wondered what it meant. Did she want him to get rid of us?

'Let's talk about that later,' Patrick said. 'I'll show you the gym.'

The gym was a couple of blocks from the house – Patrick explained how to count city blocks. It was in an old warehouse, but it looked recently painted and it was clean, the air smelling of pine and lemon. Framed posters from old boxing movies were hung high up on the walls, circling the room. Patrick walked around showing us stuff: the boxing rings, his office – crammed full of files and an old computer, boxes of protein bars and weights and sweatshirts tossed in the corner. Kids stopped and talked to him as we passed, their faces eager when they showed him a few jabs or hooks. Heavy bags were strung from the ceiling and there were large balls in corners, mats stacked against the wall, boxes spilling over with boxing gloves.

Patrick grabbed a couple of pairs and got us to put them on.

He showed us a small bag in the corner, about head-height. He said it was called a speed bag and demonstrated how to stand and hit it so it kept coming back. It was amazing how fast he was, his hands a blur.

Then it was my turn.

I was awkward at first, had a hard time finding the rhythm. The more I hit, the more I fell out of sync. I looked at Patrick in frustration.

'Hang in there,' Patrick said. 'You've almost got it.'

I tried again, tuned everything out, focusing on the ball, taking my time as I hit it with my right hand, then my left, then the right again. After a while my blows fell into a rhythm, an odd exhilaration flowing through my body each time I connected.

Dani picked it up right away, and Patrick went on about how she was a natural. 'You've got talent, kid.'

Dani smiled for the first time in a long time, her face determined when she hit the bag, the sound strong and solid and powerful. *Thwack, thwack, thwack.*

I felt good for her, my fingers itching for my camera, but I hadn't taken it out of my packsack since Brian had dropped it.

Even Courtney started to wake up when Patrick tied some gloves on her hands and showed her a couple of moves. She went over to a heavy bag in the corner and hit it in rapid succession, then kept hitting it over and over, frantic movements with no form, just hard punches that made a loud *smack*, her breath almost sobbing out of her with each blow. A couple of kids gave her curious looks but Patrick motioned them away. Tears were rolling down my face. Dani looked stricken too, watching Courtney take her grief out on the bag.

Finally she stopped. Still gasping for air, she turned to Patrick. 'Can you teach us how to take care of ourselves?'

'Sure thing – no one will mess with you girls again.'

Again. I wondered how much he guessed or knew. Would he try to find out where we came from? I hoped not. Helping scared kids was one thing. He might not be so cool if he knew I was a murderer.

'Come on,' he said, like he sensed he'd freaked us out. 'Let me show you the apartment upstairs.'

'What apartment?' Dani said, her voice suspicious.

'It's part of the gym. Tenants just moved out. It's not much, but you girls can stay until you get back on your feet. We'll work something out for the rent.'

He was right, it was just a two-bedroom apartment above the gym – you could hear the thumping below, but I liked that, the comfort of the noise, people nearby. The kitchen had a few cupboards, a scratched-up counter in pale yellow, a single sink, a small fridge and stove, and a bathroom with tiles peeling back and a bathtub stained with rust. But there were three beds with sleeping bags, a couch with one of the crocheted blankets, and a couple of dressers.

'There's some cutlery, pots, plates, things like that,' Patrick said.

180

'It's perfect,' Dani said. 'We really appreciate this.'

I pulled curtains away from the window in the back. It looked out over some houses. A woman was planting flowers in a box on her balcony. Our new apartment also had a small balcony, and I thought about getting Dani some seeds.

I looked far below. No one would be able to climb up there.

'Yeah, it's perfect,' I said.

Two days later we were having breakfast with Karen and Patrick. I stared at the laminated card, studying the name.

'That one's yours, Jamie.' Patrick passed Courtney a card. 'This one's yours, Crystal.' He gave Dani the last one. 'And Dallas.'

We'd sat up and talked in the dark a couple of nights ago, discussing our new names. Courtney had picked Crystal, after Crystal Gayle. Dani wanted to be Dallas, after Mom's favorite show. I'd wrestled with mine, testing the possibilities out on my tongue: Janine, Jennifer, Jewel, Jillian, Jocelyn, Jackie.

Finally Courtney said, 'Jamie. You should be Jamie.' Since the day at the gym, she'd been talking more. 'Like Jessie James.'

'The outlaw?'

She gave a wry smile. 'Why not?'

181

Jamie. I rolled the name around in my mouth, already leaving Jessica behind. I could be Jamie. I could make up a whole new person.

I looked at the new ID again. Jamie Caldwell. I glanced at Dani, who was staring at a photo of a boy on the kitchen wall. He looked like he was in his twenties, big like Patrick with the same green eyes but black hair. He was wearing boxing shorts and gloves, posed with his fists close to his face, his eyes serious.

Patrick followed the direction of our eyes. 'That was Stephen, my son.'

I could tell by the look on Patrick's face that he didn't want us to ask what had happened to him. Dani stared down at her ID, her face flushed like she felt bad for being caught staring. I glanced at Karen, flipping eggs at the stove. She'd mangled one and was trying to put it back together, scraping at its edges carefully, cursing under her breath.

Over the next couple of weeks Patrick showed us how to clean the gym and work the front desk. He didn't have a lot of work for three girls so we also had to get other jobs. Once we put some money together we'd be paying rent, but he'd said he'd give us a deal.

Dani and Courtney found jobs waitressing right away and worked most nights, but I wasn't having any luck and would sit awake in the apartment for hours. I wasn't used to being alone so much – every creak and noise in the building made me jump. I'd think about Dad, how we used to wait up for him when we were kids, the sound of his boots on the stairs that last night. Then I'd think about heaven and hell, wondering where I would end up now that I'd killed him, wondering if my mom would be ashamed of me.

I didn't go to bed until one of my sisters was home.

At the gym I helped Patrick organize his office and made sure people were up-to-date on memberships.

'Be nice to get this all on the computer,' he said.

'No problem. I took a class in school.' I was relieved I'd have something more to occupy my time – and my mind.

Karen showed Courtney how to teach some of the aerobics classes and she caught on fast. I liked watching her do the complicated steps, bouncing up and down to the music, her blonde hair in a ponytail. She'd dyed it platinum. Dani and I had gone the other way, darker, more of a chocolate brown. I liked how it made my eyes greener. It suited Dani too. She was still playing with her new short cut, trying different things, spiking it up or making it all messy. It made her seem older. I wanted to cut mine too but Karen said I had nice hair. She trimmed it one night for me, gave me bangs and showed me how to blow-dry it smooth and straight so it grazed my collarbone. She said the bangs made me look mysterious. I wasn't sure about that, but I liked that I looked different.

I looked like Jamie.

We practiced our new names every day, calling them out to each other, saying them over and over as we went to bed. I'd stare at Courtney, saying, *Crystal, Crystal, Crystal*, again and again in my mind, but she was still Courtney to me and I had to think about her new name every time I spoke, hesitating when we were around people. It was hard with Dani too, but her new name suited her short haircut, the way she walked around the gym in workout clothes Patrick had found for us, her hair slicked back with sweat, her tanned arms all sinews, the muscles bunching and flexing as she practiced her jabs and uppercuts for hours.

I slipped my new name on in the morning like it was a new outfit. I practiced walking different, holding myself different, my shoulders up, my eyes challenging. *Jamie*. I made myself answer the phone with a confident voice, 'Phoenix Boxing. How can we help you?' With each file I transferred onto the computer, each box that I removed, I felt more in control, more like maybe things would be okay, maybe we could build ourselves new lives. But I was still afraid – of Brian and Gavin, of the police finding us, afraid everything would fall apart.

Courtney and I shared a bedroom again – Dani

was across the hall. I woke up yelling some nights, other times Courtney or Dani woke me up yelling out. Sometimes I just heard one of them crying. I wasn't always sure which one, but it didn't matter – we shared the same pain, the same nightmares.

Sometimes I just walked around the apartment checking the locks, padding through the hall, sitting in the armchair for hours, watching the door.

We didn't talk about Dad or what had happened in Cash Creek. We didn't talk about the ranch, our old house, Ingrid and Walter and Corey. They were all gone.

Patrick and Karen never asked about the dark circles under our eyes in the morning – we often had breakfast with them at their house, which was walking distance from the gym. Karen would talk to Courtney about some music she wanted to create a routine around, and Patrick would tell Dani he wanted to teach her a new combination, and they'd pile my plate with more food, Karen laughing.

'For such a small girl you sure eat a lot.'

Patrick was teaching all of us boxing and self-defense moves. He said there were lots of programs we could take when we were a little older so we could be certified fitness instructors. He'd already signed Dani up for one.

He told people we were his cousin's kids. Both our

parents had died in a car accident and he'd taken us on until we were old enough to go out on our own.

He brought up the subject of school. 'There's one around the block, but it might get tricky if they need to see any paperwork proving I'm your guardian.'

'I don't care about school,' Courtney said. 'I was failing anyway.'

'What about you two?' he said to Dani and me.

'I'll get my GED,' Dani said.

'Me too,' I said, feeling like I was going to cry. I blinked hard.

Dani looked at me. 'But you're so good at school. You loved it.'

'Doesn't matter,' I said. 'When I'm older, maybe I'll go to college or university. I can take night classes.'

Patrick was nodding. 'Don't give up on your dreams, girls. You just might have to find another way to get there.'

When I wasn't at the gym during the day, I checked Dumpsters for cans and bottles that we could return for money, searched in the gutters and on the sides of the road, but I was nervous going down the alleys and always made sure I was home before dark. Sometimes I folded laundry for tips at the Laundromat. Dani was working hard, coming home sweaty from the gym and the restaurant where she was waitressing, taking on extra shifts when she could, bringing home leftovers she'd snuck into

186

her bag. Courtney was working at a sketchy restaurant and started hanging out with one of the owner's sons. She was getting too skinny, her face breaking out, and she'd take off for big chunks of time, sometimes not coming back to the apartment until the early-morning hours. When we got up she'd stumble out of bed, throw crumpled bills on the table, pull on clothes, and go to the gym.

Dani and I talked about it one night.

'It's drugs. I'm sure of it,' I said. 'She's doing them *and* selling them.'

'We'll talk to her when she gets home.'

We tried, but she brushed it off. 'I'm fine, it's all fine.'

'Where's the money from?' Dani said.

'I've made some new friends, don't worry about it.'

Dani followed her into the bathroom. 'It's not *fine* — we don't want this money.' She threw it on the floor.

Courtney whirled around. '*Now* you care about being legal?'

'We can't get in more trouble,' Dani said.

'*Please*, Courtney,' I said. 'If the cops catch you and they figure out who you are, we're all in trouble.'

'Fine, whatever,' she said.

She stopped bringing money home after that, just small bills from tips, but she'd still take off for hours, occasionally not coming home at all. I couldn't rest until

I finally heard the door unlocking, Courtney's purse being tossed onto the floor, the creak of her bedsprings. Sometimes she'd climb in with me, her back warm against mine, our breaths matching until we drifted off.

Other times she'd be okay for a few days, hanging around the house more, or at the gym, seeming focused, *present*. Then she'd get an angry edge to her, snapping about silly things, or she'd just be quiet, hardly saying anything, huddled on her bed for hours, drinking beer after beer, staring at the wall.

Dani gave her shit one day, accused her of spending all our money on beer.

'You're turning into a screwup.'

'Someone gave me the beer,' Courtney said. 'And I was already a screwup.' She gave a bitter smile, held the beer high in the air. 'Bottoms up.'

Soon Courtney started missing shifts at the gym. Dani flipped out, said Patrick and Karen would kick us all out, but Courtney just blew her off.

'They're not going to kick you guys out.'

'If you're not going to show up, you should just quit.'

'Fine.'

After that she only worked at the restaurant. We'd been worried that Patrick and Karen would be upset, but they seemed to understand. They'd ask how she was doing, and she was welcome for dinner anytime.

Karen would watch her with that thoughtful, troubled expression and push more food onto her plate, which Courtney barely touched. But then I had something bigger to worry about.

Three months after we'd escaped Cash Creek, I realized I might be pregnant.

Chapter Fourteen

I hadn't thought about it when I didn't get my period the first couple months. I'd never been regular – I'd missed months before – and had had some spotting, so I'd thought everything was fine. But when it didn't come the next month, I started to get worried. I waited and waited, woke up every morning certain it would be the day. I didn't say anything to my sisters for another couple of weeks, still hoping my period would come.

It didn't.

I found Dani alone in the apartment, sanding the wooden frame of a floor-length mirror. She'd been scavenging for things left in alleys and bringing them back for our apartment: old chairs, a coffee table, another couch, plant stands, and mismatched dishes. We hung tea towels up as curtains, painted the chairs and the wooden table in different bright colors, stenciled flower patterns onto the kitchen cabinets. Slowly but surely it was becoming home.

'Something's wrong,' I said.

'With Court – Crystal?'

'It's me.'

She frowned. 'You sick?'

'I haven't had my period for a while.'

She looked at me. 'What's "a while"?'

I wanted to cry. 'Not since ... you know.'

She jerked back like I'd hit her, leaned the mirror against the counter carefully, then slowly walked over and collapsed into a chair.

'Shit,' she said.

We'd never talked about getting pregnant. I remembered the look of relief on Dani's and Courtney's faces when they came out of the bathroom the first month after we left Cash Creek, but neither of them had ever asked me about my period.

'We should get a test,' she said.

I put one on the table, the plastic spinning for a moment like a compass.

'Where did you get that?'

'Stole it.'

'You have to stop doing that – you're going to get caught.'

'It was twenty dollars.'

'You could have gone to a doctor and they'd test you for free.'

I couldn't believe she was giving me shit. Then I realized she was just freaked out.

'I didn't know that,' I said.

'Have you taken it yet?'

'No. I'm scared.'

'Maybe with the stress you're just late.'

I didn't like the desperate, hopeful look on her face. The same expression I saw reflected back at me when I glanced in the mirror.

'Maybe.'

But the little line turned blue.

When Courtney came home that night, we told her. She sat down hard on the couch and looked up at us with a stunned expression.

'This is so fucked up. What are we going to do?'

Dani was sitting on the other couch, her feet under her knees. I was curled into its corner, my hand on my stomach, pressing down as though I could just squeeze the baby out of my body, feeling embarrassed, ashamed, like I had let us all down.

'Is it too late for an abortion?' Dani said.

'I don't know,' Courtney said. 'Don't some places do it later?'

I didn't like how they were talking about me as though I weren't there, not even asking what I wanted to do. I studied my bare feet – small, like my mother's, the baby toe with hardly any nail. I felt a sharp ache, wished I could speak to her.

'Maybe we should talk to someone,' I said.

We went to the free clinic the next day. A doctor examined me, took a blood test, and confirmed the pregnancy. I was sixteen weeks along, due the third week of April. I hated his hands on my body, the way he coldly asked about my period and the last time I had sex, most of all hated telling him it was a boy I'd met in the summer. I was glad Dani was in the exam room with me. She asked him about abortion, and I knew the deal by the warning tone of his first sentence, 'Past the first trimester . . .' He handed Dani a bunch of brochures. We left.

At home I locked myself in my room and read the brochures cover to cover. Courtney and Dani were in the kitchen. I could hear them talking in low voices and knew that they were waiting for me to come out so we could make a plan. We'd barely spoken on the bus ride home. I couldn't even look at them, hating the anxious look in their eyes, feeling their thoughts.

I walked into the kitchen, a blanket wrapped around me, and huddled at the table.

'Do you want something to eat?' Dani said. 'Maybe some soup or tea?'

'No, thanks,' I said.

She sat down across from me. 'That doctor was just a

jerk. You're still allowed to have an abortion. Courtney can ask her friend—'

'It's the size of an avocado,' I said. 'It can *hear* me.'

'What do you want to do, then?' Dani wasn't freaking out, but I could feel her panic.

'I don't know,' I said.

'We can't *keep* it,' Courtney said. 'We can barely afford ourselves. Patrick and Karen might throw us out.' Her voice rose, fear making it breathy. 'What if it looks like *him*?'

'I need time to think,' I said.

'You don't have much time,' Dani said. 'You're already sixteen weeks.'

'I *know*! I just need to *think*.' Doors were closing on me, slamming one after another.

'Jess, you can't—'

'Leave me alone.' I got up from the table and went back to my room.

We didn't talk about it for the next few days, but I could feel them waiting for my answer even when we weren't in the same room. I avoided them as much as possible, sat alone for hours, looking at the calendar, feeling time slipping away. I read all the brochures again and again, stared at the photos of the fetus, the tiny hands. I went back to the clinic by myself, talked to another doctor, who explained about the complications of late-term

194

abortions, the risks. I had to decide soon, but I was paralyzed with fear.

I'd wake up in the middle of the night, pressure bearing down on my chest, so heavy I couldn't breathe. I'd think about my dad. I'd already killed someone – if I had an abortion, was I killing another person? But what would it be like to give birth? Could I stand the pain? What would happen to the baby? What would happen to me?

Finally, after a week, I came out one morning while Dani and Courtney were having breakfast. They looked up at me expectantly as I took a seat at the table.

'It's too late now.'

Dani looked furious. 'If you'd dealt with it a week ago, you—'

'It was already too late,' I said. 'I'll give it away. It'll go to someone else, someone who *wants* a baby. They'd never know, and the baby wouldn't know.'

'Are you *sure* you want to do that?' Dani said. 'You want to go through all of that and then give it away? It's nine months – then you have to give birth.' Her voice hammered into me, dominating, talking to me like I was a child.

'I know what it means, Dani I'm pregnant, not stupid and It's forty weeks, not nine months.'

She looked surprised by my anger, by my newfound knowledge. She was used to being in charge, leading us into and out of battle. But this was *my* body.

'I'm going to give it away,' I said.

'You have to tell them,' Dani said, still clinging to her authority, making me be the one to tell Karen and Patrick, punishing me for going my own way, making my own decision. I felt another surge of anger. Blame whispering at the back of my brain. *If she'd listened to me before, we wouldn't have been in that town.* I pushed away the thoughts. It wasn't her fault.

The next day we told Patrick and Karen.

Karen looked flustered. 'Do you ... do you know what you want to do?'

'I'm going to give it away.'

'The father ...'

I shook my head. Courtney started to cry.

Patrick looked at her, then back at me. 'Whatever you want to do, kid. We'll help you out.'

'We can stay?' I said.

'Of course!' they said at the same time.

They looked stunned that we had worried about anything else. I felt a weight lift off my shoulders, but then an ache deep inside. It had been decided.

I was going to have a baby.

I was terrified of giving birth and couldn't read certain sections of the book Karen had bought me without my chest getting tight and panicky, overwhelmed by the feeling that I was hurtling toward something I couldn't stop – and it was going to hurt a whole lot. I already felt like my body wasn't my own anymore, like an alien or a parasite had moved in and taken over.

We hadn't told anyone at the gym yet, but I felt like everyone could see just by looking at me, and I couldn't meet their eyes. At the clinic I studied the other pregnant women in the waiting room, the rings on their fingers, the happy glow on their faces, the way they would curve an arm protectively around their stomachs. I wasn't showing yet and wondered what they'd think if they knew, if they'd think I was a slut, a bad girl. I wondered if I was doing the right thing.

By the fifth month I was starting to show a round little belly and had to wear baggy shirts and tie my jeans with an elastic band or wear sweatpants. Karen made sure I was eating right and taking vitamins. I found a new doctor. She knew I planned on giving the baby up but was nice about it, her hands gentle when she examined me, waiting for my body to relax. I would watch, detached, during the ultrasound as she talked about what stage the baby was at, pointing out the feet and hands. I tried not to think of the baby as mine, or *his*, but like I was carrying it for someone else and it was just my job to take care of it.

I'd met with an adoption agency but hadn't picked anyone yet. No one seemed good enough. I didn't want the baby but I didn't like thinking of someone being mean to it, of its getting a dad like ours. It deserved a chance.

Courtney had started sleeping on the couch. She said it was because she didn't want to disturb me when she came home late, but I was pretty sure she was angry. She never looked at my belly. Dani was okay, sometimes she was even a little nicer, making me herbal tea or bringing me an extra blanket. But I'd see her give me worried looks, the fear on her face if she glanced at my stomach.

My belly was getting huge and I'd stand in front of the mirror after a bath, staring at my bigger breasts, my disappearing belly button. The baby had started moving by then and I'd watch it roll around. In bed I could feel it kicking and stretching, sometimes clawing at my insides like it was trying to break out.

I was scared to think about what the baby might look like – *who* it might look like. The doctor had asked if I wanted to know if it was a boy or a girl but I'd said no. Sometimes when I closed my eyes I'd see Brian's face and wonder if the baby looked like him. I felt sad for the baby – it hadn't asked for this, an evil dad, a mom who didn't want it. My sisters never even talked about it, though one time Dani did mention something we might do 'after we give the baby away.'

I was hungry all the time but Dani never complained about our food bill. Patrick found me a job, doing laundry in one of the hotels – he'd helped the man's kid out. As my belly got bigger, my hips and legs ached and I walked in a swagger, but I refused to let it slow me down.

Sometimes when the baby moved I'd put my hand there, feeling a foot or a hand. I felt guilty the first time and pulled my hand away but then put it back a few minutes later, sitting quiet in the dark. We had an old TV by then, and I started telling the baby what I was watching, sometimes resting a plate of food on top of my belly. I never did it when my sisters were around, never told them when I felt the baby kick or roll, my whole belly moving as though it were doing acrobatics.

When I got really scared at night, imagining what childbirth was going to feel like, I tried to imagine how happy some couple was going to be, how they'd been waiting for years and years. I'd imagine their house, how they'd decorated a special room, the nice things they'd do for the baby, how much they'd love it.

Karen tried to talk to me about our past once, sort of feeling around about our parents.

'Were things hard for you at home?' she said.

'Yeah,' I said. 'We don't like talking about it.' I hoped that would stop the questions.

'If you ever do want to talk to someone about what happened . . .' She held my eyes for a second. 'I'm a good listener, and there are some great programs in the community, support groups—'

'We're fine.'

She nodded. 'Of course you are. But if you change your mind and think maybe there's something you want to talk about, just let me know.'

'Okay, thanks.' I knew we'd never change our minds.

She was right, though. She was a good listener. She often sat and talked to the teenagers who came into the gym about their problems at home and school. I'd listen in sometimes and wondered why she and Patrick didn't have children of their own.

'Did you want kids?' I asked.

She smiled. 'I did, but I couldn't have them. Patrick's son was from his first marriage.' They didn't talk about their past much, but a few times when we were alone together, she told me a couple of things. I figured it was because she felt bad for me or something. She said Patrick's son had gotten into drugs while Patrick was in jail and had gotten killed by some dealers – shot in the head.

'It was hard on Patrick, really hard.'

'That's why he helps other kids?' I said.

'And that's why you're all my babies.' Her eyes drifted to my belly, then looked away. 'I better get back to work.'

Dani and Courtney stayed out of the apartment a lot. Dani was usually at the gym, and Courtney was working or partying. Sometimes I wondered if maybe they didn't want to be home with me, like they were still upset that I didn't get rid of the baby. One night Courtney came home drunk and stared at my belly.

'Why didn't you say anything for so long?' she said.

'I didn't know.'

She laughed bitterly. 'Come on. You knew.'

'Leave her alone,' Dani said.

I hid in my room, crying, thinking about what Courtney had said. Had I known? Had I just not wanted to face it? I thought back to those first months of my pregnancy but I wasn't sure, couldn't remember feeling anything but fear.

Dani loved boxing and training with the other teens. She even taught a class for some little kids. I just helped Patrick in his office or worked at the hotel. When I wasn't working I studied for my GED. Courtney didn't get sad quite as often but she still partied too much. She and Dani would get in big fights. She also hung out with some of the boys from the gym who were former dealers and gang members. When Dani told her they were trouble, she just laughed at her.

'What else bad can happen?'

The months passed and I got my GED. I met with the adoption agency a couple of times, flipped through their photos of families, but I'd stare at the men's faces, wondering if they drank, if they were mean. Dani got on my case about it a lot, said I had to pick a family soon. I told her I would, but the weeks drifted past.

Late in my last trimester, I still worked every day at the hotel, and sometimes an evening shift if someone needed me to cover. One night, in the middle of April, I felt a little rush of fluid like I'd peed myself but knew I hadn't. I checked in the bathroom. My underwear was wet. I rolled it up into a ball and stuffed it in the trash. I was walking downstairs to find the manager when I felt more water trickle out between my legs. I used the pay phone to call Dani, who took me to the hospital in Patrick's van. Courtney was out.

I was terrified, the first contractions worse than anything I'd imagined, the physical exam horrible, the doctor's hands reaching up high into my body. They gave me drugs for the pain but it still hurt. I couldn't find any position to escape it, could only moan and cry. I walked the hall, soaked in the bath, nothing helped.

My body labored all night and into the morning. Nurses stared at the monitor, making notes, adjusting the strap around my belly, murmuring that I should try to rest between contractions. But by early afternoon they were too close together for that – and coming harder and harder. My throat burned with each gasp, my lips dry and chapped. Dani spooned ice chips into my mouth, her face pale. She stroked my hair back from my forehead, put cool cloths on me.

'You're doing great,' she said. 'Not much longer now.'
She'd said that hours ago.

'Is Courtney here yet?'

'She's going to come later.'

Even in my haze of pain and drugs, I knew what that meant. She didn't want to see the baby.

The contractions came in waves, urging my body forward. The nurses gripped my legs apart and told me to push. I bore down hard, felt something tearing.

They ordered me into different positions, rested my feet against a metal bar. I wanted it over, wanted it all to be over, begged them to help me, to make it stop. They urged me on. Dani gripped my hand, rubbed my forehead, whispering into my ear, 'It's okay, hang on, just push.'

The agony went on. I writhed on the bed, pleading for relief.

'Please, I can't do it. *Just get it out!*'

Then I felt something breaking free, a release of pressure from my body, and they were putting the baby on my chest.

'It's a girl!' the doctor said.

The baby was crying, her mouth open, searching. I gave her my pinkie finger, felt her little mouth latch on, marveling at the sensation. They took her away, examined her, weighed her, and cleaned us both up. I watched from the bed, her wails making me want to get up and hold her. The nurse brought her back and placed her on my chest again.

'She doesn't want to feed it,' Dani said.

I was already guiding the baby to my nipple.

'I just want to see what it feels like,' I said, even though the adoption lady was waiting outside for me to make my final decision on a family. Dani, who had called her from the hospital, stood back, her face scared.

The nurse came over, stroked the baby's head, adjusted her so her chin tilted back and her mouth opened.

'You're doing great. You're a natural mother.'

I was a mother. I stared in awe at the baby, her tiny mouth suckling at my breast, her perfect eyebrows, her damp, dark hair.

'I'll get you something to eat.' The nurse left us alone.

'You can't keep it,' Dani said.

I looked up at her. 'I know.'

'Then what are you *doing*?'

'I just needed to feed her.'

'They have bottles.'

'You don't get it.' I was crying now, my body weak from pushing the baby out, the emotions running through me, tearing me open again. 'Once I give her away, I'll never know if she's okay.'

'It's better that way.'

'For who?'

'For everyone. You're fifteen years old, Jess. Think of

the baby. She deserves someone who can take care of her.'

I felt a hot stab of anger. 'I'd take good care of her.'

'You don't have any money.'

I looked down at the baby again, blinking back tears. 'I'll do it in the morning.'

'If you wait, it will just be harder.'

'You don't know,' I said, my voice rising almost to a shout. 'You don't know what's best all the time. This is my baby – not yours.' The words hung between us. The baby mewled. Dani looked at it, tears in her eyes.

'I can stay at the hospital with you.' Her voice sounded sad, defeated.

'I just want to be alone.'

Now Dani looked hurt. 'You sure?'

'Yeah.'

She got her stuff together, stood by the doorway for a moment looking like she wanted to say something else, then turned and walked out the door.

The nurse brought me dinner. I ate with the baby still against my chest, a warm lump. The nurse told me to get some rest, and I nodded, but I stayed awake for a while, looking out the hospital window at the skyline. The world was so big. I looked down at the baby, her tiny fingernails, the soft hair on her forehead. I studied her features, looking for him. But I just saw a baby, a fragile little baby. I thought about her alone in the world, hated the helpless feeling it gave me. Who would protect her? Who would make sure she didn't get hurt?

In the morning, I reminded myself. *I have to decide in the morning.*

Part Two

SKYLAR

Chapter Fifteen

July 2015

It was slow at the gym, just the occasional clang of barbells in the background, music pumping over the speakers, but I didn't mind. It gave me a chance to search SoundCloud for some new beats – Patrick was cool with my using my laptop at the front desk as long as I greeted everyone. And it was better than sitting at home with nothing but the TV for company. Sometimes I came in on my days off to hang out. I loved talking with the regulars at the smoothie bar, hearing about their boyfriends or girlfriends, their work problems. One of them was signing in now, a guy named Dave who I thought had a crush on Dallas, but she never even looked at him.

'Have a good workout!' I said.

'Thanks, Skylar,' he said. 'That mix you made for Dallas's spin class was great. Think you could burn me a DVD?'

'Totally!'

I couldn't play at bars or clubs yet, but I'd been sharing my mixes on SoundCloud and YouTube and was getting a following. I even had a DJ name, 'Lark', because my mom used to call me 'Skylark' when I was little. It was fun, remixing popular songs or making mash-ups. I liked taking something already good and finding a new way for people to hear it.

I'd been working on a set list for the last hour, planning my next YouTube video, but now I was just doodling little stick figures all over a notepad. I needed to keep my hands busy all the time or I felt like I was going crazy. When I was a kid, Mom had taught me how to make origami birds because I drove *her* crazy with all my fidgeting – she'd grab my hands, try to hold them still.

I glanced up at a couple of boys sparring in one of the rings. One of them, Aaron, was always trying to talk to me. He caught me watching.

'Hey, Skylar! Why don't you come be my water girl?' He pretended to pose, showing off his muscles with a big grin.

I rolled my eyes and looked away. He was cute, in a street kind of way, with a shaved head and tattoos and this awesome scar that stretched across the side of his face, but no way was I going to let him know I thought so, plus he wasn't my type. Too macho, and definitely too full of himself.

I was dying to ask him where he got his scar from but that would be rude. Plus, he might think I was interested in him or something stupid like that.

I stared down at my stick figures again, drew biceps on the arms and gave them bulging quads, added a couple of double-D's to some of them. I heard the door open and glanced up. It was my aunt Crystal. She looked tired, dark circles under her eyes, probably from partying the night before. She was a bartender at a bar near Kitsilano Beach and often went out after work with the other waitresses.

'Hey, Sky. Is Dallas around?'

'She's in the gym.'

'Thanks.' She leaned over, looked down at my stick figures. 'Nice.'

'Work out every day and you too can look this good.'

She laughed. 'I'm too lazy.'

'You're prettier than most of the girls who come here anyway.'

She smiled. 'And that's why you're my favorite niece.' She grabbed a protein bar off the counter, ripped open the wrapper, nibbled on the corner.

'I'm your only niece.' I smiled back. I was happy to

211

see she was in a good mood today. You never knew with Crystal. Sometimes she'd get into these funks where she was, like, really down, or she'd come into the gym acting all crazy and laughing too loud and pissing off Dallas and my mom.

'Wicked shirt,' she said.

'Thanks.' I glanced down at it. It was a retro Bruce Springsteen concert T-shirt Mom had found at the thrift store, which I was wearing with leggings. I didn't like jeans because my legs were so long and it was hard to find a good fit.

'Is your mom working?' Crystal said, looking around.

'She's at the hotel today.'

Dallas was walking by the front desk, carrying a box of sweatshirts. She looked at the protein bar in Crystal's hand.

'You pay for that?' She said it like she was joking, but I could tell by the look on her face she was pissed. Crystal was always helping herself to stuff.

'I need to talk to you about something,' Crystal said, tossing her hair back. Now I could see the scar on her jaw where Mom burned her as a kid. When I asked Mom about it years ago she said it had been an accident with a pan, but I always figured they must've been fighting or something because she'd looked really guilty, her face flushing, and she asked me not to mention it to Crystal.

Dallas handed me the box of sweatshirts. 'Can you put these up, please? The large ones go in the back, the small ones—'

'In the front, I know.'

Dallas gave me a look.

'Sorry,' I said, hating that my aunt could make me feel like I was five years old in two seconds. She didn't smile often and she was one of the toughest woman boxers at the gym, but she was always there for me. If Mom was working late, it was Dallas who picked me up from school. When I was younger she'd looked after me a lot. I never messed around or tested her like I did with my mom – if she said it was bedtime, I hauled ass and got into bed.

'I have a class starting in a few minutes,' she told Crystal.

'It's important,' Crystal said. 'Please, Dallas.'

Dallas still looked annoyed but said, 'Let's go to my office.' So Crystal was in trouble again. I wondered what it was this time – she got fired from jobs, broke up with her boyfriends, got evicted, and took off for days. Although I liked hanging out with Crystal, it was still pretty new, ever since I got into DJing. We started talking about different bands, and I'd drop by her place after school just to hang out and listen to music. But she didn't really talk to me about her problems.

213

Dallas turned to me. 'When you're done with the shirts, can you clean the mirrors?'

'Sure, Dallas.'

Dallas and Crystal went into Dallas's office, which had a window that looked out onto the main floor. I tried to see what was going on while I hung the shirts. Crystal was talking, then she leaned her elbows on the table and put her head in her hands like she was really upset. Dallas was shaking her head and talking. I figured she was lecturing Crystal.

Dallas disappeared for a minute, then came back and handed Crystal an envelope. Crystal stood up and gave her a hug. Dallas looked like she was still lecturing, and Crystal was nodding. She must've been borrowing money for rent again. When I was little we lived above the gym with Dallas and Crystal. Then Crystal moved in with her boyfriend at the time, and Mom and I found an apartment a couple of blocks away. Dallas still lived above the gym.

I wondered how much money was in the envelope, daydreamed about what I'd do with an envelope full of cash. I had a digital mixer and some Rokit speakers on hold at the pawnshop, had to beg the owner a million times to let me put them on layaway. I went by after work sometimes just to look at them.

I'd wanted to pick up some extra shifts waitressing and asked Mom if she could get me a job. She worked at an expensive hotel downtown and had to take two buses to get there but she made great tips, especially in the summer. She'd said it was too far for me to go at night, though. I think she just wanted to keep an eye on me. At least when I was at the gym she didn't send me as many of her just-saying-hi-and-making-sure-you're-okay-and-don't-forget-to-lock-the-door texts.

Dallas came out of the office, and I focused back on the shirts, watching from the corner of my eye as she walked deeper into the gym.

Crystal came to the front counter.

'I've gotta run,' she said, grabbing a Gatorade out of the fridge.

'Everything okay?' I said.

'Sure.' She gave me a smile but she still looked kind of stressed. 'See you Sunday.' She was already pushing out the front door. She climbed into the passenger side of a blue car that had been waiting in the parking lot and took off. I got a brief glimpse of the man behind the wheel, sunglasses and a shaved head.

I glanced back into the gym. Dallas had turned around and was watching the car drive off with a worried expression.

For as long as I could remember, we had dinner over at Patrick and Karen's on the first Sunday of every month. Mom was late getting off work and when we finally got to their house that night, Dallas was already in the kitchen helping Karen, who was stirring something at the stove. I picked up a cat winding its way around my feet, and gave Karen a kiss on the cheek.

'How are you, sweetie?' she said.

'Good.' Karen didn't spend as much time in the gym anymore, preferring to do her crafts at home, but she still worked out a few times a week with Patrick.

Now Mom came over and gave Karen a kiss.

Karen gave her a look. 'You're working too much again, baby.'

'I'm fine, just hot.' She waved a hand in the air, brushing away Karen's worry. Mom did look tired, and I'd heard her walking around the apartment the night before. She wasn't a good sleeper at the best of times, often getting up in the middle of the night to watch TV, but in the summer she barely slept and hated being in the apartment on hot days, was always trying to drag me out somewhere.

'Can I help with something?' she said.

'We've got it,' Dallas said.

I glanced up at them from my perch in the living room, two cats on my lap while I flipped through TV channels. Mom was leaning against the counter, laughing at something. I knew she thought Crystal was the beautiful one, but I thought Mom was just as pretty. We didn't look alike, though. She had cute freckles, green eyes, and chocolate brown hair that was really shiny — my hair was crazy, long black curls that fell to the middle of my back and around my face. Her lips were a nice shape. I touched mine, hating my small mouth. She could get a tan in five minutes and I could spend all summer out in the sun and barely change color. We had the same nose, straight with a bit of a flare at the nostrils, but her face was rounder. Everything on my mom was curvier, same with my aunts, and they were a lot shorter. I was really tall — like, five-ten already.

Patrick came in from outside. 'Hey, sugar, I've got a new movie for us tonight.'

'Let me guess, *Rocky* part three thousand?'

He laughed. 'Shove over, kid.' I made room and he sat next to me, his big shoulders resting against mine. I leaned my head against him.

Mom and Dallas almost had the table set — Patrick and I were always on cleanup duty. Karen kept looking at the door. 'Should we try calling her again?'

'Let's just start,' Dallas said.

We sat at the table and dished ourselves out. Sounds of the front door opening, a voice calling out, 'Hello, hello!'

Crystal came into the kitchen. 'Sorry I'm late.'

Karen stood up. 'Crystal, honey. I'm glad you could make it.'

Crystal gave Karen a kiss on the cheek and plopped

217

down at the table beside me. She gave me a big smile.

'Hey, kiddo.'

Karen set another place at the table, dished out some salad.

Talk started up again but it was mostly Patrick and Dallas, discussing the gym and a boxing tournament that was coming up. Mom mentioned some of the boys at the gym, like Aaron, who she thought could win.

Crystal leaned closer, whispered, 'How was the party?'

'We had to cancel it.' My two closest girlfriends, Emily and Taylor, lived at the other end of the city and both had jobs, so we didn't see each other a lot in the summer, but we'd been planning a big party at Taylor's while her parents were away for the weekend. I was going to DJ and I'd spent hours working on an awesome mix. Then her mom got sick and stayed home.

Mom had flipped out when I asked to play at a couple of grad parties last year – even though people were willing to pay. She said there'd be too much drugs and alcohol around. I told her she could chaperone but she still wouldn't agree. She was hoping I'd go to university, and was always leaving course books around the house. She didn't know I'd started to send sample tracks of my beats to some big producers in the States. I checked my email constantly.

'We should go to the beach this week,' Crystal said.

'Sure, that'd be fun.'

I glanced at her plate. She'd only had a few mouthfuls and mostly just smeared her food around. She'd had three glasses of wine, though. Her laugh louder with each one, her face flushed, which made her blue eyes stand out even more with her tan. Dallas gave her a dirty look, but she just made a face at her.

'How are things going at the bar?' I said.

'Good. Next weekend we've got the Headkickers.'

'No way,' I said. The Headkickers were this cool indie band from Seattle that was just starting to get really popular.

Crystal smiled. 'You should come see them – I could sneak you in.'

'Awesome! That would be so—'

'No way in hell,' Mom said.

'Why not?' Crystal said.

'She's *seventeen*.'

'She doesn't have to drink,' Crystal said. 'Lighten up. We did way worse stuff when we were her age.' She laughed.

Mom looked furious now. 'Crystal, *shut up*.'

'You'll lose your job again,' Dallas said.

'The boss is away,' Crystal said. 'And if he finds out, whatever.' She shrugged. 'I'll find another job.'

'Can I go, Mom?' I said. 'You can come too.' I knew she'd be pissed I was asking in front of everyone, but that was kind of the point.

'I have to work,' she said.

'I won't drink,' I said. 'I promise.'

'We'll talk about it later,' she said, her mouth a tense line.

I already knew what that meant. Crystal gave me a sympathetic look.

I ate the rest of my meal in silence while Crystal told us about some new guy she'd met at the bar last week – he worked for a construction firm, was going through a divorce, and had a couple of kids, traveled around a lot. I wondered if that was the guy in the blue car with the shaved head. Karen was being nice, asking questions, but Mom and Dallas weren't saying much.

'He's a little rough around the edges, but he has potential,' Crystal said.

'Yeah, he sounds like a real winner,' Mom said.

'Hey, at least I try,' Crystal said.

Mom flushed. She never had a boyfriend, said she was too busy working and raising a kid, and Dallas was casual with her boyfriend. Terry was a nice guy, worked at a restaurant nearby, and they'd dated for, like, a year. Mom said Dallas was scared to commit. I think she just wasn't that into him. I'd seen him try to rub her back or hold her hand and she'd pull away.

'You should try dating somebody nice for a change,' Dallas said.

'Nice is boring.' Crystal said it with a smile but she

sounded kind of sad. I didn't understand why she was always attracted to jerks. I hadn't had a boyfriend myself yet. Well, not a real one. I'd fooled around with a few guys at school but hadn't gone all the way. If Mom had her wish I'd probably die a virgin.

Crystal poured the rest of the wine in her glass. Dallas gave her a look, and Crystal just smiled. I wished I could be like that, not giving a crap what anyone else thought. She just did whatever she wanted, whenever she wanted.

Dallas gave us a ride home. She and Mom talked in the front seat while I listened to music on my phone and checked my Facebook.

I walked into our apartment and threw my purse onto the hook, missing by a mile. It hit the floor with a thud.

'Seriously, Skylar?' Mom said.

I hung it up, then collapsed onto the couch, picked up the remote, and started flipping through the channels.

'Why can't I see the Headkickers?'

'You're underage.'

'I won't drink – I swear.'

Mom snorted. I'd been in trouble a few times for drinking and even got suspended last year for smoking pot in the bathroom with a friend, which Crystal thought was hysterical. Mom not so much. I wasn't, like, a stoner or anything, so what was the problem with getting a little buzzed now and then?

'Crystal will watch out for me.'

'Crystal will be working. Do you know how many drunk assholes will be at the bar? You have no idea how to deal with that.'

'I'm seventeen – not stupid. When you were my age, you already had a kid.'

My mom's face flushed, and I felt bad. I hadn't meant it that way, was just trying to remind her I was growing up.

'This conversation is over,' she said as she walked toward the bathroom.

Chapter Sixteen

The next Saturday night, I drove to Crystal's. I had an older red Honda Civic that Mom, Dallas, and Patrick and Karen had helped me buy for my sixteenth birthday. Crystal had been broke at the time – her boyfriend had taken off with all her money – but she'd bought me a heart-shaped air freshener that made it smell like strawberries and made me a mixed CD with some cool tunes.

Mom thought I was over at Emily's for the night. When I was younger and Mom had to work all weekend, I stayed at Emily's, and her parents had invited me on a few trips to their summer cabin. They were teachers and super-nice but they were also strict, so that made it okay with Mom. She used to call Emily's mom to get parenting advice. I hated it at the time, but now Mom didn't even follow up with Emily's mom whenever I said I was heading over there.

Crystal lived in a basement suite about twenty minutes from the gym. When I got there all her windows were open and I could hear music, something with a hard beat. I knocked a couple of times before she turned the music down and finally opened the door. She was wearing faded jeans shorts, the top button undone and the waist rolled over, and a black bikini top.

'Come on in.' She walked into her kitchen, bare feet padding on the tile, reached into the fridge, and pulled out a wine cooler. 'Want one?'

'Sure.'

She grabbed another for herself. 'Let's smoke a joint before I get ready.'

'Cool.' I followed her into the living room, where we sat next to each other on the couch.

'Your mom figure anything out?' She pulled a joint out of a little box she kept on the side table.

'I don't think so.'

Crystal lit the end of the joint, inhaling until it glowed, then held the smoke in her lungs as she passed it to me. I took a deep drag.

'God, it's hot.' She ran her hands through her hair, then took a sip of her drink.

My body felt relaxed, my eyes heavy. I sank back into the couch.

'Hope we meet some cute boys tonight,' I said.

'That hottie at the gym was sure checking you out the other day.'

'Aaron? He likes me, but it's not like that. He looks like a thug.'

'Sometimes the bad boys are the sweetest ones. It's the nice ones you can't always trust.' Her eyes were angry as she took another toke.

'Did you date a lot of bad boys when you were my age?'

'Bad ones, good ones, all kinds . . .' She was quiet for a minute, picking at the label on her bottle. 'There was one. Troy . . .' She smiled. 'Shit, we'd go at it for hours in his truck.' She took a couple of hard swallows of her drink.

'What happened?'

'He moved.' She looked sad, then shook her head, making her hair ripple. 'Fucking men, anyway.' She laughed, but it was kind of bitter.

'What about my dad? Was he a nice guy?'

Crystal's face went still. She took another swallow of her drink before answering.

'Billy? Yeah, he was a nice guy.'

'Mom never talks about him.' I used to ask her about him all the time, wanting to know every detail, but Mom didn't know much, other than his name was Billy Wilson and that he was blond – I got my height and hair from my grandfather – and he'd been into skateboarding and books. They met when he was camping for a couple weeks in the town where she grew up. When she found out she was pregnant, he was already gone and she didn't know how to find him. It upset her to talk about him, so I eventually stopped asking.

I hoped Crystal would share something else, maybe some little fact that Mom had forgotten, but she was just staring at her bottle, rolling it in her hands.

'I used to wish she'd meet someone nice,' I said. 'So I could have a dad, you know? But it doesn't look like that's going to happen.' Once I'd saved up enough for my equipment and could make more money doing real events, I was going to hire a private detective to search for my father. I didn't want to tell Crystal about that – she was cool but I had a feeling she might tell my mom.

'I don't know, Sky,' she said. 'Having a dad isn't always a good thing. He might not be who you imagined.' She passed me the joint.

'Maybe he's a jerk, maybe he wouldn't even want to meet me.' I took a drag, let the smoke out. 'But I have this fantasy that he'll come watch me DJ. I'll see him in the crowd and he'll have this proud look on his face, and I'll just know it's him.' I looked down at my pinkie finger, which bent at the top toward the one beside it. It was curved like that on both hands. I used to be embarrassed when I was little but I was used to it now. Clinodactyly, it was called, and I must have inherited it from my dad because my mom said no one in her family had it. I'd asked her, but she said she couldn't remember his hands.

I glanced up at Crystal. She was also staring at my finger, her eyes shiny.

'You okay?' I said.

She met my eyes. 'Your mom just wishes she knew how to find him for you but she can't. She feels bad about that. Maybe go easy on her ...'

I'd never really heard Crystal worry about someone else's feelings before.

She stood up. 'Come sit in the bathroom with me while I do my makeup.'

The bar was packed, the dance floor jammed with bodies, but Crystal got me a seat up at the bar where I had a great view of the band. I'd been worried I might get busted at the door, but Crystal had lent me a pair of her booty shorts and a sexy top that actually made me look like I had boobs and did my makeup so I looked older. She just walked in all confident and introduced me as one of her friends. No one asked for my ID.

We'd agreed I wouldn't drink at the bar – just in case we did get caught – but she kept me supplied with Red Bulls and we went outside a couple of times on her breaks to smoke a joint. The guy she'd told us about at dinner showed up and she introduced me. His name was Larry, and I didn't like him or the way he checked out Crystal's butt every time she turned around, but she kept giving him flirty looks. His head was shaved, so I

227

figured he was the guy who'd driven her to the gym. He also had this habit of licking his lips every time he took a sip of his drink, which was gross. He kept trying to ask me questions, but I pretended I couldn't hear him.

When Crystal was done, we headed back to her place. I drove because Crystal had had a couple of drinks at the bar. Larry came too, and the three of us sat around smoking another joint – and drinking. Crystal and Larry were really pounding them now, when they weren't busy flirting with each other. I felt like the third wheel but I couldn't go home – Mom thought I was at Emily's, and anyway I was too stoned and a little drunk.

I sat on the chair while they got closer on the couch. Larry's hand was around my aunt's waist, almost climbing up her shirt. She laughed and pushed him away, but I could tell she was into it. I stared at my drink, my face hot.

'Hey, Skylar, do you mind if we disappear for a bit?' Crystal stood and grabbed Larry's hand to pull him up.

'No, that's cool.'

They headed for Crystal's bedroom. I turned up the music in the living room, grabbed the last cigarette from Crystal's pack on the coffee table, and lit it, taking long drags and blowing the smoke out in lazy puffs as I sprawled on the couch. I didn't really enjoy smoking, but I was kind of annoyed at my aunt.

I'd finished my cigarette and had my eyes closed –

letting the pulse of the music wash over me, tapping out a beat on my leg – when I heard noises in the bedroom, kind of a thump, a muffled scream. I jerked up.

Crystal was shouting something. Larry was yelling too, but I couldn't make out the words.

I stood up and turned down the stereo so I could hear better.

Another scream, then a crash like something had been knocked over.

I raced down the hall to the bedroom, pushed open the door.

Crystal was kneeling naked on the side of the bed, punching at Larry's arms and legs as he tried to get his clothes on. The lamp was on the floor.

'Get out! Get out!' she yelled.

'I'm trying to, you crazy bitch!' he said, pulling his pants up and grabbing his shirt off the floor.

'Get the fuck out of my house!' Crystal jumped off the bed, came at him with fists flying, caught him in the corner of the jaw.

'Stop it!' I yelled.

Larry cocked his arm, smacked her hard across the face. She fell backward, hitting the wall and crashing into the night table. She tried to catch herself, but the side of her face slammed into the edge with a thud that made me feel sick. Between sobs she clutched at her face and said, 'You fucker.'

229

Larry spun around and pushed past me, knocking me sideways onto the bed. 'I don't need this shit.'

He walked out of the bedroom, still cursing as he went down the hall. The front door slammed shut.

I turned to Crystal. 'You okay?'

She was huddled against the wall, crying hard, makeup in black streaks down her face, blood dripping from her nose and the corner of her mouth.

'The door!' she said.

I ran back into the living room and locked the door, then jogged back to her room. Crystal had pulled the top sheet off her bed and wrapped it around her.

'What happened?' I said.

'I couldn't breathe. He had his hands around my throat . . . ' She reached up, touched her neck, rubbed at it. 'He thought . . . he thought I liked it.'

I didn't know what to say. Her face looked so sore. I wanted to give her a hug but didn't know if she wanted to be touched. 'I'll get you some ice.'

I went to the kitchen, put ice cubes in a towel, and brought it to Crystal's room. She was in the bathroom, now in shorts and a tank top, looking at her face in the mirror. Balls of bloody Kleenex were wadded all over the bathroom counter. Her hands shook as she touched her cheek and her bottom lip, which was puffy. I handed her the ice pack. She stared at it.

'It's for your face,' I said.

She pressed it to her cheekbone, where I could see a red mark. She was still staring at herself in the mirror. Her blue eyes huge, almost black.

'I smoked your last cigarette,' I said, trying not to cry. 'I'm sorry.'

She looked at me and started to laugh, but then her laughter turned to tears. She sat on the edge of the bathtub.

'I'm such a mess. He was right. I'm crazy.'

'No, he was an asshole.'

She wiped at her face, stood up. 'I need a drink.'

Over the next hour, Crystal drank every wine cooler in her house and finished off the remains of a vodka bottle. She kept getting up to look out the window, stumbling into everything. Then she'd stare out at the street like she was checking to see if Larry was outside.

'You sure you locked the door?' she asked several times, and even when I swore I had, she still checked. She went around and made sure every window in the house was closed and latched, though it was still hot.

I'd never seen her like this. I didn't know what to do.

'Maybe we should call my mom, or Dallas,' I said.

'You can't tell them what happened!'

'Okay, but will you please sit down?'

She sat, and before long her head started to drift lower, jerking a couple of times as she tried to fight off sleep, her chin almost touching her chest.

231

'You should go to bed,' I said.

'Come with me,' she said.

I led her down to her room and covered her with her sheet – it was a little cooler there with a fan blowing. Then I lay down beside her and drifted off.

Later, unsure of the time, I woke and glanced next to me – Crystal wasn't in bed. I sat up, looked around. The bathroom door was open slightly, letting some light into the bedroom. The drawer on her night table was open.

I headed for the bathroom. 'Crystal?'

No answer.

I pushed open the door. She was on the floor, her back against the side of the bathtub, her eyes closed and her head lolling to one side. She had a gun in her hand.

'Holy shit!'

She opened her eyes half-mast, tried to focus on me. 'Close the door. They're coming.'

'Who's coming?' I said.

'Close the fucking *door*!'

Had she totally lost her mind? I noticed a couple lines of white powder on the counter, a rolled-up bill beside them. Shit.

I knelt beside her. 'Crystal, give me the gun.'

She tucked it closer to her body, under her armpit. She was breathing fast and looking around wild-eyed.

'Did they hear us? They're going to kill us this time.'

She curled into a ball, the gun still close to her body, and started rocking back and forth, singing some song to herself.

Should I just sit with her for a while? I had to get the gun away from her somehow.

'Crystal, give me the gun, *please*.'

She shook her head. 'No. They're going to hurt me again.'

'No one's going to hurt you. *Please* give me the gun.'

She took the gun out from under her arm but was still holding it by her side. She met my eyes, and hers seemed to come back into focus for a moment.

'I need my cigarettes,' she said.

'You're out,' I said.

'I have more in my purse.'

'I'll get them.' I went into the living room, found her purse, and rummaged around, but she didn't have any.

When I went back to her bathroom, the door was shut. I tried the handle. Locked. 'Crystal? I couldn't find your cigarettes.'

'Just go home, Skylar.'

I didn't like the tone of her voice, the flatness. 'I'm not going anywhere until you come out.'

Silence.

I wondered if I should call the police or an ambulance or something.

I went into the living room and picked up my cell.
'Mom? I need you.'

I spent the·next twenty minutes sitting outside Crystal's
bathroom door. She wouldn't answer my questions, so
I babbled about the beach, how she'd promised to take
me, how we could pick up some burgers and shakes and
smoke a big joint and read dumb magazines and laugh at
celebrities. I could hear the crying on the other side, loud
sniffs, or sometimes just silence, which was worse. My
body was covered with nervous sweat, my palms sticky. I
was terrified I'd hear the click of the gun, a shot going off.

Finally, I heard a key in the front door – and my mom
calling out, 'Skylar?'

'In here!' I yelled.

Crystal was silent. I wondered if she'd passed out.

Dallas and my mom came into the room. Mom's face
was pale and her eyes looked scared. Dallas looked grim,
her mouth a hard line.

'She's so messed up,' I said. 'I didn't know what to do.'

'It's okay,' Mom said. 'Just go into the living room and
we'll deal with this.'

'No way! You can't make me leave.'

'You shouldn't have been here in the first place!'

'If I wasn't here, that guy might've really hurt her.'

Mom turned from me to the locked door. Dallas
knocked gently.

'Crystal, honey. Can you open the door?'

'She won't go to the police,' I said.

'No police,' my mom and Dallas said at the same time.

The door opened slowly. Crystal was gripping the edge, leaning against it like she could barely stand. Her face was streaked with tears, bits of dried blood still under her nose, a faint bruise already forming around one eye.

'Jesus.' Dallas stepped forward.

Crystal walked into her arms, put her head onto her shoulder, and sobbed like a little girl. Mom took the gun out of Crystal's hand, flipped something on the side of it.

'Why don't you lie down?' Dallas said, leading Crystal to the bed, where she curled up, hugging her pillow. Mom sat by Crystal's feet, her hand resting on her calf, the other still holding the gun. Dallas was rubbing Crystal's back.

'It was just like Cash Creek,' Crystal said, the words squeezing out of her like she was in pain. 'It was happening all over again.'

'Crystal,' Mom said. 'You're safe now.'

'We're never going to be safe. They're still looking for us.'

Mom looked up at me. 'Go out to the living room.'

'I want to stay.'

She got off the bed and came toward me, her face furious. 'Get out of here!'

I left and sat in the darkened living room, my face hot. I'd taken care of Crystal for hours, sat with her until they came, and now I was kicked out like a little kid. I couldn't even hear anything they were talking about, just murmurs, sometimes Crystal crying. And it was a half hour before Mom came out.

'Is she okay?' I said.

'She's calming down. Dallas will stay the night with her.'

'I want to stay too.'

'We need to go home.'

Mom gripped the wheel tight, her eyes focused on the road, but I could tell her thoughts were elsewhere, expressions flitting across her face, confusion, fear, sadness, lights from the other cars reflecting off her skin and eyes.

'What was Crystal talking about?' I said.

'She's out of it. She didn't know what she was saying.'

'What happened in Cash Creek?'

'You lied to me tonight, Skylar. I'm really upset with you.'

'You're lying to me *now*.'

She didn't say another word the rest of the way home.

*

Mom turned on the light in the kitchen and made a pot of tea, her movements jerky, agitated. She stopped, staring at the cutlery drawer like she couldn't remember what she was looking for, then finally pulled out a spoon. She dropped it with a clatter, cursed as she picked it up. I went to sit on the couch, waiting for her to order me to bed, but I wasn't going without a fight. The living room was shadowed, the streets outside our apartment quiet at this time of night except for the odd horn or siren or vehicle roaring past. Someone walked down the hall, coming home late.

Mom sat beside me on the couch, handed me a cup of tea, pulled a blanket over both of us. She glanced around our apartment like she was trying to remind herself where she was. Her gaze focused on the photo of her mom we kept on the side table in a silver frame. It was the only picture she had of her family.

'There was a reason I didn't want you to go out with Crystal,' she said.

'I was okay.'

'You could've gotten into a lot of trouble.'

'Crystal was looking out for me.'

'When Crystal gets drunk she doesn't know what she's doing. What happened to her tonight? That could've been you, and—' Mom's voice broke.

'I wasn't drinking.'

'You don't have to be drunk. It's just being in the

wrong place at the wrong time – and the bar was definitely the wrong place.'

'I'm sorry I lied,' I said. 'It just feels like you never trust me.' Mom was a pretty cool mother in a lot of ways, but she hated it when I wore anything too tight or too short, lectured me all the time about drinking and drugs, and how guys can get the wrong idea – stuff like that.

'It's not you I don't trust. It's the rest of the world.'

'You can't keep me in a box, Mom.'

'I can try.' She smiled, but it looked strained.

'Is Crystal going to be okay?'

'Yeah, she's just having a rough night.'

It was a lot more than a rough night and we both knew it.

'Who did she think was going to hurt her?' I said.

'She thought Larry might come back.'

'I'm not an idiot, Mom. She was talking like she was scared of a couple people. I know she was freaking out about something that happened in the past.'

Mom was quiet for a minute, then took a deep breath and let it out slowly.

'We met some very bad men when we were teenagers.'

'From Cash Creek? Did you go there when you ran away?' Mom had told me years ago how their mom had died in a car accident when they were growing up in Golden, and their dad had been an alcoholic. He'd gone

238

missing when she was pregnant with me. They ran away to avoid foster care and met Patrick, who gave them jobs, then they changed their names so their dad could never find them.

'Our truck had broken down, and they stopped to help ...' She took another breath, swallowed hard. 'One of them worked at the garage. We got jobs on their ranch to make some money, but they ...' She paused again, took a quick sip of her tea like her mouth had gone dry. 'They wanted more than that.'

'Did they hurt you?' I whispered, my blood whooshing in my ears. Mom was staring at the teacup in her hand.

'They got rough with us one night when we were all drinking down by a river. We managed to get away but we were terrified.' Her eyes were shiny like she was close to tears.

'What did they do?'

'It doesn't matter. We got out of town as soon as we could and we've never seen them again.' She turned to look at me, reached out to grab my hand. 'I know you think I'm too protective, and maybe I am sometimes, it's just that I see you going down the same path as Crystal, and I'm scared for you.'

'I'm not Crystal, Mom.'

'I know, baby, but bad things happen even when people are careful.'

'Why didn't you go to the cops?'

'Same reason we ran away. We didn't want to go to foster care.'

'Are they still there? Like, in that town?'

'I don't know.'

'Crystal thinks they're still looking for you.'

'That was just the drugs talking.'

'But what if she's right and—'

'They'd never be able to find us.'

'Do they, like, know your real names or anything?' I didn't even know my mom's real name. She wouldn't tell me because she was scared I might accidentally reveal it to someone.

'No, they don't.' She put down her cup. 'I'm tired, baby, and talking about this – it's really hard.'

'I'm sorry.'

'It's not your fault. I just need to go to bed.'

'Can I sleep with you?'

'Of course.' She said it with a smile, but she still looked sad.

We lay side by side, our arms touching and my head resting against her shoulder like when I was little and she used to rub circles on my forehead until I fell asleep. I could hear her breathing for a long time, not slow and measured but faster, like she was still awake.

'Skylar, you can't tell anyone about this, okay?' she whispered.

'Okay.'

'I mean it. Not Emily or Taylor or anyone else.'

'I won't.'

Finally she drifted off, but I stayed awake for a while, thinking about what might have happened down at that river. I knew Mom hadn't told me everything, had probably held back a lot, and my mind spun with questions. I couldn't stop thinking about Crystal saying, 'They're going to kill us this time.'

She'd sounded so sure.

Chapter Seventeen

I drove over to Crystal's the next afternoon. She opened the door still wearing the shorts and tank top she'd pulled on the night before, her hair a mess. Her face didn't look too bad, but one side of her bottom lip was a little swollen and she had a faint blue shadow around one eye.

'Good. It's you,' she said. 'I thought it was Dallas checking up on me again.'

'Did I wake you?' I said.

'I was just dozing on the couch. Come in.' She walked into the living room, collapsed back down onto the couch. The blinds were closed on all the windows, the room dark.

I sat at her feet. Her ashtray was full of cigarettes, and there were already two empty beer bottles on the coffee table and one on the go.

'Have you been out today?' I said.

'The liquor store,' she said with a smile. 'Had to get

my medicine.' Normally I'd have laughed, but it didn't seem funny today.

'Are you okay?' I said.

'Yeah,' she said, but she didn't meet my eyes as she sat up and reached for another cigarette.

'You want me to make some soup?' I said. 'Have you eaten anything?'

'You sound like your mom.' She leaned back on the couch, lit her smoke.

'Sorry. I'm just worried about you.'

She gave me a sad smile. 'Sorry for scaring you last night, kiddo.'

'You freaked out.' I picked up the tinfoil from an empty cigarette pack on the coffee table, started making an origami crane. The smooth foil felt comforting under my fingers.

'I shouldn't have been doing coke.'

'I didn't know you did that.'

'Haven't touched it for years, but Larry had some.' She shrugged. 'Seemed like a good idea at the time.' She looked at me. 'Boy, he turned out to be a fucker, hey?' She shook her head. 'You never know . . .'

'Mom told me what happened to you guys in Cash Creek.' I paused from my work on the bird, waiting to see how my words would land.

She took a hard drag of her cigarette, her gaze sliding away like she didn't know where to look. 'What did she

243

tell you?' She blew the smoke up toward the ceiling, showing her neck and the scar on her jaw.

'How your truck broke down and those guys picked you up, and then you worked at their ranch, but they ... they hurt you.' I didn't want to tell her exactly what Mom had said. She met my eyes, and it was like all the life had gone out of hers. They were just dark pools of pain so deep I wanted to pull away, wanted to run outside and suck in the clean air and feel sunshine against my skin.

'She told you what they did?' Her voice sounded hollow.

'Yeah, but she didn't say much. She got upset.'

She reached out and grabbed the beer off the coffee table, took a few mouthfuls, one after the other.

'What happened?' I said in a soft voice.

My question hovered between us as we sat there for an endless minute. I stared down at the foil bird, counted the beats of my heart, wondered if Crystal's was beating this fast. I wished I could reach out and snatch my question back, but I'd thought about it a lot during the night, feeling this weird mix of fear and curiosity. I needed to know what had happened at that river. I felt bad asking her when she still seemed so depressed, but that was when Crystal talked the most.

'They tied us up in the back of their truck and took us to a warehouse,' Crystal finally said. She took a drag of her cigarette. 'They kept us for five days.'

'Five *days*?' I almost crushed the bird in my hands.

She exhaled slowly, the cigarette smoke pushing into my nose.

'They were sick assholes, like, *really* sick.'

I didn't know what to say, the enormity of what she had told me sinking through me like a stone. Mom had lied. Those men hadn't just gotten 'rough' with them. They'd hurt them badly, held them captive, did terrible things.

'Do you really think they're still looking for you?' I thought about how Mom would get up in the night and check the locks. I glanced at the door now – had Crystal locked it after I came in?

'No,' she said. 'I was just messed up.'

I studied her face to see if she was telling the truth. 'How did you escape?'

'We stole their truck and got back to town. We were trying to get our truck out of their garage, but it was locked up in the back.' She was picking at the label on her beer, ripping off little pieces. 'This biker dude helped us out – he owned the pub next door. His son drove us to the bus in the morning.'

My feelings were all tumbling around inside, angry someone had hurt them, confused and upset I'd never known anything about it, but mostly I felt scared. 'It must be horrible knowing that they're still out there somewhere.'

'It's pretty fucked up.' Her eyes were shiny as she took

245

another long drag of her cigarette. She'd almost smoked it down to the filter already.

'They shouldn't be allowed to get away with it,' I said. 'I mean, I know you couldn't go to the cops. But I'd want to kill them.'

Crystal was looking at me but her eyes were vacant, like her mind was somewhere else, the cigarette still burning down in her hands.

'Crystal?' I said. 'You okay?'

'Yeah, I was just thinking about how easy you think things are going to be sometimes, how you're on this path and then all of a sudden ... ' She made a motion with her hand. 'Shit is going sideways. And you can't go back in time, you can't do it over again. No matter how much you wish you could.'

'You mean like you wish you hadn't gone to Cash Creek?'

'I wish I hadn't done a lot of stuff,' she said, staring at the far wall. A tear dripped down the side of her face. She brushed it off, took a ragged breath.

'Like what?'

'It's my fault we had to run away. I screwed up. I'm the one who *always* screws up.'

'What do you mean?'

She put out her cigarette in the ashtray, smashing the filter down with one finger, grinding it in. She lit another.

'Did you know I was going to be a singer?'

'You never said anything.' I felt thrown off again, like I'd been walking a balance beam and kept getting pushed off. We talked about music all the time.

'I could play the guitar and everything.' She pantomimed plucking strings. 'And your mom, she was going to be a photographer – she was so fucking smart. Smarter than Dallas and me in school. She could've been anything.'

I never thought about my mom having any hobbies or dreams, but she did like taking pictures – our walls were covered with her photos. I'd found an old camera one day hidden on the top shelf of her closet. I'd put it back, feeling guilty, and never asked her about it, but it was weird. Was that from when she was a kid? Crystal was right about Mom being smart, but she only had her GED. She read my homework and borrowed my books all the time.

Crystal looked at me again, tears making her eyelashes spike. 'You're a good kid, Skylar. A really good kid.'

'Thanks.'

'I mean that,' she said. 'Don't try to be like me.'

'You're not so bad.'

'I haven't done one good thing with my life.' She picked up her beer and swallowed it all, wiping her mouth when she was done.

'You've done lots of great stuff.'

'Nope.' She shook her head. 'Dallas, she's always helping people. And your mom ... she's braver than you'll ever know. I haven't done fuck-all.'

'What would you do if you could?'

She met my eyes, hers kind of vacant again.

'I wish we'd killed them,' she said. 'I wish it all the time.' She was staring through me, smoke drifting up from her cigarette.

'Crystal?'

She focused in on me, noticed the bird in my hands. 'What is that?'

'It's a crane. The Japanese call it the bird of happiness. They believe cranes live a thousand years, so it's supposed to represent good fortune and longevity or something like that. They make strings of them at funerals.'

'That must look really pretty,' she said, then smiled sadly. 'Hey, Sky. I'm really glad you came to see me, but do you mind if I just go back to bed? I've got a brutal headache.'

'Yeah, sure. I'm sorry if I upset you.'

'No, you're the best. We'll go to the beach tomorrow, okay? Give me a call in the morning.'

That night when Mom came home from work she looked exhausted, her hair coming loose from its braid, the tendrils damp, her face flushed.

'God, the bus was just gross tonight. Like being trapped in a hot tin can.' She hung up her purse. 'I can't wait to get out of these clothes.'

I made her a fruit smoothie while she was changing and brought it out to her on the balcony, where we had a little plastic table, two chairs, and a hibachi grill that we used in the summer. Mom had found a flowered tablecloth for our table and some citronella candles in pretty pots to keep away the mosquitoes.

She'd changed into shorts and a tank top and had her legs braced up on the railing, her head resting against the back of the chair, her shoes kicked off. I could see red marks in her feet from where her shoes had rubbed.

She took a sip of the smoothie. 'Yum.' She reached for my hand and gave it a squeeze. 'How are you feeling?'

'I went over and saw Crystal.'

'How was she? I tried to call from work but she didn't pick up.'

'She was probably sleeping. She seems kind of depressed. Do you think we should get her some help? Like, what about therapy or something?'

'She wouldn't go.' I could hear tension in her voice and knew she didn't really want to talk. Her eyes were closed, her head still resting on the back of the chair like it was the first time she'd had a chance to relax all day. But after my conversation with Crystal I had even more questions about what had happened.

'Crystal told me what the guys really did.'

She opened her eyes and frowned at me. 'What do you mean?'

'She told me how they kept you for days, and hurt you . . . I'm really sorry that happened to you, Mom. You must have been so scared.'

Mom looked pissed off. 'She had no right to tell you that.'

'She thought I knew. Why didn't you tell me?'

'I didn't want you to have to think about those things.'

'Did you ever tell anyone?' I said.

'No.'

'Not even Patrick or Karen?'

'We didn't want to talk about it.' Neither of my aunts or my mom had ever liked talking about their past, which made more sense now. But they barely talked about when they were kids, either. Mom had told me some things about her mother over the years, like that her name was Lillian and she'd been a good cook and liked to fish. She didn't really talk about her dad.

'Crystal said you stole their truck . . . '

'Yeah.'

'How did you get out of the warehouse?'

'Can we talk about this another time? I've had a long day.'

'You always say that when you don't want to talk about something.'

'It's always true.' She looked away, took a sip of her drink.

'Crystal said it was her fault that you guys had to run away.'

I could see a pulse beating in Mom's throat. 'She probably just meant because Dad and she used to fight a lot.'

'What about?'

'What's *this* all about?' She looked at me again.

'I just wanted to understand. Why is that so weird?' What they went through was really horrible, and I got why they didn't want to talk about it, but something still felt strange about it all, like they were hiding something else.

'Crystal doesn't think,' Mom said, her voice angry. 'She says all kinds of crap when she's in one of these moods. It doesn't mean anything.'

'It sure sounded like it meant something.'

'Who knows with Crystal?' She stood up. 'I'm going to take a shower.'

I went into my bedroom, put on my headphones, and messed around with some beats, but when I played them back they all sounded angry, chaotic, confused. Like they didn't know what they wanted to be yet.

Later that night I texted Crystal, said I was looking forward to going to the beach and asked if she wanted me to pick up anything on the way to her place.

She didn't answer.

*

Around ten in the morning I threw my bathing suit in my bag, grabbed a towel and some lotion, and headed over to Crystal's. She hadn't answered any of my texts that morning or my phone call, but I figured she might still be sleeping.

When I got to her place, all the windows were closed and she didn't answer the door. I knocked a few times and called out. Then I went around to every window, trying to see inside, but the blinds were closed. I checked around the back of the house – her car wasn't in the carport. I thought about asking the upstairs tenants if they'd seen her but it didn't look like anyone was home.

I went back to our apartment, disappointed Crystal had forgotten our plan. Maybe she had to go in to work or something. I texted her a few times that day and night, but she wasn't answering any of my messages. I checked her Facebook, mostly photos of her with different guys and shots of her at the bar or partying with friends. She hadn't updated her status since the night we were at the bar: *Can't wait to see the Headkickers! The bar will be rocking!*

'I can't find Crystal,' I said the minute Mom got home. 'We were going to the beach.'

'I'm sorry, baby. But are you really surprised?'

I knew Crystal blew off lots of people, but I was hurt she did it to me. 'She's not answering my texts.'

'I've been trying her too. She probably just forgot her cell somewhere. She'll check in soon.'

I came home from the gym the next day to find Mom watching TV and painting her toenails. She was working late that night at the hotel for a wedding.

'Mom, I need to talk.'

'What's wrong?' She looked up, her face concerned.

'I went by Crystal's a couple of times today, but she's not around. She didn't show up for work either. No one's seen her.'

'I know you're worried, Sky, but this is what Crystal *does*. You know that. Remember last year when she took off? She used to disappear for weeks and Dallas and I'd be so scared, then she'd show up like it was no big deal and we'd find out she was partying somewhere with friends or some guy.'

'Not this time, Mom. Not after the other night.'

She capped her nail polish bottle and looked at me. 'Especially this time. Dallas and I were expecting something like this.'

I chewed my lower lip. 'But she didn't tell me.'

My mom covered my hand with her own. 'She still loves you, Sky. You're her number-one niece.'

I smiled weakly. 'Because I'm her only niece.'

'Exactly.' She patted my knee and stood up. 'I better get ready for work.' She looked back at me. 'Don't worry, baby. She'll be back soon.'

While Mom went to get dressed, I pulled her key chain out of her purse and took the key to Crystal's place.

It was nine o'clock and the sun was just setting when I pulled up in front of Crystal's. There didn't seem to be any lights on in her suite. No lights upstairs, either, which was good.

I opened the front door slowly, my eyes quickly taking everything in.

'Hello?' I called out. What if she had some guy over, or came running out with a towel wrapped around her, pissed I was violating her privacy? But the place was quiet. It was a little creepy being there alone.

The ashtray on the coffee table was full; empties stood in a cluster. All the cigarette butts were her brand – Player's light, king-size. The kitchen sink was full of dishes and the garbage smelled. I pulled the bag out of the pail, tied it up, and left it by the front door. I made my way down the hall into her bedroom.

Her bed was unmade, a tangle of sheets and pillows. A beer bottle was on her night table, and the little foil crane I'd made was sitting on a Kleenex box. I picked it up, fingered the wings as I looked around.

Her perfume hung in the air. Some of her drawers were pulled out, clothes heaped in a laundry basket, but I couldn't tell if anything was gone.

I checked her bathroom – no toothbrush in the stand. I opened all her drawers. Her makeup was gone too. I looked in the shower. No razor, just a couple of almost-empty shampoo bottles and a sliver of soap.

I stood in the hallway and frowned. Where was she?

Back in the living room, I sat on her couch, put my hand on the pillow lying there. I shouldn't have made her talk about Cash Creek. I shouldn't have brought any of it up at all.

She still had two joints inside the box on her side table. I moved to her desk, rummaged through some Post-it notes, just random notes about groceries or reminders, phone numbers. I turned on her computer and checked her search history. There was some stuff about some bands, and at the top: Cash Creek.

I stared at the name, my heart beating fast. I did a search, checked the links that came up. She'd clicked on one about cattle ranches in the Okanagan. It was a listing for ranches. I scanned the names but they didn't mean anything to me.

I shut down her computer, left a note on her counter: *Please call me!* Then I cleaned up her dishes, took out her garbage, and made her bed. I grabbed the two joints out of the box – figured she wouldn't mind.

I walked back into her bedroom and checked her night table drawer, under her mattress, in her closet, searching everywhere for the gun. It was gone.

255

I wish we'd killed them. I wish it all the time.

The way she'd looked at me, like I wasn't even there.

In the morning Mom shuffled into the kitchen in her boxer shorts and tank top, her hair messy. She yawned as she opened the freezer and pulled out a box.

She glanced at my cup of coffee. 'That'll stunt your growth, you know.' She smiled at our running joke, which started after I shot up past her years ago.

She popped some Eggos into the toaster, grabbed the syrup out of the fridge, then sat across from me, using her fingers to taste some syrup from the lid.

I'd been thinking about what I'd discovered at Crystal's place, had even logged onto my laptop last night and searched again for Cash Creek. It was a really small town, only about three thousand people. Wikipedia mentioned dairy farming and cattle ranching, but when I Googled 'Cattle ranches, Cash Creek', I didn't get any hits.

Mom was talking about what we could do that day. I couldn't really concentrate on what she was saying. I was thinking about how to tell her what I'd learned but every time I opened my mouth, she went on about something else.

'Maybe we could go to Stanley Park. Do you feel like Rollerblading around the seawall?' She got up and took her Eggos out of the toaster, dropped them onto her plate, and slathered them with butter. 'Or we could go to Granville Island and walk around the stores, maybe check out the market.'

She sat back down across from me, picked up the syrup bottle.

I took a breath. 'I went over to Crystal's last night.'

Her eyebrows pulled together. 'She's home?' She set the bottle down.

'No, I borrowed your key.'

Now she looked pissed. 'You mean you *took* it.'

I shrugged. 'I needed to see inside her place. It looks like she left Sunday, maybe not long after I went over.'

'Yeah.' She took a few long sips of her coffee, watching me over the rim.

'I think she went to Cash Creek.'

She started shaking her head but I kept talking. 'Mom, listen. She was on her computer, looking up Cash Creek. I bet she was looking for those guys.'

All the color had gone out of Mom's face, and her hand was gripping the edge of the table like she was trying to hold herself up.

'Mom?'

She got up and refilled her coffee. She was stirring in sugar, only her profile visible, but I could see her eyelashes flickering like she was blinking hard.

'Crystal would never go back there,' she said.

'You don't know what—'

'I know my sister, Skylar. She wouldn't go there.'

'Her gun is *gone*, Mom. I think she went back to kill them.'

She turned around. 'That's crazy.'

'She looked them up. Why would she do that?' I couldn't tell her about my last conversation with Crystal, the stupid stuff I'd said.

'Who knows, but there's no way in hell she's gone to Cash Creek.'

'I think we should drive there and see.'

'Absolutely not.'

'Why not?'

'It's too dangerous, for one, and I can't miss work.'

'Why aren't you worried?'

'I *am* worried, okay? But Dallas and I learned a long time ago not to screw up our lives every time Crystal went off the rails. She'll figure it out and she'll come back and we'll lend her money again and she'll get another job.'

'I can't believe you're not going to look for her!'

'Skylar, you have no idea what we lived through in that town. None of us would ever go back there again.' She walked over, cupped my face. 'Trust me.'

I leaned away. 'I can't just sit around and wait for her to come home.'

'So don't. What are Emily and Taylor doing? Are they working?' She glanced at the calendar on the wall, her face slightly surprised like she'd just realized the date. 'Oh, right. Emily's going to their cabin this week.'

'She's leaving tomorrow. They invited me, but I didn't feel like going this year.' Emily's cabin was awesome and we always had fun, but sometimes it was hard watching her with her dad, how nice he was. She could be kind of mean to him, making fun of his jokes or how he dressed, acting annoyed when he wanted to take us fishing. I'd feel angry at her, then we'd get in a stupid fight.

'Call and see if you can go,' Mom said.

'You wouldn't mind?'

'I think it would be good for you to hang out with some girls your own age. You shouldn't be worried about this kind of stuff.'

'What about the gym?'

'Don't worry. I'll clear it with Dallas.'

'Maybe I'll call Emily.'

'Good,' Mom said, looking relieved. She grabbed her coffee. 'I'm going to take a shower.'

While Mom was at work that night I Googled maps and driving times, trying to calculate gas and how much money I'd need. I thought I could make it in about five and a half hours, a little more if I stopped for food or gas.

When I walked into the kitchen in the morning, Mom glanced up from pouring coffee. I'd heard the TV on late after she got home last night, and her eyes were puffy like she hadn't slept well.

I felt hot and nervous. I'd raided the cupboard for granola bars and dried fruit, any stuff that would last awhile. I planned to drive all day, stop for lunch, then get a motel room in Cash Creek – I was going to pull a few hundred out of my bank account. I'd have to work extra shifts for the rest of the summer and maybe even babysit so I could still pay for the mixer and speakers.

I poured myself some juice and sat down at the table. Mom turned around and leaned against the counter. 'Did you get hold of Emily?'

'Yeah, I can go. I'll meet them at their house in a few hours.'

'That's great, Skylar. Try to have fun and don't worry about Crystal. I'll text you when she shows up. Don't forget to call and let me know you're okay.'

'The cabin has crappy cell service, remember? I'll text when we're on the road or shoot you an email, okay?'

'Okay, baby.' She came closer, leaned down, and gave me a kiss on my lips, holding my chin like she did when I was little. 'Be safe. I'll miss you.'

'I'll miss you too.'

I watched her walk down the hall to her room.

I felt bad – I'd never lied about something so big – but I pushed it away. Mom was wrong. She didn't know everything about Crystal. She didn't know what we'd talked about that day, didn't see the look in her eyes, or how empty her house had felt. But I did, I knew. She didn't plan on coming back.

Chapter Eighteen

I left around ten, while Mom was at the gym. I'd packed my stuff, including a switchblade she'd given me years ago – Patrick had shown me how to use it.

It was already hot – I was wearing cargo shorts and a tank top, my skin sticking to my seat every time I moved. The air conditioner in my car was broken, so I had all the windows rolled down, my hair pulled back in a loose braid the wind whipped around, the stereo pounding.

The Vancouver traffic clogged the highway all the way out of the city and it was slow going at first. I was nervous about the traffic; big trucks making my car vibrate as they roared past, the tires almost as tall as my car.

As I got farther away from Vancouver and passed Hope, a small town a couple of hours out of the city, the terrain changed, getting more mountainous, with fewer signs of people. When I reached the Coquihalla, the big highway that would take me the rest of the way up to

Kamloops, the scenery had changed from cedar trees and tall firs to craggy mountaintops and high rock bluffs baking in the morning sun. It was a steady uphill climb and I passed a couple of cars on the side of the road, steam billowing out. I thought about my mom and my aunts, how scared they must have been when their truck broke down on the road.

I kept my eye out for Crystal's car as I passed gas stations and motels along the highway. It was strange, thinking she might have been driving on this road only a few days ago. I had a few photos of her on my phone along with one I'd pulled out of our photo album. If I couldn't find anybody who'd seen her in Cash Creek, then maybe Mom was right and she'd just needed to get away.

I kept going over my last conversation with Crystal. Wherever she'd gone, I was sure I was the reason she'd decided to take off. I shouldn't have said anything. What did I know? My mom and my aunts had lied to me for my whole life, every single day. It made me wonder what else they'd been lying about.

When I'd been on the road for three hours I hit Merritt, another small town. The land had changed again, getting drier, more like a desert canyon with scrubby bushes and rolling fields of brown. I stopped at McDonald's for lunch.

I ordered my food and took a table, then texted my

mom, letting her know I was almost at the cabin, sending lots of kisses and hugs and promising to text her as soon as I had coverage again. I'd texted Taylor that morning, telling her that I was going to be working some extra shifts so she wouldn't wonder if she didn't hear from me. I wasn't worried about her calling my house – my friends only used my cell. A girl came out of the bathroom with a big packsack on her shoulder, gave me a smile, and walked out into the parking lot.

I watched her go over to three guys standing by a white Jeep with a bunch of camping gear in the back. She was around my age and really pretty, with straight, almost-white blonde hair pulled into a loose knot at the back of her neck.

One of the guys handed her a cigarette, then said something as she bent forward to light it. She stepped back to blow out the smoke and turned around, walking away from them. Now one of the guys made an obscene gesture with his mouth and hand, like he was imitating a blow job. The other two were laughing.

The girl gave them the finger, then kept walking toward the highway. The guys got into their Jeep and followed her, slowing to a near-stop where she was standing on the side of the highway with her thumb out. I watched, riveted, my hand paused on my fries. What were they going to do?

The guy on the passenger side had his head out the window, looked like he was shouting something, then he lifted his arm and threw a Slurpee cup at her. She put her arm up, shielding her face, but a spray of liquid soaked her. The guys gunned the gas, their Jeep swerving on the road. The girl picked up a rock and threw it in their direction, but they were long gone.

She walked back to the restaurant and disappeared into the bathroom, her face flushed. I felt bad for her and hoped she was okay.

I was checking my map in the parking lot when she came out, wearing a different tank top, a pink one, and peered into my car.

'Hey, can I get a ride?'

I didn't really want company. I wanted to think, not have a conversation.

'Did you see those assholes?' she said. Before I could answer, she looked at the map in my hands. 'Where you going?'

'Cash Creek.'

'I'm going to Revelstoke, but if you got me as far as Cash Creek I'd be really grateful.' She gave me a hopeful smile. 'My name's Lacey.'

'I'm not sure . . .' I didn't want to be a jerk, but still.

'I'm harmless, I swear. I just don't want to end up in a ditch, you know?' She looked at the highway. 'Those guys were creepy.'

I thought about what had happened to my mom and aunts. Imagined reading in the paper about some hitch-hiker getting killed.

'Okay. But I have some stuff I have to do when I get to Cash Creek.'

'Don't worry. Soon as we get there, I'll split.'

While we drove, we talked. Turned out she was sixteen, but she looked older, with lots of makeup. She was from Hope, that first small town I'd driven through, and fighting with her parents because they didn't like her boyfriend. She was running away to meet him in Revelstoke. I thought she was crazy to be hitchhiking but she said she did it all the time. She showed me a photo of her boyfriend, who was kind of cute, with brown eyes and really white teeth. She wanted to know why I was going to Cash Creek, and I just said I was meeting up with my aunt.

I turned up the radio when a good song came on and started tapping out the beat on my steering wheel, singing the melody.

'You have a good voice,' Lacey said.

'Thanks.'

'Are you a singer?'

'No, I'm a DJ.' I felt a thrill saying the words, a little lift at the bottom of my stomach. 'I have a YouTube channel.'

'That's so cool. I wish I could do something like that.'

'You like music?'

'Yeah, but I can't sing, can't play. I'm not really good at anything.' She shrugged. 'My mom tells me all the time that I'm stupid.' She put on a harsh voice. '"You're going to end up living in a trailer park."' She laughed, but it sounded bitter, and when she looked out the window her upper back quivered like she was fighting tears. I didn't know what to say.

After a few minutes she turned back around, started singing aloud to the radio in a really goofy high-pitched voice. I started laughing.

'I told you I can't sing!'

'Wow, you weren't kidding.'

I joined in, making my voice go all squeaky, and it was kind of fun for a few minutes, until I remembered why we were on this trip. I stopped singing. Lacey glanced over, her voice drifting off. She stared back out the window.

We'd been driving for over two hours through mountains, lakes, rolling farmland, and alpine meadows when a sign with food and lodging symbols showed that we were almost at the exit for Cash Creek, which was good because we hadn't passed a gas station for miles and I was almost on empty.

The town was small, the downtown core only a few

streets. I'd only ever seen a few small towns on the way to Emily's cabin, but those ones looked cute, like somewhere you'd want to stop and get ice cream or take photos. This one looked really rough. Most of the old buildings seemed run-down, and the park benches and metal garbage bins didn't look like they'd been painted for years. Everything seemed faded, the paint on the stores, the pavement, the awnings.

'I better get some gas,' I said.

I noticed an older garage, remembered my mom's words. *One of them worked at a garage.* What if he still worked there? Should I try to find another garage? I looked down at my dashboard. The light had been on for a long time.

When we pulled up by one of the pumps no one came out, and the office looked empty. Two big shop doors were open, though.

I got out of my car. Lacey also got out and leaned against the side of the car, fanning her face. I walked over to the shop, feeling the heat radiating off the pavement through my flip-flops. My hair felt heavy and hot on the back of my neck.

A tall boy with a red baseball cap was bent over talking to another boy who was halfway under a truck. Looked like an older Chevy, and painted a gunmetal-gray with a Budweiser sticker in the back window. The truck was on a jack and huge tires with a meaty tread

268

were off and leaning against the wall. A radio on the bench was playing country music. I was relieved there didn't seem to be anyone else working.

'Can we get some help?' I said.

The boy with the baseball cap spun around. The other boy pulled his head out from underneath the truck and stood up. His eyebrows rose when he noticed Lacey, who had come to stand beside me. He had blond hair cut short on the sides and back, with long bangs brushed forward into his face. Both boys were probably around our age and looked grubby, grease under their nails, sweat stains under the arms of their dirty T-shirts, ripped faded jeans hanging low off their hips.

'We need gas,' I said.

'Shit, sorry, didn't hear you pulling up,' the tall boy with the red cap said, coming toward us while wiping his hands on a rag. Even taller than me, he had fair skin and dark curly hair winging out from underneath his baseball cap, lively eyes and a cheeky smile.

'You girls aren't from around here,' he said.

'Just visiting,' I said. I wondered if I should show them the picture of Crystal and ask if she'd filled up on gas, but wasn't sure yet how to explain why I was looking for her. I glanced over at Lacey. She'd said she was going to split as soon as we got to town, but she hadn't made any moves to hit the road yet.

The blond boy followed us out, coming around to lean against the pump, smiling at Lacey. She smiled back.

'How much you want?' the dark-haired boy said as he unscrewed my gas cap.

'Fill her up, please.' I looked around, noticed a small peach-colored brick motel across the road. Someone had put hanging flower baskets at the front entrance and the sign promised free Wi-Fi and continental breakfast. Beside the garage there was a pub with a little awning over the front entrance. There were a couple of parking spots in front of the pub, but it looked like there might be a back parking lot on the road behind.

I remembered Crystal telling me how a biker dude and his son had helped them. I looked up, noticed an open window with curtains. Did he still live there? Would Crystal have spoken to him? I looked back at the motel, shielding my eyes from the sun as I checked the cars in the parking lot. I didn't see Crystal's, but the motel might have parking in the back.

'Is that the only motel in town?' I said.

'Yeah,' the blond-haired boy said. 'We call it the Peach. There's another one north of town, like back on the highway, but it's a lot more expensive.'

'You looking for a place to stay?' the dark-haired boy said as I handed him the gas money.

'Maybe,' I said. 'Not sure yet.'

Lacey gave me a curious look.

We got back in the car and the boys went into the gas station office. It looked like the dark-haired one was putting the money into the register. They both kept glancing at us through the dirty window. The blond boy smiled, said something to the other one.

Lacey was sniffing the air through her open window. 'Oh, my God, that smells good. I haven't eaten since yesterday.'

I caught the scent of barbecued meat. 'I saw you at McDonald's.'

'I was just changing, didn't have any money for food.' She shrugged like it was no big deal. She'd told me her dad was out of work. Things must be really bad. Mom always made sure we had a full fridge even when times were tough – and she still gave money to homeless people. I asked her why one day and she said, 'You never really know someone's story.'

I glanced up, noticed the diner beside the hotel. It looked cheap.

'I'll buy you dinner, but then I have to get going, okay?' I wanted to start searching for Crystal, but I couldn't leave her starving and I was hungry myself.

'Really? That's so awesome. Thanks,'

We parked in front of the diner. Down the street a bit

farther there were a few more stores, one looking like some sort of a hardware store, with a sign for the post office and another sign showing you could buy lottery tickets, ice, and bait. A few men out front stared at us as we got out of the car. I didn't like the feeling in this town, the dust on the streets, the heat. Everything felt dirty and worn-out, and kind of creepy. I wondered if it was because I knew what had happened to my mom here, but it felt like more than that. Like this town had given up years ago.

The waitress in the diner was about my mom's age, with long black hair and short bangs. She offered us coffee, menus, and a friendly smile. We both ordered the special, chicken potpie with salad.

'Now, can I get you girls anything else?'

'No, that's good, thanks.'

We handed her back the menus. I was putting sugar in my coffee, and Lacey was staring out her window at the pub across the way.

'He's hot.'

I followed her gaze to a man working on a motor-bike in front of the pub. He had some tools out and his shirt off. He was kind of cute for an older guy, with shoulder-length blond hair parted in the middle and a close-cropped dirty-blond beard. He put his shirt back on and was walking into the pub when the waitress came back with water for us.

'Who is that guy?' I said.

She looked out the window. 'Owen? He runs the pub.'

Crystal had said that the biker guy's son had driven them to the bus station. Was it the same guy? Did his dad still own the pub? I decided I had to talk to him. If Crystal was here, the pub was probably the first place she went.

Lacey was watching me. I turned back to face her. 'What?'

'Where are you supposed to meet your aunt?'

'Not sure yet, I have to give her a call later.' I took a sip of my coffee. It was awful, grounds floating on the top, but I kind of liked the burnt taste.

'Does she live here?'

'I don't really want to talk about it. We're having some family problems.' I knew I sounded nervous, but what was I supposed to say?

'I get it, sorry.'

I texted Mom again, told her I was fine and wouldn't be able to check in for a couple of days. I'd disabled the location services on my cell phone before I left Vancouver and hoped she hadn't noticed yet.

The waitress brought our food. 'Here you go, girls.'

Lacey leaned over her plate, scooping up a huge mouthful of potpie and shoving it into her mouth. Still chewing, she stabbed her salad and brought another forkful into her mouth. I was still unrolling the cutlery from my paper napkin.

'God, this is so good,' she said.

I watched, disgusted at first – the chicken potpie looked watery, and the salad was wilted and drenched with dressing. Then I noticed the skin stretching over her collarbone, her skinny wrists and bony forearms, her pink plastic watch.

'Yeah, it's really good,' I said, digging in and taking a big mouthful.

When we were done the waitress brought our bill. I threw some money down on the table.

'Well, good luck out there.' I got up and lifted my packsack onto my shoulder – I hadn't wanted to leave my laptop in the car.

'Wait,' Lacey said. 'It's almost five. If I try to hitchhike now I might not get a ride tonight. I didn't know how small this town was – I could be stuck on the highway at dark.'

I frowned, worrying. Crystal needed me. I couldn't get sidetracked.

Lacey stood up, grabbed her purse. 'You told the guys at the station that you might be getting a motel room. Can I crash? Just for the night? In the morning I'll go over to the truck stop and I'll get a ride no problem. I'll even call my boyfriend and he can wire you some money for, like, the food and motel.'

She did have a point about getting stuck on the road. I'd only seen two cars drive down the main street the whole time we'd been there. How far would she have to walk? I glanced down and noticed her sandals, the Band-Aid between her toes.

'Okay, but just for the night.'

Chapter Nineteen

We got back into the car, heat enveloping us in a thick blanket, making me instantly miss the air-conditioned diner. The waitress had told us that the Sunshine Valley reached the highest temperatures in all of BC and I could believe it – the steering wheel was almost too hot to touch. We rolled down the windows and drove around the building, parked in front of the motel.

'Wait here, okay? I'll be right back,' I said.

'Okay.'

The woman behind the counter put down the book she was reading and looked up at me over her glasses.

'Can I help you?'

'Is a woman named Crystal Caldwell staying here?'

'Don't think so ...' She scanned her registration book. 'Nope.'

'Anyone who looks like this woman?' I passed her my photo of Crystal.

She held it away from her face, squinting. 'Looks like

the lady who's staying in forty-eight – she rented it for a week. But she's got brown hair.'

So Crystal *had* come here – she must've dyed her hair. I felt the thrill of victory – I'd found her. Then a flash of fear. Where was she?

The woman gave me the photo and a suspicious look. 'Who is she?'

'My aunt.' I had my story ready. 'She and my mom had a big fight and she took off. It was awful. I'm trying to find her, hoping to smooth things over, you know.'

The woman nodded. 'My sister and I are always fighting.'

'When did you last see her?'

'Not for a couple of days.' She shrugged. 'But I don't keep track of everyone's coming and going. She didn't want housekeeping for the week.'

'When did she check in?'

'Monday, I think.' So she must've left Vancouver Monday morning.

'Any chance I could go into her room to leave her a note?'

'Sorry, honey. But I can tell her you're looking for her.'

'Well, could I please rent a room close to hers?'

'You got a credit card?'

'No.'

'Cash up front, then. How many nights you staying?'

'Just one for now.'

'Sixty dollars plus tax.' The woman handed me a form and I wrote down my name and license plate number. I gave her the form back along with cash for the room. I wanted to ask about the ranch, but I couldn't think of a natural way. Then I got an idea.

'My friend is looking for a job. I heard there was a cattle ranch around here that hires kids.'

She nodded. 'The Luxton Ranch, only big one in town.'

'Oh, okay.' Had I found them? 'Do you know who she should talk to?'

'Brian or Gavin – they run the place.'

How could I find out if it was the same men? Maybe someone else owned it now. I tried to think what to ask next. Directions, I needed directions.

The phone was ringing.

'Enjoy your stay,' the woman said, and reached for it.

The motel room was okay, two double beds with matching blue floral covers, a tiny fridge, and a TV that looked almost as old as the one we had at home. Lacey dumped her packsack onto the bed closest to the bathroom.

'Mind if I take this one?'

'Sure.' I sat on the other bed, checked my phone. Mom had texted back, telling me to have fun and she missed me. Nothing about Crystal.

I wondered if I should leave Lacey in the room and go

278

over to the pub. I pulled back the curtain, noticed a few trucks parked outside. What if those men were there? I couldn't show the photo around – they might overhear me or recognize Crystal. I'd have to wait until morning when it wasn't as busy.

We stayed up late watching TV. Lacey talked through most of the shows, not seeming to notice my lack of response. I got up a few times when I heard a vehicle in the parking lot, looking for Crystal's car. My car was right in front of our room. I'd checked for more parking behind the building, but it just backed onto another road and I didn't think Crystal would park on the street.

I felt restless, my fingers needed to do something. I started playing around on my laptop. Lacey asked what I was doing and I showed her how to mix a track. I told her she had good rhythm, though she actually kind of sucked. She seemed so proud that I started feeling really bad, like I'd lied to a little kid and told her there were presents under a tree when I knew there weren't.

After she finally fell asleep I stayed up for another hour, thinking about Crystal, listening for cars in the parking lot. What had been her plan? If she was here to kill those guys, how would she get close to them? I checked my phone, looked up the local newspaper. I didn't see any news stories about anyone being shot or any kind of violence recently. So where was she? I was scared that something might've happened to her already,

279

that I was too late, but I reminded myself that Crystal was really smart and tough. I just had to find her.

The next day I'd talk to Owen from the pub and drive around town, looking for her car. Maybe I'd drive by that ranch — but I didn't know how I could find out if she'd been there. It wasn't like they'd tell me.

In the morning, I heard Lacey moving around in the room. I opened my eyes. She was pulling on her clothes, her back to me.

'What are you doing?' I said.

She spun around, whispered, 'I'm just going to the office to grab us some coffee and muffins before they're all gone.'

'Okay.' I shut my eyes, put the pillow over my head, and drifted back to sleep. A while later I woke up, stretched, and glanced over, expecting to see Lacey on the other bed. She wasn't there. I looked at the clock. I'd fallen back to sleep for over an hour. Shit. I sat up.

'Lacey?' I called out. Maybe she was in the bathroom. Silence.

I got up and pulled back the curtain, couldn't see her anywhere in the parking lot. Weird. Maybe she'd gone over to the diner? No, she didn't have any money. I showered, dressed, did my makeup and hair. Lacey still wasn't back, but I was kind of relieved. She must've gotten a ride when she went for the muffins.

I grabbed my purse from the floor, looked for my

phone on the night table. What the hell? I searched around on the floor, checked in the bathroom, panic beginning to take hold. Did Lacey take it? I went through my purse again – and realized my wallet was gone too. I sat on the edge of the bed, breathless and shaky like I'd just gotten off a roller coaster. She'd taken all my money and ID. Then, an even more horrible thought – my laptop. I looked in my packsack. Gone.

I sat on the floor with my back against the bed, my empty packsack in my hands, staring at it and trying to make my mind believe what I was seeing. I felt around inside the packsack again, hoping for a crazy moment that I was mistaken, that this hadn't just happened. I remembered teaching Lacey how to use my software the night before. I'd told her how my mom had used her vacation pay for the laptop, then I'd saved up for the software. She'd told me I was so *lucky*.

I tried to think how much it would cost to buy new stuff, thought about all my set lists and the beats I'd saved, all my music, all gone now. It would take me forever to replace everything – and Mom was going to kill me. I remembered how excited she'd been when we'd picked out the laptop, how she'd insisted it be brand-new even though I said used was fine – she wanted it to have a warranty.

I pressed my head between my knees, squeezed hard against my temples, and started to cry. Then I thought about how I'd bought Lacey dinner and got mad again. She said she wasn't good at anything, but she was a good thief.

I grabbed my shorts from the day before, checked my pocket. I still had a couple twenties and thankfully my car keys. I went out to my car, searched in the glove compartment and the console, under the seats, and found a five-dollar bill and some change. At least I had a full tank of gas and some food. I was also glad I'd kept my switchblade under my pillow and not in my purse.

I thought over my options. I could call Mom and tell her what happened and she might be able to wire me some money, but she'd freak out and order me home. I walked over to the office. The same woman was behind the desk.

'Did you see my friend in here this morning?'

'That blonde girl? She was hitchhiking up the road last I saw. Got picked up by a car.'

No doubt she was long gone by now. I thought about her using my laptop, reading all my emails, going through my documents. I'd been so stupid.

'Oh, that's good. I wanted to make sure she got her ride.' I smiled. Thankfully there was still a muffin in the basket and a couple of apples. I grabbed one of each, still smiling at the lady. 'Have a great day!'

Back in the room I emptied everything out of my packsack, stuffed it with a spare blanket and a pillow I found in the closet, then took it out to the car. I came back in and packed the rest of my stuff. She had my license plate number, but hopefully they wouldn't notice the missing items right away, or care enough to make a police report. I also took one of the towels and put a do-not-disturb sign on the door.

I drove to the parking lot behind the pub and waited until eleven when I figured it would open. A waitress came out and threw a bag in the Dumpster. I pushed open the back door and walked through, blinking in the dark.

Country music was playing on the jukebox in the corner. The floor was wood, looked old, but it had been painted. Beer coasters were stapled all over the walls and the air smelled of stale booze and cigarettes. Two men at a corner table gave me curious looks. I averted my eyes, wishing I hadn't worn a tank top.

A heavyset woman with short brown hair that had a purple streak in the front and a black T-shirt stretched across her breasts was pouring beer behind the counter. She glanced up at me. 'There's no way you're of age.'

'I'm just looking for my aunt.' I held out the photo of Crystal. 'She has brown hair now. Has she been in recently?'

The woman wiped her hands on a towel, took the photo. 'I think she was here a couple nights this week.'

I felt a little leap in my stomach. Before I could ask

anything else, Owen, the good-looking guy with the Harley, walked behind the bar. He narrowed his eyes when he noticed me. The bartender turned to him, showing him the photo.

'This woman was in here this week, right?'

He examined the photo, taking his time. I wondered if he might recognize Crystal from when he was a teenager – if he was the same guy who helped them – but I couldn't read his expression.

'She have dark hair now?' he said.

'Yeah.'

He passed me back the photo. 'Why are you looking for her?'

'She's my aunt,' I said. 'She's fighting with my mom and took off. I'm trying to find her.'

'You go to the police?'

'No, it's not like that. She just disappears sometimes – she likes to party.' I shrugged like it wasn't a big deal but inside I felt a nauseating rush of fear. What if he told the cops about my visit?

The bartender turned back. 'I remember now. She was sitting in the corner with the boys from the ranch on Tuesday – beer and wing night.' She laughed.

'Boys from the ranch?'

'Gavin, and a couple of the hands from the cattle ranch. They might be back tonight if you want to talk to them.' She'd met Gavin, had even sat and talked with

284

him. It couldn't be the same guy. But maybe he didn't recognize her now with dark hair?

'Did she leave with them?'

'Not sure. Gavin paid for her drinks, I remember that now.'

It didn't sound like anyone had seen her since. Did she go home with him? Then I realized this woman might tell Gavin or somebody from the ranch that I was looking for Crystal. That might screw things up – for me and for her.

'She's probably already back home,' I said with a nervous laugh. The woman went back to pouring beer, but she was giving me a strange look, like she didn't believe my story. Owen, leaning on the bar, was also staring at me.

'If she comes in again,' I said, 'can you tell her that her niece is looking for her?'

'Sure. What's your name?'

'Skylar.'

'Good luck, Skylar,' he said.

'Thanks,' I said, turning away.

I felt them watching me from behind the bar as I walked through the pub and back out into the sunlight.

Chapter Twenty

I drove down to the grocery store and bought some bottles of water and a stale sandwich, ate some of my trail mix. I had to throw out my fruit, which had already turned bad in the hot car, making it smell like rotting sweet apples and bananas. I didn't know what to do now. Where could Crystal be?

I drove around town, looking for her car – even checked at the motel outside town, just in case. I noticed another, more modern gas station with several pumps, and a strip mall with some big-name stores, but no sign of Crystal's car. I showed her photo at the gas station but no one had seen her.

How could I find out if she'd gone home with that Gavin guy? I couldn't just go to their ranch and ask. I still didn't know if he and Brian were the same men who hurt my mom. She'd said the guys took them back to *their* ranch but maybe they had just worked there. I remembered Crystal telling me how they'd been kept in a warehouse. I'd never be able to find it myself.

I decided to give it another day, see if she came back to the motel. If she didn't, maybe I'd call Mom or Dallas and tell them that Crystal was definitely here. They'd take me seriously then. But they'd probably also make me go home – and I'd be in big crap with my mom. I imagined the phone call, the anger and fear and disappointment in her voice, and felt a lurch in my stomach.

I spent the rest of the day parked on a street behind the pub where I could see the back entrance, dozing in the front seat and listening to the CD Crystal have given me. Early evening I did another loop past the motel, then parked behind the pub again. I was starting to give up hope. I hadn't seen anyone who looked like Crystal, and I had no idea what Brian and Gavin looked like.

My bladder was almost bursting and I had to sneak out and pee behind my car, hiding in the shadows. I kept watch for another couple of hours. Crystal didn't show, and I was getting sleepy. I ate my last granola bar, then pulled the blanket and pillow out from the back, reclining my seat so I was more comfortable but could still see the bar.

I heard a vehicle coming down the road, blasting hard-core heavy metal music. I tucked myself lower. It parked right behind me. I pecked over my shoulder, recognized the truck from the garage. Shit. Was it both boys? I didn't know which of them owned the truck. They turned their lights off. Two truck doors opened. The radio was still playing but at lower volume.

'Get a case of Molson, okay?' I could see the dark-haired boy from the light in the cab of the truck. He'd been driving. Another boy I didn't recognize got out of the truck and headed over to the pub.

The dark-haired boy leaned against his truck, looked down at something in his hands. I saw the glow of a cell phone. Someone else got out of the passenger side of the truck and walked around to stand by him. Blond hair in the streetlight. The boy from the garage. They were laughing and talking about some girls.

Motion in the parking lot, the other boy walking out with a case of beer. He stopped to talk to some people in a truck who'd just pulled in. He called out to the guys near me. They walked past my car. I scrunched lower, held my breath. They didn't see me, but they might on their way back. I checked behind me. They'd parked close to my bumper and I didn't have much space between me and the car in front. I heard their voices, still laughing in the parking lot.

Should I climb in the backseat? Too late. They were coming back now and would see the motion. I scrunched down, pulled the blanket over my head.

The voices were coming closer. Stopped near my car.

'Isn't that the car that came into the garage?' How

did they know that? I remembered the pink rabbit foot hanging off my mirror.

'Is someone sleeping in there?'

Rapping on the window. I didn't know what to do. If I ignored them would they go away? They rapped again. 'Hey, you okay in there?'

I pulled the blanket off, sat up, and rolled down the window. 'Yeah, I'm okay.'

'What are you doing in there?' the blond boy said. The new guy, who looked a little older with a goatee, was standing behind them.

'I was sleeping.'

'Where's your friend?' the tall boy said. He had a beer in his hand.

'She wasn't my friend,' I said. 'And she's gone.'

He was looking in the back of my car. I remembered that my clothes were all spread out.

'You mind?' I said, and he gave me a curious look.

'What's your problem?'

'I don't have a problem. Why don't you just leave me alone?'

'Sorry,' the tall boy said. 'It's just the cops patrol around here at night. You might want to find another place to hang out.'

The last thing I wanted was a cop asking any questions – I didn't even have any ID on me, thanks to Lacey.

The tall boy cracked his beer and took a sip. He gave me another look. 'You need money?'

I stiffened. Why would he ask me something like that? 'I'm okay.'

'You're sleeping in your car,' he said.

'Maybe I like camping.'

He laughed. 'My name's Riley.' He pointed to his friends. 'This is Noah and Jason.'

'Hi,' I said.

'You got a name?' Riley said.

'Skylar.'

'Well, Skylar, my dad owns a big cattle ranch. He might be able to find you some work for cash.'

No way. It had to be the same one. 'What's the name of the ranch?'

'Luxton Cattle Ranch.' He said it with pride.

I stared at Riley, trying to think whether I should ask how long they had owned the ranch. I opened my mouth but something held me back. I had this strange feeling, like I knew him from somewhere, or he reminded me of someone, but I couldn't think of who or how. I just felt really uncomfortable.

He was giving me a weird look, waiting for me to say something.

'What's up?' he said.

'I should get going.' I fumbled for my keys in the ignition.

290

'Okay,' he said, leaning down and talking into my open window. 'But if you want some work, just follow the main road past town and make a left after the bridge onto River Bottom Road. You'll see the driveway on the left – go up to the main house, my uncle lives in the lower one. Brian's my dad's name.'

'Thanks for the tip.' I felt a rush of relief when he stood back up. 'You've blocked me in.'

'We'll move. You going to be okay tonight?'

'Yeah, I'm fine.' I forced a smile. He smiled back. They all got in the truck. I watched in my rearview mirror as they drove off.

I parked behind an old school, rolled up my windows, locked the doors. I turned my stereo on, played the CD Crystal had given me. But it didn't work. No matter how I tried to get lost in the beat, I kept seeing Riley's face. He'd been nice, so why was I nervous around him? This town was making me paranoid. I turned off the stereo, ripped out the CD, and tossed it onto the floor. I made up my bed in the back and closed my eyes.

I woke with the sun streaming through my back window, the air warm and stuffy. I stretched my cramped body, felt something bad tugging at my insides. Then I remembered. Crystal was still missing. I sat up, looked around. The car, which had felt safe the night before, now seemed too small, smothering.

I changed quickly, sat on my bumper, drinking my water and thinking about what I should do. If I got a job on the ranch, I might be able to find some sign that Crystal had been there, or that they were hiding something like her car. Then I could call the police. I might even find her. But I was terrified. If they were the same men who had hurt my mom and my aunts, they might hurt me too, especially if they caught me snooping around. I remembered everything Crystal had told me, remembered the fear in her face, the dead look in her eyes.

I had to make sure they thought I had lots of family, people who cared about me, knew where I was – and I'd make sure I was never alone with either of them. I'd carry my knife at all times. I reached behind me into the hatchback, found the knife, and held it in my lap, fiddling with the switch.

I thought about talking to them, how it was going to feel, wondered if I'd be able to go through with it. What if I freaked out or had a panic attack or something? My hand was already sweaty on the blade, my pulse racing. I closed my eyes and focused on Crystal – how much I missed her, how I was the only one who could find her. I let my breath out and put the knife back under my seat, tried to tuck my fear down with it, but it was still clawing at my insides.

I went to the gas station on the highway, took a

sponge bath in the sink, braided my hair, and brushed my teeth. Then I pulled on my cargo shorts, which were a little longer than my other shorts, and a white T-shirt – it was fitted but I figured it was better than a tank top. I wasn't sure what footwear I'd need for working on a ranch, but I slid my feet into my favorite leather flip-flops with the daisy between the toes. My runners were in the car if I needed them.

I found the ranch, which was a long way out of town, on River Bottom Road. My stomach was in knots when I finally saw their sign. The fence up the driveway looked like it had been white at one time but it was dirty and peeling now, the driveway hard-packed dirt that kicked up dust behind me. I passed a second driveway that probably led to Gavin's house. I followed the signs to the office, pasture on either side of me with horses grazing in the fields.

I parked in front of a big blue building beside the house that looked like a utility trailer, the kind you see on construction sites. I couldn't make myself get out just yet, felt like an icy cold hand was holding me down, pinning my legs. I looked around, still trying to gather courage. One side had a small door with a sign for the office. Across the driveway there was a white house with a veranda that wrapped around the front. A few big maples shaded the corner. Someone had put hanging baskets on the front, and a few old tractor tires had some flowers in them on the walkway, but the house looked run-down.

If I sat there much longer, someone was going to wonder what was wrong with me. I wiped my sweaty hands on my shorts, opened my door, and forced my legs to walk forward. I peeked in the window to the side of the office door, noticed a man sitting behind a desk, his head down as he looked at some paperwork. Was it Brian? All my nerves were jangling inside me, making my mouth go dry. I took a deep breath, then knocked.

'Come in,' the man said.

The office was small, with a desk, a couple of chairs, a concrete floor. A coffeemaker perched on a small shelf, almost hanging over the edge, and a mini-fridge hummed in the corner. It was cool in the room, a welcome relief from the wave of heat that had hit me when I stepped out of my car. The man sitting at the desk looked surprised to see me and kind of confused.

'Can I help you?'

He looked a lot like Riley, though his curly dark hair was shorter and had some silver in it. But his mouth and his eyes were the same, and I had that weird familiar feeling again, like I'd met him before. Had I? Then I got it.

He had my eyes, the same dark, almost black eyes that looked back at me every time I looked in the mirror.

No.

I stared at him, taking in all the pieces, moving them around. They slid into place, a tight fit.

He sat there, leaning back, so casual. His right hand rested on top of his desk, fingers tapping impatiently. His pinkie was curved.

There wasn't a Billy, not a summer fling with a blond-haired boy who liked skateboards and reading. None of that had happened. There was this. My father.

'You all right?' he said, frowning.

'I . . .' I needed to think. Needed to be alone and cry. Needed to get the hell out of there, but I couldn't walk out now. 'It's the heat. I'm not used to it.'

He nodded. 'It's a hot one today.'

I had to say something else, had to remember why I was there.

'Your son, Riley, said you might have some work for me.' How could I still be talking, sounding so normal?

The phone rang on the desk. 'Excuse me for a sec.' He picked it up, said, 'This is Brian.' He arranged to trailer a horse for someone, then hung up.

'You from Cash Creek?' His eyes were narrowed, like he was trying to figure out if he'd seen me before. I had the panicky thought that he might recognize me, but told myself there was no way he'd put that together just by looking at me. I curled my hands in my pocket, pushed them in deeper.

I decided to be honest, in case he asked something I couldn't explain. 'I'm from Vancouver.'

'You eighteen?'

'Yeah. Riley said you can pay me in cash.'

'You run into trouble?' He was playing with a pen on his desk, clicking and unclicking it, the sound seeming to echo in the little room.

'Sort of. I got robbed.' I remembered my plan of not making myself sound too vulnerable. 'I just need a couple days' work so I can meet up with my boyfriend.' I thought of Lacey's story. 'He's waiting for me in Revelstoke.'

He stood up and I realized how tall he was, definitely over six feet. He wasn't overweight but his arms in his T-shirt were heavily muscled like someone who'd worked hard all day for years. I tried not to think about him grabbing my mom and my aunts, throwing them down ... He came around and sat on the edge of the desk, gave me another measuring look. I wanted to step back, put space between us, but I didn't want him to know how scared I was.

'You ever work on a ranch before?'

'No, but I used to work at a gym. So I'm really strong.'

'Well, if you want to give it a try, talk to my ranch hand, Theo – he's in the barn. Just walk down behind the house. He might have something for you.'

'Great, thanks.'

He gave me a friendly smile. 'You have a good day, now.'

I looked at my car as I walked by. I could just get in and drive home, pretend it had never happened. Nothing had changed. Mom and Dallas would make a police report about Crystal. They'd find her. Then I saw the flash of sun reflecting off the CD I'd tossed onto the car floor. Crystal needed me.

Theo, an older man in his fifties or so, with gray hair, laughed at my sandals, then found some gumboots in the barn for me. I tried to smile back, worried that he'd be able to see my heart thumping right through my chest, that he'd sense something was wrong. I was having a hard time following his instructions, my thoughts pulling all over the place. I watched his mouth move.

I'd never cleaned out a barn before, never pushed a wheelbarrow, and I learned fast not to load it up too much. I got used to the manure smell. It was hard work – my hand broke out in blisters, my back and arm muscles ached. My bare feet in my boots were sweaty and the heels rubbed with every step.

I kept getting flashes of Brian's face, his voice, his curved finger and dirty hands. I felt like part of me was cleaning the stalls and the other part was standing outside watching, surprised that my muscles were still working. I couldn't believe I was in that town, on that ranch, cleaning a barn while the man who raped my mother was a few hundred feet away. Sometimes I felt dizzy from the thoughts and had to stop and lean against the railing.

I wanted to call my mom, wanted to tell her what I knew and ask her all the questions piling up in my mind. *Why did you lie? Who am I?* But I couldn't, not yet. I didn't want to say the words out loud, didn't want to make it real. I'd never felt anything like this, betrayed, angry, scared, ashamed, and terrified. These were the men who'd hurt my mom and my aunts, who'd kept them trapped for *days*.

I'd tried to look around the barn, but Theo kept coming in to check on me. There seemed to be a couple of barns and some outbuildings. I didn't know how I'd be able to search them. I hadn't seen Gavin yet and didn't know if he was working somewhere on the ranch that day.

Riley came by, leaned his arms on top of the stall door, and looked over at me.

'You doing okay?'

'Yeah, thanks.' I arranged my hands on the shovel so he couldn't see my fingers.

I kept working but snuck another look at his face. We had different noses but we were both fair-skinned, and our mouths were exactly the same, his lips maybe a little thinner. It was like looking in a distorted mirror where everything that was familiar now seemed twisted. I'd wondered if my real father had other children, had thought about sitting up late with big cups of tea, getting to know each other, marveling at all the things in common, laughing at the same jokes.

I didn't want to know Riley. I wanted to walk away, never see him again.

'If you need to go to the bathroom, there's one in my dad's office. Or you can just go behind the barn.' He laughed. 'That's what we all do.'

'Okay.' There was no way I was going near his dad's office again – it was easier to think of him as Riley's father. Not mine. He'd never be mine. I kept shoveling, but Riley didn't leave.

'Sorry if we freaked you out last night,' he said.

'It's all right.'

'We're going to a party later if you want to hang out.'

I stopped. 'Listen, I have a boyfriend—'

'I'm not *hitting* on you. I have a girlfriend.'

'Lucky her.' I started shoveling again.

He laughed, then glanced around like he was making sure no one was listening. 'We've got a keg, and Noah's parents are away.' He dropped his voice. 'Don't say anything to my dad – he'll kick my ass.'

He seemed sort of embarrassed, his face flushed. I didn't know what to say. I wanted to be mean, wanted to tell him I didn't give a crap about his dad, but I couldn't afford to piss Riley off, didn't want him to know anything was going on. And the truth was, none of this was his fault.

'Your dad gives you a hard time?'

'Yeah, you could say that.' He shrugged. 'Parents, what can you do? You just live with it until you can get the hell out. You're lucky you can just do whatever you want now, and go wherever. One more year and I'm gone.'

So he was probably seventeen, the same age as me, and I remembered that he thought I was eighteen. I wondered when he was born, how close in age we really were, how his dad had met his mom. Who would want to get involved with a guy like Brian? Didn't anyone know how dangerous he and Gavin were?

'You don't have to stay working on the ranch?'

'He wants me to, but I've got other plans.' He had his chin held up high, his face kind of angry, but I could tell he was trying to act tough. 'So you feel like coming out and meeting some friends or what?'

'Thanks, maybe another time. I'm pretty tired. City girl, you know.'

He smiled. 'Did you find a place to sleep last night?'

'Yeah.' I wasn't going to share where, in case I slept there again tonight.

He pointed down the hill toward the second driveway.

'There's a creek down that way, if you want to clean up or whatever. It's on our property, just look for the side road off River Bottom Road before you get to our driveway and go through the gate. It's rough, but your car should make it.'

'Thanks.'

'Well, see you around.'

In the afternoon Theo got me to hose down all their tractors and equipment, scrubbing the caked dirt, grease, and manure off. After I was finished I walked slowly back to my car, hot, sweaty, and exhausted – I'd thought I was physically fit but this had used all new muscles. I was so hungry I felt faint. Theo had paid me some cash for the day's work and I planned on getting some food as soon as possible. I was almost at my car, which was still parked in front of Brian's office trailer, when a door slammed shut and a young girl wearing gardening gloves came out of the house. Tall and willowy, with long black hair that curled all around her face, she looked about twelve or thirteen. She looked so much like me at that age I couldn't help staring at her. And she was giving me a curious look.

'Hi,' she said.

'Hi.'

'Are you lost?'

'No, I'm working here.'

She came forward a couple of steps, leaned on a post. 'What's your name?'

'Skylar. I'm friends with Riley.'

'I haven't seen you before. You friends from school?'

'No, we just met.'

Brian came out of his office and I wondered if he'd been watching from the side window.

'Megan, you finished all your chores?' His voice was stern.

'No, Dad.' She went right back inside.

Brian gave me another friendly smile and a nod of his head, but his eyes were cold. I got into my car and drove out of there.

Chapter Twenty-one

I grabbed some food at the grocery store, barbecued chicken and a salad, fruit for the morning, and protein bars to hold me over during the day – without a cooler I didn't have any way of keeping food fresh. I also bought a few bottles of water – at the ranch I'd had to drink from the hose, hoping I wasn't drinking contaminated well water or something. I drove by the motel again, but Crystal's car still wasn't there. If she'd checked in Monday, she'd only have a couple more days.

I didn't know where to spend the night – and I really needed a shower. My feet were filthy from all the dust and my hair smelled like manure. I hadn't seen a truck stop or a public pool around town. Then I remembered Riley mentioning the creek near his house. I headed back toward the ranch and found the dirt road he was talking about. I drove slowly, the car kicking up dust behind me. I had to open a metal gate, drive through, and close it behind me.

I found a clearing on the edge of the creek and parked, got out to have a look around. The creek was shallow, but there were a couple of pools farther down and someone had built a fire. I could see a ring of rocks with blackened wood on the shore, but there weren't any empties or anything.

It was creepy, being alone in the middle of nowhere – I kept looking around every time I heard the slightest noise – but at least it was private. I hoped Riley didn't come down to look for me. To the right of the creek there was an open field with small clusters of trees and the odd big tree standing alone, but I couldn't see any houses. This must be one of the Luxtons' lower fields.

I sat on a smooth rock by the creek, still warm from the sun, and ate my dinner. After I was finished I smoked one of the joints I'd taken from Crystal's. I felt lost without my music, used to always having my headphones on, but now there was a different kind of noise in my head. I was worried about Crystal. I didn't know how I was going to be able to look around more. It seemed like they had hundreds of acres of property and God knows how many outbuildings. Somehow I had to find a way to sneak off the next day. I wondered if I could ask Riley for a tour. He should know if his family had a warehouse. I just had to figure out a way to handle things without making him suspicious.

I couldn't stop thinking about Brian's cold eyes, and what he'd done to my mom and aunts. I didn't want the images in my head, how much more real it all seemed now that I had met him. I felt shattered, like something had broken inside me, but I didn't know how to put myself back together.

I thought about that girl I'd seen who looked like me, wondered whether we had stuff in common, whether I'd like her. I imagined what it might've been like to have a younger sister, and anger grabbed hard in my stomach again.

I'd never have a father now.

I started to cry hard, and I let myself, let it all come out until my face was sore and my eyeballs ached. I felt empty and exhausted, but a little calmer.

I changed into my suit in the back of my car, left my towel on the hood, and found a pool in the creek deep enough for me to wash my hair and shave my legs. It would've been nice to have a swim, but I lay in a shallow pool with my back resting against the rocks and let the current nibble at me. I thought I heard a rumbling down the road, stood up and strained my ears.

It sounded like a truck.

I quickly got out, almost slipping on the algae-covered rocks under the water near the shore. I heard a door slam. Was it Riley?

When I walked up, I saw a tall man leaning against

my car. He was wearing loose jeans, a white T-shirt, and a blue baseball cap with a red logo on it. My step slowed. He had small mean eyes, a wide mouth, with thick lips, a bit of a gut. He looked strong. He smiled, showing lots of stained teeth.

'This is private property, you know.'

'I'm sorry. I'll leave.'

'You Skylar?' he said.

How did he know my name?

'Yeah . . .'

'I'm Gavin, this is my ranch. Heard we had a new girl. How did it go today?'

I tried to answer but my tongue was thick in my mouth. It was him. I'd never sensed so much danger from someone. It rolled off him in waves, a dark and cold energy, dirty like engine oil and cigarettes.

Gavin's smile was fading, his eyes narrowing. I unstuck my tongue from the roof of my mouth and swallowed, trying to get some saliva back.

'Good, thanks.'

I was shivering, my arms wrapped around my body, trying to hide anything he might be interested in. I hated the way he was looking at me, his eyes half-mast, his head tilted to the side, this weird kind of smirk on his mouth.

He picked up my towel, held it out. 'Well, come on, you must be cold.'

I didn't know what to do. Would he try to grab me if I came close enough to get the towel? I thought about the knife under my front seat, kicked myself for not bringing it down to the creek. I couldn't get into the car without passing him.

I walked up to him, slowly. He held out the towel, gave me a friendly smile.

I reached out, ready to run if he moved a muscle, but he stayed still. I took the towel and wrapped it around myself, wishing it was a beach towel and not a small white one from the motel. I moved around to the passenger side of the car.

He had a beer in his hand. 'Want one?'

'No, thanks.'

He pulled a red cigarette pack out of his front pocket, lit a smoke, his head tilted to the side. For a second it looked like he was checking out my legs, but then he glanced away. A shiver crawled over my scalp.

'Riley mentioned you've been sleeping in your car.' He glanced into the back of my car, stared for a second at the blanket I'd spread out. 'He said he told you that you could clean up down here after work.'

So that's how Gavin knew I was there. Why had Riley told his uncle? Was it a trap? I felt a flash of anger at my stupidity.

'I'll leave.'

He picked up the roach I'd left on the hood of my car,

gave me a creepy smile. 'Tell you what, I'll let you stay if you smoke a joint with me.'

I didn't want to smoke anything with him, but he had this angry energy about him. Like if I said no, he'd freak out. I imagined his big hands hitting me in the face, all over my body, his own face twisted in rage.

'Okay.'

He walked back to his truck. I quickly opened my car door and pulled my T-shirt over my head, grabbed my shorts and pulled them on behind the car. I could see him sitting in the passenger side of his truck, his glove box open. He was rolling a joint, but he kept glancing in my direction. When he looked away I reached back into the car, felt under my driver's seat, and pocketed my knife.

My bikini was still wet under my clothes, soaking through my shirt. I wrapped the towel around me. I looked around. No one could see me, and no one knew I was there. I'd thought that meant I was safe. I was an idiot.

Gavin closed his glove box back up, leaned over to turn the radio on. He flipped through a few stations. Country music filled the air.

He left the passenger-side door open and walked back toward me, his tongue flicking out to lick the joint's seam. He glanced up, met my eyes. I looked away. He came around to the front of the car, sat on the hood.

'Come on, don't be shy.'

I took a couple of steps closer but left a few feet between us. If he tried to grab me, should I run for the woods or my car? I should've left the door open. I fingered the knife in my pocket, the cold metal comforting.

He lit the joint and took a long drag, then passed it to me. He stared at me as my mouth circled the end. I looked down while I finished inhaling, passed it back to him.

'Brian said you were eighteen,' he said.

'Yeah.'

'You've got a boyfriend waiting for you in Revelstoke?' He took another drag, coughing on the smoke.

I nodded.

'He doesn't sound like a very good boyfriend, letting you stay out here by yourself.' He shook his head. 'Kids these days, Riley, that fuckhead Noah he's always hanging out with, they don't know how to treat a girl.' He passed me the joint. I noticed his hands, how big they were, the dirt under his yellowed nails.

I didn't say anything, just took a drag, but I didn't inhale much, didn't want to get that stoned. I needed to be sharp in case I had to run for it.

'You get cold or scared down here, you come up to the house and knock, okay? I've got a couch.'

I'd rather set myself on fire than sleep in your house.

'Thanks, I like sleeping in my car.'

'You got problems with your folks?'

'We're in touch. My mom worries if I don't check in every day.'

He gave me a measuring look. 'I bet she does.'

I wanted him to leave, but I didn't know what to say.

'Riley said he might come by later and hang out. Noah too.' It was a gamble – he might already know Riley was doing something else tonight.

'You be careful with those boys. Pretty little thing like yourself shouldn't be hanging around alone with them.'

'I'll be careful.'

His gaze slid down, leveling somewhere around my breasts as he sucked on the joint. His phone rang in his pocket. He pulled it out and checked the call display, his jaw tightening.

He answered. 'The fuck do you want ...?' He listened, his face angry. 'So deal with it ... Okay, okay ...' He ended the call, stuffed the phone back in his pocket, stood up, and handed me the joint. 'You're going to have to finish that for me. My brother needs me up at the ranch – a hose broke in the barn.'

I wanted to cry, I was so relieved, mentally thanking God and whoever else was watching over me. I was getting out of this place and never coming back.

He gave me one last smile. 'Don't forget, door's always open.'

'Okay.'

He walked toward his truck. The glove box had popped open. He made like he was going to close it, but something slid out and hit the floorboard. He picked it up and in the dim light I caught the flash of a bright blue cigarette pack, looked like Player's light – king-sized. That was Crystal's brand.

He got back into his truck and drove off, giving me a wave out the window.

The minute I couldn't hear the truck anymore, I climbed into my car and drove fast back to town. I parked behind the school again, changed out of my damp clothes and into my jogging pants and sweatshirt, and curled up into a ball, but I was still shivering. I couldn't stop thinking about that pack of cigarettes – I didn't know any guys who smoked king-sized – and his pack had been red. I couldn't leave yet. I *had* to find a way to search around his property.

I decided to give myself one more day. If nothing turned up, I'd call Mom and get out of town.

The next morning I cleaned the barn again, then Theo had me picking up rocks in the horse corrals. It was backbreaking work, bending and lifting, tossing the rocks into the wheelbarrow, then dumping them out in a pile behind the barn. My hands were so dried out I thought the skin would crack, and my nails were chipped and broken. I'd never appreciated my job at the gym so much before. I wanted to quit a million times, but I was waiting for my chance. I hadn't seen Riley all day and was starting to get worried that I might not be able to get a tour and ask him about warehouses. I had to find a way to get down to Gavin's somehow.

He'd been giving me creepy looks all day and kept coming into the barn or walking by the corral, though I didn't think he even needed to be there.

'You doing okay?' he'd ask every time.

'I'm fine, thanks.' I'd say, relieved when he'd walk away.

Once he leaned on the corral fence and had a cigarette, smoking it slowly while he watched me.

'Sure is hot out today.'

'Yeah.' I tried to angle myself so he couldn't see my butt when I bent over, but I could still feel him staring.

'Well, I better get back to work,' he said, finally leaving me alone.

Around three o'clock a woman came out of the main house with the young girl who resembled me. They got into a truck and pulled way. The girl gave me a curious look as they passed, then waved. I waved back, my face flushed. Did she notice we looked alike?

I slipped behind the barn to go to the bathroom, and startled when I heard Gavin's voice close to me until I realized he was in the feed room talking to Theo.

'How'd your date go?' Theo said.

'Bitch never showed,' Gavin said.

'Fuck her anyway, right?' Theo said.

'Damn right.' Gavin was laughing – but too hard, like something was just funny to him, his private joke. Theo laughed along but you could sort of tell he didn't really know what was so funny. Gavin seemed like the kind of guy who'd brag, not the kind who'd admit someone had stood him up. He had to be lying. Who was he talking about? I hoped Gavin would reveal something else, but they started talking about the ranch and one of the tractors that had broken down.

'I'll take a look at it tonight,' Gavin said, then he told Theo he had to go check in with Brian, that angry tone back in his voice. I waited behind the barn, peeking around the corner, and watched him walk toward the main house.

He was going to be busy tonight. It might be my only chance, but I had to be sure. When I was finished at five, I washed my hands under the hose, wincing as the water stung my blisters, then got my payment from Theo.

'I heard your tractor is broken down,' I said, trying to keep my voice casual, like I was just making conversation.

'Yeah, Gavin's working on it now. He'll get it fixed.'

'Okay, see you in the morning.'

I was starving but I didn't want to waste time driving into town to get food. I had no idea how long Gavin would be and I had to make this fast. I left the ranch and drove down the driveway, debating what to do. Should I park at the creek and hike up over the field? It was probably more than a fifteen-minute walk.

Once I hit the road I turned right but drove slowly, looking to see if there were any side roads close to the ranch where I could park. I spotted a dirt road about fifty feet down. I pulled off the main road onto the smaller one, going down a couple of feet and parking on the side. It didn't seem to be a driveway, at least there was no mailbox, but I didn't plan on being that long anyway.

As I walked down the second driveway toward Gavin's, I could see the main house at the top of the hill. It was still hot out, the air smelling like dried grass and dust. I glanced around nervously, worried that Gavin was going to drive in or that someone could see me from the house or the road.

Finally I came around the bend in the driveway and saw the second house. It was smaller than the main one, simpler, more like a basic box. You could tell a man lived alone there, with no chairs or flowers or anything on the front porch, just a stack of empties. I could hear country music, like he'd left a radio on inside. It was kind of loud, which was strange, considering he wasn't even home.

I noticed a large building slightly behind the house,

probably a shop or garage. I headed toward it. The front had two overhead doors that I couldn't slide up from the outside, and the side door was locked. I came around the back side and climbed a crate, then stood on a metal barrel and looked through a dirty window. It almost looked like there was a car under a tarp, but I couldn't see the color or anything, couldn't really even judge the size.

I got off the barrel, glanced toward the house. I wondered if it was locked. How long would it take him to fix a tractor? I'd have to be very careful – it might be hard to hear him coming up the driveway because of the radio. I walked toward the back, figuring it would be safer to find a back door in case I had to run for it.

I looked down the road again, listened. I couldn't hear anything, just the country music, louder now that I was closer to the house. I crept onto the porch, praying like crazy that he didn't have a dog. The door was locked, but I noticed a window beside it was open a little, the curtain moving in the breeze. I peeked in. It looked like a bathroom.

I slid the window all the way up. It was stiff and I had to really work it, my hands getting slivers from the old wood. I climbed in, feet first, and landed in Gavin's bathroom. It was gross, the toilet stained, the tile on the floor dingy, like he never mopped the floor. His toothbrush was on the counter, the bristles flat and the handle caked with old toothpaste, which also coated the sink. A razor was lying on its side, little bits of hair scattered all over the counter.

I crept into the kitchen, opened what looked like a closet door under the stairs, right beside his kitchen table. It was a pantry, large enough that you could walk in and move around. The house had an open floor plan – a mark on the floor and ceiling showed where a wall had been – and I could see into the living room. It wasn't very big, but he had a large TV. His couch was sagging, a blanket tossed on the side, and a fan hummed in a corner. The coffee table was old, had a full ashtray, none with lipstick, and a bunch of hunting magazines spread out.

I peeked out the little window at the front door, checking for Gavin's truck. When I turned back around I noticed some steps going down, and another door. Did it go to a basement? I opened it, looked down the dark stairs.

I stood at the top, called out: 'Crystal?'

No answer. I started making my way down the stairs, carefully holding on to the rail, each step creaking and my breath tight in my throat. I found a light on the wall, turned it on. The room was packed with boxes, old bikes, tools, garbage bags full of God knows what, camping equipment.

'Crystal?'

I couldn't see how anyone else could be down there, but I tried to walk around a little, squeezing between stuff, almost knocking over a bunch of boxes. I didn't see any other rooms. I made my way back upstairs.

The country music was even louder inside the house. Was he trying to cover something? It sounded like it was coming from an upper floor. I walked up the stairs, pushing open bedroom doors, calling Crystal's name. It was hotter upstairs, my face was slick with sweat, and the air smelled like sewer and rotten food or something. One of the rooms was empty and the other had an older bed in it, with a blanket in a camouflaged pattern tossed over it, a hunting poster above the bed. It didn't look like it was used often. There was still another room at the end of the hall. Maybe the master bedroom?

I walked down the hall, tried to turn the handle but it was locked. He was definitely hiding something.

'Crystal?' I couldn't hear anything over the radio, which was coming from that room. How could I get in the door? I examined the handle. If I could find a hammer, I might be able to smash it off – he'd know someone had been in his house, but I had to get in that room.

I walked back down the hall – I'd look for a hammer downstairs – and was almost at the top of the stairs when I heard what sounded like a truck door slamming. I ran into the spare room, glanced out the window, which was at the front of the house, and could just see the back end of a pickup truck underneath the overhang. I hadn't heard him over the radio.

I ran down the stairs, almost tripping on a pair of work boots at the bottom. I had to get through the kitchen and out the back door – no, I didn't have time. I could hear the front door opening. I grabbed the handle of the pantry door and ran in, closing the door softly behind me.

I stood still, scared to move and trying to catch my breath. The door had slats in the front so I could peek out. Maybe he was just coming home because he forgot something. I waited, listening to his boots out in the kitchen. I could see his shadow moving back and forth. He was on his phone, sounded like he was ordering parts. So he was probably done working on the tractor for the night.

I crept back a couple of feet, setting my feet down gently, praying that the floorboards didn't creak, and crouched low. I was scared to move around in case I bumped into anything. The door was letting a small bit of light in, and my eyes were adjusting. There were some cans on the shelf beside me. I grabbed one for a weapon and pulled the knife out of my pocket, my hand on the button to flip the blade.

Now I heard pans clanking, a fridge door closing, then something sizzling. The scent of meat and onions cooking filled the closet. Cupboards opening, things being moved around. Then the scrape of a chair being pulled out, sounding close, his body settling down. I realized he was sitting right in front of the closet door, could see part of his shoulder. I held my breath, terrified he'd sense my presence.

He ate for about five minutes or so, scraping his fork and knife against the plate loudly, like he was eating in a hurry, and then he got up. I could hear water running like he was rinsing his plate. He still hadn't turned the music down, and I was surprised he didn't mind the noise. I heard boots going upstairs, right over my head. Did I have time to escape? I tested the closet door, and realized something was in front. His chair from the table? It had gotten wedged under the door handle. I tried to push the door open but could only move it a couple of inches. I reached my hand out, tried to push the chair away, but I was at a bad angle. I needed to give it a good shove, but that would make noise and he might hear me. If he caught me in the kitchen, could I outrun him? He was tall and strong. My best bet was to wait until morning when he went to work.

The music turned off upstairs, startling me. I strained my ears but couldn't hear anything. He was gone for a while, then I heard his footsteps coming back down and passing through the kitchen. He turned on the TV and I could smell cigarette smoke. I needed to pee desperately and couldn't hold it any longer. I backed farther into the corner, slowly unzipped my jeans shorts, and peed on his floor, hoping it soaked into the wood and didn't roll out. It was hot in the closet, sweat dripping down my face and back, and I was thirsty as hell.

Hours later the TV was still on, but I could hear him snoring on the couch. I stayed awake in the closet, counting every moment, every beat of my heart. My legs were cramped, my back aching. I wanted to stretch but couldn't risk making a sound. I kept thinking about the room upstairs, the smell. Was Crystal trapped in there? Was she okay? Finally I drifted off, my head pressed against my knee, but I just dozed in and out, scared to let myself fully fall asleep in case I fell over.

In the morning I heard him get up, fart, and walk to the bathroom. I heard the sound of him peeing, then the shower running. He didn't go upstairs to get dressed. Maybe he put on the same clothes, which was disgusting, but everything about this man was revolting.

He was in the kitchen now, the scent of coffee and eggs and toast drifting into my closet. My stomach growled and I hoped he didn't hear it.

He sat down at the table to eat his breakfast, and I said a mental prayer of gratitude when he stood up and pushed the chair back in this time. I could see him scraping something onto a plate, then he turned around and I heard him walk upstairs. I felt a jolt of shock, followed by fear. I was right. He must have Crystal locked in that room.

A few minutes later the country music started up again. He came back downstairs, sounded like he dumped the plate in the sink, and left the room. It was hard to hear again, but I thought I heard his truck start up. I waited about another ten minutes, then pushed open the door slowly, listened. I couldn't hear anything but the music. I crept out, looked around cautiously, then walked to the living room window, peeked around the curtain. I didn't see his truck out front.

I ran to his bathroom, barely making it to his toilet, and wanted to cry in relief as I emptied my bladder. When I was finished, I tiptoed out, looking around in case he'd come back in, then crept up the stairs. I was at the top, walking down the hall, my pulse beating hard in my throat, my mouth dry. Almost there.

I tested the handle: locked again. I hit the door hard with the side of my fist, called out, 'Crystal?'

I thought I could hear something, a muffled noise, but the music was too loud for me to really tell. It also sounded like there was a fan going in the room. I had to break down the door, but I still needed a tool to knock the handle off.

I was partway down the stairs when I heard it. The front door slammed shut. I froze on the stairs. Had he been outside this whole time? What should I do? Was he coming upstairs or just into the kitchen? I turned around, tried to head back up the stairs, moving as fast as possible while not making any noise. Maybe I could make it into the spare room.

'The fuck you doing in my house?'

Part Three

JAMIE AND SKYLAR

Chapter Twenty-two

Jamie

I've been scared many times in my life, in many ways, but I've never been as terrified as when I realized my daughter was missing. When Emily first called that morning looking for her I thought it was a joke, they were just screwing around. But then I called Skylar's cell, and when it kept going to her voicemail, tried Taylor. She hadn't heard from Skylar since Thursday. It was now Monday.

I sat on my couch, heart thundering in my chest, staring at the phone in my hand. Skylar had had a pink phone when she was a baby. She used to carry it around and have pretend conversations. She'd grown up to be a teenager who never left home without her cell. Panic was sliding in and around, choking me. *Think, where could she be?* I played back our last conversation in my mind, scrolled through the texts she'd sent. She'd sounded happy. And I'd been happy that she hadn't asked about Crystal. A whisper of a thought started creeping in. No. She wouldn't.

I got out my address book, started calling all of Skylar's friends, even people she hadn't mentioned in years. No one had seen or talked to her. A boyfriend? I thought of Aaron, the boy at the gym who was always talking to her. Maybe him? No, she didn't seem interested. Someone else? She'd been secretive lately, lying more. Her sneaking out with Crystal that night. I'd lain awake for hours after I'd brought Skylar home, horrible images of what could have happened to her making my body stiff with tension. What if she'd been hurt? The whisper was back.

Crystal.

I tried her cell. It also went to voicemail.

I searched Skylar's night table, under her bed, her closet, all her drawers, my hands feeling under her pillow, the edge of the mattress, looking for notes, something. Her knife was gone, her packsack, laptop, her favorite flip-flops. Gone. I stood in the middle, looked around at the mess. She'd made her bed. Skylar never made her bed. I remembered seeing her that morning at the kitchen table, kissing her cheek. She'd smiled at me, her cheeks flushed, her eyes flitting away from mine. I'd thought it was excitement.

I logged onto the computer, checked her bank records. She'd pulled out a couple hundred dollars at a bank machine in Vancouver the morning she left, but there hadn't been any activity since. I also checked my Find My Phone app, but it wasn't working. She'd disabled the location services on her cell phone.

One of her ponytail holders was on the desk, some of her hair still twined with the elastic. I picked it up, wrapping it around my finger.

I thought again of that last conversation, how upset she'd been about Crystal. Had she reached her somehow? Had they met up? Maybe at a festival or a DJ event somewhere? Crystal knew I'd never let Skylar go to something like that. She loved being the fun aunt, the one Skylar idolized. I felt anger mixing with my fear, but then it cooled. Crystal wouldn't go that far.

I'd gone to her house the day after Skylar left, looked around. I'd checked on her place when she'd taken off in the past, watered her plants, collected her newspapers. It wasn't unusual, the sudden departure, but I was surprised the dishes were washed, the trash can emptied. I wondered if Skylar had cleaned up. Before I'd left I'd also searched for Crystal's gun. It wasn't there, but I hadn't been worried, had only thought my sister wanted it for protection. *From what?*

The whisper grew louder. Skylar had thought she'd gone to Cash Creek. *What if ... No, don't think that.*

Skylar had probably just gone to a concert, or was DJing at a party somewhere to earn more money for her equipment.

But Skylar had been worried, really worried. She'd been angry at me for not going to Cash Creek. *I can't believe you're not going to look for her . . .*

The whisper became a scream.

I knew where my daughter had gone.

My hands were shaking so much I had to dial the gym's phone number twice. Dallas answered right away.

'Skylar's run away.' My voice was high, the words strained and unnatural-sounding.

'What do you mean?' Dallas sounded wary. 'You sure?'

'I think she's gone after Crystal.' I told her what I'd discovered. 'She must've decided to look for her.' I thought about my daughter alone in that town, felt another wave of horror and panic. 'Can I borrow your car?'

'Crystal wouldn't go back there.'

'It doesn't matter. Skylar thought she did.'

She paused for a long moment. 'I'm coming with you.'

'We can't both leave,' I said. 'What about Patrick?'

'Let me think. We have to tell him something. He'll wonder why we need a couple of days off suddenly.'

'I wasn't on the schedule. Can you tell him you're sick?'

Dallas snorted. She'd probably called in sick once in her life.

'What if we told him Skylar's sick at Emily's cabin and we have to get her?'

'He'll wonder why we are both going – and he knows Crystal took off again.' Dallas took a breath. 'I'll have to tell him part of the truth. Maybe just that Crystal's taken off to Cash Creek and Skylar's gone after her.'

'He'll be worried,' I said.

'Yeah, but he's smart. He knows some bad shit went down in our past, and the less he knows, the less trouble he'll be in for helping us out.'

'Get here as soon as you can.'

We hadn't driven east in eighteen years, but neither of us was admiring the scenery. Dallas was behind the wheel, and I was riding shotgun. While I was waiting for her at my apartment, I'd stuffed a few things into a bag, blindly grabbing clothes and snacks, and pulled out the cash I'd hidden in the freezer in case of emergencies. I also checked Skylar's Facebook page. No status updates since the day she'd left Vancouver, no comments on anyone's wall, no activity. Crystal hadn't updated hers since the night they'd gone to the bar.

Dallas said she'd called Terry, her boyfriend, and told him we were going to pick up Skylar from the cabin because she wasn't feeling well.

'He didn't ask many questions,' she said.

'How was Patrick?'

'He's worried, but I promised we'd be careful and we'd keep in touch.'

I took some deep breaths, told myself that everything was going to be okay, we'd find them.

'Do you really think Crystal's in Cash Creek?' Dallas said.

'I never thought she'd go back, but Skylar was convinced.'

'Crystal was so depressed when I talked to her on Sunday,' Dallas said, 'but I thought it was just her usual shit.'

I stared out at the road, the highway signs flashing by. I'd been annoyed at Crystal, tired of dealing with her crap, angry that she'd involved my kid. 'I should've paid more attention. I can't believe this is happening.'

'We still don't know if either of them is there.'

'Then where are they?'

Dallas sped most of the way and we made the drive in a little over five hours, only making one stop at a gas station in the town before Cash Creek to grab some sandwiches and coffee and fill the car up – we didn't want to have to go to the garage in Cash Creek. Dallas also bought a pack of cigarettes, lighting one as soon as she got to the car. I hadn't seen her smoke in years.

As we got closer to town, Dallas lit another cigarette, her hands shaking as she held the lighter. I was still gripping my phone, my nails digging into the plastic. My body tensed as we passed the garage. A tall, gangly young man with dark hair under a red baseball cap was having an animated conversation with a blond boy. They were laughing about something, the dark-haired boy's mouth open in a big smile. He reminded me of Brian, and I had to look away.

The pub was still beside the garage and I was hit with a new wave of memories: the boy standing outside, his father leading us up the back stairs a week later, the rifle gripped in my hands, the overwhelming fear that the men were coming for us. Those hours after we escaped were still a dark cloud, hazed over with shock and trauma. I hadn't let myself think about it for years, had worked hard to forget everything that had happened. It hadn't been easy.

The first year of Skylar's life had been a blur of sleepless nights and nerve-wracking days when I never knew if I was doing the right thing, all the while knowing I could never tell my sisters how difficult it was, how sometimes I just wanted to run away from it all. Karen kept me sane, took over when it got to be too much. Often I'd take Skylar over to her house just so I could rest for a few hours, and we'd end up staying the night. I'd never told anyone how sometimes I'd wondered if I'd made the wrong decision, if Dallas had been right and Skylar would have been better off with a real mother, a woman who was older and knew what to do. But whenever I felt Skylar's tiny body next to mine – we slept together for years – or I nursed her in those quiet hours, I couldn't imagine my life without her.

As she got older, she started looking more like Brian. Sometimes she'd turn and gaze at me a certain way, her dark eyes sparkling, or laugh in a certain pitch and tone, and for a terrifying moment it was like he was there in the room with us, looking at me. I'd go into the bathroom, shut the door behind me, and run water to cover the sound of my crying. I'd wonder again whether I'd done the right thing, whether I'd made a mistake. But then she'd knock on the door, her little-kid voice saying, 'Momma!' Or she'd push it open, look up at me, and say, 'Why you crying?' and reach for me with her chubby arms for a hug. I'd pick her up and she'd rest her head in the crook of my neck, tickling my nose with the baby-fresh scent of her silky hair, and I'd be filled with such love, such sweet joy.

As the years passed, I didn't see him in her face anymore, didn't hear him in her voice or laugh. She was only my Skylar.

When she started asking about her father I told her the first name that sprang to mind – Billy, my childhood friend. I'd just wanted to give her some sort of happy story she could believe – a story I could also believe.

Once Dallas realized I was keeping the baby, she took over, bossing me around, telling me what diapers to buy, helping me give Skylar baths. But I'd seen the haunted expression on her face sometimes when she was looking at Skylar. I'd seen her turn away and gather herself, coming back with her face calm, like nothing was wrong. But then love had won out with her too. Her fridge was covered with every drawing Skylar had ever made her. She'd come to all her school plays, fretted along with me when Skylar was sick, shopped for days to find her the perfect Christmas or birthday present, then played with her for hours.

Crystal never helped with Skylar, had never really bothered with her much at all when she was a child. I hadn't thought she'd ever really let herself love her like Dallas and I had. But then Skylar had become a teenager, had gotten more into her music and started challenging me on everything, getting in trouble at school. Crystal and her had been drawn together, had become friends.

And now she'd drawn Skylar into danger.

We debated about whether we should try to find Allen at the pub first or see if Crystal had checked into the motel. We didn't know how many were in town now, but we remembered one on the main drag.

'She's not going to want people to know she's here,' Dallas said. 'I don't think she'd have talked to Allen. Least not right away, not unless she needed information.'

'She'd have to stay somewhere, unless she drove straight to the ranch.' I tried to imagine Crystal showing up, gun in hand, and couldn't see it. 'Skylar would need a place to sleep too, but she only took a few hundred out of the bank. Wouldn't she have run out of money by now?' I refused to think about what that meant, was determined to only keep one thing in my mind: Skylar and my sister were okay and we were going to find them soon.

Nothing else was an option.

'Let's ask at the motel before we talk to anyone else,' Dallas said.

We drove there but didn't see either of their cars in the parking lot.

'I'll ask at the front desk,' I said.

Dallas parked the car. 'I'll come in with you.'

A woman was watering plants behind the front desk while she watched a small TV in the corner, shaking her head at something a newscaster was saying. A plastic rack with postcards and homemade greeting cards spun around lazily, pushed by a fan on the floor.

She looked up with a smile. 'Can I help you?'

'We're looking for some people,' I said. 'A woman in her early thirties, blonde and very pretty, and the other is a teenage girl, tall, with black curly hair.'

She was already nodding. 'The girl stayed here one night – stole a blanket and a pillow! The other woman's not blonde anymore.'

I couldn't breathe, couldn't think for a moment. I'd been hoping I was wrong, that she hadn't seen either of them. That they were somewhere else.

'What do you mean?' Dallas said.

'She's got brown hair.' The woman gave us a suspicious look. 'The girl said she was her aunt. What's this all about?'

'Is the woman still staying here?' I said.

'She rented the room for a week, didn't want housekeeping, and I haven't seen her since. She should've checked out a few hours ago. We're going to have to clear her stuff out if she doesn't come back by the end of the day.'

'When was the last time you saw the girl?'

'Friday morning, I guess. She was in here asking about her friend.'

'Her friend?'

'She had a blonde girl in the car with her, but she split the next morning.'

I exchanged a look with Dallas. Who the hell had Skylar been traveling with? And why had she stolen a blanket? Was she sleeping in her car?

'The woman, what name did she check in under?' Dallas said.

335

'I can't give out information like that.'

'We're her sisters.'

'Doesn't matter. I've got to protect the privacy of my guests.'

'The dark-haired girl is my daughter, my *seventeen-year-old* daughter,' I said. 'We need to find out where she went.'

The woman looked nervous now. 'Maybe I should talk to the police.'

Dallas reached into her purse, pulled out a couple of twenties, and slid them across the counter. 'Maybe we can work something out?'

The woman looked at the money, glanced around as she picked it up.

'She called herself Courtney something or other, can't remember the last name.' She looked down at her registration book, flipped through some pages.

'Here it is. Courtney Campbell.'

She'd used her *real* name? What was going on with my sister?

'We'll pay for the room for another night,' Dallas said.

'Room's sixty bucks a night,' she said. 'And that girl stole from me.'

I counted out five twenties and she gave us a key.

We pushed open the door, blinking from the bright light outside until our eyes adjusted. Clothes were strewn around, some shoes in the corner, and the bed was still unmade – there'd been a do not disturb sign on the door. Crystal's old suitcase was in the closet, one of her T-shirts tossed onto the bed. I pressed the shirt to my face, smelling her perfume, the scent faint but so familiar it brought tears to my eyes. Where was she?

Dallas was in the bathroom.

'Her makeup bag's still here,' she called out.

'Crystal would never take off without her makeup and it doesn't look like she's been back here for days. I think we need to talk to the police.'

'They'll want to know why they came here,' Dallas said, coming out of the bathroom.

'If Skylar's looking for Crystal, she's been asking around about her. God knows what she's been telling people – or who she's been talking to.'

'That's why we need to stay calm and think this through,' Dallas said. 'We don't know what happened at this point.'

'If Brian's figured out who Skylar is ...' I couldn't finish the sentence.

'There's no way he could, and Skylar could be on her way home, for all we know. Crystal could've hooked up with someone you know how she is.'

'She wouldn't do that in this town.'

'We don't know *what* she'd do. When she's in one of her fucked-up moods all bets are off. That's why we shouldn't jump the gun just yet.'

I thought about how Crystal had used her real name. She definitely wasn't thinking straight.

'So what's our next move?' I said.

Dallas thought for a moment. 'Let's ask at the restaurant first. Maybe someone saw something.'

Chapter Twenty-three

Jamie

We snagged a seat by the front window. The restaurant was starting to fill up, loud with clanking noises from the kitchen, the cook yelling out orders. The air smelled of burnt toast.

'Be with you in just a minute,' a waitress with black hair and blunt-cut bangs said as she walked by with some plates for another table.

I glanced at my watch, feeling restless, agitated. It was only quarter after four, but I wanted to find the girls before it got dark, didn't want to be in this town at night. I looked around the room at the other diners and caught my breath when I saw the back of a tall man with dark curly hair and a baseball cap. My heart started to race. I tried to find my voice to warn Dallas, but I couldn't speak.

Dallas was giving me a strange look. 'What?'

'Is that . . . '

She turned to see what I was looking at, then sucked in her breath.

The man looked to his left and I caught his profile.

'It's not him,' I said. But Dallas was still staring, like she couldn't hear me. All the color had gone out of her face.

'It's not him. Hey, look at me.' I grabbed her shoulders, forced her to face me. 'It's not *him*.'

She finally met my eyes, heard my words. Her face relaxed, but her breath was still rapid. 'Jesus,' she said. 'I thought . . . I thought he was going to turn around and see us . . . '

'I know.' I looked around for the waitress. I needed water, had to get rid of the acid taste of fear in my mouth.

'Do you think he still works there?' Dallas said. She was staring out the window at the garage. The boy I'd noticed earlier glanced toward the diner as though he felt us watching him.

'I don't know,' I said. 'But we should find out.'

The waitress came back carrying a coffee carafe and menus for us. 'Sorry about the wait, ladies. Coffee?'

'That'd be great,' I said. 'And some water, please.' While she poured coffee into the cups on our table, I added, 'You didn't happen to see a teenage girl in

340

here recently, did you? She's tall, with black curly hair.'

'Oh, yeah, she was here with her friend a few nights ago.'

I felt a stab deep inside, pain mixed with hope.

'Her friend?'

'A pretty blonde girl.' The waitress laughed. 'She was talking the head off the other one.'

'Did you hear what they were talking about?' I said.

'No, but the dark-haired girl asked me about Owen.' She pointed across the street. 'He was outside working on his Harley.'

We both looked at the pub. Owen. He was still there.

'Does his dad still own the pub?'

'Allen passed away about ten years ago. Owen's been running it ever since.' She gave us a curious look. 'You girls from around here?'

'We've been through a few times.'

'The girls you asking about okay?' the waitress said.

'Yes, one of them is my daughter.' I gave her a pained smile. 'You know how it is with teenagers.'

The woman smiled back. 'Got two girls myself.'

'If she comes in again, please let us know.' I wrote my cell number down on a napkin, passed it to her.

'Sure thing, sweetie. Maybe talk to Riley and Noah over at the garage. They know lots of the local kids.'

'Thanks. We'll do that.' As she walked off I looked

341

at Dallas. 'Who the hell is this girl Skylar was traveling with?'

'Maybe she picked up a hitchhiker.'

'Should we ask about Crystal?' I said.

From the corner of my eye, I noticed the waitress bend down and say something to a table full of women. They glanced in our direction.

Dallas had also noticed. 'I think we should just get out of here.'

'Let's talk to Owen,' I said.

We dropped some money on the table for the coffees and left before the waitress could come back. I worried that Brian and Gavin would hear that two women were looking for a runaway girl. What would they do if they had her?

Don't go there. We don't know what happened yet.

We pushed open the door and were instantly hit in the face with the smell of beer, greasy pub food, and body odor. The music was loud and lots of the tables were full. Men watched us walk in, shoulders hunched as they leaned over their beers, hats pulled low, faces leering. I glanced around, nervous that Gavin or Brian could be in the pub. A woman with a purple streak in her hair looked up from behind the bar as we got closer.

'What can I get you ladies?'

'We need to talk to Owen.'

342

Her gaze flicked over us. 'I'll see if he's available.'

She came out from around the bar, walked down the hall, and disappeared into a room on the left. She came back out a minute later.

'He's in the storage room.' She pointed down the hall.

'Thanks.' We walked down to the room I'd seen her enter. The walls were lined with bottles of liquor, the floors stacked with a few kegs. A man with shoulder-length blond hair was crouched down, making notes on a clipboard.

He glanced up at us. 'Can I help you?'

I froze, staring into his eyes. He cleared his throat, startling me out of my thoughts. 'Do you remember us?' I said.

He stood up, his body filling the small space. I stepped back, bumped into Dallas, who was standing slightly behind me. His eyes locked on mine, the moment stretching out, then realization spread across his face.

'You're those girls.'

He was a lot taller than when we'd met him years ago, his legs long in faded blue jeans, a black leather belt with a Harley buckle wrapped loosely around his waist, reminding me of his father. He'd filled out, too – his arms and shoulders in his white T-shirt looked like they were solid muscle. He had a beard, slightly darker than his hair, which he ran his hands through as he stared at us.

'We better go into my office,' he said. We followed him farther down the hall. I noticed the back door, the stairs leading up to the apartment, and pushed away the memories, the fear. We filed into his office. He sat down at an oak desk, which had seen better days, the finish worn off in spots, but it was organized. His pen holder was a piston, and he was using a model of a Harley as a paperweight. A huge shelf against the wall beside him was stacked with books.

'Close the door,' he said.

As I shut it behind me, I noticed the woman at the bar watching. She glanced away. When I turned back around, Owen was looking at me.

'I always wondered what happened to you ...' His face was curious, then turned worried, his eyebrows pulling into a frown. 'What are you doing here?'

'We're looking for my daughter, Skylar – she's seventeen, tall, has black hair. We think she might be looking for our sister Crystal.'

'Yeah, Skylar came in here, said she was looking for her aunt.' It was strange to hear him say her name.

'Had you seen Crystal?' I said.

'She was here a couple of nights this week. The bartender said she was sitting with Gavin and some of the guys from the ranch. Shit ...' He sat up straight. 'I didn't know who she was.'

I stared at him. She'd been talking to Gavin? Was she

fucking nuts? He must not have known who she was, at least not at first. What had she been thinking?

'Does Brian still work at the garage?' I had to force the name out.

'He runs the ranch with Gavin now – they live on the property.' He looked back and forth between us. 'What are your names?' he said.

'I'm Jamie,' I said. 'This is Dallas.'

'Do you know where Skylar went after she talked to you?' Dallas said.

'No idea.' He shook his head. 'I'm sorry.'

'What about Crystal? Did you see her leave?' I said.

'No, the bartender didn't either.' He met my eyes. 'Why is she back here?'

I looked away, my face flushing. The room felt hot, the walls pressing in on me. I remembered him helping that night, his eyes staring at our wrists.

'We don't know why she's here,' Dallas said. 'But we'd appreciate if you kept this to yourself for now.'

'The waitress at the diner said we should talk to Riley and Noah at the station,' I said. 'Do you know anything about them?'

'Yeah, they're good kids. But Riley's Brian's son.'

The tall boy with the dark hair. Skylar's *brother*.

'Does he . . . does he have any other kids?' I said.

'A daughter, around twelve years old. Riley's

seventeen.' He looked hard at me. 'Skylar said you and your sister had a fight.'

'Our sister has a few problems,' I said.

'Is she looking for more? Because talking to Gavin is a good place to start. He's bad news.'

'We know,' I said.

'There's been talk about him getting rough with women over the years. Nothing's stuck, but he got arrested a few times. Brian, since he got married, he's calmed down some, but I've heard he's a real asshole to his wife and kids.' He looked at me steady, his eyes narrowed. I held my breath, waiting for him to ask how old Skylar was, to put it together, but he just said, 'You think Crystal and your daughter got tangled up with them?'

I didn't know how to answer, my mind still racing over everything he'd said, panic hitting hard and deep in my guts.

'We don't know what happened,' Dallas said. 'We just know those men are dangerous.'

'Have you talked to the police?'

'Not yet,' I said. 'We were hoping to find Skylar and Crystal first.'

'We know the Luxtons have that big ranch,' Dallas said. 'Do they have any other properties? Maybe an old warehouse?'

I felt light-headed, could almost smell the rotten fruit, the musty mattress.

'The Luxtons own a lot of land,' Owen said. 'I think they have some out toward Armstrong. What are you looking for?'

'We're not really sure yet,' I said. 'We just wanted to get a sense of what we're dealing with.'

'We should talk to Riley and Noah,' Dallas said. 'They might know something.'

'Be careful,' Owen said. 'Whatever you tell them will get back to Brian.'

'We will,' I said.

'If I can help in any other way, let me know, okay?' Owen wrote his cell number down on a piece of paper and handed it to me. 'I live right upstairs.'

'Thanks,' I said, standing up.

'I'll let you out the back.'

Chapter Twenty-four

Skylar

I scrambled up the stairs, but one of my flip-flops caught on the edge of a step and I fell, landing hard on my knee. I kicked the shoes off and bounded up the last few steps, taking them three at a time, heavy footsteps thudding behind me.

I was in the hallway, my hands reaching for the spare bedroom door, when Gavin hit me so hard in the back I was slammed into the wall. He wrapped his arm around my throat, pressing against my windpipe. I fought for breath, feeling like every bone in my throat was being crushed. I tried to get my knife out of my pocket but his right hand gripped my arm, bending it behind my back. I reached over my head with my left, smacked the heel of my hand into his nose.

'Motherfucker!' His grip loosened.

I jammed my hand under his arm and pushed out fast, forcing him to release me, then spun around and kicked him in the crotch.

He dropped to his knees, cupping his groin.

I pushed past him and started running for the stairs, digging for the knife in my pocket. I could hear his steps. He was on his feet again.

'You fucking bitch!'

I was leaping down the stairs, knife in hand. I was almost at the bottom, but he was too close. I could feel him behind me, heard his breath wheezing out. My head snapped back. He'd grabbed my hair. I lost my balance and fell hard, the edge of the steps hitting my lower back. Pain shot up my spine.

His arm was around my throat again as he tried to drag me up, but this time I used the knife to stab at his forearm. He yelled and let go. I got to my feet, jumped down the last couple of steps, sprinted through the kitchen. He was following, fast. I was almost at the front door.

I was grabbed around the waist, tackled to the floor, his weight on top of me, squishing all the air out of my lungs.

He gripped my wrist, slammed my hand over and over into the floor, bent my fingers back until I had to let go of the knife. He picked it up.

I took in a strangled mouthful of air, clawed at the floor with my free hand, trying uselessly to pull my body away. I shrieked, 'Help!'

His hand slapped down over my mouth. I tried to bite the hand but it was pressed too hard and I couldn't get my teeth onto any skin. My mouth filled with the bitter taste of salt and grease. His other hand was holding my wrists behind my back. I kept kicking out, hearing grunts every time my heels connected with his legs, the blows sending shock waves of pain up my shins.

He leaned down, spoke into my ear. 'I'm going to move my hand. If you make one noise or kick me again, I'm shoving this knife into your guts, hear me?'

I whimpered.

He pulled me to my feet, his left arm around my neck, holding me in a headlock. He walked me backward, half carrying me, his arm pressing hard against my windpipe. We were in the kitchen. I glanced around for a weapon, saw the pans drying in the rack, but I couldn't reach them. I flailed out with my arm, lunging in the direction of the pans. He pulled me back with the arm around my throat, making me gasp for breath. I scratched at his arm, tried to pull it off.

'You move another muscle and I'm slitting your throat.'

I froze. Should I try to fight anyway? I heard a drawer open.

Suddenly his left leg was coming around the front of mine, sweeping my feet out from under me. I fell onto the floor, my bones jarring. I tried to scramble away but a boot stepped hard onto my back and pressed down for a few seconds, crushing. Then he was kneeling on the back of my legs, holding me in place. My arms were wrenched painfully behind me. Sounds of tape unwrapping. He bound my wrists, pinching the skin, making my watch dig in. My shoulders strained, the muscles tearing.

His weight shifted, and the pain in my legs eased as he stood up. He gripped my bound wrists.

'Get to your feet.'

I got to my knees, and he pulled me up the rest of the way.

He wrapped his left arm around my shoulders, holding the knife to my throat with his other hand, pressing the cold blade against my skin.

'We're going upstairs. If you try anything, I'll cut your throat.'

I was frantic as we walked up the stairs. If I smashed my head back I might be able to break his nose, but then he'd probably stab me. We were in the hallway now, moving toward the closed bedroom door.

I was almost hyperventilating, my breath getting stuck in my throat, making me choke. *Calm down, you have to calm down.*

351

He was going to kill me.

We were at the door. He lowered the hand with the knife, and I heard jingling noises behind me, like he was digging for keys in his pockets.

I only had a second. I smashed my head back, felt a hard thud, blinding pain down my neck. He must have been looking down and I hit the top of his head.

'You stupid bitch!'

He grabbed the back of my hair, slammed my head into the doorjamb, stunning me. I felt my knees give out and hit the floor.

I tried to get onto my feet, but my legs weren't working right. I collapsed onto my stomach, fighting to stay awake, my vision blurring.

Sounds above my head, a key going into a lock, the door opening.

Hands were gripping my shoulders, dragging me into the room. I was groggy, floating in and out. I tried to focus, told myself to fight, but my body felt sluggish, my legs and arms not working properly.

Rough hands flipped me over, hauled me up to sit with my back leaning against the wall. The room spun, my vision coming in and out for a moment.

'Wake up! You've got some questions to answer.'

I focused on Gavin's face in front of me, my vision clearing, then looked around frantically, getting quick snapshots of images. It was dark – the window seemed to be boarded over, the only light coming from the open doorway.

There was a big bed, and in the middle, a body. I could only make out a figure, saw movement as though someone was struggling to get up. Then I realized whoever was on the bed was tied to the wooden bedpost. The figure stood.

Crystal.

She was naked, her hair straggly and matted. Rope was tied around her neck like a collar and leashed to the post. Her face was contorted in fear. She was gagged but not with tape, looked like some sort of fabric, and her hands were tied behind her back. I screamed, the sound shrieking out of me. I tried to get up to run to her but Gavin pushed me down. He grabbed my face, grinding my teeth together.

'Shut the fuck up!'

I couldn't get my breath, my body heaving with each gasp, snot dripping out of my nose and mixing with the sweat rolling down my face. Crystal looked frantic, pulling on her leash as far as she could. She was down on her knees, shoulders shaking as she cried.

'*Shut up.*' Gavin let go of my face and slapped me hard. I still couldn't stop screaming and he slapped me again.

I tried to get my breath under control, whimpers

leaking from my mouth. My body was vibrating, something warm pooled under my legs and I realized I'd peed myself. Gavin looked down.

'Jesus Christ.' He looked at Crystal. 'What the fuck are you doing? Get back on the bed.'

She didn't move, still staring at me, her eyes panicky and full of tears.

Gavin walked over and slapped her hard in the face.

I screamed as her head rocked back. He turned and glared at me.

'You scream like that again, I'll shove my foot down her throat, get it?'

'I'm sorry. Please don't hurt her!'

Now he was looking back and forth between us, his eyes narrowed, and I realized my mistake. He'd figured out that there might be a connection between us. He walked over to the stereo, which was sitting on an old wood dresser, and turned it down. Then he flipped on the light.

I could see it all now – the plastic bucket in the corner, the messy bedding, the pale blue blanket ripped and stained – and gasped when I got a better look at Crystal. Marks covered her breasts and stomach, looked like bites. Her face was bruised, her top lip scabbed and puffy.

'I said, get back on the bed,' he said again. She climbed onto the bed, watching us with a horrified expression on her face.

He came back to where I was sitting. Knelt in front of me.

'Why were you in my house?'

'I was going to rob you.'

'Bullshit.' He looked at Crystal, then at me. 'You two know each other?'

'No,' I said. He stared at me. I tried not to look away, but his eyes terrified me.

He walked over to Crystal, grabbed her rope leash, and pulled her off the bed. She stood up, and he turned her to face me, standing directly behind her. He started to pull the rope tight around her throat.

'Who the fuck are you?' he yelled at me.

Crystal was trying to shake her head, signaling me not to say anything, but her face was turning red, her eyes bulging.

'She's my aunt!' I yelled back, sobbing.

Gavin let go of the rope. Crystal fell to the floor, wheezing for air.

'Your aunt.' Gavin stared hard at my face again, realization spreading across his. He came closer, grabbed my chin, turned my face side to side.

'How old are you?'

Crystal was shaking her head again. Gavin stood up, took a lunging step toward her, and kicked her in the ribs. She cried out, curled into a ball.

'Stop!' I yelled. 'I'm seventeen.'

He walked back toward me, crouched down so he could see behind me. I felt his hand on mine, bending my fingers.

'You're his kid.' His face was so close to mine I could smell his breath, coffee and cigarettes. 'Which bitch is your mother?'

Tears filled my eyes. I'd screwed everything up.

'The youngest one.'

I couldn't read his expression, anger but almost a weird sort of triumph, then it turned mean. My body tensed, waiting for the blow.

His phone rang. He stood up and took it out of his pocket, looked at the screen, then answered it. 'Yeah, I'll be there in a minute.' He stared at me while he listened. 'I said I'll be a fucking minute. Had an issue with the truck . . . No, I fixed it.' He ended the call, shoved the phone back in his pocket.

Suddenly he kicked me hard in the side. I cringed against the wall, trying to get away from his heavy boots. He glared down at me.

'You can thank your daddy for that.'

He left the room, locking the door behind him. I was shocked he hadn't tied me up. As soon as I heard his footsteps going downstairs I got to my feet and hobbled over to Crystal, who was still on the floor. I dropped down beside her and got our bodies close, even though we couldn't wrap our arms around each other. I could feel how frail her body was, how she'd lost weight. We pulled away, looked at each other.

'I'm so sorry,' I said. 'I messed up. I was trying to rescue you.'

She was making grunts and moans behind her gag, her eyes questioning. I had no idea what she was saying.

'Mom and Dallas don't know I'm here. I ran away.' I was crying, realizing how stupid I'd been. 'But when I don't come home she'll figure it out. They'll come looking for us.' I prayed it was true. But Mom wasn't expecting me home until Thursday. What would happen to us until then? Would they kill us?

Footsteps coming back up the stairs, sounds of the door unlocking. I cringed beside Crystal. She pushed me behind her with her shoulder, like she was shielding me.

'Isn't that sweet,' Gavin said when he walked in.

He was carrying a coil of rope, some fabric, a bottle of water. He took off the cap and held it to my lips, letting me drink, but he poured it so fast it bubbled out of my mouth, making me choke, running down my body.

'You shouldn't waste that, going to be awhile before you get more.'

He threw the bottle into the corner of the room near the door. Then he grabbed my arms and dragged me to my feet, walked me toward the end of the bed.

He set the fabric down on the blanket, put the rope around my neck, like a lasso, and tied the other end to the bottom bedpost, wrapping it around under where the railing joined so I couldn't slide it up. He checked the length to make sure I couldn't reach the door or the stereo, pushed the bucket between me and Crystal, who was tied to the same side of the bed but on the opposite end.

'Here's your shitter.' He stood in front of me, grabbed my face again, squeezing with his hands. 'Where's your car?'

'I hitchhiked here. It ran out of gas in town this morning.' I said it fast, my words mangled because he was still squeezing my face. 'I left it on the side of the road.' I had another idea. 'The cops will probably impound it.'

'Bullshit. You were in my house all night.' He shoved his hands in my pockets, grabbing at my ass and crotch, his face so close to mine I could see every bead of sweat, the dark stubble, the faint scar on his chin, his bloodshot eyes.

He pulled out my keys, jingled them in front of my face.

'You think I'm stupid?'

I shook my head. 'No!'

'I pulled my truck behind the shop to grab some tools. If I hadn't come back in, you'd have screwed everything up.'

358

'I just wanted to find my aunt,' I said.

'Well, you found her.' He smiled. 'Now where's your fucking car?' He gripped my face again, making tears come to my eyes.

'I told you. It's in town.' The car was my last chance at being found.

He let go of my face, and for a second I thought it was going to be okay, he'd believed me. But then he walked over to Crystal, spun her around, and bent her over the bed. He pulled hard on the leash around her neck, making her back arch. She was making horrible sounds behind her gag, muffled screams and cries.

'You want to try again?' he said over his shoulder to me. He gave the leash another tug.

'It's on the side road!' I shouted. 'Let her go!'.

He yanked on Crystal once more, then released her. She collapsed onto the bed, slid down to the floor.

'What road?' He turned back to me. 'Don't lie to me again.'

'It was on the other side of the main road, close to the driveway.'

He nodded, like he knew the spot, then picked up the bundle of fabric and walked toward me.

'I won't scream,' I said when I realized he was going to gag me again.

'You girls always scream,' he said.

He shoved the fabric in and tied a long strip around

359

my head, holding it in place, then knotted it at the back of my head, pulling it tight. It made my lips feel like they were being stretched wide. I gagged a few times, choking on the cloth.

He stepped back, looked at the both of us, and smiled big, showing all his yellowed teeth. 'I'll see you girls tonight after work. We'll have a party.'

He walked over to the stereo, which was an ancient-looking ghetto blaster covered in beer stickers, and turned up the country music, then gave a little jig at the door and pretended to tip his baseball cap at us.

He flicked off the light and closed the door. I couldn't hear him locking it but I saw his shadow under the door, then it disappeared.

I turned to Crystal, who was still sitting on the floor. I could just make out her shape in the dim light – some sun was streaming through the cracks in the boards on the window and underneath the door. My eyes were adjusting to the dark and I could soon see her better. She looked defeated, her shoulders slumped.

I tugged at my hands, twisting them in different directions, straining at the tape, but he'd tied me tight. I tried to walk closer to Crystal, hoping she could use her hands to untie the gag around my neck, or my rope, but he'd been smart and only given me enough to get within a foot of her. I met her eyes.

She was shaking her head, her face sad. Then she

screamed into her gag, a harsh, raw animal moan of despair. Her face red, and tears rolling down her face.

I dropped to my knees and gave over to my own tears.

Chapter Twenty-five

Jamie

The boys were working on a truck, both their heads bent over the engine. They heard our feet on the concrete and looked up.

'Can I help you?' the dark-haired boy said, wiping his hands on a rag. He had to be Riley. I couldn't get over how much he looked like Skylar, the way he moved, how his mouth lifted when he spoke. He also looked like Brian, but softer somehow. Dallas was staring at his face too.

Riley looked confused now, waiting for us to speak. I found my voice.

'We're looking for my daughter – her name is Skylar.'

His eyes widened, and he glanced at his friend, then back at us.

'Skylar?' he nervously licked his lips. 'Did she, like,

run away or something?' I searched his expression, looking for signs that he was faking his question, trying to act innocent, but he looked genuine.

'Yes.' Not sure what she might have told them, I decided to keep it simple. 'She took off a few days ago. No one has seen her since.'

Riley glanced at Noah, then back at me. 'She was working up at the ranch, but I don't think she showed up today. Least she wasn't there when I left this morning.'

She'd been working at the *ranch*? I felt like I'd been punched in the guts with steel gloves.

'When did you last see her?' I said.

Riley was hesitating, like he knew something but was scared to say it.

'It's really important we find her,' I said.

'Yesterday after work.'

'Do you know where she was going?'

'No, but I think she was sleeping in her car. I told her she could swim at the creek on our place but I don't know if she went there.'

The creek. Memories flashed – running, falling to the ground, Brian's body on top of me. *Focus on Skylar.*

'Did you tell anyone else she was going there?' I held his gaze.

'No.' But he'd looked away. He was lying, I was sure of it.

'And you have *no* idea where she might be now?' I

363

said, still staring hard at Riley, wondering if he knew what kind of man his father really was.

'No, I told you,' Riley said, but he didn't sound annoyed, more worried, like maybe he was just figuring out he might've been the last person to see Skylar.

A car pulled up in front of the garage.

'I've got to help these customers,' Riley said.

'If you think of anything else, please give us a call.' I scrawled my number quickly across the back of a pad of invoices lying on the bench.

'Hope you find her soon,' Riley said as he ran out.

As we were walking back to the motel, I said, 'We have to tell the police Skylar was working at the ranch – and what the men did to us.'

'They're going to have questions.'

'We just have to tell them enough so they know Brian and Gavin are dangerous,' I said. I wasn't sure how I was going to be able to speak about what had happened to us, but I had to somehow find the strength.

'I don't trust Riley,' Dallas said.

'You think he could be involved?'

'We know his dad's fucked up, and he was nervous. Something's weird.'

Could we have it all wrong? Could it be Noah and Riley who did something to Skylar? But why would Riley admit he'd seen her?

'That's why I want to talk to the police,' I said. 'They'll be able to figure out if he's lying.'

'There's a risk they could start looking into our past.'

'They have no reason to at this point, no way of knowing about Dad.' I still had nightmares sometimes, could hear him calling me 'Peanut.' I would stay awake for hours, replaying that last night, wondering what would have happened if I'd just injured him, where we'd all be now. And I often worried about what Skylar would think if she ever found out. I told myself that I'd had no choice, but I was haunted by the idea that everything that had happened in Cash Creek was a punishment somehow, that our lives had been broken that day.

'We need to make sure we have our stories straight,' Dallas said. 'And whatever we do, we can't let them know Crystal had a gun.'

We walked into the station together. It was an older square building with white wood siding, looked like it had been built in the seventies and smelled of burnt coffee. It wasn't very big, and only a few police cars were in the parking lot. On the way we'd talked over a few things they might ask, worked on our cover story, but we knew it was the things we weren't thinking about that might screw us up.

I told the woman behind the counter that we wanted to report some missing people, and an officer came out a couple minutes later. He introduced himself as Sergeant McPhail and led us to a small interview room with a table and a few chairs. He sat on one side, the two of us across from him. He was an older man with snow-white hair, brown eyes with eyebrows that slashed down at an angle, a long nose, and a stern mouth. He reminded me of an eagle, the way his eyes stared intensely at one of us, then flicked to the other. I got the feeling he didn't miss much, which was good if it meant he could find the girls faster but bad if he sensed we were lying about parts of the story.

'You want to file a missing persons report?' he said, making notes on a pad of paper.

'Yes, my daughter and our sister,' I said. 'We live in Vancouver, but they were staying here at the motel.'

'Their names?'

'Skylar and Crystal Caldwell. Skylar is only seventeen.' I curled my hand into a tight fist, digging my nails in hard, focused on the pain.

'When did you last hear from them?' he said.

'We haven't heard from our sister since Sunday. Skylar texted me after she left Thursday morning, but I haven't heard from her since and their phones are just going to voicemail. We went to the motel ... ' I couldn't go on, kept seeing Crystal's shirt lying on the bed like she'd planned on coming back at any minute.

'Crystal's things are in her room,' Dallas said, 'but

the lady at the motel hasn't seen her all week and she should've checked out today. Skylar stayed only one night there. We think she started sleeping in her car after that.' Usually it pissed me off when Dallas stepped in and spoke for me, but this time I felt a wave of gratitude that she was there, that I had her strength to lean on.

'Was Crystal's purse in the room?' he said.

'No,' I said.

'Why were they in Cash Creek?'

'Eighteen years ago we passed through town ...' My skin was on fire, my face burning hot. For a minute I couldn't find my breath, felt like a hand was clamping down over my mouth. I wondered if I was having a panic attack. 'Our truck broke down.'

'Brian Luxton and his brother picked us up and took us back to their parents' ranch so we could make some money,' Dallas said, speaking fast and angry. 'They attacked us one night and took us to an empty warehouse. They raped us. They kept us there for five days.'

The sergeant sat up straight in his chair, his eyes watching us intently.

'Did you report it?' he said.

'We were too scared,' I said. 'We just wanted to get away from this place. What the men did to us—' I broke off, caught my breath. 'It's still very hard for us to talk about.'

367

'We don't want to press charges,' Dallas said. 'We just want you to know that they're dangerous. We believe Crystal came here to confront them, and Skylar followed. We think Brian and Gavin have done something to them.'

'We know Crystal was at the bar at the same time as Gavin Luxton, and we know Skylar was working at the ranch but she didn't show up this morning,' I said. I told him everything we'd learned from Owen and Riley.

'You need to search their properties,' Dallas said.

'Before we can do anything, I need some more information from you,' the sergeant said. 'What were the girls driving?'

'Skylar has a red Honda Civic, and Crystal drives a black Acura.'

'Do you know what they were last wearing?'

I shook my head. 'No. But Skylar was probably wearing shorts and flip-flops. She has a leather pair with a daisy on them, between the toes.' I swallowed hard against the tears building in my throat. 'She wears them all the time. Crystal often wears yoga shorts and tank tops.'

'We'll find out if the motel has a surveillance camera. We'll also ask local businesses in the area. I'll need a recent photo and the girls' descriptions, names of their friends, any associates or employers.'

I gave him Crystal and Skylar's details, their dates of

birth, names of their friends. 'I have some photos on my phone,' I said.

'Can you email me?' He gave me his address and I sent him the photos.

'Crystal's hair is dyed brown now,' I said.

'Where's Skylar's father?'

'He's not in her life.'

He looked up, met my eyes briefly. I wondered if he was going to ask for her father's name or contact information, but he just made a note.

'How did Skylar seem the last time you spoke to her?'

'She was upset and worried about her aunt, but she told me she was going to stay with a friend at her lake cabin. She lied to me.'

'Has she run away before?' he said.

'Skylar's never done *anything* like this,' I said.

'What about their lifestyle? Any medical conditions? Drug use?'

I thought about what to say. 'Skylar's a good kid. Crystal's had a few problems, but she wouldn't just disappear on us.'

'You said Skylar was worried about her?'

If I told him the truth, would he not take things as seriously? Would he just think Crystal was a flake or a screwup? I had to say something.

'Crystal had something upsetting happen to her that weekend, a fight with a guy she was dating. We think that opened up some of her feelings about what happened to us when we were teenagers, and that's why she came back here.'

'Any indication she may be suicidal?'

I thought about Crystal locked in the bathroom, a gun in her hand.

'No.'

He made another note. 'You said you went into her motel room. Did you see any signs of a struggle?'

'No, but it was messy,' I said.

'We'll check it out – don't enter the room again.'

'We'll get another room at the motel.'

'I'm going to need their cell numbers – we'll ping their phones.'

'What does that mean?'

'If they don't have GPS, we can see where their phone last bounced off a cell tower and triangulate the signals. It will give us an indication of where they might be located, but if there isn't any cell coverage or their batteries are dead, it won't help us. We'll still get an idea of where they might've been recently.'

'That's good,' I said, starting to feel hopeful they'd find them soon. I glanced over at Dallas. She gave me a small smile.

'We'll pull their text messages, but that might take a couple of days to get from the phone company. Their description and vehicle will be entered on CPIC, the

Canadian Police Information Centre. We'll also notify other detachments.'

'When will you talk to Brian and Gavin?' I said.

'As soon as possible. We still need to go through the process. I understand your concern about the men, but we can't pigeonhole our investigation because of your bad history with them. If we put all our focus on them and they don't have the girls, we'll have wasted a lot of time and the girls could still be in trouble.'

'Will it be on the news?' I said.

'We probably won't release it to the media right away. We'll start our investigation and see what we discover by canvassing. If the men do have them, we don't want them to react in a dangerous manner.'

'You're worried they might kill them,' I said, a stab of fear thrusting deep into my guts. I stared hard at his face, trying to find some hope, reassurance.

'We just want to proceed with caution at this point,' he said.

'You *need* to find that warehouse,' I said, frustrated by all these delays. I knew who had the girls. I just needed him to find them.

'There are too many in the area, so that's just not practical use of our manpower. We need to canvass, talk to people, and see what other leads turn up.'

'So you're just going to walk around?' Dallas said, her tone making it clear she was not impressed. 'That's going to take too long.' I loved her for her bluntness, her ability to say exactly what we were both thinking.

'We're going to do everything we can to find them quickly. If you hear anything, let us know, and we'll keep you posted. I'll give you my cell number.'

'What should we be doing?' I said.

'Call their friends, see if anyone has heard from them. If you decide at a later date that you want to press charges against the men for the assault, we can pursue that matter. Right now let's focus on finding your daughter and sister.'

I walked out of the station with Dallas on shaky legs, the heat coming up off the pavement making me feel sick. When we got to the car, Dallas opened the doors.

'We should let it cool off for a minute.'

We leaned against the side, the metal hot against my back even through my shirt. Dallas's hair was damp at her forehead, her eyes red-rimmed. She lit a cigarette, taking long inhales, her fingers pinching the cigarette like it was a joint.

'You okay?' she said, her shoulder bumping against mine.

'Yeah. What about you?'

She nodded, took another drag of her cigarette. It was so familiar, the way she held it, the tilt of her head. I felt like a kid again, watching my big sister.

'Give me one of those,' I said. Dallas passed me a cigarette and the lighter. I hadn't smoked since I'd found out I was pregnant. I felt the smoke burn down my throat, my head instantly light from the rush of nicotine. I blew the smoke out, studying the police station, still trying to get a grip on my emotions. I felt busted open, scraped raw, dirty, like I wanted to take a long shower.

'I wonder what they'll think after they start talking to Crystal's friends and co-workers,' I said. We both knew the cops might find out Crystal was always taking off and getting into trouble.

'I don't know, but they still have to see it through.'

'I'm pissed they can't just search the ranch.'

'Hopefully the men will screw up on something when they talk,' Dallas said. 'That's all it takes sometimes. Then they can get a search warrant.'

I wanted to think positive, but I couldn't shake the terrible feeling that we had just exposed ourselves and put Skylar in even more danger.

'What if he's right? What if the guys do flip out and they kill the girls?' I put my head in my hands, took some deep breaths, trying to get a grip.

'You can't think like that,' Dallas said, resting her hand on my shoulder. 'The cops will find them. *We'll* find them.'

I looked up, met her eyes, and gave her hand a squeeze, grateful again that she was there with me, then

373

took a hard drag of my cigarette. 'I still can't believe Crystal came to this hellhole again.'

'I can.'

I turned to her. 'You've thought about killing them?'

'Haven't you?'

I remembered the rifle jamming in my hands, Brian down on the floor.

'Yeah. I've thought about it.'

Chapter Twenty-six

Skylar

I turned my head away from Crystal and closed my eyes tight. I couldn't believe we were both trapped. I should've just left the night Gavin found me at the creek. If I'd called my mom or the police, they might've been able to find Crystal. My chest was so tight it felt like someone was squeezing it. I couldn't get a breath. I sucked desperately at the air. *Stop, Skylar, just focus, see if there's a way out.*

My body shook as I looked around frantically at the door, the boarded-over window. I could see sheer curtains at the top, in a burnt-orange color. They must be hanging on the other side of the boards. If anyone looked, they'd just see the fabric.

I'd never be able to rip the boards off with my hands

tied. I tried to wiggle my hands over my butt, so I could slide my legs through, but he'd rotated my arms when he taped them, forcing my back to arch painfully. I couldn't bend my arms enough to step through. Crystal was watching me, her expression sad.

The country music was giving me a headache. He hadn't turned on the fan and the room was sweltering, making the odor coming off the bucket even worse. I had to try hard not to throw up. My lips were already hurting, and my tongue felt swollen. I was thirsty and I wondered if I'd die of dehydration.

I stood up and looked around the room again, trying to focus on the details. The bed was in the center of the back wall – the only window was on its left side. Crystal was sitting on the floor in a small stream of light, watching me. The foot of the bed, where I was tied, was closest to the door. It looked like there was a closet to the left, with two bi-fold doors. A closet meant coat hangers, which we could maybe use for weapons or something, but we had to get there.

The dresser was in the opposite corner from me, near the closet. The room itself was fairly large, obviously the master bedroom. I could make out a deer head and a few paintings on the wall, hunting scenes.

He liked to kill things.

I sank to the floor, my back against the mattress, and pressed my head into my knees, my mind spinning with panicked thoughts. What would he do with my car? What was he going to do to *me*? I looked at Crystal again. She had her arms wrapped around her legs, but I could still see the bruises on her body. Would Gavin rape me too? Did Brian know Gavin had Crystal? Did Riley know?

I thought about my mom. What would she do when I didn't come home Thursday? Would she call the police right away? Would it be too late?

I'd been so stupid. I thought of all my lies, how clever I'd thought I was to disable the location services on my phone, throwing her off track.

I tried to stay calm, tried to think what my mom would tell me to do. *Wait, Skylar. Think. Plan your escape. Don't give up. I'll come find you.* It comforted me, thinking of my mom searching. She was smart; she'd know what to do. They'd track Crystal like I did, they'd talk to the lady at the motel, they'd find out somehow that I'd been working at the ranch, they'd get the police to search for us.

Then I thought about how Gavin had looked at me, how he'd realized I was Brian's daughter. Would that change things? Maybe Brian would let me go? My hopes plummeted. Of course he wouldn't, not after I'd seen Crystal. If he knew I was his daughter, he might even kill me sooner.

He wouldn't want anyone to ever know about me

*

As the hours passed, the room got hotter, the stench from the bucket making my eyes water and my stomach surge into my throat. Flies buzzed in the window and into the bucket, an incessant hum. I couldn't stop thinking about water, how good it would taste, how dry my mouth felt. I hadn't eaten for twenty-four hours.

We were both sitting with our backs against the bed. Sometimes Crystal would rest her head on her knees, like she was sleeping. A few times I caught her watching me, tears in her eyes. I wondered what she'd been doing every day, imagined her lying on the bed, sleeping or staring up at the ceiling, wondered if she'd been hoping we'd rescue her or if she'd just wanted to die. I felt another wave of shame. It was my fault that she was here, and now it was my fault she didn't get rescued. I *had* to find a way to get us out of here.

I studied the bed, the bottom of the posts, hoping there were some wheels we could get off, some metal parts I could use to slice the tape, but it was solid wood. If I could get to the fan I could use the cord to choke Gavin, or maybe bash him over the head with the stereo, but both were out of my reach.

I stood, motioning for Crystal to do the same. I leaned down and pressed my shoulder into the side of the mattress, pushed with my body. She understood quickly what I was trying to do and started pushing. We used our bodies to shove the bed toward the other wall.

I was closer to the fan and stereo, but they were still a frustrating foot away no matter how hard I strained.

We pushed the bed back into place. My bladder ached from holding on for so long, pains shooting through my stomach. I hooked my thumbs in the back of my shorts and tried to shimmy them down so I could use the bucket, but they were too tight. I had to pee my pants again, feeling ashamed and dirty. Crystal looked away, like she was trying to give me privacy. I tried not to think about it, tried to focus on escaping.

I wondered if Crystal had tried anything yet and wished we could talk. What should I do when Gavin came back? Try to fight or beg for my life? I had to get him to untie me somehow.

The room was even hotter, sweat dripping between my shoulder blades, my hair wet at the back of my neck and my forehead. My shorts were damp and uncomfortable. I could smell the sweat and urine on my body. Flies were walking around the edge of the bucket, some landing on Crystal, crawling on the bite marks, but she didn't move, not even a twitch. I worried she'd get an infection, then I thought maybe she didn't care anymore, maybe that's how she'd been surviving. She'd looked terrified earlier, but now she just seemed kind of out of it.

Flies were buzzing near me now, circling and landing on my jeans shorts. I wiggled my body, trying to get them off.

I remembered the waitress telling me about the record heat waves in the Sunshine Valley. *Gets so hot around here you can fry an egg on the sidewalk.* Was Gavin just going to leave us up here to die of starvation or dehydration? I imagined my body turning to a husk, my skin cooking, the flies eating at my eyes.

The hours passed slowly. He had to be getting off work soon. I strained my ears, wondering if I'd hear his footsteps over the music. I figured I was in some sort of shock, my body breaking out into waves of shivers, and then a numb feeling coming over me. I felt faint sometimes, my head woozy if I moved too fast. It was weird not being able to talk to Crystal. She'd cry sometimes, looking at me, then I'd start crying too.

It felt late in the day now, seemed like I'd been trapped for hours and hours, but I'd lost all sense of time. I had my head resting on my knees when I noticed the doorknob turning. I looked up with my heart beating fast.

Gavin walked in, gave us a smile as he turned down the music. He was still wearing work clothes, his jeans covered with dirt, his red T-shirt stained with big sweat circles under the arms. He smelled like manure.

He was also carrying a couple of sandwiches, the bread squished in his big hand, and two bottles of water.

'Sorry I'm late, girls. Had some business to take care of. Goddamn, it's hot in here.' He set the water and sandwiches on the dresser, took his baseball cap off, and rubbed at his sweaty hair. 'Miss me?'

I glared at him. Crystal was watching, a nervous expression on her face.

He sniffed at the air. 'You girls stink.' He came over with the water and the sandwiches, squatted in front of me, sniffed again. 'Guess you couldn't get your shorts off, hey?'

He undid my gag. I inhaled deeply, finally able to suck in a big lungful of air. My mouth was sore from being stretched for so long, my tongue thick and swollen. I licked my dry lips, the salty sweat at the corners of my mouth.

He reached up and grabbed one of the bottles, fed me the water. I sucked at it desperately, trying not to let any spill out, swallowing it all down. When the bottle was empty he shoved a sandwich into my mouth, let me take a bite. It was dry, tasted like old meat and cheese, but I bit and chewed as fast as I could.

He replaced the gag then moved on to Crystal and repeated the process. Then he stood up, threw the bottles toward the door, and came over to me.

'Get on your feet.'

Fear rushed through my body. Was this it? Was he going to kill me? I glanced over at Crystal. Her eyes were terrified again.

'Don't look at her.' He gripped my arm, pulled me

to my feet. 'I found your car. You won't have to worry about the cops impounding it.' That mean smile again.

His hands were at the front of my shorts. I screamed behind my gag, tried to step backward. He grabbed my rope leash, gave it a quick snap. The rope tightened around my throat.

'Unless you want more of that, stand still.'

I froze, tears forming in my eyes and dripping down as he undid my button and zipper, staring into my face, his tongue licking his lips.

He stepped back, lowered my shorts, leaning over slightly, his face brushing against my crotch. I closed my eyes. My body was shaking violently.

'Lift your feet.' I lifted them one at a time. He took off my shorts, threw them into the corner. 'Going to have to burn those.'

I felt him step closer, felt the heat of his body. He put his finger inside the waistband of my underwear, and I flinched. He circled his finger around to my lower back and then the front again.

'You like that?'

My eyes were still closed. I was crying so hard I wondered if I'd suffocate.

Now he was pulling my underwear down, slowly. He let out a whistle.

'Aren't you sweet.'

He made me lift each foot again. I kept my eyes

closed, didn't want to see him staring, didn't want to see the look on his face. Something landed in the corner, probably my underwear. I heard him step back.

'Open your damn eyes.'

I opened them, my whole body heaving with sobs.

'Your daddy was being a right prick today.' He reached out, gave me a hard slap across my face. I stumbled backward, trying not to fall onto the bed, my face stinging from the blow.

I heard noises, like Crystal was screaming into her gag. Gavin lunged toward her as she ran at him, hit him hard in the chest with her shoulder.

He grabbed her and threw her onto the bed, sprawled on top of her. Her legs were kicking at his backside. He slapped her hard a couple of times, the sick sound of flesh meeting flesh ringing through the air. She stopped kicking.

I screamed helplessly into my gag, tried to get closer, wondering if I could use my rope and get it over his head and choke him, but I couldn't reach that far.

He had one forearm pressing down on Crystal's throat, his other hand undoing his jeans. I sank to my knees, turned my back on the scene, and closed my eyes. I chanted over and over in my head, trying to drown out the noises, the sound of the bed slamming against the wall, animal grunts from Gavin.

It's going to be over soon. We're going to get out of here.

We'll find a way. My mom is going to find us any minute. She'll kill him for this.

Finally Gavin let out a groan and was silent, the sound of his breathing filling the room. I could hear small whimpers from my aunt. My eyes were shut tight, holding back tears that leaked out anyway. I thought about my mom and Dallas, how they'd lived through this. I hadn't really understood before.

I heard Gavin get off the bed, the sound of his zipper.

Footsteps coming closer now. I heard him squat in front of me, felt his presence. I opened my eyes, braced for him to slap me.

'I've got to get ready to go out, but you and me, we've got a date later.'

He turned the music up, gathered the empty water bottles, and left. I got to my feet, looking for Crystal on the bed to see if she was okay. She rolled on her left side, so that her back was facing me. Her shoulders were shaking.

I wanted to comfort her, but I couldn't do anything. I slid back to the floor.

I thought Gavin was gone for the night, but he came back a little while later, rifle in his hand. I scrambled to my feet. I heard Crystal move on the bed and glanced at her. She was in a sitting position, her body turned to the side like she was trying to shield herself. He wasn't even looking at us, though.

384

He walked over to the stereo, turned the music down. He seemed agitated, his movements jerky, his face flushed and his breath heavy like he'd run up the stairs. He walked back to the door, then turned around.

'You two make one sound, I'll kill you.'

He locked the door again. I heard his footsteps going down the hall, then another door opening. He must be in the spare bedroom. I remembered how the window looked out to the front of the house. Was someone coming?

I heard a vehicle pull up, a car door slam shut. Knocking on the front door.

The doorbell rang. I waited, expecting Gavin to run downstairs, but I didn't hear his footsteps. Was he going to shoot whoever was at the door?

Silence for a few more minutes, then knocking on the back door. It sounded like it was almost right under our window.

A voice called out, 'It's Sergeant McPhail with the RCMP. We'd like to talk to you for a minute, Mr Luxton.'

I wanted to scream – help was so close. I looked at Crystal. She was on her feet, staring at the window. I motioned to her that we should try to lift the bed. Maybe if we dropped it a few times the posts would make some noise, but she shook her head, looking toward the door. She was right. Gavin would hear.

A couple of minutes later, I heard a car door slam again, then the sound of the car driving away. I felt desperate, helpless. We'd been so close.

Gavin came into our room. He still looked nervous, but his breathing wasn't as fast as before. He paced around a bit, glancing at us every once in a while like he wasn't sure what to do next. He stopped and looked at us.

'You bitches are lucky,' he said. 'You get to live a little while longer.'

He turned the music back up, flicked the light off, and left the room.

I sank back down to the floor. No one was going to come now.

Chapter Twenty-seven

Jamie

We drove back to the motel when we were finished at the station and rented a room close to Crystal's.

'I don't want to just sit around waiting,' I said.

'What do you want to do?'

'Maybe we should stake out the ranch, see if they leave.'

'We can't – not if that sergeant is heading out there.'

'Then we should try to find the warehouse. But I don't know how.'

'I saw a flyer up at the station,' Dallas said. 'It was for a town barbecue in the park today at five. There'll be lots of locals there, right?'

I glanced at my watch. 'It's almost seven.'

'They had a band playing too. Might go on for a while.'

387

'Think we should ask around?' I said.

'Someone might've seen them in town. Maybe it's like that cop said, we shouldn't rule anything out, you know? We could at least ask people to check their properties and see if anyone knows of any old warehouses.'

'It's worth a shot,' I said. 'But what if the men are there?'

'We'll get the hell out as fast as we can.'

Balloons and streamers were strung up at the park and a country band was playing on a small stage, a few couples dancing to the music. It looked like some of the booths were being dismantled, but a few still had barbecues going and people were handing out small plates of samples. You could tell things were winding down, the garbage bins were overflowing and litter was scattered on the ground, but there were still quite a few people standing around or sitting on picnic tables.

The officer had called to tell me he'd gone out to the ranch, but neither of the men was home. He was going to try again later. We kept our eyes peeled for them as we walked around, showing a photo of Skylar and Crystal that I had on my phone to people in the lines, asking if anyone recognized the girls or knew of any abandoned warehouses or buildings in the area. No one knew anything.

Disheartened, I was turning away from one booth, when a man stepped in behind me.

'Heard you were asking about some girls?'

I looked up. 'Yes, we—'

Brian. Those black eyes, the small mouth.

I glanced down, tried to think, but my nerves were on fire, everything in my body telling me to run away. 'We're . . . we're hoping someone might have seen them.' I stared at my feet. *Please, please don't recognize me.*

'That a photo?' He had his hand out for my phone. He must've seen me showing it around. I couldn't refuse now.

I passed him my cell, noticed his chipped nails, remembering them digging into my thigh. I felt shaky and light-headed, my skin clammy. I was worried I might be sick. Glad I was wearing sunglasses, I tried to see where my sister was. Dallas had a beer in her hand and was walking my way. I had to warn her somehow, but she wasn't looking at me, she was staring at her phone.

Brian was talking, 'Pretty girls. I haven't seen the blonde, but the dark-haired one worked at my ranch for a couple of days.' His voice was casual, almost pleasant and friendly. 'I'm sorry. I didn't know she was missing.'

I was stunned he was admitting he'd seen Skylar, and that she had even worked at his ranch. I didn't know how to respond.

Now Dallas was next to me, still looking down at her phone, her warm arm bumping into mine. 'I was thinking we should talk to some of the regulars at the pub,' she said. When I didn't answer, she glanced up from her phone and said, 'What do you—' She stopped as she noticed Brian, gave a little gasp.

He looked back and forth between us, his face confused as he registered our fear. The moment stretched out, settled around us. His eyes narrowed, his gaze lingering on our faces. Then the flash of recognition, followed by shock.

He stared down again at my cell in his hand, like he was trying to understand what was going on. I could see his gaze focus on Crystal.

He looked back at us, handed me the phone. 'If I see them around, I'll let you know.' He walked toward a small group where a woman seemed to be waiting for him. Her soft brown hair was pulled into a low ponytail, some of it coming loose around her face. She looked sweet but a little haggard.

A tall girl was standing beside her and I sucked in my breath. She could have been Skylar's twin a few years ago. The girl was younger, maybe twelve or thirteen, and they had different noses and a slightly different face shape, the girl still with the round face of a pre-teen, but there was no doubt they were related.

As he got closer Brian paused, watching someone walking toward him.

Gavin.

He was heavier now, his belly rounded, and wearing sunglasses and a baseball cap, but I'd recognize his walk anywhere. He had on a white T-shirt with a Budweiser logo, faded jeans, cowboy boots. He moved quickly, like he was late or something, his skin flushed and sweaty.

Dallas was staring at him, her face pale. She swayed on her feet, and I grabbed her arm.

'You okay?'

She wrenched her body free and started walking so fast she was almost running back to the car. I pushed through the crowd, trying to catch up. I kept glancing back over my shoulder at Gavin. Brian met him partway, said something.

Gavin turned around, and looked straight at us.

I got to the parking lot, my breathing loud in my ears.

'Those fucking assholes,' Dallas said.

I leaned against the side of the car, the solidness, the hot metal, reassuring, but my legs still felt weak.

'The way he was staring at the photo?' I said. 'He looked *surprised*, Dallas.'

'I know. Let's get out of here.'

Chapter Twenty-eight

Skylar

When Gavin left there was still some light shining through the boards on the window, but the bedroom was mostly dark. I could make out Crystal's shape on the bed. I wished we could at least touch. I felt ashamed sitting on the floor, in just my T-shirt and no underwear, hated having to use the disgusting bucket.

I tried to be hopeful. A policeman had come to the house. He might come back. We just had to figure out a way to signal that we were inside. But I didn't know what we could do that wouldn't alert Gavin. Maybe we'd get lucky and he'd come back when Gavin wasn't home. We could try to knock something over, or ram the bed into the wall. It felt like a good idea, and I clung to it.

Police meant *someone* was looking for us. I had to believe that.

After what felt like a couple of hours, Gavin opened the door and flicked on the light. I closed my eyes against the sudden brightness, waited for them to adjust, then looked back at him. Something was different, I sensed it right away. A weird energy was radiating off him, anger but also excitement.

It was the excitement that scared me the most.

He walked in a few feet, his body swaying like he was really drunk. His eyes were glassy, his face sweaty. He was holding a beer.

'Shit's hit the fan, girls.'

Gavin turned the music down, paced in front of us, staring at us as he took swills of his beer. He set the bottle down on the dresser by the stereo and lit a cigarette, leaning against the dresser as he watched us. He was thinking about something, but I didn't know what. My body was crawling with fear.

Sounds outside, like a truck pulling up.

Gavin stood up straight. 'What the fuck?'

He walked out of the room, closed the door, but I didn't hear it lock this time. I heard his unsteady steps down the stairs, then another man's voice.

'Where the hell are they?'

Brian?

'Get out of my house, you asshole.' Gavin's voice, thick and slurring.

'I know you have them,' the other man said. Sounds of boots walking downstairs. Doors opening. Was he checking the basement? More arguing in the kitchen, then boots running up the stairs – and heavier ones following behind.

I stared at the door, terrified and hopeful. Was someone going to rescue us? What was going on?

Boots running down the hall, stopping at the other rooms, doors opening and closing, then our door burst open.

It was Brian. He stopped still, stared back and forth between me and Crystal, his face shocked. I stayed huddled on the floor, trying to cover myself.

Gavin came in behind him, his chest heaving. 'Get the hell out of my house,' he said, giving Brian a shove in the back.

Brian spun around. 'You *idiot*. You have them *here*?'

'Screw you,' Gavin said, walking toward the bed. I strained my neck to the side, watching him. What was he going to do?

He sat beside Crystal, making the mattress sag, and put his arm around her shoulders. 'You remember our little friend.' He pulled her face close, gave her face a wet kiss. 'She missed us.'

'You have to get rid of them,' Brian said.

'I'm not doing anything.'

'The police are going to come here, you dumbass.'

'They already did.'

'Are you shitting me?' Brian said, his face enraged.

'I didn't answer the door.'

'They're going to come *back*.'

'Doesn't mean they can search my place.'

I looked back and forth between the men, their anger scaring me. It made the air feel thick and dangerous.

'How the hell did you even find them?' Brian said.

'This one found me,' Gavin said, smiling down at Crystal. 'She had plans to kill us, but I got her first. The other one broke into my house.'

Brian was shaking his head. 'I can't believe you brought this shit onto our property. You're going to get us arrested. I have a wife and kids, you asshole.'

'You have more kids than you know about,' Gavin said with a sneer.

'What the hell are you talking about?' Brian said.

Gavin walked toward me, grabbed me by the hair, and pulled me up. Then he turned me toward Brian.

'Don't you see it?' he said, his voice mocking.

'See what?' Brian looked me up and down, his gaze lingering between my legs. I wanted to cover myself, hating that I was standing there half-naked in front of my father, who was staring at me. I started to cry.

'The other one is her aunt,' Gavin said.

'So fucking what?'

'So she's your fucking *kid*,' Gavin said, letting go of my hair and moving to stand beside me. I tried to slow my sobs, tried to catch my breath.

Brian stared at my face. 'Bullshit.'

'She looks just like Megan,' Gavin said, his mouth twisting into a satisfied smile. 'And she has a fucked-up finger like you.'

Brian looked at me again, studying my face. 'Jesus Christ.'

'The young one was her mother. You took her cherry and gave her a daughter.' Gavin laughed. I flinched.

'Why did she come here?' Brian said.

'Looking for her.' He pointed at Crystal. 'I checked the registrations in their cars. Names are Crystal and Skylar Caldwell. They live in Vancouver.'

'So that's where the bitches ran off to,' Brian said. 'They sure looked terrified to see us tonight. Scared the shit out of me, too.'

My mom and Dallas were in *town*? I felt a surge of hope, then fear. What did Brian mean, they were terrified? What had happened?

'What did you do with their cars?' Brian said.

'They're in the garage.'

Brian shook his head slowly, his mouth opening, then closing, like he was so furious he couldn't find the words. 'You goddamn fool.'

'Relax. I've got a plan,' Gavin said, staring at me again. 'It's freaky how much she looks like Megan,' he said. 'Your girl's going to be a looker.'

Brian glared at him with a disgusted expression.

'What kind of sick fuck are you?'

'She's not *my* daughter.'

'If I ever catch you looking at Megan like that, I'll beat the shit out of you.' Brian glanced at me again. 'Give her some pants or something.'

'Jesus Christ, you're a pain in the ass,' Gavin said, but he walked over to his dresser and pulled out some boxer shorts. He brought them over to me, made me step in each leg and pulled them up, then turned to Brian. 'That better, asshole?'

Brian was staring at Crystal on the bed, his eyes half-mast and his face thoughtful. He looked at Gavin. 'We'll take them to the warehouse tomorrow afternoon – after Theo's gone. I can't do it tonight. Jenny's waiting.'

'I like them right *here*.'

Brian grabbed his brother by the throat and backed him against the wall. I moved away as far as the rope let me, wondering if they were going to fight.

'We're taking them to the *warehouse*,' Brian said. 'I don't give a shit what you do to them there, but they're not staying here.'

He let go of Gavin, who rubbed at his neck, his face red. 'Screw you, Brian. I'm not taking orders from you.'

397

Brian took a lunging step toward Gavin, his fist raised in the air like he was going to hit him. Gavin stumbled backward.

Brian dropped his hand. 'Don't go anywhere tonight and stay away from those other bitches.' He walked toward the door, never even glancing back at me once. There'd still been a part of me that had hoped when he realized I was his daughter he might help me, might feel *something*. But I was nothing to him.

He just wanted us gone.

After Brian left, Gavin paced the room, his face furious and his hands clenched. 'Fuck you, Brian,' he said, weaving on his feet. 'Who the hell are you to tell me to stay home?'

He stumbled toward the stereo, turned the music up, then walked out, flicking off the light before slamming the door.

In the last second of light, I noticed the beer bottle sitting by the stereo.

Chapter Twenty-nine

Jamie

I sat on the bed, staring out the window at the garage. I could see Riley's red cap as he ran out to a car. I turned back to Dallas, who was lighting a cigarette.

'What if we were wrong?' I said. 'What if they don't have them?'

'Where else could they be?' she said.

'I don't know, but his face . . .'

'I know. He was shocked.' She took a long drag of her cigarette. I motioned and she tossed me the pack. I lit one.

'The cop asked if Crystal was suicidal,' I said. 'She was in her bathroom with that gun. What if she came back here to . . .' I couldn't say it.

'I used to worry about it every time she went on one

of her benders or took off for days,' Dallas said, 'but she always came back.'

'This is the first time she came *here,* though,' I said. 'What if she wanted to *die* here?' I held her gaze, hoping I could see something that would make me feel better, make me believe that it wasn't possible, but she just looked worried.

'We can't think like that,' Dallas said. 'Let's just sit tight and wait for McPhail to call. They might find their cars soon or someone who saw them.'

Waiting was agony. I paced, watching the clock. After an hour, I called, but McPhail's phone went to voice-mail. I left a terse message.

'Nothing?' Dallas said, and I shook my head.

Another hour ticked past.

'Let's get something to eat,' Dallas said. The last thing I wanted to do was eat, but it was better than this end-less pacing and staring out the window.

'Let's order something and bring it back to the room,' I said, and Dallas crushed her cigarette in the ashtray and stood.

The pub was full. I scanned the crowd, searching the faces. Strangers stared back at me with curiosity. Lots of guys wearing baseball caps, but none of them were Brian or Gavin. Still, I was uneasy as I took a seat next to Dallas at the bar.

'Can I get you something?' Owen said.

'We'd like to order takeout,' I said.

He handed us menus, then poured us a couple of shots.

'Looks like you girls could use something a little stiffer,' he said when I looked at him.

'Thanks,' I said, but pushed mine away. Dallas drank them both.

He gave us a smile and walked back down to the cash register. We ordered burgers from the waitress, a younger one this time with messy blonde hair, too much makeup, and a pierced nose.

Owen came back awhile later and leaned his hands on the bar in front of us. 'You girls doing okay?'

'We're hanging in there,' I said.

'Any news?' he asked.

I glanced at a man sitting at the end of the bar, staring up at the TV screen in the corner, and lowered my voice. 'Nothing yet, but we made a police report.'

'Sergeant McPhail's a good cop. He'll find them.'

'Thanks.'

The waitress brought us a couple of Styrofoam containers. 'Here you go, ladies.' She moved off, started putting away some glasses behind the bar.

'Get you anything else?' Owen said.

'We're good, thank you,' I said.

We got up from our stools, put some money down for our meals.

401

'Don't worry about it, ladies,' Owen said. 'It's on me.'

'Thanks,' I said.

We let the pub door fall closed behind us and stood on the sidewalk, the cement still radiating heat and the air warm though the sun was going down. A few vehicles were parked on the road in front of the pub.

Dallas stepped onto the road. I followed her, glancing both ways. We were in the middle of the road, headed across to the motel. Down the street a little was a pickup, parked on the side. I couldn't see the sides, just the front grille and the hood. It looked like a black truck. Then I heard the engine gunning.

'Dallas,' I said in a warning tone.

She followed my gaze, and her step slowed. 'Is that ...?'

The truck gunned its engine louder. Then I saw the cigarette smoke blowing out the window. A hand came out next, pointed at us like a gun.

'Get moving,' Dallas said.

We hurried the last few steps, weaved around and between all the vehicles in the motel parking lot. We kept glancing back but didn't see the truck. Finally we were at our door, Dallas fumbling for the key.

'Open the door!' I said, looking over my shoulder again. We pushed ourselves inside, slamming the door behind us, both breathing heavy.

I walked to the window, pulled back the curtain an inch. A car drove by, but there was no sign of the truck.

'Where the hell did he go?' I said. We waited in silence for a couple of minutes, still watching the road.

'He must've driven in the other direction,' Dallas said.

I heard a noise, a tapping sound, coming from behind us. We turned around.

'What was that?' Dallas said.

'The bathroom window?' I said, moving a little closer, but slowly.

Three loud noises now, like someone had slapped their hand on the window. I stopped walking, a scream building in my throat.

Dallas grabbed my arm. 'Don't move.' She went over to her bed and unzipped her suitcase. 'I'm going to check it out.'

Now I saw what she was holding. A handgun.

'Holy shit. Where'd you get that?' I said.

'Doesn't matter.' She walked toward the bathroom and slowly pushed the door open, gun pointed. 'Stay away from us,' she yelled out.

We waited, listening.

I heard a truck. 'You think that's him?'

'Maybe.'

'We should let McPhail know,' I said. But when I called him, he didn't answer the phone. I left a message asking him to call back as soon as possible.

Dallas sat on the other bed, the gun still gripped in her hand.

'Why didn't you tell me you had a gun?' I said.

'I didn't want to freak you out.'

'I'm glad you brought it.' I was surprised she'd never mentioned that she owned a gun. I hadn't touched a gun since we left Cash Creek the first time, but I kept a knife and mace in my night table and carried them with me at all times. I thought of the knife I'd given Skylar, wondered if she'd taken it with her.

We spent the next twenty minutes listening to every vehicle that pulled in and out, waiting for our back window to get smashed in. Both of us tense, smoking cigarettes, not talking much. Sergeant McPhail finally called at ten.

'Gavin Luxton threatened us,' I said. I told him what happened.

'Did you actually see him?'

'No, but I'm *sure* it was his truck.'

'We'll take a few patrols by the motel tonight.'

'Did you go back out to the ranch?'

'I spoke to Brian and he let me look around his property, but Gavin wasn't home. We've asked him to come in tomorrow morning.'

'He wasn't home because he was in town trying to scare the shit out of us. Did Brian admit Skylar worked at the ranch?'

'Says she worked there a couple of days but didn't show up this morning. She told him she was trying to make money to meet up with a boyfriend. He figures she just continued on.'

'That's a lie. She doesn't have a boyfriend.'

'We'll look into it,' he said, but I was getting a horrible feeling he believed Brian.

'What about Crystal?'

'Claims he's never seen her before.'

'That's bullshit. We worked there – I can describe their barn.' I thought of something else. 'Theo, they had a ranch hand named Theo.'

'I'll look into that, but at the moment we still don't have enough to get a search warrant.'

'We told you Gavin was seen talking to Crystal at the bar. Isn't that enough?'

'Unfortunately, no one saw her leaving with him that night. We need solid evidence.'

'What about Riley? I think he knows something.'

'We've also asked him to come into the station in the morning. Hopefully he'll give us more to go on – we'll keep you updated. In the meantime just stay in your room.'

We spent the night taking turns keeping guard. One of us sat on the bed with the gun while the other tried to sleep but mostly tossed and turned. McPhail had called back, told us there was no sign of Gavin near our motel.

It didn't bring me comfort, knowing they hadn't seen him. He could still be outside waiting.

I sat with my back pressed against the headboard, the gun gripped tight in my hands and my head turned toward the door, staring at the handle.

Chapter Thirty

Skylar

We had to get to that bottle. The room was almost dark now and I had no way of communicating with Crystal, but we had to drag the bed closer somehow.

I thought about the layout of the room. The dresser was in the far corner to the right, opposite the side of the bed where I was tied.

When we'd tried to push the bed before, we did it from the side only and pushed across. This time we had to spin the bed around so the bottom faced the other wall – then I might be able to knock the bottle off the dresser.

I managed to grab my rope with the back of my hands, then walked forward toward the wall on the left side, dragging the bed behind me, hoping Crystal would realize what I was doing. I heard her feet land on the floor, then the bed started to move easier – she was pulling too. It was hard work, and I felt faint from the heat, sweat dripping down my face and stinging my eyes. The rope pulled my arms back, stretching all my tendons and ligaments. But we managed to drag the bed a few feet.

I stopped, tried to catch my breath, inhaling through my nose. I could also hear Crystal breathing in the dark.

The next step was to spin the bed around. I had to push from the bottom end, which meant Crystal couldn't help. I leaned down, put my shoulder into the side of the mattress near the end of the bed, and pushed forward. I felt the bed move on her side too and stopped pushing. How could I tell her to stop?

I thumped the floor a couple of times with my foot, and when I started pushing again, she didn't push from her side.

I had to stop a few times to catch my breath, and worried about Gavin walking in, but I couldn't give up now. That bottle was our only hope.

Finally I got the bed pointed in the direction of the bottle. I walked around to the bottom of the bed and grabbed the rope behind me again, pulling forward like a workhorse, leaning all my weight into it. I hoped Crystal realized that I needed her to get behind the headboard. I felt the bed move – she was pushing forward while I pulled. She must have seen the bottle too.

We had the bed within a couple of feet of the dresser. My eyes had adjusted slightly and I could make out the shape. The opposite bottom corner of the bed was closer, but could I reach it? I climbed on top, tried to crawl to the other side. Then I lay on my back and stretched my foot toward the dresser.

I could just stretch my toes out and touch the bottle, but I might knock it off. We needed the bed closer.

I got off and wedged my shoulder into the side of the mattress again, pushed with all my strength, felt Crystal doing the same behind me.

The bed moved another foot. I heard the bottom bedpost hit the dresser and held my breath, but the bottle stayed where it was.

I climbed back onto the bed and stretched my feet out carefully, feeling around with my toes, praying that I didn't kick the bottle. When I felt my toes graze the cool glass, I pressed my feet against the sides of the bottle, cradling it in my arches. *Slowly, slowly.* I lifted with my feet, curled my legs into my chest, and turned my body to the left, dropping the bottle down onto the mattress. Beer spilled out, soaking my foot with cold liquid. I wished I could drink it.

I used my feet to push the blanket up around the bottle so it couldn't roll anywhere, then got off the bed.

Now we had to put it back into place – which seemed to take twice as long but I'd lost all sense of time. All I knew was I had to get the bottle and break it before Gavin came home. I crawled across the mattress. I could sense Crystal's presence at the other end of the bed. There was still a small bit of light coming in through the boards, but it wasn't helping much.

I tucked the bottle under my chin, sank to my knees, and lowered my head down, carefully standing the bottle on the floor. How was I going to break it? I sat on the floor, curved my feet around it, then smashed down, but it wouldn't break. I thought for a moment. Maybe if I smashed the bedpost down on it.

I stood up, used my foot to move it near the bedpost, and held it in place. Then I squatted, lifted the bed with the back of my hands, and used my foot to slowly push the bottle under the post. Still holding the bottle in place with my foot, I slammed the post down on it with all my strength. It didn't break. I tried three more times, my triceps and quads shaking from exertion. I couldn't give up.

On my fourth try I heard the bottle break and wanted to cry with relief. I felt around with my feet, nudged some bigger pieces, and squatted down to pick one up, using the back of my T-shirt to protect my hands. It was hard to cut the tape behind my back – I had to curl my hand around in an awkward position, blindly sawing at

410

the bindings. I poked myself a few times and had to take it slower. I was terrified Gavin might come home any minute.

Finally I felt the glass cut through and I was able to pull my wrists apart, though tape was still stuck to them. I shook my hands out, rotated my arms, then undid the gag at the back of my neck.

'I did it!' I said. 'Hold on. I'm coming.'

Crystal's eyes were excited, but she glanced toward the door. I needed to get her free, fast.

I tried to undo the rope around my neck but it was tied in some sort of lasso and I couldn't figure out the knot. I walked to the end of the bed, sweeping my feet around so I didn't cut them on glass. I managed to untie the rope from around the bedpost, but it wasn't easy – my arms and wrists were sore, the tape still stuck around them, and my fingers fumbled with the knots. *Come on, come on.* I got the last piece of rope undone, and I was free.

I ran over to the light and switched it on.

Crystal shielded her face with her knees. I raced back to her and undid her gag, pushing it down around her neck.

'Skylar!' she said, her voice so dry and raspy it made my own throat hurt. 'You shouldn't have come here.' She started crying.

'I had to find you.' I wrapped my arms around her

and hugged her tight. 'I'm so sorry I screwed up and got caught.'

'You have to get out,' she said, still crying. 'He'll come back.'

'I'm not leaving you.' I sawed at the tape with my chunk of glass. She brought her hands forward, her face twisting as she moved her shoulders. She touched my face, my hair. Her eyes searched mine.

'I can't believe you're here,' she said. 'Are you okay?'

'Yeah. What about you?' I grabbed her hand, inhaled sharply when I saw her wrists. The skin looked red and raw, maybe infected.

'It's okay,' she said. 'I don't even feel it anymore.' I knew she was trying to reassure me but I just felt more scared. I had to get us out of there.

'I'll untie your rope from the bed.' But when I tried, the knot was too tight. 'I can't do it,' I said, panicking.

'We'll have to cut it,' Crystal said.

I grabbed two big pieces of glass and handed her one, then started sawing, but it was thick rope and slow going. Crystal was also struggling. She had to use the corner of the blanket to protect her hand and she kept dropping the glass.

'My arms and hands are too weak,' she said, stopping to rest. 'Go. Get help.'

I tried the door handle but the door wouldn't open. I slammed my body against it a few times. 'It won't budge!'

I ran to the window, tried to pry off a board. 'They're hammered on.'

'He could come back any minute,' Crystal said. 'We won't be able to hear him over the music. You have to hide the broken glass, make it look like you're still tied up, and when he goes to sleep tonight, we'll work on my rope.'

'But what if he rapes us?' I couldn't breathe for a second after I said it.

'I'll make him angry at me. It's not hard.' She gave a bitter smile.

'Maybe I should try to ambush him when he comes in,' I said. 'I'll wrap the rope around his neck and strangle him from behind.'

'He's too strong, Skylar. We both need to be free – our only hope is two against one. We just have to wait for our chance and get him before Brian's here.'

'I'm scared, Crystal. I don't want him to hurt you.'

'I'm scared too,' she said. 'But we're going to be free soon. Now, quick, clean up the room. You have to try to tape your hands back together.'

I scraped the broken glass under the bed after putting some bigger pieces near Crystal's end. If things got really rough, maybe she could use one to stab him in the eye or something. I also put one down by my side of the bed. There were a few marks in the hardwood from the bed moving, but I hoped he didn't notice. There was also a damp spot on the bed from the beer. I moved the blankets around, trying to hide it. I had to turn off the light soon.

I ran over to Crystal, gave her a kiss on the cheek. 'I love you,' I said.

'I love you too,' she said. 'Remember, wait for the right moment.'

'Okay.'

I made it look like her hands were still taped, hiding the rough-cut edges underneath each other, but she could still get her hands free if she needed them. I slid the gag back up over her face, then mine, and turned the light off.

I stumbled back to the bed, feeling my way, and looped my rope around the bedpost and the railing. Then I wrapped my wrists back up, but I wasn't sure if I'd hidden all the rough edges and prayed that he wouldn't notice.

We sat in the dark again. I wished we could speak, but I felt a tiny spark of energy. We had a plan. We were almost free.

After what felt like another hour, our door flung open. I shielded my eyes against the light, peeked over my shoulder. Gavin was looming in the doorway. He stumbled in, obviously drunker than he had been earlier. He walked over to me, knelt down, and gave me a smile. He reeked of booze and cigarettes. He took one out of his pocket, lit it, and blew the smoke slowly into my face. It went right up my nose – I coughed, couldn't get my breath for a minute.

'I saw your mommy tonight,' he said.

I looked into his eyes. Was he telling the truth? What happened?

'Scared the shit out of those bitches.' A mean laugh. My thoughts scattered in a million directions. Had he hurt my mom and Dallas? I wanted to rip my hands free and strangle him, but I couldn't do anything – not yet.

He licked his lips, looked at my legs, traced his hand down to my foot and back up toward my thigh. I was filled with terror and rage, had to fight the urge to kick him in the face even though everything in my body wanted to run away.

He gave me a blurry-eyed leer. 'Think I'm too drunk to enjoy you tonight, but your time's coming.' He stood back up, let out a loud burp, and looked at Crystal. 'Don't worry, sweetie. You're still my favorite.'

He stumbled over to the stereo, turned the music down. 'This shit's giving me a headache.' Then he flicked off the light and left the room. I could hear him locking the door, swearing like he was struggling with the key.

I waited until I heard his steps go all the way downstairs, then gave it awhile longer, hoping he'd pass out. Finally I decided it was time.

I pulled my wrists free, removed my gag, and untied

my rope from the bedpost. I crept over to Crystal, feeling for her in the dark, and undid her gag and wrists.

'I put some glass under your corner,' I said, already climbing up on the bed to start cutting her rope.

'Cut at the end behind the post, not in the middle,' she whispered. 'In case we have to tie it up again. We don't want him seeing the cut marks.'

While we worked, we talked in the dark.

'How did he get you?' I said.

'I was stupid. He didn't recognize me, so I picked him up at the pub, told him we should go down to the river – it's where those assholes attacked us when we were kids. He was getting some pot out of the glove box. I had the gun in my hand.' She was quiet for a moment, then said, 'I think he saw the reflection in his window, because he turned around, yanked the gun out of my hand, and hit me in the head. I woke up in here, and—' Her voice broke. 'I'm so sorry, Skylar.'

'It was my choice to follow you. I was worried.'

'How did you know I was in Cash Creek?'

'I broke into your house. I saw what you were looking at on your computer.'

'I should've cleaned that out.' She sounded really upset.

'Mom said you'd never come here. She thought you'd just run off.'

'I wish *you* hadn't come.'

'But now I can get us out.'

We lapsed into silence, the only noise the glass scraping over the rope.

'I'm worried about Mom and Dallas,' I said after a minute.

'It sounds like Dallas and your mom reported us missing,' Crystal said. 'Brian and Gavin aren't going to hurt them – not when the cops are involved.'

'But he said that they were scared.'

'He was just trying to get to us.'

I took a breath. 'Okay,' I said. 'And we're going to get out of here soon too.'

'I'm going to make *sure* you get out,' Crystal said. 'No matter what.'

'What do you mean? We're *both* getting out.'

'That's the plan,' she said. 'Keep working on the rope.'

It took us the whole night, and we were exhausted by the time we finally cut Crystal loose. The light was starting to creep in through the window. Gavin might be up soon. We plotted in the dark.

'He'll come with breakfast and water,' Crystal said. 'When he leans over to feed me, see if you can get the rope around him from behind. Then I'll stand up and get mine over his head. We can wrap the rope around the post for leverage, then we'll strangle him – it won't take as much strength that way.'

We gagged ourselves again, wrapped the rope loosely

around the bedposts, taped our wrists. Then we waited.

Finally I heard noises downstairs, a toilet flush. Then loud voices – he'd turned the TV up. A few minutes later I thought I heard a truck start but wasn't sure. It could have just been the TV. I looked at Crystal and she shook her head.

As it grew hotter and brighter in the room, I began to wonder if he was going to come up that morning. What if he was waiting until Brian came? What were we going to do?

After what felt like a couple of hours, the TV was suddenly turned off, the silence startling. I held my breath, stared at the door. I heard his boots stumbling up the stairs, and sounds of him unlocking the door. He flung it open. His face was pale and grizzled, but he was wearing a dress shirt, his hair slicked back.

'Got to run up to the ranch for a few minutes and look at the tractor. Brian can't seem to do fuck-all by himself if I'm not around. You girls be good, now.'

He turned the music up, then walked out and closed the door behind him.

I looked at Crystal. She shook her head again, telling me to wait. I watched her, ready for the signal, but I was getting frustrated. A few minutes later, Crystal pulled her wrists apart and yanked her gag down off her mouth.

'We need to be sure he's gone,' she said.

'We don't have enough time,' I said. 'He might come

back with Brian. Then they're going to take us to the warehouse.'

Crystal's face was grim as she thought for a couple of seconds, like she was considering our options.

'We have to bust through the door.'

Chapter Thirty-one

Jamie

I woke up on the bed, still dressed in all my clothes, my mouth tasting like dry cotton. I glanced at the clock. Seven-thirty. Dallas was standing by the window.

'It's going to be really hot today,' she said.

She'd brought back muffins and coffee from the front office. I sipped at the coffee, tried to choke down some of the muffin, but everything tasted like paste. At nine-thirty my phone finally rang. It was the sergeant.

'Did you speak to Gavin?' I said.

'He came in this morning, but he won't let us search the property.'

'He must have something to hide.'

'Not necessarily. Lots of people don't like the police.' A long pause. My body stiffened as I realized he was about to tell me something I wasn't going to want to hear. 'Crystal's phone was found on the side of the road near the river. Looks like it might have been smashed with a rock.'

I sucked in my breath. 'Brian and Gavin took us to that river when we were teens. That's where they attacked us.' Dallas sat up on the other bed.

'We don't know how the phone got there at this point, but the last place Skylar's phone pinged was off a cell tower on the highway toward Vernon.'

'She didn't go to Vernon – she doesn't know anyone there.'

'We still need to follow through on that lead.'

'You don't believe me.'

'Parents don't always know everything that's going on in their kids' lives.' His patronizing tone was starting to really piss me off.

'You're wasting time. I'm telling you – she *never* left this town.'

'I'll keep you updated on what we find.'

I hung up the phone, and yelled into the air, 'Fuck!'

'What's going on?' Dallas said.

'They found Crystal's phone smashed down by the river, and they think Skylar's in Vernon – her phone pinged off a tower.'

Dallas looked confused. 'Do you think maybe she got away from them?'

'They're still in this town. I can *feel* it.'

'Maybe it has something to do with that hitchhiker.'

I spun around. 'Shit, she probably stole Skylar's phone or something. And now the cops are going to change their whole investigation.'

Dallas narrowed her eyes, thinking. 'We should stake out the ranch and tail them if they go anywhere today.'

We were careful when we left the room, checking for Gavin, but we didn't see anything. We grabbed some bottles of water from the corner store and were soon parked on a side road where we could see if anyone left the Luxton Ranch.

'I hope those assholes don't have a back driveway,' Dallas said.

'Shit, I never thought of that.'

'Let's just keep an eye out and see what happens.'

We took turns, one dozing while the other kept watch, both of us still exhausted from our sleepless night at the motel. No one left the ranch, and not many vehicles drove past. It was a quiet road.

Finally, at ten-thirty, a navy-blue truck came down the driveway. I elbowed Dallas, who was asleep behind the wheel.

'Look.'

We lowered ourselves as the truck roared past. I couldn't see who was on the passenger side but I caught a flash of the driver's profile and dark hair. It was Brian.

'Was that Gavin with him?' I said.

'I don't know, the sun was glaring off the windshield,' Dallas said.

'Let's see where he's going.'

We followed the truck to the bus station and parked around the back side, where we could watch the truck in the parking lot. Brian's wife got out of the passenger side and went into the station. She was wearing a pretty sundress. His daughter, in shorts and a T-shirt, climbed out of the backseat but stayed by the truck. Through the window we watched his wife go up to the ticket agent.

'Can you see how many tickets she's buying?' Dallas said.

'No.' I was worried about the fact that we'd left Gavin back at the ranch. What if he went out to the warehouse and hurt the girls? I reminded myself that he probably wouldn't go without Brian.

A few minutes later the woman walked out to the parking lot. Brian was helping the young girl bring a suitcase out of the back of the truck. He also handed one to his wife, then gave her a hug, but it was perfunctory. The wife and daughter walked toward the waiting bus. His wife looked back at him, her face anxious as she climbed aboard. I wondered what he'd told her.

Brian was leaning on his truck, watching the bus. It started up and he glanced at his watch, like he couldn't wait to get out of there. He looked back at the bus, gave a smile and a little wave. I could see the girl waving back from the window, her dark eyes big. I thought of Skylar.

The moment the bus was out of sight Brian's smile disappeared. He walked into the building.

'Where the hell is he going?' I said.

'Maybe he's using the bathroom?'

We stared at the door, waiting for him to come back out.

Suddenly his face was at Dallas's open window. We both jerked back in our seats.

'Why are you following me?' His voice was cold. His eyes flicked around, checking to see if anyone was watching.

'We know you have them,' I said.

'I don't know what you're talking about.'

'Where *are* they?' My voice shook with rage. A woman walking by looked at us curiously.

'I told you already, I don't know.'

'The cops are talking to your son today. He was the last person to see Skylar. If anything's happened to her, he'll be blamed.'

'Still don't have a clue what you're talking about,' he said, bending down and peering into the car. 'Sorry to disappoint you, but I'm married now.' He held his finger up, showing his ring. 'So if you were looking for a little repeat ...'

Dallas's face was flushed and angry, like she was going to explode any minute. Her hand reached under her seat where she'd put the gun.

He straightened, stepped away a couple of feet.

'Go back to wherever you've been hiding, girls.' He walked to his truck, climbed in, and roared off.

Dallas was silent all the way back to the motel. She whipped open the door, tossed her purse onto the bed, and started pacing, her hands on her hips, her jaw clenched. 'Fuck,' she said, shaking her head. 'It should have been me.'

'What are you talking about?'

She sat down on the edge of the bed, ran her hands through her hair. 'I should've come here years ago and finished those scumbags off. That's why I bought the gun – I just never had the balls to see it through.'

'It was smart you never came back. Look what's happened now.'

'Yeah, they've got Crystal and Skylar ...' She turned away, hiding her face. She got up and grabbed a cigarette from the pack.

'It's not your fault.'

'I should've killed Dad, it should've been *me*. I screwed up, and I screwed up when we got to Cash

425

Creek. I didn't protect you.' She sat back on her bed.

I didn't know what to say, had never heard Dallas talk like this.

'You always look out for us,' I said. 'We know you tried.'

'I just want to kill those fuckers and make it right.' She took a drag, blew it out in an angry rush.

'Nothing will ever make it right,' I said. 'It happened. We just have to find the girls and get out of this shitty town.'

She looked down at the cigarette in her hand, rolled it between her fingers, her eyes narrowed. 'We should go back to the ranch, wait until Gavin leaves, then sneak onto his property. We have to find out if the girls' cars are there.'

'You think they would've kept them?'

'Maybe this all came down on them too fast,' Dallas said. 'They haven't had time to deal with everything.'

'Bring your gun,' I said.

We drove down the same side road and stared at the driveway. My temple was pounding with a headache, all the muscles in my body tense. We assumed Brian lived in the bigger house with his family and Gavin lived in the smaller one below. We figured we could cut across the field and avoid the driveway after he left.

We sat in the car for an hour. We were hot, sweaty,

and smoking too many cigarettes. My throat was dry, my head aching. I glanced at my watch. It was almost one, and there'd been no sign of them. We'd brought water but had almost drunk all of it when we finally saw Gavin's black truck pulling out of his driveway, and then going up to the main house, a plume of dust behind him.

'He might be gone for only a few minutes,' I said.

'It might also be our only chance,' Dallas said.

'Okay, let's go.'

We climbed the fence and cut through a lower field, trying to stay on the edges of the ranch until a house came in sight. 'That must be Gavin's,' I said.

The front doors on the shop wouldn't slide up. We circled the garage and tried the side door, but there was a big padlock on the door. We noticed a window at the back. Dallas hoisted me up. I wiped at the dirt on the window.

'Can you see anything?' she said.

'It's dark, but it looks like there are two cars – they're both under tarps.' I looked around. 'And some cutting tools on the bench! Shit, I think they're stripping the cars.'

Dallas lowered me, and we looked for a way to break into the garage.

'Maybe we could smash the padlock with a rock,' I said.

Dallas was staring at the house. 'Listen how loud that music's playing.'

'Should we try to break in?'

She looked down the driveway, then in the direction of the ranch.

'This might be our only chance,' I said.

She nodded. 'Let's do it.'

I tried the back porch door. Locked.

Dallas was looking up at the porch roof. 'Do you hear something? Like underneath the country music?'

The music was even louder near the house.

'That thudding sound?'

'Yeah.'

We were both quiet, but we couldn't hear the sound anymore.

'Maybe we should smash one of the windows,' I said.

'Let's check the front first.' Dallas was walking around the corner of the house when she stopped suddenly. 'Crap, I think a truck's coming!'

We ran for the back of the garage, keeping low. We'd just made it when I heard the truck pull up. We leaned against the wall, our bodies tucked behind some old barrels, staring at each other. The truck shut off and a door opened.

'Wait.' Dallas peeked around the corner. I held my breath. 'Okay, let's go.'

We were crossing the field, trying to get to a cover of trees, when a shout rang out behind us.

'What the fuck are you doing?'

I glanced back and saw Gavin running down the hill after us. I started sprinting, Dallas running hard beside me, our feet thudding on the compact ground. I looked over my shoulder, almost tripping on a rock. He was slowing down, then stopped in the middle of the field, watching us.

'That was really stupid, bitches!' he yelled.

We clambered through the fence, dashed across the road, jerked open the car doors, and jumped in. Dallas tore off down the road.

I looked out the rearview mirror. No one was following.

'We can never go back now,' Dallas said. 'He'll be keeping watch.'

'He has their cars,' I said, starting to cry. 'That's why Gavin refused the search – he must have them in the house.'

'We have to tell the cops,' Dallas said. 'They can get a warrant.'

I called McPhail as soon as we got within range.

'We found their cars,' I said.

'Where?' He sounded surprised.

'In Gavin's garage. We snuck onto the property. There

are two cars under some tarps, and cutting tools out on a bench. We also heard thudding noises coming from inside the house. We think he has the girls. Can you get a warrant?'

'Not if you didn't see the actual cars. A vehicle under a tarp isn't enough.'

I closed my eyes. Shit. Shit. Why hadn't I lied?

'What about the noises we heard? He has country music on really loud too – like he's trying to cover something up.'

'The noise could've been anything, even a washing machine out of balance. And if the music was that loud, how can you be sure what you heard?'

'We *both* heard it.'

'You need to let us do our jobs,' he said. 'Putting yourself in danger is not helping. You're just interfering with the investigation.'

'You're not finding any fucking evidence!'

'Look. We have to do this the right way. If we force our way onto the property and find something we didn't lawfully obtain, the whole case could get thrown out.'

'I don't give a shit about some court case,' I said. 'I want my daughter *now*.'

'Stay away from the Luxtons,' he said. 'If you're caught on the property, they could press charges. I don't want to have to warn you again.'

*

430

Back in the room, I looked out the window and saw Riley across the street helping a customer.

'We need to talk to Riley again,' I said.

'The police aren't going to like that,' Dallas said.

'I don't care. He knows something.'

I'd wondered if Noah was going to be a problem, but as we walked over I could see him through the glass windows of the office, talking on his cell phone, turned away from us. We headed quickly to the shop. Riley was putting away some tools in the garage.

'We need to talk to you,' I said.

He spun around, his hand on a wrench.

I held my hands up. 'Whoa.'

'Sorry.' He set the wrench back down, picked up a rag, and started wiping his hands. 'What are you doing here?'

'We want to ask you some questions. It's really important, Riley.'

'I already told the cops everything.' He looked uncomfortable but not hostile. I stepped closer.

'I don't think you hurt Skylar, but I do think you know something that could help us find her.'

He was shaking his head. 'I wish I knew where she was.'

'Years ago, your dad and uncle hurt me and my sisters – and now they're going to hurt my daughter.' I was going out on a limb saying this stuff but I needed to see his reaction to know if he was part of it.

431

He jerked back, his eyes wide like I'd hit him. 'That's a lie!'

'There are two cars under tarps in your uncle's garage – and cutting tools on the bench. *Their* cars. I'm sure of it. Just look and you'll see.'

'You have to leave.' He looked angry now, his face red. I saw the resemblance even more between him and Brian and had a flash of fear.

'You know it's true. Your dad's violent with your mom, isn't he? Maybe your sister?'

'Fuck you.'

'What if your sister went missing?' I'd been thinking about the young dark-haired girl but now I realized I'd spoken true words. Skylar *was* his sister. 'What if she disappeared and the one person who could tell you something wouldn't?'

He picked up the phone.

'If you know what happened and you're covering for your dad, the cops are going to throw your ass in jail too,' Dallas said. 'Your life is screwed.'

'I'm calling the police.' He was dialing now.

'Let's get out of here.' Dallas grabbed my arm.

'Just look in the *garage*!' I yelled as she pulled me away.

Riley slid the shop door down hard until it crashed to the ground, almost catching our feet. We walked quickly across the road.

*

432

We'd only been back in the room for ten minutes when my cell rang. It was the sergeant. My breath lifted into my throat, hope and fear tangling up in my head. *Please let it be good news.*

'I told you to stay away from the Luxtons,' he said as soon as I answered. 'Riley says you were harassing him at the garage.'

'He *knows* something,' I said.

'This is an active investigation. As soon as we have—'

'This is my *family*. I'm going to do everything I can to find them.'

'I know you're concerned, but we can't have you getting involved in the investigation. When you go around talking to people and sneaking onto their property, it makes our job harder. You need to understand—'

'No, *you* need to understand. They're going to *kill* my daughter and sister. So you need to hurry the hell up and find them!'

'Listen,' he said, sounding furious now. 'If I see you anywhere near that ranch, or you come within two feet of *any* of them, I'm arresting you on the spot.'

He hung up. I tossed my phone onto the bed, punched my fist into the mattress a couple of times. 'Shit, shit, shit!'

Chapter Thirty-two

Skylar

I paused from kicking the door. 'Did you hear someone yelling?'

'I don't know,' Crystal said. 'It's hard to tell over the music.' She was too weak to kick the door for long, her muscles cramping from dehydration. I'd been kicking at it for a while, still hoping to break through even after I knew it was a lost cause. It was solid wood.

'Maybe we should get back into position,' I said now.

'We're going to have to go with our first plan,' Crystal said.

I nodded and pulled up my gag, stuck my wrists back together, and loosely coiled my rope around the bedpost.

Just in time – Gavin came in a couple minutes later. He was out of breath, his sweaty skin a grayish green. He had to bend over and rest his hands on his knees, catching his breath. He straightened up, gave me a dirty look.

'Your mother's becoming a problem.'

My *mom* had been here?

He was pacing around now, looking agitated. He kept taking his cap off and rubbing his hands through his hair, his face stressed, like he was trying to figure something out. He wasn't coming close enough for us to put our plan into action, and I was scared we weren't going to have another chance.

He pulled his cell out of his pocket, punched in some numbers.

'It's me,' he said. 'I caught those two bitches snooping around, think they were looking in the garage ... No, they're covered with a tarp. We should move the girls soon ... Come down when he's gone.'

I remembered the yelling I'd heard. Was that my mom, trying to find us? I wanted to cry, thinking how close we'd come to freedom.

Gavin glanced at us. 'Just a little longer, girls, then we're going to set you up somewhere real nice.' He smiled at Crystal, then left the room.

We sat on the floor waiting for what felt like hours. Judging by the heat in the room it was now afternoon. What if Gavin didn't come alone again? Brian had said they were going to move us in the afternoon. Would we be able to fight *both* Brian and Gavin? We hadn't had water or food since the night before. Crystal was weak, and I was losing confidence with every minute that passed.

Gavin finally came in with some bottles of water. He gave me mine, then moved on to Crystal. I watched, my muscles tense, ready to break free of my bindings, but he stopped suddenly and stood straight, looking toward the door.

He walked over to the stereo and turned the music down. I shifted my body so I could see what he was doing.

Now I heard the noise outside. Sounded like a dirt bike or an ATV or something. Gavin leaned back against the dresser, lit a cigarette. He was watching the door, just waiting. It had to be Brian.

'You're not answering your phone,' Brian said, walking into the room.

'I'm sick of you calling me every goddamn minute.'

'We had shit to talk about,' Brian said.

'So talk,' Gavin said.

'Let's go downstairs.'

'I'm staying right here.' Gavin took a long drag of his smoke, then nodded at us. 'We've got no secrets.'

'Fine, whatever,' Brian said. 'We've got to get rid of the cars.'

'I've been stripping them.'

'That's not fast enough. We have to hide them on the

property. We can use the backhoe and bury them in one of the lower fields.'

'What about these two?' Gavin gestured in our direction.

'Change of plans,' Brian said, his eyes cold as he stared at me.

Chapter Thirty-three

Jamie

We took turns pacing and looking out the window, like the street might reveal something. I couldn't stop thinking about those thuds.

'We should just go to Gavin's house with your gun and force ourselves inside,' I said. 'By the time the cop catches us, we'll already have the girls.'

'What if they're both there?' Dallas said. 'What if they're both armed?'

She had a point. 'I know where we can get another gun.'

'Where?'

'Owen – his dad used to keep one hidden under the cabinet, remember?'

'Okay, but he's not just going to give it to us.'

'Maybe he would. We have to at least try.'

'He could report us.'

I shook my head. 'I don't think he would.'

She took a breath and stood up. 'Fine.'

We found Owen working at the bar. I looked around, saw a few people nursing their drinks.

'Hey,' I said. 'Have a minute?'

'Sure.'

'Could we talk to you in private?'

Wiping his hands on a towel, he gave me a curious look. Then he called to the waitress at the other end of the bar. 'Cover for me.'

We went into his office and he closed the door. Pulling out the chair from behind his desk, he sat. 'What's going on? Did you find them?'

'We're not sure,' I said. 'Look.' I took a breath. 'I know you don't really know us, but we need your help.'

'Okay,' he said slowly.

I glanced at Dallas, who was watching me. I turned back to Owen. 'Could we borrow a gun?'

He sat straight. 'What?'

'Gavin came by our hotel last night and threatened us. We know the girls are out at the ranch, but the cops can't get a search warrant.'

'How do you know the girls are there?' He was frowning.

'We found two cars covered by tarps in their garage and we heard thudding sounds from inside the house.'

'And you need a gun because . . . ?'

I debated lying. We could tell him we just needed it for protection, but I didn't think he'd believe me. 'We're going out there and getting our girls back.'

'We won't say you gave us a gun,' Dallas said. 'We'll say we stole it.'

He was shaking his head. 'Sorry. No. You're going to get killed.'

I leaned forward. 'We are going with or without your help. But if you give us that gun, we might walk out of it alive.'

'Your dad helped us once,' Dallas said. 'Remember?'

'We don't know if the girls are okay. We don't—' My voice broke and I turned away, trying to get my emotions under control.

'Shit,' Owen said. 'Meet me out back in ten minutes, by the silver truck.'

He came out carrying a hockey bag, looked around before walking over to where we had parked under the shadow of a tree. He had his keys out, put them in the door of his truck with his back to us, dropped the bag on the ground, and reached in like he was getting something from behind the seat. 'Put the bag in your car,' he said.

Dallas looked around and quickly put it in the backseat.

'It's unregistered.' He turned around and met my eyes. 'Good luck.'

Chapter Thirty-four

Skylar

'What the hell do you mean, change of *plans*?' Gavin said.

'We can't move the girls – and you can't keep them here.'

'So what are you saying?'

'We have to kill them, bury their bodies on the property, get rid of any sign of them before the cops descend on this place.' Brian said the words so casually that it took a moment for my brain to comprehend what I was hearing. Then it hit. I looked at Crystal, knew she'd get what I was thinking.

Should we go for it now?

She shook her head, just a slight movement. She wanted to wait, but I felt desperate, time slipping away. We had to do something soon.

'Cops need a search warrant,' Gavin said. He took the last drag of his smoke and ground it out on top of the stereo speaker.

'They might be getting one,' Brian said. 'You were seen at the bar with her, you idiot. And we don't know what those other bitches saw today.'

'I told you the cars are covered with a tarp.'

'You caused this, you clean it up.' Brian took a handgun out from behind his back and handed it to Gavin. Blood roared through my head.

I looked at Crystal, who nodded. This was it – we had to go for it. I was about to pull my wrists apart when Gavin hit Brian across the head with the gun, the crack echoing in the room.

Brian stumbled back, his hand to his head. Then he rushed forward and tackled Gavin, slamming him into the closet door behind him.

Locked in a hold, they fell to the floor, rolling around and punching each other. They were partly behind the bed. I could hear grunts, boots against wood, heavy breathing as they struggled. My hands were undone. I looked at Crystal. She was reaching for her rope. I glanced at the open door. Could we make it?

I tried to pull my rope free from the post, but it was caught somehow. I looked at the men, terrified one of them would notice.

They'd moved away from the bed. Brian was on top

of Gavin, hitting him in the face, loud smacks over and over. Suddenly there was a shot. The room exploded with the noise, making my ears ring. I couldn't tell who'd been hit.

I gave my rope another yank. Crystal was beside me now, trying to help.

Brian rolled off Gavin and leaned against the dresser, clutching at his stomach – a bloom of red. He looked stunned, then his body slumped to the side.

'Shit,' Gavin said.

Finally my rope came free. I took off for the door, Crystal following. From the corner of my eye I saw Gavin getting up, gun still in his hand.

'What the fuck!' he yelled.

We were at the door. Now running down the stairs. I heard Crystal stumble behind me and reached behind, felt for her hand, pulling her along.

'I can't keep up, I'm holding you back.'

'Come on!' I yelled. 'We're almost there.'

We were at the bottom. I heard Gavin trip and fall at the top of the stairs, heard his body hit hard. I prayed it would buy us some extra time.

We ran through the kitchen, heading to the front door. I let go of Crystal's hand and wrestled with the front door handle, got it open. I glanced over my shoulder to see how close Gavin was and saw that Crystal had stepped back.

I reached for her hand. 'Let's go!'

She pulled her hand free and pushed me out the door. 'Run, Skylar!'

'What are you doing—' She slammed the door shut. I pounded on it, heard the lock sliding into place. 'Crystal!' I screamed.

'Get out of here!' she yelled.

I ran to the living room window, could just make out her naked form grabbing a knife from the kitchen counter, then I saw Gavin emerging from the bottom of the stairs, the gun still in his hands.

'Crystal!' I yelled, slamming my hands on the glass. I looked around, but there wasn't anything I could use to break the window.

I turned back just in time to see Crystal run at Gavin. They were struggling over the knife, his hand gripping her wrist. I had to help her.

I raced to the back of the house.

Chapter Thirty-five

Jamie

Dallas sped around the corners, almost losing control of the car a couple of times. She slowed down after we nearly hit someone passing on a motorbike coming toward us in the opposite lane. I braced one hand against the dashboard, the other tightly wrapped around the rifle.

We roared up Gavin's driveway. I was sitting forward in the seat, ready to jump out and run. Dallas pulled her gun out from her waistband with one hand.

Gavin's truck was in front of the house, an ATV parked beside it. Was it Brian's? We came to a stop, the car skidding on the dirt. Through my open window I could hear screaming.

'Where's that coming from?' Dallas said.

'Sounds like the back of the house!' We jumped out of the car and started running. Dallas led the way, holding her gun out in front of her. I had the rifle against my shoulder. We kept to the edge of the house, ducking below the windows. When we came around the side, Skylar was standing on the porch, throwing her body at the door.

'Crystal!' I heard her scream.

'Skylar!' I shouted.

She spun around, and I gasped at the sight of my daughter, the rope around her neck, the stained shirt, the boxer shorts, the tape stuck to her wrists. Her face was streaked with tears and her eyes looked frantic.

'Crystal's inside,' she cried out, then started sobbing hysterically.

'Where are they?' I said, running up the steps with Dallas.

'Gavin shot Crystal,' she said, crying so hard I could barely make out the words. 'I saw through the bathroom window. I saw her fall.'

The air rushed out of my body. 'Is she okay?'

'I don't know,' she said between sobs. 'She stabbed Gavin. I think he's dead.'

Dallas grabbed Skylar's shoulders. 'Where's Brian?'

Skylar looked like she was in shock, her face ghostly white, her body shaking violently. 'He was upstairs – Gavin shot him.'

I put my arms around her, held her close. 'It's going to be okay.'

Dallas leapt off the porch and grabbed a big rock, then ran up and smashed the bathroom window. She reached in, unlocked it, then slid it up and climbed inside. I tried to hold Skylar back but she wrenched out of my arms and clambered after Dallas through the window. I followed behind.

I'd just stepped onto the bathroom floor when I heard a scream, then Dallas shrieking, 'No, no, no!'

I rushed out of the bathroom, found Skylar and Dallas in the kitchen on their knees by Crystal. She was naked, a thick rope around her neck, her skin a myriad of bruises. Her chest was covered in blood.

Dallas was holding her body in her arms, cradling her. Skylar was on the other side of Crystal, her hands over her mouth and her eyes stunned.

'Oh, God.' I dropped to my knees beside them. I gripped Crystal's hand, horrified by the raw skin around her wrists, the tape stuck to her flesh.

'Crystal, sweet Jesus, what did they do to you?' I moaned, feeling for her pulse, my fingers pressing desperately, praying.

'CPR. We have to do CPR.' I tried to pull her out of Dallas's arms.

We tugged over her for a moment, me crying and Dallas yelling, 'It's too late!' I thought of every minute we'd spent in town, every second we'd wasted. We should've gotten here sooner. We could have saved her.

'We have to *try*,' I screamed back, my throat so choked with tears I thought I'd strangle on them. I ripped my shirt off, pressed it against the wound on Crystal's chest, crying even harder as it turned bright red.

Dallas let go and I lay Crystal down, bent her head back, started blowing in her mouth. Dallas began chest compressions. I knew Crystal was gone, could feel her mouth turning cold underneath mine, but I couldn't let go, couldn't stop breathing for her. *Crystal, no, please, come back. We need you.*

Dallas stopped the compressions. She wrapped her arms around me, tried tugging me away. I fought back.

'No!'

I hit my hand down on Crystal's chest, screamed in her face. 'No!'

'Stop,' Dallas said, her voice anguished. 'Stop.'

She grabbed me harder, pulling me away. I collapsed backward into her arms, my body wrenching with gasping sobs. 'Oh, no,' I said. 'No, no, no, no.'

I could feel Dallas's body shaking behind me. I turned to Skylar, reaching for her. She was rocking back and forth, her head bowed, hands to her face. Her body sagged sideways, leaned into mine. Dallas encircled both of us in her arms, her face pressed between ours, my tears wetting her cheek.

449

Crystal was lying in front of us. I didn't like her hand resting alone on the floor. I held it, so she was still with us, so she wasn't left out. It was always all of us. I didn't know what the world looked like without her in it. She was our light, our dancing light.

I glanced to my left, barely able to see through my tears. Gavin was lying on the floor a couple of feet away, a knife sticking out of his chest.

'She locked me out,' Skylar said. 'Why did she lock me out?'

I was helpless to explain, couldn't take my eyes off Crystal, her beautiful face. I heard a noise and turned toward the front door, saw someone stumble out.

'Dallas!' I said. 'Brian just went out the front!'

She let go of us and got to her feet, her shirt covered in Crystal's blood and her face enraged. She ran to the door, the gun in her hand. Now I could hear a motorbike and the faint sound of sirens, coming closer.

I picked up the rifle, following her. Dallas was almost out the front door. I stepped onto the porch. Brian was in the driveway, trying to get onto his ATV, his body bent over, a trail of blood behind him. It looked like he was fumbling for keys. A motorbike was coming up the driveway. The rider skidded sideways and fell next to the ATV. He got to his feet and ripped off his helmet. It was Riley. He ran for his dad. Dallas let off a shot aimed at Brian's back, but he turned at the last minute and she hit

450

the ATV. Brian grabbed his son by his shirt and dragged him toward the motorbike, using him as a shield.

'Dad! Stop!' Riley yelled as he tried to pull away.

Brian threw his son down onto the ground, picked up the motorbike, and started it up, fishtailing as he roared down the driveway.

I aimed at the tires, but missed.

The sirens were getting closer. Dallas took another shot. The bike swerved, and Brian tumbled to the ground, the motorbike's engine still whining.

Now Riley was running toward him, and cop cars were racing up the driveway, swerving to avoid Brian and Riley. They pulled up in front of the house. An officer got out, saw us holding guns, and drew his.

'Everyone get down!'

Chapter Thirty-six

Skylar

I pressed my forehead against the cool glass window, looking out at the highway, the big trucks passing our car. I was trying not to think about Crystal but I kept seeing flashes of her face, the blood on her chest, her head lolling to the side.

Mom was holding my hand in the backseat. I could feel her looking at me once in a while, could feel her concern, all her emotions pressing into me. She'd asked if I wanted to talk, her eyes serious and sad, her mouth trembling when she looked at the bandages on my wrists, her hands patting and touching and stroking my skin like she had to keep feeling me to believe I was alive.

'Not yet,' I'd said. I felt like I was swimming under-water and if I opened my mouth it would fill up and I'd drown. I kept getting flashes of images, but they were foggy, surreal, like I was having a horrible nightmare I kept waiting to wake up from, but it just went on and on.

I remember walking out of the house with one of the cops, seeing my mom in the back of a police car, Dallas in another, lights flashing, men talking into radios, their faces serious. Riley was kneeling on the ground. An officer was crouched down talking to him, a hand on his shoulder.

I remember trying to run to my mom, seeing her anguished face through the glass. The officer pulled me away, saying something about having to take me to the hospital and that I could talk to my mom later.

At the hospital, they treated my wrists and neck, asked me all kinds of questions. I tried to answer, tried to focus my thoughts and explain how sorry I was for running away, how it was my fault Crystal was dead, but then I heard a buzzing, a fly trapped against the window, and started crying so hard they had to give me a shot to calm me. Finally, I fell asleep.

The hospital kept me overnight to treat me for dehydration. In the morning I asked for my mom, but an officer said they needed to ask me more questions first. A woman officer drove me to the station and brought me into a room. She was nice, smelled like pine needles and forest and fresh air.

She asked me to go through everything, starting from why I decided to drive to Cash Creek. I didn't know if they'd already found out about my mom. Didn't know if it was still a secret, didn't know what was a truth or a lie anymore.

'I don't want to talk,' I kept saying.

'We know about your mother,' she said in a soft voice. 'We know Gavin and Brian hurt them. It's okay for you to talk to me. You won't be in trouble.'

I looked at the door, wished I knew if she was telling the truth. I felt like I couldn't trust anybody.

'Where are Brian and Gavin?'

'Gavin died at the scene and Brian's in the hospital, but he's going to recover. We want to make sure he's punished for what he did. That's why I need you to tell me everything that happened – so he can't hurt anyone else, okay?'

I took a breath and started talking. I had to stop a few times because I was crying too hard, but she was really nice and waited until I calmed down. She kept bringing me water. I drank glass after glass. I never wanted to be thirsty again.

'Is everyone going to know he's my father?' I said at the end.

'That's not for the police to disclose. It's your private information.'

She explained about Victim Services, then another

nice lady came in and talked to me about counseling and told me who to contact when I got back to the city.

'You'll feel better when you're home,' she said.

We passed a McDonald's on the highway. I remembered picking up Lacey only days before, how I'd been so sure that I'd find Crystal and bring her home. I'd thought I could do it all on my own. My eyes stung with tears.

'I know he was my father,' I said. 'I know it was Brian.'

Mom sucked in a breath beside me. 'Skylar . . . I'm so sorry.'

I turned to look at her. 'Why did you *really* run away? What did Crystal do?'

Mom hesitated for a second. I glanced in the rearview mirror, saw Dallas watching. She looked back at the road.

'Our father was really violent,' she said. 'We were terrified of him. We had to leave.'

'It was more than that, Mom. Crystal felt guilty about something. What was it?'

Mom's eyelids were flickering, like she was thinking hard.

'She . . . she'd been seeing a married man. Our dad was late coming home from camp, but we thought he'd be back any day. If he found out what Crystal had done, he'd beat her. We had to get out of town as fast as possible.'

455

'What were your real names?'

'Our last name was Campbell. My real name was Jessica, Dallas was Danielle, but we called her Dani, and Crystal was Courtney.'

I spent a minute thinking about that, trying to fit these names to my mom and aunts. They felt all wrong, all bunched up and stretched out, both at the same time.

'Were you really from Golden?' I said.

Mom sighed. 'Littlefield.'

'Why did you lie?'

'I was trying to protect you.' Her eyes were shiny with tears.

'You lied about *everything*.' My voice broke.

'Baby, you don't understand. You were just a child—'

'I don't want to talk anymore.'

'Honey . . .'

I turned away. 'I said I don't want to talk.' I focused on the wheels of a big truck passing, swallowing hard against the lump in my throat.

No one spoke for the rest of the drive home.

We'd been back a couple of weeks when I ran into Aaron – the guy with the big scar across his face who trained at our gym – leaving Victim Services one day. I had a flash of remembering how Crystal had said he liked me.

'What are you doing here?' I said. We were standing on the front steps of the building in the shade. It was

456

nice, after the heat inside. I couldn't be in hot rooms anymore, ran around at home opening all the windows.

'My shrink's here,' he said.

'You see one of the counselors?' My counselor, Tina, was okay. She was an Asian lady, maybe around my mom's age. It was still hard to talk about what happened, but it was getting a little easier.

'Yeah, because of my dad.'

I nodded, not wanting to ask about his father, and definitely not wanting to think about mine. I looked down at my sandals, the tan line on my toes, and wondered what had happened to my daisy sandals.

'You haven't been at the gym,' Aaron said.

'No.' I'd come in one day when we'd been back for about a week, thought it might help me feel better, but it was worse. The way people looked at me, either like they were trying too hard not to act weird, or being way too nice.

'You all right?' Aaron said.

I looked up at him, startled. People didn't ask me that. Well, Mom did, but that was like almost every day, which was annoying. I snapped at her every time she asked, then she'd get a hurt look, and I'd feel like a jerk. Patrick didn't ask me anything, so I liked going over there. We watched movies while Karen cooked and Mom hovered in the kitchen, looking over at me when she didn't think I could tell.

'Things are pretty messed up,' I said. I was surprised I was being honest, but Tina had told me it was okay to tell people how I was really feeling.

'Sorry about your aunt,' he said.

'Thanks.' I squinted at a car, a blonde woman driving with sunglasses. I saw Crystal everywhere, in stores, on the street, turned to say something, then remembered. We hadn't had a funeral yet – Mom and Dallas weren't ready to say goodbye. I wasn't either. I went down to the park sometimes, smoked a joint, and thought about her. Sometimes I'd tell her stuff. I tried to just focus on the good memories, like watching her behind the bar, how she'd make drinks so fast while laughing and joking with everyone, or hanging out at her place, music on loud.

'What are you doing now?' Aaron said. 'Like, this afternoon?'

'I don't know, going home, I guess.'

'You want to time me? I've been running the stairs at the park.' He put his hands up like he was boxing. 'Training Rocky-style.'

I rolled my eyes.

'You going to help me or what?'

'I should go. My mom's waiting.'

Mom wanted me to go back to school in September and I'd agreed to give it a try. She said it might be good for me to be around my friends again. I wasn't so sure about that. Emily and Taylor had come over once, but it was weird, like I didn't know what to say to them. I just felt tired and kind of distant. I don't sleep very well anymore. Tina said that was normal. I have a lot of messed-up dreams, like Crystal is in my room staring at me, blood all over her chest, or I'm in Gavin's house, tied to the bed, and the rope is getting tighter around my throat.

Sometimes when I woke up, I'd hear Mom walking around. I got up one night after we'd been home for a few days, found her sitting on the couch, all the lights off.

'Did I wake you?' she said.

'Couldn't sleep.' I sat beside her. She looked like she wanted to ask what was wrong, but she just reached out, held my hand.

I took a breath. 'I'm ready to talk about it.'

I told her everything that had happened, how Gavin had caught me in the house, what he'd done to me in his bedroom, how scared I'd been, how brave Crystal had been, how she'd tried to protect me.

I was glad Mom and I were talking in the dark, so we couldn't see each other crying – I wouldn't have been able to finish – but I could hear her sniffling when I told her how I'd realized that Brian was my father.

'Did you ever regret keeping me?' I said.

459

'No! Not for one minute! The moment I saw you, you were mine. I couldn't let anyone else have you.'

'If you'd given me away, Crystal might not be dead.'

'Oh, Skylar, you can't think like that. We don't know what might've happened. Life just goes a certain way sometimes and it's not anyone's fault.'

She said she was really sorry about lying to me, and I said I was sorry for lying too. Even though we had that big talk, I still felt like I didn't know who I was. It was hard, knowing that my father was that horrible person.

What did that make me?

A week before school started, Mom and I went to the gym so she could get her paycheck. I needed some new clothes. As if it mattered. I waited outside, sat on the hood of the car in the shade. It was still hard being at the gym, looking up every time the door opened, thinking Crystal was going to walk in. I felt bad too when I saw Dallas, how sad and tired she looked. I worried about all the years she had known who my father was, wondered how she really felt about me.

Aaron came out of the gym. He was walking past when he noticed me and walked over. 'You working today?'

I shook my head.

'Want to run some stairs? I'm going to the park later.' I gave him a look. 'No?' he said. 'You could still come and time me. I'm training hard.'

'Let me guess, Rocky-style,' I said, my voice mocking.

He just laughed and leaned against the side of the car, close to me. He was all sweaty, but I didn't mind it for some reason.

'So how are you doing?' he asked, and I shrugged. He opened his water bottle, started drinking. His jaw muscles flexed, making his scar move. I remembered how I didn't want to ask how he got it, how I thought it would be rude. I didn't care what he thought about me now.

'How did you get your scar?' I said.

Aaron looked surprised, swallowed, then said, 'I got between my dad and a knife. He's in prison now.'

'Does that bother you?'

'When he first went in I thought everyone would think I was bad too.' He stared ahead, screwing the cap back on his bottle. 'Then I figured out I was just being an idiot. I'd never do what my dad did, you know?'

'Yeah.' I thought about Riley. Did he feel ashamed like me? After my mom had told him about the cars in Gavin's garage he'd rode his motorbike there, snuck onto the property, and checked it out — he had a key to the shop. He then rode back into town and called the cops from his cell. I don't know if he figured out that I was his sister, but I don't want to talk to him, not yet at least. I think about my half-sister sometimes, but she's just a stranger to me.

Aaron turned and looked at me. 'You think I'm bad?'

461

'No. You just had a bad thing happen to you.' I remembered my counselor saying something similar to me. I hadn't understood then.

He smiled. 'See, the good people get it. Screw the rest.'

I smiled back, reluctantly. 'Yeah, screw them.' Our eyes met, and I felt kind of weird. I looked away. 'We can go to the park Saturday – but it has to be early. Meet me at six-thirty.'

'Man, you're tough.' He got to his feet. 'See you there.'

I watched him walk back into the gym. Maybe I'd tell him someday.

Chapter Thirty-seven

Jamie

I wandered around the house, sat in the living room, the TV off, listening to the music coming from Skylar's room. I did that a lot, savoring her noises. Even when she was skulking around the kitchen or snapping at me, I was still so grateful she was home. She hated how protective I was being, but I couldn't help wanting to make everything better for her, couldn't help worrying if I didn't hear from her for too long. I tried to ease up on the text messages, and she was good about answering, but it was going to take me a while to let go. She didn't know this yet, but I was seeing a counselor too. I'd had my first appointment yesterday.

Skylar hadn't said much when we got home from the mall, but she seemed in a better mood. I'd seen her outside with Aaron. I didn't pry, but I was curious what they talked about. I knew he'd had a hard life and problems with his father. I hoped he could be a friend to her, or maybe more. Crystal had given me shit once when I expressed concern about Skylar dating boys from the gym.

You have to let her live her life, make her own mistakes. Then she'd smiled her beautiful smile and said, *Don't worry, she won't turn out like me.*

I felt a sharp pain under my ribs, the familiar breathless ache I got every time I remembered Crystal was gone. I still couldn't believe I'd never see her again. Dallas and I had gone over and cleaned out her place, stayed there for hours after everything was packed, just sitting on the floor with her things all around us. Most days I swung back and forth between grief and anger, struggling to understand. I was still so pissed at Crystal for going to Cash Creek, but mostly I was pissed that she hadn't run out the door with Skylar.

I hoped wherever Crystal was she was finally at peace.

The phone rang. I glanced at the call display.

Owen.

He'd called after we first got back, checking that we were okay. And we'd spoken a few times since about how things were going. I didn't know why he was calling this time and didn't really feel like talking, but maybe he'd heard something about the case.

'Hi, Owen.'

'Did you see the news?' he said. He sounded serious.

I sat up straight. 'What?' *Please, God, don't let Brian be on the run.* He was still in Cash Creek last I heard, out on bail and waiting for his trial.

'A body was found in Littlefield a couple of days ago. They think it might be a guy who went missing years ago . . . ' He paused. I waited, my heart thudding. 'They had photos of his daughters, asked if anyone had seen them.'

Maybe it was a mistake. Maybe it was someone else.

'Where was he found?'

'On a farm, I think. The new owner was clearing the land or something. I don't know if the police have positively identified him yet.'

It was true. They'd found him. I stared down the dark hall leading to Skylar's room. I was going to lose my daughter. I was going to lose everything.

I'd checked the Internet every day when we first got back, watched the news every night, worried about Skylar's identity being exposed, that someone would realize who we were and connect us with Dad's disappearance, but as the days passed, I'd gotten busy with other things. I'd thought we were safe.

'I better call my sister.'

'Okay.' He paused. 'Hang in there. Call if you need me.'

'Thanks, Owen.'

*

I phoned Dallas. She was home with Terry. They'd been spending more time together lately. She stepped outside and I told her about Owen's call.

'McPhail's going to realize we're those missing girls,' I said. 'He knows we passed through eighteen years ago – that same summer.'

'Dad's body was found in Littlefield.'

'Doesn't matter, they all talk.'

'Just stick to our story. They can't have any proof.'

Maybe they didn't need any. 'I have a bad feeling, Dallas.'

'It's just fear. Remember – they have nothing on us.'

'I have to tell Skylar. She's going to have questions.'

'What are you going to tell her?'

'I don't know.'

I knocked softly on Skylar's door. She turned the music down, opened the door.

'What's up?'

'I need to talk to you.' I sat on her bed and patted the other side.

She sat beside me with a frown. 'What's going on? You're acting weird.'

I took a breath. 'I got a call from Owen. My dad's body has been found in Littlefield. I don't know all the details yet, but the police will probably want to talk to Dallas and me.'

'Did one of you do it?'

'Skylar . . . '

'You said he was violent, and Crystal, she was really weird about that scar on her face – was it self-defense? Is that why you ran away? She killed him?'

I couldn't do it. I couldn't look in my daughter's eyes and lie to her again.

'It was me, Skylar. I shot him.'

She sat back. I tried to reach for her but she shook me off. 'Why? Why would you do that?'

'He was drowning Crystal in the toilet.' I told her what had happened that night when our dad came home, how it had ended with my shooting him in the bathroom. How we'd covered it up.

'I had no choice.' I searched her face. She had to believe me. She had to understand.

Skylar was pale, her dark eyes huge, but she just looked worried and shocked. 'Are you going to go to jail?'

'No, they'll probably just have a few questions.'

'You have to get a lawyer.' Skylar's voice broke like she was fighting back tears. 'I don't want you to go to prison.'

'It's going to be okay.' I grabbed her hand.

'How can you say that?' She was crying now. 'Crystal's dead and now you're going to jail. I won't have anyone.'

'They don't have any proof.' I thought of the hole in

the wall, the garbage we hid, all the things we may have missed.

'I *need* you.'

I pulled her in for a hug. She rested her head on my shoulders, even though she was inches taller, and I stroked her hair like when she was a little girl.

'Skylar, it's going to be okay. I promise.'

'If you go to jail, it will be like Crystal died for nothing! She wanted to do something good with her life. She wanted to make it right.'

'Some things can't be made right.'

'This is my fault,' she said, pulling away and standing up. 'They wouldn't know where you were if you hadn't come to Cash Creek looking for me.' Tears were streaming down her face. 'I screwed up everything.'

I stood, held her hands. 'This is *not* your fault.'

She pulled free, grabbed her coat by the door, and ran out of the room. I chased after her. 'Where are you going?'

'I need to go for a walk.'

'I'll come with you.'

'I want to be alone.' She slammed the door, leaving me in the suddenly quiet apartment, crowded with my thoughts, fear pressing in.

'It's *my* fault,' I whispered to the closed door.

I called Dallas back and we talked late into the night. The next morning a police officer called while Skylar was still sleeping. He asked that we come into the Vancouver police station that afternoon to talk about an important matter.

I knocked on Skylar's door, told her I had to go to the station. She didn't answer.

The police took us into separate rooms.

The officer who was going to interview me introduced himself as Corporal Parker from the Littlefield detachment. He was a younger man, maybe in his mid-thirties, with black hair slicked back with gel, and his navy-blue suit perfectly pressed – the seam still crisp down his pants leg. He had polished shoes, a shiny watch, and a serious expression.

'First I want to let you know that you are free to leave anytime. You don't have to talk to us and you're not under arrest, but we need to clear up some things and we're hoping you can help us. Do you understand?'

I nodded.

'A couple of days ago a body was found in Littlefield. We're still waiting for dental records to make a final ID, but a wallet in his pocket identified him as Roger Campbell, who was reported missing eighteen years ago.'

His wallet. We'd been so careful but we never thought to check his pockets. I thought of his old leather wallet, how it had worn smooth.

'Do you recognize that name?'

I could tell by the look in his eyes that he already

knew who we were. If I lied now, he wouldn't believe anything else. 'He's my father.'

He nodded, his mouth pulling into a grim line. 'I'm sorry to tell you that it looks like he was murdered.' He explained that an excavator had dug Dad up in the old pig field – and that he'd been shot in the head. I didn't want to fake tears, so I tried to just look stunned, shocked by the events. It wasn't that hard to do.

'What do you know about his disappearance?' the officer said.

'We thought he'd left us.'

He held my gaze for a minute. 'During the investigation in Cash Creek, an unregistered .22-caliber rifle was found among some other items that we believed belonged to you, camping equipment, clothes. Brian Luxton denied any knowledge of the gun and it was sent to Ballistics to check for matches.'

The rifle. The assholes had kept it. Heat infused my face.

He was staring at me, waiting for me to say something, but I kept quiet, trying to think what this meant. What should I do? Should I ask for a lawyer?

'Nothing turned up, but when we found your father's body we ran another match. The same caliber of bullet was found lodged in his head,' he said.

I stayed mute.

'We've talked to your old neighbors. We've read the

police reports. We know your father abused you girls. We also know that your sister, Courtney, was involved with a married man and that your father told his friend he was going to beat the crap out of her. We know something went down that night, Jamie.'

I stared at him, my legs starting to shake under the table. This was it. It was finally coming out. We were screwed.

'I know this has been weighing on you for years,' he said, his voice sympathetic but his eyes still fixed on mine. 'You've probably wanted to share your story with somebody for a long time. I'm a pretty good listener.'

I knew what he was doing, and what he wanted me to say. I took a breath, thought about my conversation with Dallas the night before, what we'd agreed. It still didn't seem right, but it was our only option. I remembered again what Skylar had said. *If you go to jail, it will be like Crystal died for nothing.*

I held the words close, focused on an image of Crystal's face, how she would smile when she played the guitar, how much she loved us. Tears rose in my throat. I pushed them back down. I couldn't cry now.

'I don't know what happened,' I said. 'Dani and I were out one night and when we came home, Courtney said she'd had a fight with Dad about her boyfriend but he wouldn't be hurting us anymore.' I realized I'd slipped into using our real names, but it had felt more natural.

471

'What did you think she meant?'

'We didn't ask.'

'You didn't *ask*? What about when he didn't come home for days?'

'He always took off after fights. We thought she'd just told him to leave us alone, or threatened to call the cops – she and Dad were always fighting.'

'Did you see anyone else at the house that night? Maybe this married man she was seeing?'

'No, no one.'

'Did you notice anything out of place when you got home? Any signs of a fight? Blood on your sister's clothes?'

'No, nothing.'

'And she *never* told you anything else?'

'Nothing,' I said, holding his gaze.

'The woman who owned the ranch said Courtney showed up with a burn and that you had a nasty bruise. Said they heard shots the night before.'

'We'd been shooting rats – it was a week after Courtney and Dad fought. Walter came down, checked up on us. The sergeant came by the next day.'

The officer was watching me steadily. 'Whose idea was it to run away?'

'Courtney's. She said Dad probably wasn't coming back this time and we should leave before we got sent to foster care again.'

'And you didn't ask what that meant?'

'We didn't *care* what happened to him,' I said. 'He beat the crap out of us whenever he was home, especially Courtney. We were just happy he was gone.'

'Do you think Courtney *could* have killed him?'

I thought about that night, remembered her legs kicking out, how the gun had felt in my hands, the shocked look in Dad's eyes.

'She hated him, hated what he did to all of us.'

'I need to talk to your sister.'

He was gone for a long time. I sat numb, thinking about Dani, thinking about Courtney, how young we all had been.

The officer finally came back and sat down.

'Your sister confirms your story. She says that neither of you knew what had happened to your father.'

I felt a surge of relief, forced myself to stay calm. 'What's going to happen now?'

He looked thoughtful, his eyes focused on the file he was holding. 'We'll never be able to truly close the case – Courtney's gone and she can't tell her side of the story – but there's enough evidence to suggest that it was likely her and we won't be pursuing this matter any further.' He flipped through the file, pulled out a few documents, glanced at them, then back up at me.

'You kids went through a lot.'

The tears I'd been fighting rolled hot down my

cheeks. The sympathy in his face, the understanding, shattered the wall I'd built around me.

I thought about all the years we had lived in fear, how many beatings we had taken, everything that we had lived through in Cash Creek, and how it had felt like we were never going to be free of our past.

'You have no idea,' I said.

Epilogue

Dallas

I've been angry as long as I can remember. Even before our mother died, I remember being angry. Angry at our father, and angry at our mother for not leaving, for always giving him another chance. I'd cried at her funeral, holding Crystal's and Jamie's hands, felt their bodies shaking beside me. Then I stopped. I just fucking stopped.

I didn't cry at that crap foster home when they made me work so many hours that my hands were raw, or when the wife smacked me with the wooden spoon across the back of my head, or when I had to sleep in the barn with the horses who shuffled their hooves all night long. Not when Dad beat us, punching us so hard we lost our breath, or when Jamie shot him, then looked at me with huge eyes, as if asking me to make it better. But how could I? I knew our life was never going to be the same. I knew that it was over. Whatever pitiful happiness I had managed to scrape up for us had blown away the second that bullet hit my father's head. I knew I'd never marry Corey and have his babies and rock on the porch and laugh. Crystal would never move to Nashville and become a singer. Jamie would never get to travel the world and take photographs.

And I damn well didn't cry when Brian and Gavin raped me, their sweaty hands all over me, their disgusting breath in my face, when they twisted me around and hurt me in ways I didn't think possible. I just got angrier. All I've ever felt was rage. Deep, deep dark rage. It consumed me.

I tried to drown it out at the gym, took it out on my opponents, on the heavy bags, on myself, but it never went away. It was always there, simmering.

The thing that made me the maddest of all was Crystal dying. I mean, what did she ever do? She'd never hurt anyone. All she wanted was to sing and have fun, but that asshole Gavin killed her. I'd held her in my arms when my mom brought her home from the hospital, and I held her in my arms when she died. I hadn't told Jamie that I'd felt the last breath leave her body, felt her go. I'd wanted to scream at her to come

476

back, made deals with God, but she left anyway. Left us behind. She wasn't supposed to do that. We were three. Not two.

I glanced over at Skylar and Jamie as we got out of the car.

'Ready?' Jamie said.

I nodded, but I wasn't ready. I'd never be ready to say goodbye. It was just something we had to do. We got the boxes out of the trunk.

It had taken almost a week to make the origami cranes. We had a thousand by the time we were done, three hundred and thirty-three brightly colored birds strung on three different lines. Skylar kept the extra one. We'd spent hours threading the string through the cranes, fitting each one inside the other and carefully staggering the colors until they made a beautiful rainbow. Skylar had told us that the Japanese believed that the wings of cranes could carry souls up to paradise. I hoped it was true.

You weren't supposed to spread ashes in a public place, so we'd come down to the beach early in the morning, the grass still damp with dew. There were so many birds we each had to carry a box to the shore, then carefully take the string out. We had to let most of the string drag behind as we took our sandals off and waded into the cold water, sand squelching between our toes. When we'd gone a few feet, we stood in a solid line, pulled our strings closer, so they were floating in front of us, then let go so that the waves could take hold.

With our hands over our eyes, blocking the sun shining off the water, we watched them crest, then disappear, then come back up. They floated together, some of the strings tangling, making one brightly colored line on top of the wave.

'They look pretty,' Jamie said.

I had the fleeting thought as they floated away that I wanted to run after them, wanted to dive into the water and swim hard. I wanted to bring them back.

'I should get the ashes,' I said.

I walked toward the picnic table on the shore, where'd we left the cedar box. I held my hand on top of the box for a minute, the wood smooth and warm in the sun. It seemed so small, too small to hold such a big spirit.

When I came back to stand beside Skylar and Jamie, I slowly opened the box with the little plastic bag. I realized, with surprise, that my hands were shaking slightly, and I fumbled for a second with the tie around the top.

I got the bag open, leaned over the water, and let it flow out. The ashes were delicate, a soft gray. Some sank down, but some of the particles floated on the surface. The waves pushed them closer, and they wrapped around our legs. None of us moved. Another wave came and pushed the ashes away.

Jamie and Skylar had their eyes closed, their faces

lifted to the sun, their hands clasped tight. They looked at peace. The wind was moving Skylar's hair, blowing a curl across her face. She brushed it away, reminding me for a minute of Crystal, how she'd toss her hair over her shoulder.

I'd watched Skylar the few times she'd come into the gym that summer, noticed how quiet she was, the dark circles under her eyes. I'd worried, remembering those early days with Crystal when we'd escaped from Cash Creek years ago, her depression, the drugs. But since Skylar had gone back to school, she was coming around. Jamie said she was getting into her music again.

I'd never really worried about Jamie, not the same way I had Crystal. Jamie was strong. The strongest of all of us.

The wind had calmed down, the water smoothing out. I watched our birds far in the distance. I felt someone looking at me and glanced at Skylar, who was staring at me, that serious look in her eyes again.

'You okay?' I said.

'Do you hate me?' she said.

I was startled. 'Of course not.'

She took a quick breath, like she was bracing to say the next words. 'I'm his daughter.'

'You're ours,' I said fiercely. 'You were *never* his.'

Her chin started to quiver, then her eyes filled with tears.

'I'm sorry I didn't save her. I'm really sorry, Dallas.' Her shoulders were shaking now, her hands coming up to cover her face. Jamie started to reach for Skylar, but I stepped forward, wrapped my arms around her tight.

'She didn't want to be saved, Skylar,' I said. It hurt me to say it, but it was true. Something shifted deep inside me, a strange sort of relief rising into my chest, pushing through the rigid muscle and bone. My eyes were burning. I fought, still trying to hang on, scared suddenly that I'd be swept away.

'I love you, Dallas,' Skylar said, her cheek pressed to mine.

It broke then, the tears. They swelled up, surged through my body, flooded down my cheeks, mixed with the salty air, blended with Skylar's on my face. I couldn't stop, my body shuddering, my breath coming out in strangled noises.

'It's okay,' Skylar said.

Her voice was so sweet, so gentle. I sobbed, everything blurring together in my mind, how I'd held Jamie and Crystal as we'd buried our father, how I'd promised them it was going to be okay. That's all I wanted, to take care of my sisters and keep them safe. We had to stay together. I'd tried to hang on to them tightly, but Crystal was always twisting and pulling, going her own way, and Jamie had been angry at me so many times. I couldn't let them see that I was also scared. So scared that if I stopped being angry, there'd be nothing left of me.

I wiped at my eyes, blinked at the horizon. Over Skylar's shoulder I saw the string of birds disappear. We'd come here to release Crystal, but she was the one who had finally freed us. We'd lived for so long in fear. But we could do things now. Jamie could become a photographer and go back to school. I could have a farm, could marry. I could have a baby. The thought almost stole the breath out of my lungs. I hadn't known I'd still wanted that, felt a tug inside me pulling me toward something hopeful.

Skylar and I pulled apart. I wiped my face again, embarrassed. Jamie touched my arm, gave it a squeeze.

We walked back to the car, Skylar's long legs gliding through the water. She jogged ahead, noticing an old man on the beach who'd dropped his hat, the wind sending it tumbling down the shore. She chased after it.

'I still can't believe she's my daughter sometimes,' Jamie said, beside me.

Skylar had caught the hat, brought it back to the man. She turned and smiled at us, her hair blowing wild.

'She's the best part of all of us,' I said.

Jamie turned to me, her forehead creased like she was trying to place my words, then I saw the memory take hold, softening her eyes, her mouth. She also remembered what our mother used to say. *You three are the best part of me.*

481

'Yeah, she is.'

Skylar met us at the shore, looped her arms through ours. We walked back to the car together. Three of us, once again.

Acknowledgements

I'm enormously grateful to the following people:

Jen Enderlin, my brilliant and fabulous editor at St. Martin's Press, who, among other things, helped me figure out the second half of this book. You always find the missing piece of the puzzle. The incredibly talented team at St. Martin's Press: Sally Richardson, Dori Weintraub, Lisa Senz, Nancy Trypuc, Kim Ludlam, Kelsey Lawrence, Angelique Giammarino, Elizabeth Catalano, Caitlin Dareff, Katie Bassel, Jeff Dodes, Laura Clark, and the entire Broadway and Fifth Avenue sales force. Thanks again to Dave Cole and Ervin Serrano. In Canada, many thanks to Jamie Broadhurst, Fleur Mathewson, and the wonderful group at Raincoast.

Mel Berger, my amazing agent, who also has excellent taste in sushi restaurants. I've enjoyed our walks on the busy streets of NYC. Kathleen Breaux, thanks for all your help and your cheerful emails. My gratitude also to Ashley Fox, Erin Conroy, Tracy Fisher, Laura Bonner, Raffaella DeAngelis, Michelle Feehan, James Munro,

Cathryn Summerhayes, Annemarie Blumenhagen, Covey Crolius, Margaret Riley King, and the rest of the team at William Morris Endeavor Entertainment in New York and Los Angeles.

Carla Buckley, my critique partner and sister of my heart. Do you mind proofing this for me?

Constable J. Moffat, Virginia Reimer, Renni Browne, Shannon Roberts, BJ Brown, Matt Enderlin, Jonathan Hayes, Bruce McPhail, Murphy Unischewski, Steve Unischewski, Stephanie Paddle, and Kendra Hadley, for all their professional advice.

My husband, Connel, and my daughter, Piper. I love you both more than I can say.

Chevy Stevens grew up on a ranch on Vancouver Island and still lives on the island with her husband and daughter. When she's not working on her next book, she's camping and canoeing with her family in the local mountains. Her debut novel, *Still Missing*, won the International Thriller Writers Award for Best First Novel.

DON'T MISS OUT

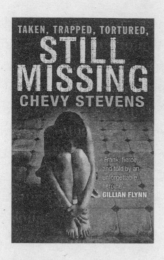

When a van pulls up outside the house she's selling, Annie Sullivan thinks it's her lucky day. But nothing could be further from the truth . . .

At thirty-four Sara Gallagher is finally ready to hear the truth about her birth parents, but some questions are better left unanswered.

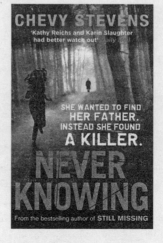

ON **ANY** CHEVY

You can't run, you can't hide . . .

ALWAYS WATCHING

'A harrowing tale . . . that got under my skin'
Linwood Barclay

CHEVY STEVENS

As a psychiatrist, Nadine Lavoie wants to help people, but she has dark troubles of her own – some she can't even think about and some she can't even remember . . .

Toni and her boyfriend Ryan were wrongly convicted of the murder of her younger sister seventeen years ago. Now she's out on parole and back in her hometown, but she must take a terrifying stop back to her past to find out the truth and clear her name – before it's too late

FROM THE BESTSELLING AUTHOR OF STILL MISSING

They said she was a murderer
They said she killed her sister

THAT NIGHT

CHEVY STEVENS